Natural Born Skinhead 1971

John M. Tallon

NATURAL BORN SKINHEAD 1971
(Revised and reprinted April 2015)

Copyright © John Tallon, 2014

Cover art, Adam Tallon, copyright © 2014

All rights reserved in all media. No part of this book may be used or reproduced without written permission, except in the case of brief quotations embodied in critical articles and reviews.

All characters and places are entirely fictitious. Any resemblance or similarity to persons living or deceased is purely coincidental.

Also by this author:

Something to Do – 1972
and
Never a Dull Moment – 1973

Available on Kindle and in Paperback
at Amazon.com and Amazon.co.uk

Find us on facebook @
John M Tallon

or

https://www.facebook.com/pages/Something-to-Do-1972/427764967346581?fref=ts

To all those who have ever
played the game

CONTENTS

PREFACE

CHAPTER 1 – In the Summertime **1**

CHAPTER 2 – Everybody's Talkin' **29**

CHAPTER 3 – Natural Sinner **64**

CHAPTER 4 – I'm a Neanderthal Man **92**

CHAPTER 5 – Within You and Without You **123**

CHAPTER 6 – O Fortuna **154**

CHAPTER 7 – Get Down and Get With It **184**

CHAPTER 8 – Wand'rin' Star **214**

MUSIC (**end pages**)

GLOSSARY

Preface

Natural Born Skinhead 1971 is the prequel to both the popular novels 'Something to Do 1972' and 'Never a Dull Moment 1973.' It is in effect the 'first' and final book in this trilogy, which describes the harsh reality of the world of Jay Mac and his Crown Skins team mates, as they perceive it, recounting their often violent struggle not to be overwhelmed and desperate attempts to be recognised as somebody.

Their membership of the large Skinhead gang or 'team' that to a great extent controls every aspect of their teen life on the bleak housing estate where they reside, is vital in providing them with an identity and sense of purpose. For Jay Mac, the non-resident, outsider, being accepted and acknowledged as a legitimate part of the crew is his own Holy Grail quest, one that he will face any challenge and risk all to achieve.

To explain why these disparate youths should allow themselves to be impelled by this dangerous dynamic, 'Natural Born Skinhead 1971' begins in the final significant years of their senior schooling, where the brutal educational regime they have endured draws to a close precisely at the moment when the aggressive youth cult of the Skinhead is at its zenith. When these two worlds collide, the result can only be the creation of a raging, violent, nihilistic; testosterone fuelled enfant terrible whose cropped head and cherry red boots will strike fear into the heart of a complacent, uncaring society.

As with 'Something to Do 1972' and 'Never a Dull Moment 1973' the following preface should be considered as a content advisory notice. This is a graphic tale depicting incidents that range from the seemingly innocuous to the extremes of sadistic violence, including that of a sexual nature.

Throughout the circumscribed world of the youths is detailed, reflecting the fashion, the music and the aggression. Set in the period immediately after the close of the idealistic 1960s; the 'Summer of Love' has ended and there will be several 'winters of discontent' to follow during the transitional epoch at the beginning of this pivotal decade.

The youths follow a particular stylistic trend, they like the look of the Skinhead fashion popular at the time, the opportunities for aggression that it offers and the respect they believe they receive from other members of society. There is no racist, neo-Nazi, Fascist agenda, overtones or undertones, they are a working class proletariat group and identify themselves more along social class lines than any other differentiation.

From the start there are references to the prevailing cultural mores and perceptions of that time. There is no attempt to glorify them in any way but rather to reflect the formative climate in which the youths have developed and, find themselves living in. The atmosphere is essentially machismo-driven, homophobic and misogynistic and, by today's standards would be totally unacceptable but arguably renders a true portrait of that time, 'warts and all.'

The three books of this trilogy may be read as individual volumes, each with self-contained tales and conclusions, or as one continuous narrative. Together they provide a complete picture of the colourful, exciting, violent world of the Original Skinheads and the spirit of 1969.

NATURAL BORN SKINHEAD

Chapter 1

In the Summertime

Sunday 18th July 1971

Sunday 18th July was that rarest of things, a scorching hot, English summer day. By midday a blazing sun burned with an uncomfortable, angry intensity in a cloudless sky. Jay Mac and six of his Crown Skins team mates where sitting on the continuous concrete sill of the semi-circular library building situated at the eastern end of the drab dilapidated shops. They were enjoying the partial shade of the overhanging maisonette flats built above, while exchanging philosophical observations about life in all its multi-faceted minutiae.

"Fuck me its hot!" said Jay Mac, lazily raising his left arm and scratching the back of his recently cropped head.

"Too fuckin' hot mate, for my likin'. What we need is a good storm to clear the air." Irish replied as he lit another cigarette from a twenty pack of Senior Service 'lifted' a short time earlier from the newsagent and tobacconists, while the vendor was distracted trying to watch the other crew members crowding into his small establishment.

All seven youths were similarly coiffured displaying varying degrees of their requisite haircut; a 'number one Perry Como with razored trench' and all wore the full Skinhead uniform, again with only the slightest of individual variations. Short sleeved Ben Sherman or Jaytex shirts either checked or plain, accompanied by well-scrubbed, eighteen inch parallel, Wrangler blue jeans bearing half inch turn ups, supported unnecessarily by similar width elasticated braces in red or black with metal clip fastenings, worn at just the right height to almost fully display the classic ubiquitous eight eyelet Dr. Marten Airwair 'bouncing soul' boots. Competitively polished to a parade ground finish in cherry red, with the exception of Irish's dull black version, zealously guarded

Natural Born Skinhead 1971 ●2

differing combinations of Tucson redand Kiwi oxblood, produced a variety of lustres and depth of shine.

"D'yer think it gets this hot in Spain?" asked the somewhat slower witted Brian 'Brain' Dent, genuinely, fully earning his usual epithet.

"Fuckin' hell Brain, are you jokin' or what? This is like a winter's day in Spain mate," Stevie 'Johno' Johnson, the immensely strong farm-labouring youth, who having left school the previous summer, had been working for almost a year, replied with a wry smile.

"Why d'yer ask anyway Brain?" the blond haired Glynn, next youngest of the group enquired.

"Well, I was thinkin' of goin' there and gettin' a job as a bull-fighter y'see, I've had enough of the panel-beatin'." Brain replied, astonishing them all.

"Is there any actual reason that yer decided on this line of work Brain, or did yer just wake up this mornin' and think 'yeah, I feel like havin' a scrap with a fuckin' big beast with massive sharp horns'." Jay Mac asked smiling.

"I saw it on the telly like an thought it looked alright." Brain replied honestly.

"Fuck, that must 'ave been a brutal episode of *'Watch With Mother'*." Jay Mac observed.

"Nah it was on that *'Whicker's World'* show. Yer know the one with the toff in the big specs?" Brain responded unfazed, in his monotone manner.

Irish suddenly stopped in the middle of his regular pass-time of attempting to blow consecutive smoke rings and said "Brain, you get in the ring with one of those mad cunt bulls and it'll hit yer so fuckin' hard yer bollocks will go back up inside and come out through yer mouth."

Brain looked suitably impressed. "Fuck me, can that actually happen, Irish?"

"Happens all the time mate, you ask anyone in Spain if yer do go there." Irish replied smiling slyly.

"Yeah, it's called 'talkin' bollocks'." Jay Mac added, grinning.

"I think I'd better leave it then." Brain replied convinced that his friends' dire warnings were genuine; the whole crew laughed.

Natural Born Skinhead 1971 • 3

"I'm fuckin' starvin' is anyone else starvin'?" Billy 'Blue' Boyd the more corpulent member of this group of generally rangy, athletic-looking youths announced.

Jay Mac looked out into the blinding sunlight which bleached the colour even from the drab, dark grey concrete high-rise tower blocks nearby and the gaudily painted frontage of the otherwise bland Eagle public house across the road from where they were seated. He noticed several sheets of discarded greasy newspaper wrappings, which lacking even the slightest breeze to animate them, had totally capitulated in the relentless heat and lay perfectly still surrounding a small mound of partially digested chips and peas that some unfortunate reveller had regurgitated the previous evening.

"Hey Blue, there's a chips and peas dinner on the deck over there. Gerrin there mate, while it's still hot, before them fuckin' flies have it away." Again all the crew laughed including Blue, who nevertheless eyed the steaming remains hungrily.

"Anyone fancy a bit of mindless vandalism?" Irish inquired casually.

"I don't mind, it'll pass a bit of time until the alehouse opens." the permanently unemployed Joey 'Tank' Turner replied, adding "but what's left to do?"

"What about the windows in them new houses down by the bus sheds, we haven't done them for a bit?" Johno offered, hoping to ensure that the crew kept well away from his part of the large council housing estate.

"Why not, it'll be a laugh." Glynn concurred with the same reason in mind.

After a short discussion they all rose to their feet and prepared to move off, hoping for a brief distraction from their usual routine.

Just at that moment the distinctive, throaty sound of several two-stroke scooter engines, could be heard coming in their direction along the main central road that bisected the bleak estate into its eastern and western halves. With this announcement of their imminent arrival, only briefly preceding the actual appearance of a dozen heavily adorned, sleek Lambrettas the seven Eagle crew members stood transfixed, abandoning their immediate plans to await developments.

Natural Born Skinhead 1971 •4

Even the harsh sunlight failed to mute the colours of this noisy cavalcade, presenting them starkly in glorious *Technicolor* against the bleak, drabness of the post-war, utilitarian housing and served only to enhance their gleaming chrome accessories. After bumping his machine, a magnificent LI175 up onto the kerb and riding across the litter-strewn and chewing gum patinated pavement towards the youths, the apparent leader of this Lambretta crew brought his vehicle to a stop directly in front of them.

Applying the brakes though keeping the engine idling with occasional revs of the throttle, he placed his Airwair clad feet onto the ground straddling the scooter, pulling down a red scarf which covered the lower half of his face as he did.

"Alright lads, what's happenin' busy are yer?" the smiling rider who they all recognised as Tony (G), a particularly vicious street fighting Skinhead, asked.

"Never a dull moment round 'ere Tony." Jay Mac replied, pleased to see an acquaintance of his from the lower edge of the estate whom he had struck up a friendship with over a period of time, simply by virtue of the fact his route from the bus stop took him past Tony (G)'s lodgings and he, Jay Mac, had expressed a genuine appreciation for *his* LI 175 on passing.

"That's what I thought Jay Mac. Anyway if you lads can tear yerselves away from all this excitement for a bit, we've got a Southport run on and there's a few spare seats goin'." Tony offered generously then added by way of further inducement "There's bound to be yards of snatch there today, with this weather."

While he was speaking the other riders continually circled about on their machines, either racing in and out of the ever-empty car park of the eponymous alehouse, or performing sharp U-turns and skids in the deserted main road. It was a primal display of young warriors that would have been recognised by anthropologists studying any society, in any age. Like a retinue of knights mounted on their metal chargers, they were announcing their presence, inviting any challenge, hoping to attract any suitably nubile females.

Their scooters were exclusively Lambrettas. It was not that they held a lesser opinion of Enrico Piaggio's Vespa, they just happened to prefer the look of Ferdinando Innocenti's vehicle;

Natural Born Skinhead 1971 • 5

Palavicino and Torre's machine appealed to them more than D'Ascanio's, the aerodynamic Milanese model won, over the Tuscan 'Wasp'.

Mostly brilliant white in primary hue with slim two colour side panels the top half either of iridescent cobalt blue or cadmium red, with matching front shield central columns; they were a backlash against the sombre, monochrome greyness of the era and bland housing of the bleak proletarian ghetto. They all displayed a selection of long and short chrome front racks; aluminium mud guard rails and raking Florida bars sweeping along and up their sides. Some had attached a dazzling array of headlamps or mirrors, or a combination of both; each proudly displayed either a half Perspex fly screen or the newer 'bubble' variant. Golden adhesive backed letters advised which models were LI's; SX's; TVs, or GPs and declared their club affiliation, if any, or Skinhead crew membership.

While Jay Mac did not hesitate to accept his friend's offer, Irish was a little more circumspect and had been attempting to identify some of the riders, without much success, with their facial features obscured under their white Centurion with black peak helmets and scarves worn like bandits in a Hollywood western.

"Where's yer main man, Quirky? I can't seem t'see him about." he asked curiously.

Everyone knew Georgie Quirk the six foot, thirteen stone, insane leader of the Hounds public house crew and from time to time its associated scooter boys; he assumed the leadership of the latter by default even though he did not personally own a scooter. His penchant was extreme violence and the focus of his uncontrollable rage was usually the police; consequently he often spent time residing at Her Majesty's pleasure; this was one of those times.

"Quirky's not our leader, well only some of the time, anyway he's not with us today, that's why we've got a few spaces. Him and four other lads went into town last night; got thrown out of a couple of alehouses and ended up layin' into some bizzies. Nothin' unusual for Quirky, the mad cunt". Tony (G) advised smiling.

Jay Mac was pleased that the crazed Quirky was absent. Though he had never met him and only ever seen him briefly in

Natural Born Skinhead 1971 •6

action at a safe distance, he had a bad feeling about the dangerous maniac, having no desire to cross his path or be in his company.

"Ok lads we've got five places goin' so make up yer minds and we're off." Tony offered once more pointing to the vehicles, seven of which already had pillion passengers.

It was a simple choice, either a potentially exciting day away from the grim estate, or, stay within its claustrophobic confines as usual; yet both Brain and Tank were unsure. Jay Mac was already on board Tony (G)'s machine and strapping on the spare helmet that was secured to the chromed backrest, when he called back to the two waverers "Alright Tank, Brain, if yer can't make yer minds up yer better off stayin' here, see yers."

Irish, Johno, Blue and Glynn followed his lead and quickly mounted the four remaining spare positions to the rear of each vehicle, as they obligingly pulled alongside.

Within moments the colourful, gleaming convoy roared away from the deserted central shopping area, blasting their air horns as they did. The speed of their departure caused such a flurry of exhaust fumed air that finally, the tired, discarded newspaper fish and chip wrappings experienced an invigorating gust sufficient to animate them into a defiant swirl about the legs of the two remaining Eagle players.

"I never did like that Southport place" Brain, who hardly ever left the estate, said as he watched the column of riders disappear from view.

"Me neither, I'd rather sit here and wait for the boozer to open. There's nothin' excitin' about goin' to Southport, better off here." Tank concluded before sitting back down onto the concrete sill of the library, preparing for his long wait.

Brain joined him on the sill and continued his ruminations about possible career changes.

◇◇◇

Travelling along on their twenty-mile journey from the Crown Estate to the Victorian seaside resort of Southport, although they were actually moving through space and time they might as well have been passing through a portal to another dimension. Not long after leaving their own grim urban conurbation, having sped past that of their nearest southerly rivals, the huge walled Ravenshall

Natural Born Skinhead 1971 • 7

Estate, they entered the tree-lined avenues of the more salubrious Walton Hall district, surrounded on both sides by pleasant human-scale red-brick rows of 1920s semi-detached dwellings.

The further they travelled in this other world of rising hierarchical affluence, the more alien their own dystopian landscape appeared in contrast. By the time they had reached the approach road to their destination and were passing by the hugely expensive, detached, Edwardian villas and immaculate presented, well-maintained Art Deco bungalows of the Formby region, the transition from one dimension to its exact opposite was complete; they were now strangers in a strange land.

"Fuckin' houses round here mate, thee must be worth a fortune!" Jay Mac shouted to Tony (G) when they were briefly stopped at a traffic light controlled junction, this being one of the few opportunities when brief exchanges of conversation may actually be heard.

"Yeah mate, they're all minted cunts out 'ere. You'd 'ave to win the fuckin' Pools to get one of these houses, or be a footy player!" Tony shouted back in reply before moving off, still at the head of the strung out column.

Although they were keen to arrive at their destination, no one was in a hurry. Travelling on this uber-cool form of transport was never about getting there but all about being seen on the way to the scene. They had received many positive verbal responses from small groups of females throughout their journey, whenever the youths had spotted them, making sure to attract their attention by blasting their air horns loudly as they approached.

Glynn however, had noticed that as they now passed these more sophisticated dwellings, they appeared to be receiving diminishing returns in response to their brash hailing of the local females.

"What's wrong with these fuckin' birds, they're not interested in us?" he shouted to his 'driver' at a similar junction.

"They're too fuckin' snooty round 'ere, yer need a Bentley or a Roller for these birds to even look at yer." Stevie (B) the driver shouted back, adding reassuringly for the dismayed Glynn's sake, "Don't worry mate, there'll be loads of lively minge at the fair, so fuck these snooty bitches."

"That's what I was hopin' to do." Glynn called back but his words were lost as the column moved off from the lights.

Natural Born Skinhead 1971 •8

A short time later their leisurely journey was nearing its end as they cruised along the sand blown coast road, with the fresh smell of salty sea air borne in on a light welcome breeze. Jay Mac could have carried on without stopping; he was entirely in his element. Although he was looking forward to 'All the fun of the fair' and the speculative promise of a casual encounter with some or any obliging females, sitting back against the rest, riding on that gleaming Lambretta with its dazzling chrome accoutrements, at the head of eleven equally brilliant machines, was in *his* mind, about as good as life got.

The splendid attractions of the well laid out town with its pleasant shopping boulevards and floral displays were of no interest to the youths; as a consequence they circumvented this and headed directly for the famed extensive fairground.

"Pull in 'ere!" Tony (G) shouted, holding up his right arm momentarily then turning across the oncoming traffic and into a sandy clearing between two of the lofty grass topped dunes, partially fenced along its frontage by a rickety stick and chicken-wire arrangement, bearing a sign which read "PARKING ALL DAY 4s." An entrepreneurial elderly male, wearing a knotted handkerchief on his head, clasping an old briar pipe between his dentureless gums and sitting in a worn, striped deck chair, was clearly the 'owner' of this unofficial parking lot.

"Four bob all day, no half days, park at yer own risk." he called opening only the side of his mouth to speak 'Popeye the sailor' style.

All eleven vehicles followed Tony's lead and shortly were parked in a neat row with each scooter diagonally facing into the dunes behind. After securing their helmets as best they could to the backrests of their scooters, they straightened up from their journey, checked their appearance and those who had shades, if they were not already wearing them, now slipped them on. Jay Mac and a few others also gave their cherry red Airwair a quick wipe to remove any dust acquired during their trip.

Tony then approached and spoke to the proud proprietor "Alright old timer, here's ten pence off each one of us for the twelve bikes. If yer fancy earnin' another fifty pence, just keep an eye on our gear and we'll give yer it when we get back." he offered

Natural Born Skinhead 1971 ● 9

generously, hoping to confuse the older man, whom he thought may not yet have fully grasped the newly introduced decimal monetary system.

"'Ey lad, don't try to take the piss out of me. I'm seventy-eight years old; I was in the bloody trenches in the 'Great War'. I've seen off more than the likes of you." He paused and angrily sucked on his pipe. "Four bob's twenty pence not ten. This bloody decimal system's not gonna fool me. Now give me what's due and if yer make it an extra pound, that's twenty shillings to you, I'll guard yer bikes with me life."

Tony and the crew laughed as they produced the necessary funds for the spritely, septuagenarian 'businessman'.

The twenty-four Skinheads now strolled nonchalantly towards the beckoning entrance to the fairground oozing confidence and thinly veiled machismo arrogance, they knew they were top of the food chain and it showed.

Within moments they had joined the bustling crowd and where immediately engulfed in the full visceral experience of a scorching summer's day at an English provincial seaside fair. It was a sensory bombardment particularly of sounds and smells, with stall holders and ride operators shouting at the top of their voices trying to tempt the army of prospective punters. The pungent aroma escaping from the hot dog vendors' merchandise, dominated by that of frying onions, vied with the sickly sweet temptation of the sugary, swirling, candyfloss stalls. As if trapped in a late 1950s time warp, the blaring music from the garishly painted, colourfully lit, thrilling rides played a constant selection of classic 'Rock-n-Roll' tunes, punctuated by the shrill screams of some of the riders. While the crew strolled about scanning the crowd of mostly carefree civilian family types, they looked for two potential outlets for their raging testosterone, sex and violence.

There were several groups of females who giggled as the Skins passed by but it was clear even with their ridiculously short skirts, dresses, high heels and excessive, almost theatrical make-up, they were on the wrong side of the age of consent, even though the boys were little older themselves.

"Lot of fuckin' jail bait so far." Tony (G) noted.

"I might dive in there, I'm only just sixteen meself." said Glynn grinning lasciviously.

Natural Born Skinhead 1971 ●10

"D'you want yer fuckin' arse popped in the nick, you'll be jail bait yerself if yer tap any of that pussy." Irish warned.

Just then the loud crack and immediately following metal ping of airgun pellets being fired at obliging targets attracted their attention, prompting Johno to speak, "I fancy a go at this rifle range so I'm gonna hang on 'ere, ok?

Jay Mac and the other Eagle players decided to remain also and the two-dozen strong cohort split into four smaller groups of five, six, or seven a piece, each going their separate ways.

"Listen, we're gonna have a blimp round, might 'ave a go on the dodgems, we'll see if we can get any snatch there. If there's any trouble shout out or sprint over, alright?" Tony advised before moving off with six of his scooter boy companions.

While Johno and three other Eagle crew members tried to outshoot each other on the range and knock down the surprisingly resistant targets, Blue sought out the nearest fast food vendor to satisfy his most urgent need.

Shortly after the Skinhead marksmen had exhausted several rounds of expensive ammunition and their patience with the stoic metal targets that refused to go down, Blue returned holding two huge sticks of pink candyfloss and with two young girls linking his arms, also engaged in licking their way suggestively through similar mounds of the sticky sweet wisps of blown sugar.

"Look what I've found, say 'ello to Janice and Carol." he announced with a beaming smile.

"Say piss off more like." said the dour Irish. "D'your parents know yer out on yer own girls?"

Jay Mac was studying them both and felt that Irish was being over cautious as he viewed them as close to their own age. What concerned him more was their attire, these were not the usual ridiculously underdressed Lolitas that they wisely steered clear of. Their short aggressive hairstyles; checked, short-sleeved Ben Sherman shirts, red half inch elasticated braces and blue eighteen inch parallel Wrangler jeans, worn with oxblood coloured loafers, suggested they were part of a Skinhead team.

"On yer own are yer girls? Or are yer fellas hangin' around nearby?" he asked curiously.

Natural Born Skinhead 1971 • 11

"We don't know what yer mean but if you're too scared to come for a walk with us, maybe one of yer good lookin' mates here has got the balls."

Glynn did not need any further encouragement and instantly joined Carol offering his arm to her. "See yer lads, don't wait up, you keep playin' with yer air rifles", he shouted back as he, Blue and their two recently introduced female companions strolled away laughing.

"Fuck, I would've knobbed the pair of them, why did you an Irish 'ave t'go and piss on things?" Johno said angrily.

Irish and Jay Mac did not reply, their five year incarceration in the *'Cardinals' School for Catholic Boys'* only recently ended, had provided no academic education but inadvertently taught them enough brutal lessons to qualify them as graduates of the University of Life.

"Come 'ed let's try the Waltzer, there's bound to be loads of birds there, if nothin' else, yer guaranteed a good blimp." Jay Mac offered lightening the mood.

For once he was entirely correct surprising even himself, when they approached the iconic fairground ride. With Dion's *Runaround Sue* just beginning to blare out from the sound system, several attractive unaccompanied females of differing ages had taken their seats in the metal carriages and after having the safety rail pushed into place across their laps, the leering thirty-something attendant, began spinning each separate carriage of three to five girls. Whirling and hurling about in a spastic sequence of violent movements, the brightly painted metal carriages gained momentum, passing time and again in front of the mostly male appreciative onlookers.

As the prevailing fashion for girls and women still favoured the 1960s almost obscenely short skirts and dresses, or bottom-hugging hot pants, legs and underwear were often on show even as a result of normal everyday activity. Now with being forcibly thrown about at sharp inclines, elevated above eye line, nothing much was left to the fevered imagination of the excited youths. Screams of delight from the girls were matched with appreciative cheers from the boys.

"I fancy that one there." Johno pointed as a carriage of three pretty females spun past close to where they were standing.

Natural Born Skinhead 1971 •12

"Which one did yer mean?" Irish enquired unable to avert his gaze from the colourful spectacle.

"Fuck me, the blonde one with the black knickers." Johno replied indelicately.

"Nicely put Johno, a bit obvious like, I'm favouring the brunette in the pinks at the moment, a little more subtle than your obvious black pair, I'd say." He paused as they passed by again then added, "That leaves the virgin whites for you Irish, they'll match yer own."

"Piss off cunt. I don't care what colour knickers they're wearin' I'll have them down soon enough." Irish replied boastfully.

"Here's yer chance mate, the rides comin' to an end, we better step in quick before the pervy fairground feller knobs the three of them." Jay Mac warned smiling.

"Nah, he's not a leg man, he's after that one with the bouncin' tits in the next carriage. I've nearly been goin' blind meself watchin' them; they're like two bald fellers tryin' t'get out of her vest." Irish observed with a wry smile.

Even as the ride came to a halt and before the thirty-something ex-Teddy Boy with his greased back D.A. style blue-black hair, drainpipe jeans and open to the waist dark blue short-sleeved shirt, revealing a dazzling array of colourful tattoos on his chest and arms, could make his move, Jay Mac pushed forward to assist the still shaky girls in walking down the wooden stairs. The lecherous roustabout was only momentarily fazed then swiftly transferred his attentions to the girl with the wobbling chest, chivalrously ensuring that he provided a steadying encircling arm about her slim waist, just below her considerable bust and a helpful pat on her equally well-rounded bottom.

"Alright gorgeous me name's Jay Mac, watch yer don't slip there, I wouldn't want yer t'fall, unless I was underneath t'catch yer when yer landed." Jay Mac offered as an opening to the brunette with the pink underwear.

She smiled and took his hand and the youth beamed in return as he helped her step back onto the sand dusted floor.

Johno and Irish followed his lead with similar successful results; the day was improving rapidly.

Natural Born Skinhead 1971 • 13

"These are me mates, Johno and Irish", Jay Mac began by way of formal introduction. "The thing is we've been wantin' to go on that scary Ghost Train but we're afraid of the dark. So we wondered if you kind ladies would come with us and hold our... hands, what d'yer think?"

The girls giggled and returned the introductions.

"I'm Sharon and this is Michelle and Linda. We've just finished our exams and we're here with our friends celebrating," Sharon paused then asked genuinely "We're all going back in September for sixth form, so we're really going to let our hair down this summer, are you all sixth form boys?"

"Oh yes very much so. You can't beat a good bit of studying we always say." Jay Mac replied.

"What is it you're studying?" Linda asked curiously.

"Er... well... form mostly, except for Mr Johnson here, he's more what you call the hands on type."

Johno followed his friend's lead, "Very true Jay Mac, I do love to get me hands on whenever I can."

Looking from one to the other the girls laughed and said in unison, "Why not?"

Michelle turned to Irish who as usual was unsure and reticent in his approach to females, still deeply affected by the hellish experiences of their five years in the 'Brothers' institution. "What's the matter, are you the strong silent type, is that it?" she asked softly.

Irish nodded in agreement and Michelle caught hold of his hand.

"Irish is a feller of few words; he's more a man of action, if yer know what I mean?" Jay Mac advised.

"Good, I like that." Michelle said smiling, adding "Now what about that Ghost Train, we'll look after you?"

All three boys found it difficult to suppress their elation as they led the girls towards what they hoped would prove to be a truly thrilling ride.

Moments later they joined the small queue of other scare-seekers. These were mostly teenage boys and girls eager to experience a brief period of relative privacy in the semi-darkness of the cavernous attraction. Genuine screams and artificial wails announced the return of the previous riders, who emerged suitably

Natural Born Skinhead 1971 •14

red-faced and dishevelled with a thump of the rubber-clad doors, splitting the hand-painted less than convincing ghost in two as they did.

"All aboard who's gettin' aboard!" shouted the cheery operator whilst collecting the fares.

The Crown Skins shuffled forward with their smiling female companions. Just as they were about to take their seats in the next available carriage, Glynn came running towards them displaying a bloodied nose and split lip.

"They've got Blue, these lads, they've got Blue!"

"Fuck, I don't believe this." Jay Mac shouted in exasperation, "Who's got 'im, where are thee?" he asked angrily.

"There's six of them, they're Skinheads, thee was with those girls waitin' for us in the arcade. Thee've took Blue round the back."

"An you ran off an left 'im?" Irish snapped.

"I had to get help, they're big lads." Glynn replied.

Jay Mac, Irish and Johno glanced at the girls then back at Glynn's bloodied face.

"Sorry girls we'll 'ave t'go" Jay Mac said, adding, "We'll be right back... honest."

"Don't bother, you go and play with your friends, some other time maybe." Sharon said dismissively.

All four team mates raced at break-neck speed to where their friend was being held, pushing other civilian punters out of their way en route. With Glynn pointing the way they soon arrived at the arcade, one of several dotted about the site, each containing a variety of slot machines and simple mechanical games with their own distinct sounds and arrangements of flashing lights. Turning the corner of the building they sprinted to its rear, from where they could already hear the sounds of cruel laughter from males and females and Blue's desperate pleadings. All rational thought was abandoned as they ran into the distressing tableau of their friend standing with his back to the rough plastered wall, his face bleeding from numerous wounds and being slapped, punched and kicked by six tall Skinheads and their two young girl counterparts.

Natural Born Skinhead 1971 • 15

This was one of the instances when Jay Mac's natural cowardice and self-preservation instinct was overwhelmed by his furious rage.

"Hey you fuckin' cunts, come 'ed!" he bellowed as he sprinted towards the momentarily startled group.

The incensed Johno gave no advance warning, pushing past Jay Mac and leaping forward to deliver a bone crunching head butt, onto the right cheek of the tallest Skinhead tormenting their friend. With Irish, Jay Mac and Johno fully engaged with the six males, the hesitant Glynn held back and instantly fell victim to the vicious assault of the two females. As a consequence he was soon on the receiving end of their painfully accurate punches to his face and body, supplemented with kicks to his legs and groin.

Blue was seemingly unable to commit himself to his own rescue and the initial advantage gained by his friends' sudden ferocious attack now dissipated. It began to appear as if those same rescuers may soon be in need of assistance themselves. These local Skinheads were all aged between seventeen to nineteen years; of tall, rangy build with 'number one' crops complemented in some instances by thick bushy sideburns and all were wearing the full kit, including the obligatory cherry red Airwair. The latter were being brought to bear with increasing efficacy when Jay Mac went to the ground grappling one of their number and began receiving a good kicking from two others, while Irish traded punches with a wild individual standing toe-to-toe and Johno similarly engaged with his initial adversary as *his* immediate crew mate was attempting to apply a headlock to the immensely strong farm labourer. The hapless Glynn was in the sorriest predicament of them all, trying to throw his own ineffectual punches whilst receiving the Skinhead girls' vicious blows.

"What the fuck's goin' on 'ere!" Stevie (B) shouted as he and his Scooter Boy contingent discarded the remainder of their fish and chip meals, in their newspaper wrappings and leapt into the fray. With the arrival of these new Crown Team players the dynamics were totally changed, as eight against four became ten against eight. Kicked, punched and head butted, the locals soon tired of the fight, with only the two spitting 'she-cats' still displaying the raging desire to continue. The leader who had

Natural Born Skinhead 1971 •16

received by far the worst injuries from his encounter with Johno, signalled to them all to make their escape.

"Go'ed, fuck off while yers still can!" Stevie (B) the powerfully built, ginger haired scooter boy called after the rapidly departing locals.

"I'll be back with me cousin and his mates, you wait, yer gonna get fucked!" their leader retorted.

"Nice one tit, bring yer fuckin' Ma as well next time, she might do better!" Stevie (B) concluded, having the last word.

"Thanks lads." Johno said, speaking for all five of the Eagle players, bearing several bleeding facial cuts of his own.

"That's alright, remember, we're all from the same team, the Crown, yeah." said Stevie (B) magnanimously.

Though they were considered part of the Crown Estate's auxiliary force as Scooter Boys, they were above all Skinheads who happened to ride scooters, not scooter enthusiasts who dressed as Skinheads.

Jay Mac smiled and laughed with the rest of the crew but he knew that though he may fight with them, the rules of the original teams' founders meant that he could never be officially recognised as part of the Crown Team. He did not live on that estate but instead came from its vast sprawling rival, that of the Kings. He would always be classed as an outsider.

"Picked up any birds yet?" Stevie asked casually.

"Nah, almost but we had to let them go because of these two knobs." Jay Mac replied smiling, though genuinely regretting the missed opportunity. "What about yerselves, Stevie, 'ave yous had any luck?"

"Not really, we've had some crackin' blimps though, knickers all over the place." Stevie replied with a grin, adding, "Tony (G)'s done alright. His crew's got off with some older local skanks, late twenties types, a bit rough like but worth a poke. They've taken them over to the sand dunes to give them a good seein' to."

"The jammy bastards." Jay Mac concluded, adding enviously, "Late twenties birds ey? Fuckin' hell, they'll be experienced alright; I could just do with a bit of mature woman meself."

"Yeah, yer like them sort don't yer Jay Mac?" Irish observed without any further explanation. His friend did not respond.

Natural Born Skinhead 1971 • 17

After a few more brief exchanges on the virtues of 'older' women, the two groups went their separate ways; the Eagle crew in search of deep fried sustenance which cheered the shaken Blue considerably.

"I'm fuckin' starvin'." he announced, wiping his face with the soft polish-stained cloth that he also always carried, attempting to remove some of the dried blood.

"Blue, I wish I had a pound note for every time I've heard you say that, yer greedy git." Jay Mac observed as they marched over to the nearest fish and chip stall, whose salt and vinegar fragrance was leading them irresistibly towards its greasy wares.

Within a quarter of an hour, having gorged themselves on several large portions of steaming, golden battered cod and soggy, thick cut chips, the momentarily satisfied crew were strolling back towards the arcade that had most recently been the scene of Blue's rescue.

"Ah, that's better," said Johno belching loudly as he finished the last drop of his Pepsi Cola from its distinctive glass bottle.

A rapid encore followed from his companions, each striving to outdo the other in volume and duration.

"Yer can't beat the taste of Pepsi, that's another great thing about America..." Jay Mac began about to extol his perceived virtues of life in the United States.

"Jay Mac, not now mate, don't get started on yer favourite topic 'why the States are best', no one's in the mood for it." Irish advised his friend, sensing the generally sullen atmosphere, regarding their total failure to secure any female company.

For a short while they tried to find substitute amusement by: attempting to sink 'enemy battle ships' with glowing rapidly travelling electric light torpedoes moving under the shimmering glass top of a games table; or winning a small fortune on the 'one arm bandits,' or by becoming 'pinball wizards' themselves. Jay Mac laughed to himself as he thought of the words to a musical soundtrack album that one of his elder cousins often used to play on her record player, *There is Nothing Like a Dame* from the Broadway hit show *South Pacific*, he mused at how painfully accurate the lyricist had been. Just then a pleasant female voice disturbed Jay Mac from his reflections "What about that ghost train ride you promised us?"

Natural Born Skinhead 1971 •18

Quickly turning about, having only just successfully sunk the Scharnhorst after previously dispatching the Bismarck, Graf Spee and Gneisenau, Jay Mac was delighted to see the pretty brunette Sharon standing immediately behind him with Michelle and Linda close by.

"As soon as you're ready ladies, your carriage awaits." he replied, gesturing to Johno and Irish to also secure their prizes quickly.

"Are you three gettin' off with these birds and leavin' us?" Blue asked, concerned that the local crew may return.

"Too right we are." Irish replied.

"Yeah, and if there's any trouble, remember... don't call *us*." Jay Mac advised, adding, "Have a wander around, am sure yer'll find something to do.

The girls were quickly whisked away to the much anticipated ghostly ride and eagerly assisted into the first three available carriages by the excited Skins.

Jay Mac and Sharon were in the first carriage and he wasted no time in putting his arm around his partner's shoulders.

"Just in case I get scared," he said smiling.

"I think it's me who should be scared," she replied giggling.

When the poorly executed, vague representation of Frankenstein's monster burst forward from its dusty alcove, almost losing the badly fitting Beatles wig that it wore at a jaunty angle, Jay Mac pulled Sharon closer to him feigning shock at the arrival of the creaky automaton. He could feel her soft shapely form through the thin material of her gingham patterned mini dress, which looked like an exact copy of one of their Jaytex or Ben Sherman shirts. The hem of this short flimsy item had risen by only a couple of inches but this was sufficient to almost fully reveal Sharon's pink underwear, worn over her dark tan tights.

Jay Mac was finding it increasingly difficult to divert his attention away from this enticing image and focus on the artificial thrills of the spooky ride. As a sheet of stringy cobwebs replete with a selection of rubber spiders fell down across their faces, he leaned into the startled girl and kissed her softly on her full moist lips. Sharon responded enthusiastically and, conscious of the limited time available before their 'train' journey came to an

Natural Born Skinhead 1971 • 19

abrupt end, Jay Mac lightly passed his right hand down across her small pert breasts, letting it come to rest mid thigh. Other than breaking away from their passionate kiss the breathless girl made no reaction, Jay Mac was emboldened but only moved his hand a short distance further along her smooth, warm thigh.

The sudden rising with accompanying moans of a life-size grinning, plastic skeleton, eyes flashing like red hot coals, from a lidless dark wooden coffin, provided the perfect opportunity for the excited youth to press on and seize his prize. As Sharon screamed at the appearance of the erect fleshless cadaver, Jay Mac pushed his hand up between her thighs and firmly grasped her most private parts through her pink panties. A second more piercing scream followed and after delivering a stinging slap to the right side of the youth's face with her left hand, she grasped his offending paw with her right.

"What d'you think you're bloody doing, you dirty git?" she asked indignantly. "When I said I was going to let my hair down this summer, I meant that was all I was going to let down, nothing else!"

An uncomfortable silence hung between them with only the mechanical sounds of the eerie ride to be heard, until a pair of similar outraged screams erupted from the female occupants of the two carriages following. The three Crown team players had struck out and now could only hope for a rematch.

When the ride ended and the couples had returned to the sand dusted floor of the fairground, Jay Mac made one last attempt to retrieve the awkward situation. "Listen... there's been a bit of a misunderstandin' so no hard feelings, let's start over again." He paused to gauge their reaction but their impassive poker faces gave no clue.

"How d'yer fancy some candyfloss and a ride on those dodgems?" he offered.

"Alright," Sharon began, "but the three of you better keep your hands to yourselves, or we're off."

"Oh yes, of course, understood." said Jay Mac; Irish and Johno nodding sheepishly in agreement.

A few minutes later after the girls had been supplied with towering columns of sticky, sweet candyfloss; they arrived at the dodgems' location. With Chuck Berry's *No Particular Place to*

Natural Born Skinhead 1971 •20

Go, replacing Eddie Cochran's *Summertime Blues*, on the sound system, the couples took their places in the immobile electrically powered cars to await the start of the their bumpy ride. The amiable atmosphere had almost returned and the boys hoped that they may yet obtain a favourable result. A crackling blue-white spark from the top of the pickup rod at the rear of each car, set them all in motion and with the boys assuming the driving position in each car, they immediately began steering violently into other vehicles, hoping to hit without being hit.

Apart from the other riders being entirely comprised of 'civilians,' initially the large crowd of spectators were mostly holiday-makers and day trippers. Shortly, however, when Jay Mac and Sharon became temporarily stalled in the centre of the conductive arena floor, after a particularly violent hit from Johno and Linda's car, the youth noticed disturbingly that the enthusiastic onlookers were now almost entirely mid to late-twenties males, dressed in dirty black, white or grey tee-shirts; sleeveless leather vests and filthy oil-stained jeans. With their unkempt, long, straggly, greasy hair, goatee beards and bare arms displaying extensive colourful tattoos of deaths heads, daggers piercing bleeding hearts and naked buxom ladies, they left no doubt that they were the Skinheads' antithesis and mortal enemy, 'Greasers.'

Standing close to one of these leering, hard-drinking, screwing and fighting motorcycle enthusiasts, was the leader of the crew of Skins that had previously attacked Blue, wearing a prominent swollen, bruised cheek bone as a result of his contact with Johno's head. He was grinning broadly with grim satisfaction as he pointed directly at Jay Mac, Irish and then Johno. Both of Jay Mac's Eagle crew mates had by now become aware of their dire predicament and were desperately racking their brains for a solution that would get them and their female partners safely away from this band of Greasers. The girls realised something was seriously amiss, beginning to become fearful themselves.

"What do they want, what's going to happen to us?" Sharon asked wide-eyed.

"Nothing, you three are safe, we won't let anythin' happen to yous." Jay Mac replied calmly, trying to reassure the nervous girl.

Natural Born Skinhead 1971 • 21

The ride ended and they had no alternative other than to try to push their way through the tightly packed encircling bikers.

"Come on little fuckin' pinheads; bring those three girls with their sweet young pussies over here, so they cam find out what it's like to get poked by grown men." a grinning male with two gold teeth positioned where his upper canines should have been, called lecherously to them.

"Leave the girls alone, they've got nothin' to do with it." Jay Mac heard himself say, though he knew there was little he or his two friends could actually do.

One of the Greasers reached out for Linda, trying to put an arm around her waist but Johno grabbed his wrist in a vice-like grip and threw his outstretched limb aside. Instantly he was punched in the side of the head and back by several heavy fists bearing numerous metal rings. The girls were close to tears as they finally managed to step down from the arena platform to the floor outside. Jay Mac scanned the crowd, which had now lessened to some degree with the approach of evening, for signs of the other Crown team players and was dismayed to see them also being corralled by the throng of Greasers, herding them in their direction.

"Right pinheads, now that yer all here we're gonna go over to the dunes and have us a party. Move yer fuckin arses!" the proud owner of the gold canines ordered.

Nobody interfered, any civilians nearby quickly moved on, the ride operators looked the other way anxious to resume business as usual.

Forced unceremoniously out through the previously welcoming entrance, the Skinhead cohort knew they were in a difficult position with limited options. Above all they did not wish to reveal the presence of their prized scooters a few hundred yards on from the fairground, in their secluded clearing. Only Blue and Glynn had escaped unnoticed, their next choice of action would be crucial if their friends were to have any hope of assistance. Slipping out from the rear exit of the fair, they raced to the top of the nearest dunes searching for Tony (G) and his crew, who Stevie (B) had previously said were being entertained by some local 'ladies'.

Natural Born Skinhead 1971 •22

Having abandoned their obliging female consorts after an invigorating afternoon, Tony (G) and his crew had ventured into the town in search of some much needed liquid refreshment. As they were sauntering back to the fair through the sand dunes lazily swigging the last of their warm ale from dark brown glass bottles, they saw Blue and Glynn running towards them. It was now Blue's turn to deliver the news of someone else's capture.

"Thee've got the lads! A load of Greasers! Thee just rounded them up and their takin' them away from the fair over to the dunes, on the other side."

Tony (G) quickly absorbed the information and assumed command, "How many of them was there, Blue?"

"I dunno... about thirty probably." Blue replied honestly.

"Ok, they've got fifteen of our lads and there's nine of us 'ere, that's not bad odds. We need some weapons to even things up a bit, 'ave a look round for anythin' useful." Tony instructed coolly.

This was one instance where they were unfortunate not to be fighting on their home ground, the Crown Estate, where assorted debris from a throw-away society could always be fashioned into impromptu weaponry. In the absence of artificial, man-made items, they settled for the ancient natural resources, large round pebbles and other pieces of rock. Armed with their primitive 'tools', supplemented with their empty ale bottles, they ran as fast as they could across the soft, yielding sand, intent on rescue and giving a good account themselves.

Even while Tony's lightly armed commandos were racing to the scene, Stevie (B), positioned close to the Eagle players, who were trying to keep the terrified girls safely in their midst, had his own ideas on the best course of action.

"Listen lads, the way I see it, if they get us and these birds over behind those dunes, we're all really fucked. Out 'ere on the main road we've at least got a chance of doin' some damage and the birds could get off."

"I'm with you Stevie, I don't fancy gettin' tortured or even worse for these girls, so say the fuckin' word when yer ready." Jay Mac replied with Irish and Johno adding their agreement.

As they were being herded along the seafront they passed by the Greasers' bikes parked obliquely to the road. These were an

Natural Born Skinhead 1971 • 23

impressive assortment of Triumphs, Nortons and B.S.As, the least powerful of which could have easily outraced the fastest of the Skins' scooters. The boys looked at them appreciatively even though they were the vehicles of the enemy captors.

"Crown Team c'mon!" Stevie (B) shouted striking the nearest Greaser to his left side and sending him crashing into the closely packed bikes. His crew smashed into those escorts who were guarding that flank, while Jay Mac, Irish and Johno broke to the right out onto the road, forcing an opening for the girls.

"Go 'ed girls, gerroff, run for it!" Jay Mac shouted pushing Sharon through the temporary gap.

All three ran screaming for help along the main road, oblivious to the traffic travelling in both directions.

"Fuck off yer greasy bastard!" Johno roared as he delivered his bricks of fists into the face and body of his nearest opponent.

This was a close-quarter brawl, a hand-to-hand mêlée, where punching, butting, kneeing and eye gouging were the order of the day. All three Eagle players and the Scooter Boys lashed out as if their lives literally depended upon it, they expected no quarter.

Initially the Greasers' numbers frustrated their attempts to subdue the wild Skinheads. While they had organically formed into a tight cluster, the Greasers raging about hampered each other in their determination to break through. Like the massed ranks of attacking Persians at ancient Thermopylae, while Leonidas and his Spartan hoplites held, their ranks too proved impenetrable. Oppressive, baking heat and a dry dusting of swirling sand generated by this violent action surrounded these warriors also. Noses were broken, lips split and eyes blackened, their faces awash in a sticky mix of snot and blood.

Realising that the battered though resolute Skins were determined to resist and worried that someone may send for the police, depriving them of their anticipated entertainment, the gold canine wearing Greaser, cousin of the original Skinhead assailant, signalled to some of his forces to fall back and resort to their primary weapon. Removing their thick leather belts, which bore extensive metal studs along their length and ended in heavy metal buckles, they decided that striking from arms length with these armoured lashes may prove more effective.

Natural Born Skinhead 1971 •24

"Whip these fuckers, make the pinheads bleed," their leader shouted.

Covering their heads and faces as best they could with their already bloodied hands to avoid the devastating lashes, the beleaguered Skins were unable to strike back, or defend their now exposed abdomens and groins from the vicious kicks of the Greasers' deep soled, dark motorcycle boots. Reduced to their knees, hands covered in bleeding wealds, constantly being kicked and punched, the Skinheads knew they were almost spent, unable to last much longer. As if sensing their enemies' stoic resistance was nearly at an end, the Greasers redoubled their efforts trying to flay the flesh from the battered, beaten crew.

"Crown Team!" Tony (G) bellowed enraged, as his troops unleashed a salvo of large round pebbles and rock fragments onto the heads and backs of the surrounding, frenzied Greasers. Leaping down from the dunes they stormed into their foe using their ale bottles as glass clubs. When the whip-wielding bikers turned to face these new arrivals, their raging, bloodied victims sprang into them determined to exact their revenge.

"Fuck these smelly bastards!" Stevie (B) shouted unnecessarily.

The odds were now more even, though still in favour of the Greasers, who were mostly as yet uninjured. Despite their valiant rallying and arrival of their Skinhead comrades, the superior strength of the older males began to dominate and looked as if it may prove to be the deciding factor.

When Tony (G) was downed by the grinning leader of the bikers and fell beneath their heavy boots, the fighting heart of the Skinheads had almost beat its last.

"Let's have it yer greasy twats!" shouted the first of the Mods to charge into the fray, grappling their enemies' leader to the ground, then delivering a series of rapid punches to his no longer grinning face.

"Come on Mods, these are nowt, let's fuckin' do them!" another Trilby-wearing, late-twenties male exhorted, following on with a dozen more uber-cool scooter riders. With the tables now turned and the Greasers facing men of their own age and older, they quickly began to lose interest in the fight. When the usual blaring discordant two note siren conveniently announced the imminent arrival of the police, they wisely chose to run for their motorcycles and rapid escape.

Although the bikers could have continued if they had wanted, they felt there was nothing more to be gained, they had had their fun, no point in risking possible arrest. By the time the one solitary panda car arrived, the only trace of the Greasers' presence was a thin vapour trail from the exhausts of their powerful bikes, hanging in the warm air for a few moments before it too vanished from the scene.

"What the bloody hell's goin' on here? We've had reports of a mass brawl between your lot and a gang of Rockers." the exasperated, sweating, red faced police officer enquired angrily, as he squeezed his considerably overweight frame from the tiny vehicle.

"There's nowt goin' on officer, yer've been misinformed. We just stopped to have a talk like, with some younger Scooter Boys, that's all." the apparent leader of this group of Mods replied in a broad Lancashire accent, smiling at the perplexed officer. "We saw some Bikers but thee weren't Rockers, only a bunch of daft lads pretendin'."

Seemingly satisfied the officer felt there was no reason for him to remain and squeezed himself back into the vehicle, preferring to return to the comfort and enticements of the station canteen.

"Right, well, when you've finished your little chat move on, we don't want any trouble round here." he advised.

As the driver turned the patrol car about in the road the lead Mod continued, "Aye, if they had've been Rockers, we'd all have been fucked and you lads woulda been goin' home in ambulances, not on your scooters."

The Crown Skins thanked their rescuers who were their immediate stylistic forebears, the Skinheads having in part emerged from the later manifestation of the cool youth cult, the Hard Mods.

"How did yer know we were Scooter Boys and in trouble?" Tony (G) asked curiously.

"We were in't cafe down road havin' cup-a-tea, when yer birds came runnin' in, shoutin' about some Scooter Boys gettin' done over by a gang of hairy scruffs. Well we knew thee didn't mean

Natural Born Skinhead 1971 •26

fuckin Hippies and we couldn't have that... our boys gettin' a kickin' off greasy bikers." the lead Mod advised then added "y'girls are over there, we gave them a lift back up 'ere, yer should be bloody grateful to them, their grand lasses."

The whole crew strolled over to the Mods' scooters parked nearby, these were a magnificent eclectic mix of Lambrettas and Vespas all presented to the highest showroom standard, each was distinctive with its own unique features, either in additional chrome fixtures or paintwork. One bore Union Jack side panels, another a 'Who' logo with 'My Generation' in gold above this and 'Don't get Fooled Again' below.

Their leader, who had been talking to them, introduced himself as Baz 'The Ace Face' then pointed to his immaculate SX200 which bore four Aces on each side panel, one for each card suit, alternately red and black.

"No disrespect like... Baz, but how come yer all still Mods ridin' round on yer scooters, didn't yer fancy changin' movin' on?" Jay Mac asked politely genuinely interested.

Baz, the Ace Face smiled "We're Mods that's it, always will be. It were never a fad for us, it's a way of life." He paused to check the rest of his crew were ready, "Ok lads, we're gonna get off now, we've got a bit t'go before we get home t'night." Baz mounted his machine after kick starting it into roaring life, adding several revs of the throttle for good effect. "See yers, don't f'get, stay cool and keep the faith."

With that he pulled out onto the main seafront road at the head of the column and was followed by a colourful cavalcade of thirteen equally splendid machines.

"Where's your bikes?" Sharon asked, now sufficiently calmed to revert to her own natural curiosity.

Jay Mac was uncomfortable, having previously told Sharon that he, Irish and Johno were Skinhead Scooter Boys, not just the pedestrian variety.

"Yes, where is your bike Jay Mac?" Tony (G) asked with a grin, leading the way to their parking spot.

When they arrived at the clearing between the dunes, the old curmudgeon had gone, clearly favouring his supper over the possibility of extracting the promised pound note from the boys.

Natural Born Skinhead 1971 • 27

Their scooters, however, were untouched with their helmets still secured to the backrests and each rider approached their own machine. Jay Mac had no option but to confess to the waiting girls, while Irish and Johno studied the floor.

"What it is, yer see Sharon... is... well... we're sort of... between scooters at the moment."

Sharon spoke for her friends in return, "Well, here's some news for you, yer sort of between girlfriends at the moment as well then... see yer... bye."

Tony (G) following the old adage that 'all's fair in love and war,' quickly seized the opportunity. "Listen, are you three girls in need of a lift, cos we'd be more than happy to help yer out."

The girls smiled coquettishly as Sharon replied, "Gosh that would be really nice, we all live in Formby, if that's not out of your way."

"Ladies, your wish is our command. We might need a cup of tea when we get there cos driving's thirsty work." Tony replied, smiling slyly.

"Of course, you must come in; Mum and Dad are away on a cruise at the moment, so we've got the house to ourselves."

"Even better... I mean, what a pity, we would've loved to have chatted to them." Tony said accepting their tempting offer then turned to the crestfallen Jay Mac, Irish and Johno, "No hard feelings lads, yer alright for the train aren't yer, the stations not that far from 'ere. The boys'll get Blue and Glyn back, thee look a bit worse for wear."

"Brilliant Tony, yeah that's really ace, nice one mate." Jay Mac answered through gritted teeth, forcing a smile.

The giggling girls mounted the three machines that had originally conveyed the unlucky Eagle players. As they did their short dresses and micro-skirts rose up, affording the delighted boys a generous flash of their pink, white and black underwear, reminding Jay Mac, Irish and Johno of what might have been.

A second colourful line of scooters moved off, this time heading in the opposite direction. They blasted their air horns as they passed the three Eagle players trudging dejectedly away from the buzzing fairground, now fully lit for the evening. The girls did not wave or even glance in their direction. With hearts as heavy as the dark rumbling clouds that were beginning to roll in off the Irish

Natural Born Skinhead 1971 •28

Sea, nobody spoke, the boys accepted they had had some thrills and a few scares but the 'tunnel of love' was firmly closed to them.

<><><>

By the time their train had reached Liverpool City Centre, those same dark rumbling clouds were preparing for a dramatic entrance. As the Skins walked down from Exchange Station to the Pier Head bus and ferry terminus, there was a sudden single blinding flash of sheet lightning, immediately followed by a deafening crack of thunder, the heavens opening within seconds releasing a hammering downpour.

"Give us a fuckin' break will yer." Jay Mac shouted in exasperation.

"What a shit end to the day." Johno concurred.

Only Irish seemed pleased, "That's better, much more like it, I said it was too fuckin' hot anyway." he said with a wry smile.

Chapter 2

Everybody's Talkin'

TWELVE MONTHS EARLIER - Friday 17th July 1970

It was four o'clock the last bell of the school day had just rung, for Jay Mac, the fifteen year old Skinhead it was High Noon. Mr Leonard 'Lenny' Wilkinson dismissed the class of thirty-two boys from the claustrophobic, dilapidated room with its yellowed, peeling paint and seriously cracked plaster, that exposed the rough brickwork below, after his hour long drone on the relative merits of the parallelogram of forces in relation to the physical world, finally ended. Both teacher and pupils were keen to be free of that tiny box where the one iron framed, louvered window, with its broken catch and layers of crusty paint rendering it un-openable, trapped and refined the noxious fumes escaping from the unwashed armpits and marginally wiped backsides of them all, Lenny included, on this mid-July day.

Though glad to have escaped from this mind-numbing lecture that he had endured innumerable times during the past four years and the farmyard smelling classroom, this was one school day that Jay Mac was not praying to end. Pushing his way with the rest of the jostling horde along the narrow, low ceiling corridor that somehow always managed to smell of rotten fish mixed with bad eggs, he was reminded by his friends of his imminent brawl.

"You've got to do this cunt, Jay Mac." Irish advised.

"Yeah, this is the one where yer make yer fuckin' name." Terry (H) added.

The more prosaic desire to actually survive the bout with both eyes, all his teeth and a functioning pair of gonads was more prominent in the youth's mind but he acknowledged their support and the magnificent opportunity he was being afforded.

"Can't wait, let's have it." he heard himself say, though his stomach was churning and his rational mind offering dozens of reasonable excuses for flight.

Being close to the end of term and the school year, this was the traditional time for old scores and new rivalries to be settled. Although there were countless scuffles, violent assaults and brutal beatings every day before, during and after the statutory hours of

Natural Born Skinhead 1971 •30

learning, these tended to be impromptu, ad hoc, loosely organised affairs; the end of term encounters were far more structured with some semblance of rudimentary rules expected to be followed. The proprieties must be observed at all times by the combatants and their seconds.

"Yer better watch this dirty cunt, Jay Mac, if he gets yer down, he's a real ball grabber." Liam McCarthy warned. He was one of Jay Mac's closest friends and a formidable Skinhead, whose one ambition in life was to become a Royal Marine Commando, he was also topping the bill on this afternoon's fight card.

Passing by the doorless entrance to the lavatories, which alarmingly where placed close to the canteen, prompting generations of boys to question why the foul tasting fare was not just poured directly into the sluices, thereby avoiding the uncomfortable digestive process, Jay Mac and friends held their breath. Even after four years they still had not become inured to the distinctive fragrance emanating from the six separate toilet cubicles that were woefully inadequate for the urgent needs of six hundred male pupils and smelled as if this was the confluence of a thousand sewers and they had all erupted violently.

Moments later they strolled out of the main entrance under the imposing school motto carved in gold letters on a deep red mahogany plaque, above the two ancient wooden doors which proclaimed 'In serving Christ we learn'; though most boys preferred '*Christ*, we've learned to serve.' The Brothers who ran the institution had their own more immediate physical instruction method, enthusiastically proclaiming 'punishment is good for the soul' as they strapped, caned, slapped, battered and occasionally, when trying to secure redemption for the soul of a particularly recalcitrant boy, punched unruly pupils for any number of minor infringements of a code that only they seemed to be privy to.

Once outside on the old cobbled street, the boys quickly made their way to the venue. Conveniently situated close to the school, the 'arena' was in fact a large quadrangle with a crazed concrete floor, surrounded on all four sides by rows of condemned, derelict terraced houses awaiting clearance.

Natural Born Skinhead 1971 • 31

"C'mon Mack, yer shit-house." Vinny 'Vox' O'Connor, shouted on seeing Jay Mac and his fellow Skinheads entering via one of the passages located at each corner of the quadrangle.

A fair size crowd of mixed partisan supporters and neutrals, drawn mainly from their own year but also from that above and below, had already gathered taking their places around the edge of the actual 'ring,' which was chalked out on the floor by one of the assistants to the referee.

Vox had removed his black blazer and colourful striped school tie and stood waiting in the centre dressed exactly like Jay Mac his opponent in a white short sleeved Ben Sherman shirt, grey sixteen inch parallel trousers and gleaming cherry red Airwair. His dark cropped hair was fractionally longer than Jay Mac's more recent number one but this aside; they both looked almost identical and were well matched.

While Vox swung his arms about his head then jumped on the spot catching his knees at chest height, Jay Mac passed his blazer to Irish, his official second. He scanned the expectant faces of the crowd, feeling the heat of the July sun on his head, shoulders and back as he stretched his arms and loosened up ready for the fight.

"One last chance Mack, take off those fuckin' boots, tell everyone yer not a Skinhead an yer can walk away." Vox offered grinning.

"Fuck you arse bag." Jay Mac replied, having no intention of complying with Vox's instruction, this being the original cause of their bitter disagreement. He knew that when he recently acquired the last piece of his Skinhead uniform, the core element, as vital as the distinctive haircut, a pair of cherry red Dr. Marten's Airwair boots with 'bouncing souls' his transformation was complete. He was no longer John Mack, schoolboy but Jay Mac the Skinhead. The territory, the obligation, the basic fundamental requirement that came with this lifestyle choice, was that he would not only look the part but become the character. His alter ego, like those of his favourite American comic book super heroes, must stand his ground, never back down and accept any challenge. At least that was the theory.

Standing now frozen in the microseconds before the bout began all sound suspended, other than that of his own heartbeat and rapid breathing, he almost wavered; almost.

Natural Born Skinhead 1971 •32

"Right lads, get stuck in when I say, no backin' off, if yer've had enough, shout out. No eye gougin' and no bollock rippin' and before yers start, leave any weapons with yer mates." the referee appointed from the Fifth Form spectators advised, before stepping quickly to the side.

Instantly Vox leapt forward crouching and swinging wild punches as he did. A left hook caught Jay Mac on the right cheek but he countered with two close range jabs of his own to the body and face of his opponent. They both stepped back a pace then closed again, exchanging a flurry of blows that struck arms, abdomen and head. For the first couple of minutes they continued in this fashion, allowing their rage and adrenalin to dominate, without any clear objective other than to pound the enemy into submission.

Cries of "Go in with yer head!" and "Boot the cunt!" arose from the well meaning crowd, anxious for the sight of first blood from either. Vox was clearly listening, immediately changing tactics, grasping Jay Mac by his shirt front and launching his head onto the youth's nose, the audible crack and resultant stream of bloodied mucus pleased Vox's supporters and they urged their man to finish the stunned Jay Mac.

"Grapple 'im Vox, ground 'im, body slam." one fan of Saturday afternoon televised wrestling shouted.

Vox went for the throw trying a side sweep but was unable to successfully complete the manoeuvre without being brought to the ground himself, as Jay Mac caught *him* in a headlock, no stranger to the popular television programme either.

Both combatants crashed onto the hard, unforgiving floor surface and began rolling about delivering short range punches without a moment's respite. Briefly Jay Mac gained the upper dominant position, bringing his own fists to bear on Vox's mouth and nose, drawing blood from each target.

"Keep poundin' the fucker, don't let 'im breathe!" Terry (H) called to his friend.

Vox took the punishment swallowing his own bloodied phlegm, before spitting it back into Jay Mac's eyes. Quickly he dislodged his foe and threw him to one side then rose over him. Forcing his left forearm across Jay Mac's throat, he pushed with all his

Natural Born Skinhead 1971 • 33

strength, trying to choke the youth hoping to make him black out. He was lying fully prone on top of Jay Mac pinning him with his weight.

"Come on, give it up. Say yer not a Skin, shout it out before I fuckin' choke yer, say it!" he demanded.

Jay Mac did not reply but forced a grin onto his purple face as he fought to stay conscious.

Sliding a little to the side of his prostrate opponent, Vox furtively brought his right hand into contact with Jay Mac's groin, covering his action with his own right thigh and began wrenching the youth's testicles violently, as if to trying to tear them from his body.

"Give it up yer shit-house, yer not a Skin, yer nothin'." he demanded.

Jay Mac was in excruciating, unbearable agony but still refused to comply. Instead he quickly caught hold of the back of Vox's head with his right hand, pulled him downwards and drove the fingers of his left into *his* eyes. Vox screamed in pain, instantly releasing Jay Mac's genitals.

"He's blinded me, he's fuckin' blinded me!"

Foul was called by the referee, who in a less than impartial effort to separate both combatants began booting the supine Jay Mac.

Liam now intervened having watched every move of the fight intently. He grabbed hold of the angry adjudicator and threw him into Vox's vocal supporters, advising, "That cheatin' cunt of yours he's been tryin' to pull Jay Mac's balls off and you've done fuck all about it. Make another move against 'im and I'll put you away fuckin' permanently."

Each contingent quickly raised their own man to his feet and claimed a victory. The referee was forced, reluctantly, to declare a draw. Vox, whose temporary blinding had done little to assuage his anger, called over to Jay Mac, "This isn't over Mack, I'm gonna take them fuckin' boots off yer and prove yer not a Skin."

Jay Mac was in agony from his groin injury and was leaning on Irish for support when he called back, "I am a Skinhead alright, an I'll finish yer with these boots the next chance I get."

Both Jay Mac and Vox were now consigned to the sidelines as the much anticipated main event was about to begin. While Liam

Natural Born Skinhead 1971 •34

the aspiring Royal Marine Commando prepared for the bout loosening his muscles and joints, jumping on the spot, Paul 'Sharkey' Sangster casually removed his blazer then passed it to his second. He smiled broadly looking across directly at his opponent, revealing his large trademark teeth, which were so badly chipped that they appeared as if they had been deliberately filed to razor edge points, resembling those of his deadly namesake.

The contest was attracting the high stakes gamblers to wager considerable sums. Large numbers of cigarettes were being offered against hard cash amounts with the minimum opening bet being the princely sum of half a crown, or two shillings and sixpence; serious money for these youths.

"In the centre lads, when yer ready." a replacement referee from the Fifth Form shouted, anxious to get the proceedings underway.

Liam briskly marched into position then stood at ease awaiting Sharkey's appearance. At five foot ten, he was the same height as Jay Mac, though stockier in build with a shock of fiery red hair, that he always kept cropped to no more than a number one length. He had adopted the skinhead lifestyle almost by osmosis, being an established, formidable fighter who accepted any challenge and already bore every hallmark, all he had required was the distinctive kit. Within weeks of the first reported appearances in the press of *'Wild Skinhead Gangs Assaulting Peaceful Hippies in Hyde Park'* by excited hack journalists anxious to coin a new name for an old phenomena in the summer of 1969, Liam, whose elder sister had left home to live and work in London securing a shop assistant's position in Carnaby Street, began to send him much appreciated clothing parcels, containing the prerequisite items to equip him for this latest youth fashion. The young Liam could rightly claim to be one of the first Skinheads in Liverpool, with his Ben Sherman shirts, half-inch red or black elasticated braces, Sta prest cream sixteen inch parallel trousers and original eight eyelet red Dr. Marten's Airwair. Jay Mac who was keen to become a member of a 'team' emulated his style, listened to his advice and aped his aggressive manner. Waiting now on the sidelines with his friends, he was looking forward to receiving a master-class in Skinhead combat from his idealised role model.

Natural Born Skinhead 1971 • 35

"Come on Sharkey yer fat bastard, let's have it." Liam called, becoming impatient, eager to begin.

"Can't wait t'get yer fuckin' ginger head kicked in can yer?" Sharkey responded strolling towards the centre of the 'ring'. At six foot one inch tall and close to thirteen stone in weight, he was one of the biggest boys in the school; he too was a capable scrapper and violent Skinhead.

"Alright lads, toe the line." the referee advised quickly chalking a rough white stripe on the concrete floor between them. He repeated the rules as in the first bout and then also quickly moved away to a safe distance.

Sharkey was big but he was also fast and he came on with speed intending to grapple Liam, trap his arms and quickly squeeze the air from his lungs. Liam's instinctive reflexes, however, were even faster, he dodged to one side pounding his right fist into Sharkey's gut as he did; receiving a thumping right hook from his opponent's meaty fist in return. Darting about, up on his toes like a professional boxer, Liam launched painfully accurate hand-grenades of punches onto his chosen target, either Sharkey's head or body, then quickly moved out of range of his heavy atomic bomb responses, knowing full well that if one of these were to connect they would cause more than just collateral damage.

While the aspiring Royal Marine was cheered on by his supporters, largely comprised of Jay Mac's fans from the earlier bout and some previous undecided neutrals, Sharkey's crew, drawn mostly from Vox's crowd, remained silent, until they were presented with an opportunity to personally intervene. Stepping quickly back out of his enemy's range, after delivering another double-fist salvo, Liam came just too close to Sharkey's contingent, one of whom caught hold of him momentarily by his braces without being observed by the referee. Those decisive few seconds of unbalancing restraint deprived him of his momentum, jarring his carefully choreographed movements.

"Fuck off, yer ginger twat! Now I've got yer." Sharkey announced delighted as he smashed his left meat hook of a fist into Liam's face, drawing the all-important first blood in response.

Liam was released from the prejudicial grip but it was too late he was hemmed in against the 'human ropes' receiving blow after blow, whilst keeping his arms raised and elbows tucked in. With

Natural Born Skinhead 1971 •36

his remaining air rapidly departing from his emptying lungs as every new body-shot pounded his aching ribs, Liam brought his right knee up into Sharkey's groin connecting sharply with his testicles. Though this action gained him a momentary respite, it failed to stall his opponent long enough to enable *him* to move beyond his range. Changing tactics Sharkey now reverted to his original plan flinging his brawny arms around Liam in a powerful bear hug then lifting him from the ground, fully applying his awesome strength.

"How's that feel 'ey, can't get yer breath can yer?" Sharkey taunted applying more pressure to the hold.

Liam did not reply conserving what little air he had left.

"This is what that slag of a sister of yours is gonna feel like when I'm doin' her." Sharkey continued, grinning as he spoke, exposing his ugly jagged teeth while referring to the original cause of their disagreement.

Liam's one sibling, his elder sister, had enclosed within a recent parcel of fashionable clothing, some colour photographs of herself dressed in a figure hugging, dazzling, psychedelic print micro-mini dress. When Sharkey snatched one of these photographs while Liam was showing them to Jay Mac and the rest of the crew, the heavyweight Skinhead began making disgusting, provocative remarks about what he would like to do to Liam's sister. Reminding his ensnared rival of his vile threats at this point was not the wisest of actions. Summoning every last vestige of his own considerable strength, Liam drew back his brick of a head before projecting it with straining muscles onto Sharkey's nose at the bridge, almost flattening the bone and cartilage as he did. For the second time this afternoon a sickening crack was heard and the usual nasal stream of snot and blood began to flow.

The crowd fell silent, both sides frozen in anticipation of their man's reaction. A wild cheer arose from Sharkey's fans on seeing that his python-like grip held and as he responded to the devastating head butt by unleashing his own primary weapon, his razor sharp teeth. Launching his head along the right side of Liam's, he bit into the raging Skinhead's ear, drawing a mouthful of warm blood as he did.

Natural Born Skinhead 1971 • 37

"Foul!" C'mon ref, fuckin' foul, stop the fight!" Jay Mac and the rest of Liam's supporters roared incensed by Sharkey's vicious illegal move and the referee's lack of intervention. Their rage was further exacerbated when the supposed arbitrator mimed a gesture as if to suggest he could not see clearly and was unsure what was actually happening.

Surging forward Liam's supporters swarmed around Sharkey, lashing out at him from every angle, causing him to disengage from his immediate opponent, though bringing part of Liam's ear with him. Vox and his crew now also leapt into action and for a few moments a general mêlée raged about the two original combatants, both of whom were standing apart completely still and grateful for the brief respite.

"Get back t'yer fuckin' places... move, the lorra yer!" Liam bellowed, his face purple imbued by a righteous anger, as the scarlet stream flowed from his mutilated ear. Startled though they were both sides complied with his urgent instruction, resuming their spectator role waiting for further developments.

"Come to it yer fat sack of shit." Liam demanded and Sharkey happily obliged almost running towards his fate. Exploding into the raging heavyweight Liam abandoned all caution. Boxing skills were forgotten and British Army 'milling,' continuous punching without respite or retreat, came to the fore. Now it became a case of who wanted victory the most. Relentlessly pounded with his own blows seemingly ineffectual, Sharkey began to show signs of weakening, his will to win deserting him. When he slipped and stumbled onto one knee, an almost tangible sense of expectation swept over the whole crowd.

"Gerrup Sharkey, Gerrup quick!" his supporters shouted.

"Boot his fuckin' head in!" Liam's fans exhorted.

Sharkey could not manage to follow the advice of his section of the crowd; Liam enthusiastically did as instructed repeatedly bringing his prized Airwair into violent contact with his enemy's face. Soon split bleeding lips, closed eyes with reddened swollen lids and a fractured cheekbone joined Sharkey's already crushed nose. Liam drew back filling his lungs with revitalising air while his kneeling foe swayed from side to side, with blood pouring from his unrecognisable mush of a face. After stepping away a precisely measured distance, Liam bounded forward to deliver his coup de

Natural Born Skinhead 1971 •38

gras, a final devastating boot to the gaping mouth of his battered opponent, with such force and accompanying crunch as to lead the crowd to believe Sharkey's head would actually be disengaged and leave his heaving sack of a body.

"That's the end of yer fuckin' rotten shark's teeth, yer fat cunt. I've saved yer from goin' the dentist." Liam announced triumphantly, standing over the crumpled, unconscious body of his totally defeated foe, he cared not whether his words could be received but was happy to have said them.

With Vox and other members of the fallen, now toothless, Sharkey's contingent trying to revive their man, various lucrative wagers were being collected by the more pragmatic, avaricious element of the crowd, before Liam and his fans strolled away from the scene basking in the glory of a stunning victory. After exiting through the alley by which they had previously entered, they came to a halt close to the main entrance of their school. Their much sought after contraband tobacco prizes were distributed amongst them, either for personal consumption or, as in Jay Mac's case, for subsequent exchange for hard cash.

Casually leaning against the rusty iron railings of the school perimeter, holding a blood soaked formerly checked handkerchief to his mutilated ear and smoking a cigarette that Irish had lit for him, Liam was in good spirits, "Ahh, that's better. Yer can't beat a ciggie after yer've just fucked some cunt, or, had a good hard shag."

Jay Mac quickly noted "Sounds like yer describin' the same thing mate."

Liam laughed on realising what he had said but pressed on regardless, "Aren't yer havin' a ciggie yersef, Jay Mac?" he asked smiling, knowing that his friend never smoked, despite constant pressure from his peers.

"Nah, that shit's not for me, it just fuck's up yer lungs." he replied genuinely expressing his personal view.

They all laughed at this seemingly ludicrous suggestion.

"Yeah, yer see that's where you go wrong Jay Mac, yer fuckin' think too much about things instead of just doin' them." Liam the philosopher advised then turned to Terry (H) for support, "Am I

Natural Born Skinhead 1971 • 39

right Terry or what?" he asked, continuing once again on receiving a positive nod from his fellow accomplished brawler.

"Now yer take the likes of me and Terry 'ere, well we just go for it, ciggies, pussy, or scrappin'. We don't give a fuck, we say, so what? Ciggies might kill yer, the pussy might be a bit ripe and yer could get a dose, or the lad yer scrappin' with could be a right 'ard bastard..., who cares? Just dive straight in, fill yer fuckin' boots and fuck tomorrer." He paused again after delivering his inspiring, edifying eulogy, then sought general confirmation, "Am I right lads or what?" he asked once more, this time rhetorically, expecting no dissent.

Acknowledgements of "Oh aye yeah, totally Liam," and "Too fuckin' right Liam," emerged as a general consensus before they all gradually dispersed, strolling away to their own particular bus stops, having concluded a successful day's learning.

Liam caught Jay Mac by the arm prior to departing and said "You've got the makin's of a real Skin, John. Just remember what yer've seen t'day an 'eard, when the time comes do the cunt whoever thee are, take them out good style, don't think about it, yeah?"

Jay Mac thanked his Skinhead mentor and walked away with that well-meant advice and images of the brutal conflict continually playing over in his mind. He would always remember that day.

Liam too had his own permanent souvenirs; a mutilated, part chewed right ear and a pair of cherry red Airwair containing several embedded teeth fragments, which he kept long after their famous patented soles had finally worn away.

◇◇◇

Forty-five minutes later, having left Irish and Terry (H) to catch their bus to the Crown Estate, Jay Mac disembarked from the double-decker green Atlantean vehicle that had brought him to his destination, the vast, sprawling Kings Estate. Containing four huge concentric housing developments simply known as: North, South, East and West Kings, each of which was greater in size and population density than its nearest rival, the Crown and surrounded by a dark grey perimeter of smoke belching, monstrous factories that required a captive workforce of drones to service its needs

Natural Born Skinhead 1971 •40

twenty four hours of every day, this industrial megalopolis dwarfed any other contender, both regionally and nationally.

Having entered his low-rise tenement block at the ground floor he made certain to re-lock the heavy, sheet-metal covered front door then bounded up the two flights of concrete stairs, to the small council flat where he lived with is aged aunt and World War Two veteran uncle. Even as he closed the door to this bijou apartment, Jay Mac heard the dreaded sound of his cousin, former infant phenomenon and idolised daughter of his guardians, Margaret, in full flow delivering an extended encomium on her favourite subject, herself. Before he could turn and flee from the property, his arrival was noticed; he was ensnared and summoned to join the appreciative, fawning audience which consisted of his aunt, uncle, Margaret's three year old daughter and infant son, who was in the process of having his overloaded nappy changed.

"I wondered when you'd show y'face. I've been hearing all about this gang business that you've been getting involved in and I'm going to give you a piece of my mind." She paused just long enough to catch her breath, while her own mother kindly obliged by disposing of the reeking diaper.

Jay Mac seized the opportunity, interrupting her flow, "Are yer sure y'can spare a piece, yer've not got that much t'start with?"

"You cheeky swine, I'll give yer the back of me hand in a minute." Margaret blurted angrily.

"No yer won't those days are over. Anyway close yer mouth will yer, yer breath's makin' that nappy smell fresh." Jay Mac quickly responded, then sauntered into the tiny kitchen.

"Tell him dad will yer, I'll not be spoken to like that by the likes of him, he should know his place." Margaret demanded furiously.

Her father quickly suppressed a smile that had revealingly and unconsciously arisen, as he considered Jay Mac's retort to his precocious daughter. Sucking loudly on his old briar pipe, he shrugged his shoulders as if resigned to the fate that the situation was hopeless, the incorrigible Jay Mac was a lost cause.

Standing in the kitchen preparing a corned beef sandwich for himself, the youth had already switched on the radio and tuned it to the Radio One frequency. *Green Tambourine* was currently

Natural Born Skinhead 1971 • 41

playing on Tony Blackburn's selective turntable and Jay Mac increased the volume before sitting down to eat at the small, Formica-topped table.

"Don't you ignore me." Margaret began, having followed him into the room. "Look at the state of yer, cropped head, braces and bloody big red clown's boots."

"'Ey, leave the boots out of it, thee've done nothin' to you, yet." Jay Mac replied with a grin.

"Are you threatening me, because if Charlie finds out he'll give yer a bloody good hidin'." Margaret responded, adding, "Looks as if someone else has already done that judging by the state of your face."

"I had a nose bleed in class actually, I was studying that hard." Jay Mac lied.

"Well I didn't think you'd been fighting, you couldn't punch y'way out of a paper bag, you couldn't punch a hole in a wet *Echo*..." Margaret was interrupted in mid-flow of her comic exemplars of amusing, imaginary tasks that her cousin would find overwhelming, as he raised the volume of the radio to its maximum with Traffic's *'Hole in My Shoe'* now replacing The Lemon Pipers.

"Turn that bloody noise down before I come out there!" the old soldier shouted from the living room.

Jay Mac knew the boundary to which his uncle's limited patience could be extended and his explosive rage if that was even marginally exceeded; he wisely did as instructed, Margaret beamed with a smug grin spreading across her chubby face. Never quite reaching five foot in height, rotund in figure and with a non-descript, mop top of a hairstyle, that even an early day's Beatle would have rejected, she was not quite the voluptuous, curved, sex symbol that she imagined herself to be. These physical limitations, however, failed to detract from or diminish in any degree her phenomenal ego driven self-perception, one bizarre manifestation of which was her willingness to dispense unsolicited fashion advice.

"You know what you need; a complete change of wardrobe," she began, addressing the totally disinterested young Skinhead, who replied sarcastically "I wouldn't mind just havin' a wardrobe

Natural Born Skinhead 1971 •42

in the first place, seein' as how I have to keep me gear in the old junk cupboard."

Margaret ignored his remark and pressed on, "First thing, grow that bloody hair, at least to shoulder length, then y'could get it styled, properly. You know I'm an agent for Littlewoods catalogue, y'could order some new trendy clothes from that."

Jay Mac smiled slyly now intrigued by his cousin's remarks. "Go 'ed, let's hear it, sounds interestin'."

"Well, they've got some very nice floral patterned satin shirts, some with a frill down the front and you could match one of those with a pair of crushed velvet bell-bottoms." She paused awaiting Jay Mac's reaction.

"Go on, this is good stuff." he said, smiling insincerely, adding "What about me boots?"

"Obviously they'd have t'go, a nice pair of shiny wet look, pull-on Chelsea boots with silver buckles, would just finish things off."

'An me' Jay Mac thought but said instead, "Hang on, I'll just get a pen and paper."

"Good, I'm glad you've been listenin'." Margaret beamed with self-satisfaction.

"Oh yeah, I've been listenin' alright, I just wanna write it all down in case I've missed anythin', cos yer never know when yer might just need to spot a total, fuckin' wanker." Jay Mac announced and risked turning up the volume of the radio to drown Margaret's outraged screams.

He stood up to leave the room and his cousin made to slap his face but he quickly moved aside. "Don't do that, like I said, that's all over now."

"I'm only trying to help you and that's the thanks I get, one things certain, you'll never get a girl dressed like that." Margaret called after him, almost in tears with rage.

"'Ey, the only thing I'd be gettin' if I dressed like you said, would be a sore arse." Jay Mac replied, hoping to end the matter, until his persistent cousin suddenly caught his attention once more. "And to think I came here today to offer you some money."

Intrigued Jay Mac turned to face her once more, "Go on, spit it out, what is it yer want? What's the catch?" he asked.

Natural Born Skinhead 1971 • 43

"It's just that me and Charlie are goin' away with the kids the week after next, to Llandudno. We were wondering if you'd like to mind the house and look after the dog and the cat." Margaret offered.

"What's it worth?" Jay Mac enquired, ever mindful of his lack of funds.

"Well we were thinking one pound, how does that sound?" Margaret asked.

"Yeah, well think again, it sounds like someone is gonna end up with nobody mindin' their house. I tell yer what make it three quid and I'll even take me boots off *before* I get into bed." the youth offered in return.

"Two pound and that's me final offer." his cousin snapped.

"Two pound it is, up front, cash, now." Jay Mac agreed, smiling, stretching out his left hand, palm upwards.

Margaret hesitated for a few moments then realising there was no room for further negotiation took two, one pound notes from her well stuffed purse and handed them to the smiling Skinhead.

"Right that's settled, I'll be down at yours the week after. Am gonna take the dog out before I go t'me mates. Smells like she needs a good crap, or is that your breath again, Maggie?" Jay Mac called before whistling Patch the old mongrel, who had also been speculatively wondering where the 'pleasant' aroma, which filled the tiny room was coming from.

"Get out you cheeky devil, before I change me mind!" Margaret shouted after him as he quickly left the flat with his faithful canine companion.

"What a fuckin' bitch." he said, "No offence girl."

◇◇◇

Several hours after clinching his business deal with his frustrated cousin, Jay Mac was sitting on the concrete sill of the small, semi-circular library building at the end of the dilapidated, regularly vandalised shops in the centre of the Crown Estate. A number of his associates from the Eagle crew, one of five similar gangs each named after the public houses of the estate that together comprised the Crown Skinhead Team, were also present on this humid, still evening.

"Yeah, it's fuckin' ace workin' on the farm, outdoors all day, in the sun, better than bein' stuck in some shitty factory or worse in

Natural Born Skinhead 1971 •44

some office like a fruit." Johno announced having recently secured a full time labourers position at one of the few remaining farms, dotted along either side of the Lancashire highway that bisected some of their larger fields.

"I bet yer won't be sayin' that when the fuckin' winter comes on, freezin' yer bollocks off." Irish warned cynically.

"I'll take me chances Irish, at least I'm still not trapped in school like you poor cunts for another year." Johno responded smiling, effectively closing the subject, knowing they all envied his early escape from the stultifying, repressive, status quo perpetuating, national education system.

Several other friends of the youths had also taken advantage of being able to leave school at fifteen years of age, before proposed legislation would eventually end this practice.

Jay Mac and the rest of the Eagle Skins present were envious of Johno's premature release from that grinding regime but even more so of the fact that he could now become a fully fledged member of the Crown Team, he was no long to be considered a 'Junior' as they would all remain until they too 'escaped' from their schooling.

Even Terry (H) who was favoured by the team leaders, being sometimes allowed to accompany them on their own violent missions, due to his acknowledged, formidable fighting prowess, could not be officially invited to join the Senior crew while still technically a schoolboy. It was one of the few but fundamental rules that the team founding fathers: Dayo (G), Tommy (S), Devo (S), Quirky and Gaz had decided upon when establishing their Skinhead gang in the summer of 1969, just as the new youth movement was sweeping the country and they were completing their own formal education. Unfortunately for Jay Mac who had been regularly visiting his school friends on the Estate for several years and was well known by many of the crew, one of the other principal tenets held that no one who lived outside of that bleak housing development could ever become a full member of the Crown Team. Jay Mac was welcome to fight their enemies alongside them, take part in any organised vandalism, or other random, mindless escapades as they arose but he could only ever be considered an auxiliary, never one of the troops. It was his one

Natural Born Skinhead 1971 • 45

ambition to somehow reverse that rule, overcome that obstacle and, as he saw it, break the glass ceiling, the desire to belong; to be recognised would drive him along a deadly highway.

"Y'done alright today Jay Mac." Terry (H) began. "Yer just needed to drop that cunt before he got yer down. Snot the fucker first, then gerrin close and pound their ribs, don't let them breathe, then switch back to the face." Terry ended his brief but fascinating talk on his recommended method for quickly despatching an opponent and also finished one of his cigarette 'winnings' from Liam and Sharkey's bout earlier that day.

Jay Mac had already sold the bulk of his stock and was pleased with the increase in his coffers. Feeling generous with no more than a handful of cigarettes left, he distributed them amongst his friends freely.

"There y'go lads, do yerselves more damage if y'want. Don't say I didn't warn yers." he said passing the last smoke to Brain, who responded "Thanks Jay Mac but yer must be wrong mate. If the ciggies was no good for yer, or did yer some 'arm, the people that makes them would tell yer, wouldn't thee?"

"Fuck Brain, that's why thee don't tell yer. Just think what would 'appen to their sales if thee told people, no fucker would buy them anymore." Jay Mac concluded, revealing which of the two youths was the more naive.

"'Ello boys and girl." said a gruff voice announcing the arrival of Yad, one of the three Heron Public House crew leaders, with his two fellow commanders, Macca (G) and Weaver and some of their followers.

Yad was the younger brother of Dayo (G), the powerful, vicious, gorilla-like co-founder of the team. With his dark cropped hair, single continuous black eyebrow, downturned mouth and premature heavy stubble, he looked exactly like his older sibling, as if he were his chronological twin. He was a difficult, taciturn character and primarily owed his position within the team to the fearsome reputation of his brother. He took dislikes to other crew members as his whim directed; above all he hated Jay Mac.

"Well, if it isn't little Jay Mac, the Kings' rat back 'ere again. What's the matter, 'ave yer got lost, or can't yer stand them queers tryin' t'bum yer all the time?" Yad asked, laughing at his own humorous remarks.

Natural Born Skinhead 1971 •46

"Yad, if the Kings Estate *was* full of queers, you'd 'ave packed y'high heels and moved there years ago." Jay Mac responded immediately.

The Eagle Crew laughed at Jay Mac's reply, frustrating the angry Heron co-leader further.

"Watch yer mouth Jay Mac, remember who I am. I'd give yer a slap but it looks like one of yer rough boyfriends has already done that." Now Yad's fellow commanders and crew laughed in return. Before Jay Mac could respond Terry (H) intervened, "Y'know what Yad, I was talkin' and you just butted in, don't ever do that again, or I'll forget who yer brother is, right?"

The sneer on Yad's face changed to a scowl but he was wise enough not to respond to Terry (H)'s warning. "This lad's been scrappin' today against a right 'ard bastard." Terry began again, "That's somethin' I can't remember seein' you do for some time, if ever, yeah?"

Yad did not reply but changed tack instead, "Nice new pair of Airwair Jay Mac, have thee started wearin' them now on the Kings? I thought thee was all still goin' round dressed like fuckin' Mods."

Jay Mac smiled but remained silent on seeing another group of new arrivals positioning themselves behind Yad.

"What are you goin' on about soft lad? I hope it wasn't somethin' bad about bein' a Mod, cos remember that's what we used to be, before we was Skins and I wouldn't like that." Dayo (G) Yad's brother and Crown team leader asked, standing directly behind his sibling looking like an older, far more dangerous twin. Dressed in his Levi's denim jacket with bleached collar and pocket flaps, eighteen inch parallel blue Wrangler jeans and gleaming cherry red Airwair, he stared at Yad intently waiting for a reply. Alongside him was his vicious lieutenant, Gaz, similarly dressed and equally unsmiling. Just beyond them to the rear, were two females with pretty faces that were unfortunately overwhelmed with makeup, wearing very short mini dresses and oxblood loafers, they both smiled and giggled while the whole group waited for Yad's reply.

Natural Born Skinhead 1971 • 47

"I was just... sayin' to this Kings' rat here... about them all still bein' Mods on that shit-hole estate... nothin' else about you." Yad offered now more subdued.

"Listen Yad wind yer fuckin' neck in, yer really startin' t'piss me off. Yer supposed t'be a leader of the Heron crew, start actin' like it. The way you're goin' yer not even gonna make the Senior team, never mind lead a crew." Dayo warned ominously.

Yad said nothing more but his brother continued, "See this lad Jay Mac, well Terry (H) here tells me he's sound, gives me his word on it and that's good enough for me." Jay Mac was momentarily elated until Dayo added, "He knows he can never be part of the Crown Team but he'll get stuck in all the same, ok?"

Yad smiled slyly on hearing these words and felt he had been entirely vindicated, having gained a better result than he could have hoped for.

"Right Johno, big night for you lad, yeah?" Dayo began, waiting for the farm labourer now come of age to rise to his feet.

"Yeah, too right." Johno acknowledged.

"Ace, well let's not fuck about. Welcome to the Crown Team Senior's Johno, yer done well." Dayo said with a smile then made to punch the excited youth in the stomach with his left fist but slapped his face with his right instead. "Now get the back of that denim marked up with a black feltie, so that everyone knows yer a proper Crown Skin."

After giving that specific instruction and acknowledging the gratitude of Johno and his Eagle Crew friends, Dayo, Gaz and their female companions were about to depart for an evening's entertainment, commencing with several rounds of drinks in the eponymous alehouse situated across the road from where they were presently gathered.

Suddenly the distinctive sound of a two-stroke scooter engine could be heard speeding towards them, from the eastern side of the estate. With a loud blast of twin air horns, the rider raced up to where the group was standing, pulling in at the edge of the kerb before coming to a stop in front of Dayo (G).

"Alright Floyd, what's happenin' lad?" Dayo asked recognising the elusive Crown player who was only rarely seen on the estate, preferring to keep company with friends of his own a long way from the bleak housing development.

Natural Born Skinhead 1971 •48

"It's all good my man." Floyd announced in his best affected American soul singer drawl, displaying his trademark ingratiating smile after removing the scarf that was covering the lower half of his face.

Jay Mac was studying the mysterious, enigmatic rider and his immaculate machine; both presented a matched, uber-cool pair. Apart from his peaked Centurion helmet, which was decorated in a U.S. stars and stripes paint scheme, 'Easy Rider' style, Floyd wore the usual hand-scrubbed full denim 'suit,' consisting of Levi's jacket and eighteen inch parallel Wrangler jeans but instead of the ubiquitous cherry red Airwair, he preferred a spotless pair of original, white, Chuck Taylor, Converse All Stars, or 'keds'.

"Where yer off Floyd, just cruisin' or what?" Dayo asked.

"You know me Dayo, I'm mixin' a bit of business with pleasure and you ladies know it's my pleasure to do the business." he answered smiling, fully revealing his slightly prominent but otherwise perfect teeth, instantly reminding Jay Mac of a young version of the famous film star James Coburn. The girls giggled coquettishly as if suddenly overcome with shyness.

"We all know what *you're* like Floyd." Dayo's female partner advised, much to the annoyance of the team leader.

"Well don't let us keep yer mate. There must be some pussy waitin' t'be filled somewhere, I'm sure." Dayo said curtly.

"Ain't that the truth my man but there's no rush, treat them mean t'keep them keen, yeah?" Floyd paused to survey the crew. "Any of you boys need anythin'; aftershave, smokes, watches, I'll do yer a special price if yer interested, saves me some petrol?"

Everybody either shook their heads or replied that they had no immediate requirements, particularly in respect of cigarettes.

Jay Mac who had been admiring Floyd's scooter with its highly polished scarlet and white side panels and dazzling array of chromed accessories including mirrors and spot lamps attached to the front rack, now spoke, "Nice bike man, looks really cool."

Floyd instantly directed his attention to the youth, "You like scooters man, know anythin' about them?"

"Er... well I'd say this one was a '62-'63 Lambretta TV175, mark III, with..."

Natural Born Skinhead 1971 • 49

"Whoa, I'll stop yer there man, that's good enough, how d'yer know about these?" Floyd asked intrigued.

"Me cousin's husband, he likes workin' on motorbikes an scooters, I've been on the back of most of them since I was a kid." Jay Mac replied.

"That's cool, I'll keep that in mind, I'm lookin' to trade up to a '68 SX200, let me know if y'come across anythin' that would suit." Floyd answered then turned back to Dayo. "I like this kid, is he part of the team?"

"Nah, Jay Mac's a good lad but he's not from 'ere, he's from the Kings and you know the rules." Dayo advised.

"Yeah, well sometimes rules need to be broken, anyway, be seein' yer people, stay cool." With that he kick started his machine into life and roared away from them, up along the main central road out of the estate.

"Where does he go, that crazy fucker?" Gaz asked his fellow senior commander Dayo, "Fuck knows, we've been askin' that since school. Ever since that time with Devo... anyway, who gives a shit?"

Jay Mac and the rest of the Eagle crew caught Dayo's remark but *he* had no understanding of what this meant and instantly dismissed it from his mind.

Yad was watching the youth as he casually followed the scooter rider's route until he was no longer in view. "Hey look, Jay Mac's got a new boyfriend, yer well in there lad." he shouted with a grin.

Dayo turned about sharply just as he was crossing the road, heading towards the Eagle, "Yad! Go home will yer, it's way past yer fuckin' bedtime."

Everyone laughed, even Yad's fellow commanders Weaver and Macca (G).

Saturday 1st August 1970

"Pass us that toque wrench will yer John, so I can finish up here." Charlie asked, completing a rear hub oil seal replacement on a workmate's Lambretta LI150.

Jay Mac did as requested watching intently while Charlie, the long suffering husband of his cousin Margaret, ensured that he tightened the hub to just the right torque for its degree of cone.

Natural Born Skinhead 1971 •50

A short time later with everything reassembled in its correct order and the sleek, royal blue and white side panels refitted, the well presented scooter was removed from Charlie's shed 'repair shop', placed against the rear wall of the small end terraced corporation house and covered with a dark, protective tarpaulin sheet.

"Right, Joey's callin' round for his bike on Wednesday night and we'll be back by then, so I'm takin' the keys with me. You won't need t'move it, so no point in leavin' temptation in yer way lad." he said smiling, wiping his oily hands on an equally stained rag.

"As if Charlie, y'know me." Jay Mac answered in mock astonishment.

"Yeah exactly, I know you. Listen we'll be gettin' off shortly, when Margaret's finished arsin' about, stuffin' the kids and the gear into the car. I've left some bottles of beer in the fridge, help yerself but don't drink the fuckin' lot, ok?" Charlie advised, waiting for the summons from his Harpy of a wife. Having spent his two years National Service attached to the R.E.M.E. he had been given the opportunity to develop and refine his own natural mechanical aptitude, however, when he returned to civilian life and full time employment on the assembly line of a local car factory, though reasonably well paid, once overtime and shift allowances were included, his passion for vehicle maintenance was never quite fulfilled. Consequently he spent every available opportunity repairing either his own bikes or those of friends, he would much rather be spending his few days leave from work engaged in this satisfying pastime, than the next five days in a cramped caravan on a site in North Wales trapped with Margaret, former infant phenomenon and their two screaming children.

"C'mon Charlie, what's keeping you?" Margaret called from the road, "He's not causing trouble already is he?"

Jay Mac strolled through to the front doorway and shouted to his cousin "Now don't you worry about a thing Maggie. When me mates have gone and the orgy's finished, I'll make sure I give the place a quick goin' over, once I've thrown out all the prossies."

"You little swine, I should never have asked you. You're no bloody good, just like your drunken mother and non existent

Natural Born Skinhead 1971 • 51

father." she paused, lowering her voice conscious that the neighbours may be listening and to catch her breath, exasperated as she was. "Just you make sure you look after Alfie and Mrs Mills while we'er gone and don't annoy the neighbours, cos I've told them to give me a full report when I come back."

Smiling broadly while watching the disheartened Charlie start the engine in their filled to capacity Hillman Imp, Jay Mac raised two fingers in victory salute and waved goodbye with this hand.

"Right Alfie." he began, addressing the four year old white English Bullterrier, with his two jet black erect ears that looked like devil's horns. "Me and you can 'ave a drink, listen to a few records then we'll get out and about for a stroll and see if we can find some pussy." He paused and looked across at the large, overfed Persian cat sitting on top of the refrigerator, as she in turn circled her tail about ominously, staring back at this uncouth boy in disdain. "An when I say pussy, Mrs Mills, you don't need t'worry, I'm not talkin' about you."

Within half an hour, having drunk two bottles of pale ale, part shared with Alfie, demolished several heavily laden ham and crisp sandwiches and loudly played some of his favourite tracks from his own Motown Chartbusters albums, that he had wisely brought with him, Jay Mac was preparing to take his canine drinking companion out for a casual inspection of the neighbourhood.

His cousin happened to live at the southern most edge of the city, close to the border of the extremely affluent county of choice for the well-heeled, Cheshire, with its much sought after splendid housing. Living in such close proximity to this desirable upper middle class utopia, could easily delude even a marginally self-obsessed aspiring individual into believing they were also actually part of the county set. Driven almost entirely by her unbridled ego, the pretentious Margaret had been suitably beguiled and seduced, swiftly adopting the mannerisms and prejudices of her immediate neighbours and 'betters'. Margaret could hardly bear to visit her own parents on the vast, sprawling blue collar ghetto of the Kings housing estate, which she felt was almost as diametrically opposite both socially and culturally as it was geographically, located at the furthest northern edge of the city. The perceptive Jay Mac was aware of her raging snobbery, provoking her whenever it became too glaring. Now, however, as he strolled along passing under

Natural Born Skinhead 1971 •52

ancient, spreading sycamore and elm trees with his companion Alfie the Bullterrier wearing his thick, black leather, with silver studs collar attached to a short, heavy shank, metal chain, Jay Mac dressed in his full Skinhead 'uniform,' began to feel a little self-conscious, becoming increasingly aware that *he* was a fish out of water.

After sprinting across one of the several large recreational parks in the area and throwing a selection of fallen tree branches of varying diameters for his excited, eager friend, he suddenly stopped close to the neatly painted iron railings encircling the perimeter convinced that he could hear a familiar sound in the distance. Squeezing out through a convenient gap in the fence he stared away up the steep, leafy avenue beyond with the sound coming closer all the while. Out of the dappled shade randomly lit by shafts of bright sunlight, that dared to penetrate the dark green canopy, there emerged more than a dozen gleaming scooters, both Lambrettas and Vespas. While they where stopped at the traffic lights at a crossroads junction some twenty yards from Jay Mac, the mesmerised youth stood gazing at this impressive convoy of cool. Even as he recognised one of the lead riders at the head of the extended column, so too he was noticed. After crossing the junction, the driver of the foremost scooter, an immaculate Lambretta TV175 with scarlet and white side panels, indicated for them all to pull in by the grassy kerb immediately alongside Jay Mac.

"Alright Jay Mac my man. What's happenin' Skin and what the fuck is that evil beast yer've got with yer?" Floyd asked after pulling down the plain white scarf that covered the lower half of his face.

"Yeah it's goin' good man." Jay Mac began, trying to mimic Floyd's affected drawl. "I'm just stayin' at me cousins for a bit, this is their dog. He looks bad but he's a bit of a soft shite really." The youth was cautious in his answer not wishing to reveal that he had an entire house to himself. "What are you doin' round 'ere anyway? It's a fuckin' long way from the Crown."

"I go all over the place Jay Mac. Today I'm just cruisin' with the 'Cloud', we're goin' on a North Wales run along the coast to Rhyl, might even do Llandudno." Floyd replied smiling.

Natural Born Skinhead 1971 • 53

Jay Mac looked along the line of pristine scooters with their gleaming chrome accessories and colourful fly screens, noticing that they all displayed the words 'Cloud Nine' in gold adhesive-backed letters either around their edge or across their centre. He was surprised he had not registered this vital detail on first meeting the mysterious Crown player previously.

"I didn't know you were part of this top scooter crew Floyd." Jay Mac announced, nodding towards the red bubble fly screen of Floyd's machine.

"Nah, yer wouldn't I've not long put these letters on. Y'see man I do a lot of private business and that's the way I like it, so do me a favour, keep this t'yerself, yeah?" Floyd responded, momentarily losing his trademark smile.

"Floyd, it's like I've never seen yer man, y'can trust me." Jay Mac replied smiling while still attempting to mimic Floyd's affected American accent.

"Good man Jay Mac, I like your style. I think we could do a little business sometime. Anyway we're off, the snatch is callin' to us and we wouldn't want some other pricks t'get in there first." He paused glancing down at Alfie the bullterrier sitting patiently by Jay Mac's legs, panting heavily as if grinning with his lolling tongue hanging from his powerful jaws. "Pity yer smiley friend's with yer or I would've said come with us but I don't think we've got a helmet to fit him." Floyd observed then casually looked over his right shoulder before giving the signal to move out, shouting back to Jay Mac as he did "Yer've got company man... be lucky!"

With a fanfare of multiple blasting air horns the crew roared away from the kerbside and down the steeply sloping main road intent on reaching the RuncornBridge, gateway to North Wales.

Jay Mac's gaze followed their departure briefly, more interested now in Floyd's final words. As he spanned the immediate horizon he was pleased to see two girls of about his own age standing with a King Charles Cavalier Spaniel, in the dappled shade of a huge sycamore tree directly opposite him across the other side of the wide thoroughfare. Instantly he shouted after the scooter column "See yer lads! Sorry I couldn't make it today but if y'get into any trouble come back and get me straight away!" As if he had only just noticed the two smiling girls he called to

Natural Born Skinhead 1971 •54

them, "Hello ladies, didn't see yer there, no need t'be scared, everything's alright, just seein' me lads off."

The girls both giggled, one of them answering, "We were gonna come over and say hello but we were worried about yer dog."

"It's fine, this feller does what I tell him, he knows who's boss, come over, let's have a chat." he replied, smiling broadly.

As they were crossing the road walking towards him, Jay Mac studied their pretty faces and slender figures, deciding which one would be his most likely target. At first he thought he was mistaken on seeing that not only were they dressed identically in matching blouses with sleeveless Fair Isle jumpers, Prince of Wales checked micro skirts, dark tan tights with knee length white 'virgin' socks over them and Cuban heeled, shiny oxblood slip-on shoes adorned with faux gold chains of four intersecting rings across their front but their pleasant faces were also almost perfect copies of each other.

"Jay Mac's the name, nice to meet you girls. Do yer both like scooters?" the excited youth enquired.

"I'm Lisa and she's Laura, I'm the oldest by twenty minutes and yeah, we do like scooters." Lisa answered, casually flicking her long blonde hair away from her smiling face as she spoke.

'Twins!' Jay Mac thought, 'fuckin' jackpot.' All manner of lurid, sexual fantasies sprang into his adolescent, hopeful mind, 'Twins! Three in a bed? Blonde, I wonder if collar and cuffs match. And if I bang one of them, does the other one feel it' were principal amongst these stimulating questions. For a few moments he forgot to speak, mentally salivating lost in his own enjoyable thoughts.

Laura broke the comfortable silence, "Are you a proper Skinhead? Cos we like Skinheads, especially if they ride scooters."

"Oh yeah, totally a full Skinhead me, yeah from the Crown Team and I'm with the Cloud Nine Scooter Boys, sort of their leader y'might say." Jay Mac responded quickly, believing that if he was going to lie there was no point in using half measures.

"Where's your bike then? How come you're not with y'mates today?" Lisa asked curiously.

Natural Born Skinhead 1971 • 55

"Me Lambretta's off the road, done it in racin' some sweaty Greasers last week. Me cousin's doin' it up for me now, so it can go even faster." he replied; the lies kept growing, taking on a life of their own.

"So you race Greasers on their massive bikes with your scooter?" Laura asked sceptically.

"Yeah all the time, yer've got to when yer the leader of a crew. Like I said me scooter's bein' suped up, so it's mad fast." He could tell that they were intrigued and quickly pressed home his advantage, "It's only down the road at me cousins, yer can come in and see it if yer like."

"Alright we'd like that." Lisa replied for them both.

Alfie was busily engaged in sniffing the obliging female spaniel's backside, while she politely returned the gesture.

Jay Mac glanced down at the two canines wagging their tails excitedly, hoping for a similar result himself with the captivating twins.

A short time later as the eager youth was trying to entice the girls into his cousin's home, they became suspicious of his motives.

"Who else is in this house, y'have got a bike haven't yer?" Laura asked before entering over the threshold.

"There's no one here but me and me bike's round the back, so don't worry girls, yers can have a quick look then gerroff, ok?" he replied.

Seemingly reassured, the twins walked through the doorway and along the short lobby to the kitchen then out into the yard behind. After putting down two bowls of water for the dogs to drink, Jay Mac threw back the tarpaulin to reveal 'his' Lambretta, the girls were suitably underwhelmed.

"Is this it?" said Lisa, staring disappointedly at the plain, unadorned scooter which, belonging to one of Charlie's workmates and being used entirely for its original intended purpose, transportation, carried no unnecessary accessories.

"Yeah, that's it girls, yer see I don't wanna attract the attention of the bizzies, so I keep it on the low, good ey?" Jay Mac quickly answered.

Natural Born Skinhead 1971 •56

"Never mind the bizzies, am surprised you get any attention with it lookin' like that." the cynical Lisa retorted, adding "We might as well gerroff Laura."

"Whoa, hold on ladies, don't be too hasty, yer haven't even sat on it yet, me scooter I mean." he offered desperately.

"Let's have a go on it then... yer scooter I mean." Laura responded disinterestedly.

Jay Mac quickly assisted her in assuming the correct riding position, leaning closely, taking full advantage of any tantalising glimpses offered by this intimate proximity. Casually allowing his hands to make as much accidental contact with thighs and bottom as possible and receiving no objection, he began to feel that his exciting fantasies may yet become a reality.

"Listen girls, I don't fancy sittin' in 'ere all evenin' on me own, I get really lonely, so how's about stayin' on for a bit listenin' to a few records and havin' a couple of drinks?" he suggested hopefully.

The girls smiled to each other then agreed, with Lisa speaking for them both, "Go on then, we'll keep yer company for a bit but keep yer wanderin' hands t'yerself.

Soon all three were seated in the rear parlour on Margaret's cherished plumb coloured, stretch cover embalmed comfortable sofa listening to The Four Tops' *Still Waters (Love)* and drinking the remaining supply of Charlie's ale.

Jay Mac the Skinhead thorn was happily wedged between the two pale roses who were becoming increasingly intoxicated, the unscrupulous, scheming youth having furtively added a considerable amount of Margaret's own personal stock of London Gin to their drinks.

"Is it warm in 'ere? 'Ave you turned the fire on?" Laura asked, slightly slurring her words.

"No, you're right, it is warm, must be the weather. Why not take off yer jumpers, I'll help yer if y'like." Jay Mac offered kindly, pleased that all was proceeding according to his fiendish plan.

Lisa removed her woollen Fair Isle and fell back against the sofa, her head lolling onto Jay Mac's right shoulder, her twin sister to his left, quickly followed suit.

Natural Born Skinhead 1971 • 57

Feeling that the opportune moment had arrived; the youth carefully dislodged himself from between the two almost sleeping beauties. After propping Laura into a reasonably comfortable position, he leaned across and kissed Lisa on her full moist lips. Disturbed from her alcohol induced partial slumber, she murmured softly before responding passionately to his advances. Spurred on Jay Mac deftly moved his left hand across Lisa's breasts, letting it linger over each as he did. The girl moaned and moved herself forward meeting his touch, arching her back, Jay Mac was delighted. After carefully opening the buttons of her thin, short sleeved blouse, he briefly admired her bosom held up as if for inspection in a simple white, underwired bra. With Lisa's breathing becoming more deep and heavy as Jay Mac released her small, firm orbs from their restraint, he immediately transferred his mouth from her willing lips to her expectant breasts. Shuddering with delight as each new thrilling wave passed over her; she caught hold of the back of his cropped head pulling him to her, encouraging his movement from one to the other of her aroused nipples.

Even in the midst of his enjoyment, greed began to torment his fevered brain, 'Why concentrate on one twin when I could do them both?' was the burning, pertinent question he asked himself. Before he could tear himself away from the delights of Lisa, however, her identical sibling joined in the fun without requiring Jay Mac's prompting. He was surprised and delighted to suddenly find her embracing him, moving her left hand eagerly across his torso feeling his lithe, athletic firmness. Soon Laura had opened his short sleeved, red, white and blue checked Jaytex and slipped her exploratory hand inside.

'If I'm dreamin' please don't let me wake up.' he thought, the adventurous Laura having now moved her probing hand from inside his shirt to the groin of his straining jeans. As she tugged at his zip fly, preparing to unleash his throbbing erection, Jay Mac passed his left arm back behind him across hers and deftly placed his hand between her soft, warm thighs. Both girls were now moving their undulating bodies, against him moaning as they did.

'This is too good t'be true, it can't last' he thought, almost approaching the point of no return. He was right, it was and it did not.

Natural Born Skinhead 1971 ●58

Lisa was the first to pull herself away and deliver a stinging slap, followed almost immediately by Laura, who threw his probing hand to one side then also slapped his reddened face.

"Well you dirty pig! Trying to get us drunk so you could have your way with us, filling our glasses with more Gin than pale ale, y'could smell it half a mile away, never mind taste it." Lisa began.

"We wondered how far you'd go before we had t'stop yer." Laura added.

Jay Mac sat upright and adjusted the zip fly of his jeans without looking at either girl, deciding not to offer any defence.

"We're the Maloney twins, ask anyone round here, they all know us, our Da runs the Red Ensign alehouse, we've been knockin' it back since we were little kids." Lisa advised. With Laura quickly adding, "Yeah, we could drink *you* under the table anytime soft lad! C'mon sis let's gerroff."

Both girls rose to their feet, straightened their clothing and made for the door.

Jay Mac tried to follow them as best he could hampered by his enthusiasm, which was only just deflating. "I suppose a quick toss is out of the question?" he called smiling.

"Hey lad, just be grateful if you don't get a visit from our arl feller, when we tell him what y'tried to do to us. He'll knock the shite out of yer." Laura warned.

"Yeah, we'll remember this address alright, don't you worry." Lisa noted, adding, "Now where's Poppy got to, c'mon girl we're leavin'." A bedraggled Poppy scampered out of the kitchen where she had left a steaming reminder of her presence after being rudely entertained by the 'grinning' Alfie.

Later that evening as both boy and dog sat in the living room with the colour television blaring away in the background, Jay Mac having located Charlie's vital, secret pornography magazine stash, was casually studying some of the more imaginative, enticing images within. He glanced across at Alfie the bullterrier who was vigorously humping a particularly attractive red velour covered cushion, with provocative gold tassels, that he had been eyeing for some time from afar, normally confined as he was to the floor area. Now with Jay Mac kindly relaxing the usual administration's

Natural Born Skinhead 1971 • 59

house rules, Alfie was at last united with his foam-filled fancy and was taking full advantage of the unique opportunity.

"Go'ed mate, get stuck in there, at least one of us is gettin' a bit of relief." Jay Mac called, lazily swigging from the last remaining bottle of ale. "Throw us one of them cushions will yer mate, I think I'll join yer."

Sat on the top shelf of Margaret's recently acquired, trendy, teak veneered display unit, Mrs Mills the pampered, overweight Persian cat looked down on their antics in disgust, slowly circling her tail as an indication of her feelings, registering her annoyance.

Sunday 2nd August 1970

Sunday morning arrived with a sky filled with heavily laden clouds and a torrential downpour of rain, as an opening promise of more to come. Jay Mac would have been well advised to consider this a portent. Instead, almost oblivious to the prevailing weather conditions outside, he was singing loudly to Desmond Dekker's *'Isrealite'* currently and appositely playing on the radio, whilst preparing a huge fried breakfast for himself and his 'grinning' canine dining companion.

By mid-afternoon the heavy rain having finally slowed to a light drizzle, Jay Mac decided to take Alfie for a walk in the opposite direction to the previous day's expedition, down towards the dockyard waterfront. After a quick polish of his gleaming cherry red Airwair and donning his Levi's denim jacket, Jay Mac clipped Alfie's thick leather studded collar to his heavy shank chain lead and set off.

As boy and dog strolled along through the damp grey afternoon, the Crown Skin reflected philosophically on the events of the previous day. 'Not a bad swap really, well worth a couple of slaps.' he mused, feeling that the twins' physical reprisals and verbal warning had been a fair exchange for such a stimulating experience, one which would furnish him with useful, pleasant memories for some time. Within a quarter of an hour their meandering route had taken them from the fairly spacious, predominantly semi-detached and town house 1930's development of Margaret's domain, to the more densely grouped rows of dilapidated Victorian terraces, which had originally been constructed to house an army of dock workers and their families.

Natural Born Skinhead 1971 •60

Jay Mac had noticed with passing curiosity that several vacant, weathered, old common brick constructed properties, some now missing their roofs, were daubed in white or black paint with the letters 'S.D.S.' He unwisely gave this little thought until he began to observe some examples with additional words appearing under these specific bold letters, which read 'S.D.S Rules OK!' and 'S.D.S Only Keep Out!'.

"I think this is about as far as we're goin' mate." he said to his grinning canine companion, fully discerning the meaning of these cryptic messages. 'I'm in the grounds of the South Dock Skins Team' he thought, deciding to turnabout half way along a red engineered brick lined arched passage that spanned a redundant railway viaduct above.

"Alright lad, where y'from mate?" the taller of two Skinhead's blocking Jay Mac's exit called to him, his voice echoing with a hollow resonance as it bounced from the walls of the vaulted passage.

Jay Mac did not answer and turned back to face the way he had previously been travelling, only to find two other similarly dressed youths barring his way forward also.

One of these now called to the Crown player, "'Ey lad, you with the pig on a string. Did yer hear what he said? Where the fuck are yer from, let's have it."

Both groups approached within a few yards of Jay Mac and he could clearly see that they were in full Skinhead 'uniform', almost identical to his own. He also registered them as being somewhat older, possibly seventeen or eighteen years of age.

"Am from the Crown Team, on the north side of the City." he answered as firmly as he could.

The second inquisitor laughed, "Never fuckin' heard of them, thee must be a shit team, full of queers, am I right?"

Jay Mac did not reply but stared directly at the speaker, the first questioner pushed him from behind and said "'Ey, dickhead that's Kav of the South Dock Skins talkin' to you there, so fuckin' answer him."

Jay Mac continued to look at the youth now identified as Kav, a tall, rangy Skinhead with a dark crop, bushy sideburns and

Natural Born Skinhead 1971 • 61

distinctive large, flat protruding ears set perpendicularly to his acne-scarred face.

"Yer'll have t'come back with me to the Crown Estate Kav and tell the lads there what yer think. They'd probably find that really interestin'." Jay Mac answered with a grin.

Kav was momentarily surprised by this challenging reply then said to his team mate standing behind Jay Mac, "Tony see if this cunt has got any team markings on the back of his denim, cos I can't see any from here on the front."

Tony did as instructed, quickly calling back, "Nah, he's lyin', he's not part of any team, only a soft kid pretendin' to be a Skinhead."

Kav sneered at Jay Mac saying, "Alright kid, am gonna be decent with yer. See those new pair of Airwair yer've got there, well you don't need them cos yer not really a Skin, so do yerself a favour, take them off, pass them over t'me an yer can gerroff with yer pet pig, wirrout gettin' a kickin', deal, ok?"

Of all the items that Kav could have asked for from the youth, whether wallet, or watch, if he had worn one, he had picked the one thing that Jay Mac would never willingly surrender. When in the summer of 1969 he had first read newspaper reports about Skinheads and determined to become one, he set out to acquire the distinctive kit any way that he could. The one vital element that he desperately needed to be fully acknowledged as a legitimate Skinhead, a pair of Griggs' original, 1460, eight-eyelet, cherry red Dr. Marten's Airwair boots with genuine bouncing soles, was the most expensive and difficult for the cash-strapped schoolboy to obtain. After months of running errands and carrying out any menial task, he finally had sufficient funds to buy his first pair of the famous footwear. They gave him recognition, status and identity and could not be given up lightly.

"Ok mate, I don't want any trouble, hang on I'll unlace them and give them to yer." he called back to the sneering South Dock Skin.

Kav looked from one to the other of his friends, pleased with Jay Mac's passive response, "See I told yer lads, yer can always tell a real shit-house, yer can almost fuckin' smell them."

Natural Born Skinhead 1971 •62

While gloating he made the crucial error of momentarily glancing away from his intended victim; it was a mistake that always resulted in pain.

Crouching down low Jay Mac quickly unclipped Alfie who appeared bemused by what was happening around him. In a flash the Crown player sprang forward with the heavy shank, metal dog chain wrapped around his fist and smashed a thumping right hook into Kav's unprotected face.

"'Ere y'go, smell this yer cunt!" he shouted letting his school friend, Liam's advice guide his actions, having split Kav's nose and lips and now concentrating on pounding his ribs with both fists. Self-confessed coward as he was, he also recognised that he was trapped and would take a beating either way, therefore, he might as well do some damage of his own, seeing attack as the best form of defence.

It was a bold but futile gesture; these were four experienced scrappers that he was facing. For a few fleeting moments Jay Mac provided a tour de force display of one determined individual holding off a group of equally committed attackers. Stepping back from the bloodied Kav, he released the chain to its full length, holding on to its leather strap handle and began lashing faces and limbs as they came within painful range. All the while Alfie, the bullterrier, wandered about inspecting the pavement and crumbling brick walls of the terrace facades for interesting traces of previous canine visitors.

"Get this fuckin' cunt!" Kav ordered, enraged, "Everyone jump in, fuck the lead, just get him down."

After repeatedly kicking Jay Mac from all sides, particularly striking at his legs to weaken his stance, all four leapt upon him and dragged him to the ground. He knew the drill, four years in the Cardinals' institution had taught him well. Quickly he assumed the foetal position, tucking his head in between his raised forearms and drawing up his knees into his chest.

The raging quartet of South Dock Skins went insane in their efforts to kick him to death. Boot after boot struck the human football, covering him with stripes of ox blood polish, almost spinning him around where he lay on the wet pavement. As Kav and Tony diverted to stamping rather than kicking, their two team

Natural Born Skinhead 1971 • 63

mates carried on as if trying to score winning goals. Jay Mac turned and turned about receiving blow after blow without making a sound, he had also learned long ago never to cry out. He maintained his determined silence until a particularly violent kick caught him between the legs, in his testicles.

As Jay Mac let out an agonised howl of gut wrenching pain, Alfie pricked up his ears, turning to study the scene more closely. The bullterrier had had quite enough. He had dismissed the name calling and accepted the interruption to his afternoon stroll with good humour but this unprovoked attack on his travelling companion and friend was too much. Snarling angrily so that all may observe his magnificent full complement of flesh-tearing, bone crunching teeth, a gesture which also served as formal announcement of his intentions, he tapped into the rich vein of his canine gladiator heritage and unleashed the awesome warrior from within. Letting out a terrifying guttural roar, he leapt into the action. Springing forward with all the coiled strength his powerful musculature could generate, he threw himself into the fray, literally tearing into his enemies with lightning speed and vicious ferocity.

While a much relieved and amused Jay Mac lay on the hard, wet pavement where he had been thrown, watching Alfie leaping from one to the other of his attackers, bellowing with indignant rage, the wild bullterrier ripped through prized, well-scrubbed jeans at leg and buttock height. Minor flesh wounds and torn fabric were the order of the day, serving as sufficient trophies for the triumphant hound, putting all four youths to flight, howling in pain and running from the scene of their intended robbery.

Jay Mac staggered to his feet aching in every muscle and limb, caught hold of Alfie and re-clipped his lead then firmly patted the animal's brick of a head. "Good lad, well done mate." he said grinning broadly.

Alfie responded with a classic bullterrier 'smile', wagging his stick of a tale vigorously in return as if to say, "What a tale I'll have to tell that bloody snooty cat."

"Let's go and see what booze Margaret's got left in that cabinet of hers, cos me and you deserve a stiff drink." Jay Mac said with a pained grin.

Natural Born Skinhead 1971 •64

Chapter 3

Natural Sinner

Autumn 1970-Summer 1971

Friday 4th September 1970

A long hot summer gradually faded into a warm, early autumn, beginning with a pleasant September, marred only by the obligatory return to school of Jay Mac and friends for their final year. The youth cult of the Skinhead was at its height both nationally and locally, with small neighbourhood crews merging into larger parochial, or estate teams. On the bleak Crown Estate, all five public house crews; The Heron; The Eagle; The Unicorn; The Hounds and The Bear adopted the unifying title of Crown Skins and generally accepted the over lordship of three of its most formidable fighters: Dayo (G), Tommy (S) and Devo (S), respectively: Graham Day, Thomas Southern and Sean Devlin. The latter two individuals of this terrifying triumvirate were universally acknowledged by all the subordinate players as being the most dangerous, though paradoxically they were a disparate, incongruous pair.

Sean Devlin was a wiry youth of average height but he bore the battered countenance of a seasoned scrapper, particularly his prominent damaged brow ridge and right orbital socket. He was also the son of a well-known if minor player, Michael Devlin or, Micky (D) who had been part of the Crown's original Teddy Boy gang during the early 1960s, favouring the use of a knife wherever possible. Devo (S) was dangerous, not just because of his lineage and scrapping abilities, which were nothing unique on a large, proletariat housing estate overloaded with 'baby boom' angry young men but because even amongst a number of undiagnosed clinical psychopaths, he stood out as the most unhinged.

Tommy (S) was an entirely different character both in build and temperament. At five foot nine he was marginally below the average five foot ten to six foot height of the majority of the crew but in a very positive sense, there was nothing else average about him either. Of stocky build in the human form of the proverbial brick out house, he displayed an incredible density and solidity for his size, possessing the heavy musculature of a young Olympic gymnast and two large brick fists at the end of his brawny arms. Although his black hair was always cropped to no more than the length of a number one cut, it was clear that if it were to grow out, it had the propensity to become thick and bushy. Surrounding his thin-lipped, hard, angular face, was a pair of impressive Victorian mutton-chop sideburns, which were only prevented from being a full beard by a one-inch gap beneath his chin. Set deep under his prominent brow, were two small, triangular, steel-grey eyes that looked more like splinters of glass when they caught the light. Only a fool would not have recognised this youth as a potentially awesome fighting machine, yet several fools chose to dispute this obvious fact, until they learned a brutally painful lesson.

Unlike the unhinged Devo, Tommy (S) was calm, balanced and above all courageous, he had heart in abundance; the Team recognised it instinctively and would follow his direction without question. The zones of command jurisdiction tended to be split amongst these three individuals, with Devo and his followers occupying The Unicorn at the southern boundary of the estate, Tommy (S) encamped with his loyal retinue in The Eagle and Dayo (G) choosing The Heron at the lower, northern edge of the estate for his base of operations.

As Jay Mac's school friends from the Crown lived close to the Eagle public house, it was this eponymous crew that he was desperate to join, hoping that eventually by performing some daring feat of arms, he would be accepted, at least as an honorary member of the Crown Team.

Opportunities would present themselves but first he had to concentrate on surviving one final year in the hellish environment of the Cardinals' Institution, replete with its own, ever-changing, hierarchical pyramid of fighting prowess, built from the living, bloodied blocks of determined, testosterone driven young males hoping to be placed at its pinnacle.

"Help me, help me please!" screamed the terrified First Year pupil on reaching the school yard and what he mistakenly believed to be the relative safety of an area predominantly occupied by Fifth Formers.

Natural Born Skinhead 1971 •66

"What the fuck are you doin' here, you little puke?" Terry (H) asked as he casually passed a cigarette that he was sharing with some of his crew, to Liam.

"Please, the third years are after me, they're gonna take me to the bogs for duckin'." the skinny eleven year old pleaded, near to tears.

Within moments a gang of six Third Year boys burst into the yard looking for their prey. They knew the rules, the far corner of the coarse, gravel covered, enclosed rectangular exercise area, was reserved for the upper school youths only and they were wary of trespassing into the territory of the densely packed ranks of these aggressive males, most of whom were Skinheads.

"He's over 'ere, y'can come and gerrim if yer want." Terry (H) called to them.

The terrified, hysterical boy ran along the line of grinning Fifth Formers and caught hold of Jay Mac, even as the posse of hunters closed on him. "Please don't let them take me... please, I've got asthma, I can't go down those toilets... please."

Jay Mac grasped hold of him by his colourful striped tie and pulled the boy towards him, "Hold yer fuckin' breath then," he snapped, adding, "Next time thee come for yer don't run this way."

The tearful boy was seized and lifted from the floor as he was dragged away to undergo the time-honoured initiation ritual, that awaited all those who could not elude capture by the 'hunters'. His face would be pushed down into a reeking toilet bowl filled with urine, packed with a flotilla of faeces, generously donated by several contributors. When the chain was pulled and the W.C flushed, he must hold his breath until the heavily stained bowl finally cleared of its stinking contents. Jay Mac, like the rest of his peers, watched dispassionately while the screaming, struggling boy disappeared back through the doorway and into the main corridor which led to the lavatory block. The Crown player remembered how, when it was his turn four years earlier, he had fought like a crazed, cornered animal and used his natural survival instincts to escape by running into an open classroom, leaping from a desk onto a high windowsill and dropping to the relative safety of the cobbled street, twelve feet below. Risking a broken ankle and receiving the punishment of the Brothers for leaving the school

Natural Born Skinhead 1971 • 67

without their express permission, was a price he was willing to pay.

"Poor little cunt, I almost felt sorry for 'im." Jay Mac said casually to his friends.

"That's cos yer too soft Jay Mac, yer need t'fuck that off." Liam the Skinhead sage advised.

"Get yer ciggies out lads, don't fuckin' keep me waitin'." Michael 'Mitch' Mitchell warned as he passed amongst the Fourth and Fifth Form throng, gathering the weekly 'protection' fee for his monstrous master, Robert 'Stamfo' Stamford, king rat and cock of the entire school.

Both Mitch and Stamfo enjoyed a successful symbiotic relationship, feeding each other's particular desires to their mutual benefit. Mitch was a deeply disturbed individual who was obsessed with 'Men's magazines' that featured stories and ghoulish, colourful, artists imagined scenes of sickening torture, particularly if practiced on women, supposedly by evil Nazis or leering Japanese troops of World War Two. Though his fellow pupils often suffered excruciating pain at his hands, Mitch's principal victims were more usually small animals or birds, his main delight being found in blinding cats and decapitating pigeons.

His business partner and protector, Stamfo was a lugubrious, apathetic giant of a youth, who gained some small amusement from watching or listening to detailed descriptions of Mitch's sadism, using the licensed torturer more as a debt collector than in any other capacity. If Tommy (S), the undisputed master of the Crown estate may be considered as a pocket battleship then the six foot two Stamfo, who appeared physically several years beyond his chronological age, was the fully-gunned destroyer of Liverpool's Skinhead fleet.

Jay Mac often mused over the potentially spectacular clash of Titans that would occur, if ever these two devastating scrappers were to confront each other. Surely, he thought it would be akin to a Ray Harryhausen stop-frame animation depicting two awesome, mythological creatures tearing into each other, the carnage would be Biblical.

Fortunately for Jay Mac on this collection day he had the required tobacco insurance payment to hand, having lifted two of his aunt's king size, filter tipped Embassy cigarettes the previous

Natural Born Skinhead 1971 •68

evening. Mitch was clearly disappointed, almost saddened as each pupil paid their contribution, stuffing his blazer and trouser pockets with contraband. Finally, much to the torturer's relief and delight, a Fourth Year boy failed to produce the goods and was quickly pushed by Mitch to the far corner of the yard, behind the milling crowd, where his punishment could begin. Screaming in agony as his testicles were being wrenched and twisted from side-to-side, whilst simultaneously receiving a series of unbearably painful sharp stabs in the buttocks, with the needle point of a pair of compass, he writhed about, involuntary tears streaming down his face, adding to the grinning Mitch's pleasure.

Not quite saved by the bell, more by an impromptu fight, one of the dozens that flared up throughout every day, the agonised youth was left crumpled on the floor holding his groin, receiving only the briefest of kickings from Mitch who, like the rest of his peers, was mildly curious as to what was occurring in the central arena of the yard.

Encouraging shouts of "Boot his fuckin' head in!" and "Knock his fuckin' teeth out!" abounded as the tight circle of eager fight fans drew around two Third Years who were vigorously laying into each other, both equally desirous of scaling that blood-drenched pyramid of fighters.

"Two ciggies on the blond lad!" Terry (H) offered, opening the betting.

Wagers were quickly placed, gamblers fearful that the bout may come to a premature end before they could secure a piece of the action. Stamfo, who rarely moved from his usual position, slouched against the rear wall, authorised his settler to offer five to one odds in favour of the stockier, dark-haired scrapper, whose nose was already clearly broken and streaming with scarlet fluid. Some unwise individuals took these seemingly generous odds, most however politely declined Stamfo's sporting gesture.

Jay Mac was watching the fight with renewed interest, curious as to Stamfo's uncharacteristic behaviour, having known him since their primary schooldays; when they had been the best of friends living in very close proximity to each other, in the old Victorian slum heartland of the city, he also knew that *he* only ever bet on certainties.

Natural Born Skinhead 1971 • 69

For a few moments it appeared this was going to be a unique occasion where Stamfo lost his 'money'. Then, suddenly the blond boy, now also bloodied, stepped away exhausted after delivering several powerful kicks to his kneeling opponent's face, only to receive a thumping strike to his own unprotected groin. Collapsing to his knees, he was immediately seized by his foe, thrown onto his back and straddled. Time after time his head was pounded into the coarse gravel-covered floor, reddening his fair hair with each sickening thud. Finally it was over, the stocky victor favoured by Stamfo, rose to his feet and in a traditional gesture of triumph, booted his fallen adversary in both sides of the head then spat into his bloodied face. As if officially finishing the bout, the bell rang to end morning break and the six-hundred plus boys casually formed into their allocated class lines, to await the arrival of one of the Brothers, or a member of the secular teaching staff, to admit them all back into the main building.

"Not a bad mornin' so far," Liam said with a grin as he stepped into place behind Jay Mac.

"No, still plenty of time for more entertainment, we've got Sir Wanker Watts next for French, that's always bleedin' good for a laugh." Jay Mac replied smiling.

Two of the stern faced, black cassock-wearing Brothers arrived, sweeping into the yard like a pair of huge menacing crows. All the boys, whether Skinheads or not, knew better than to trifle with these ecclesiastical tough guys, they may theoretically be men of God but they could unleash the fury of the devil if roused. Brother Mulcahy, the senior of the two now present, known by the pupils as 'The Boss,' addressed them before dismissal.

"Well, yer wretched creatures a new term has only just begun and already yer doin' Satan's work for him, fightin' in the yard, gamblin' and smokin'. We see *all* yer wickedness, don't you worry and even if we missed any of yer sins, He doesn't, He's always watchin' yer night and day."

"Some of these teachin' cunts in 'ere are totally fucked then." Jay Mac said in a whisper to his friends.

Quiet as he was, his murmuring was not missed by The Boss. "Mack, did you speak boy? Because I will happily flay the hide from yer with my friend here." he warned, producing his favourite

Natural Born Skinhead 1971 •70

three-foot long cane from within his gown, with a theatrical flourish.

"No Brother, not really... I was just sayin' Amen... Brother." Jay Mac replied straight faced.

A suppressed ripple of laughter spread through the ranks but the Brothers ignored this for the moment and dismissed the assembly line by line, in ascending chronological sequence. As Jay Mac's Fifth Form crew passed by The Boss, he struck with lightning speed, slapping the youth hard across the face, knocking him momentarily to one side.

"What's that for Brother? I haven't done anythin'." Jay Mac asked curiously.

"Have yer not boy? Ah well, I'm sure yer were thinkin' of doin' some devilment." The Boss paused then shouted along the length of the corridor "Remember boys, punishment is good for the soul."

Geoffrey Watts, foreign languages graduate and teacher of French at the Cardinals' was reluctantly making his way slowly towards the Fifth Form bottom set group, which included Jay Mac and friends, his anxiety growing exponentially with each laboured step. Less than affectionately known as 'Sir Wanker Watts-a-lot" or more simply Wanker Watts. He was entirely the proverbial 'square peg in a round hole,' both when facing his dreaded pupils and amongst the secular teaching staff, who were almost exclusively ex-military, either World War Two veterans or more recently National Service conscripts. Too young for the former conflict and judged too frail to serve in any capacity for the prescribed two years of involuntary duty, he was quiet, reserved and bookish, his only real passion being the study of languages. At the Cardinals' he was totally in the wrong place at the wrong time and he knew it, as did the waiting Fifth Formers, with their Skinhead majority, watching the classroom door for his arrival.

"Bonjour la classe." Mr Watts greeted them as he stepped into the room, "comment allez vous, ce matin?" he enquired politely.

The replies that he received from those who could be bothered to answer, were mostly in the form of an earlier vernacular Anglo-Saxon dialect containing a clear instruction, though tempered by a few less aggressive, "piss off wanker" responses. He knew it was going to be a long morning, particularly with this being a double period immediately preceding the eagerly anticipated lunch break. Bravely, or foolishly, he attempted to address the class and outline the supposed edifying content of the day's lesson, 'conjugation of French verbs'. Not one pupil glanced in his direction, most were sitting with their feet up on the desks displaying their contempt and gleaming Airwair boots, while a number of well-used copies of Mayfair and Playboy were being passed around, a sizeable card school was in progress and several keen students of the Sun newspaper's relatively new feature, the Page Three topless model, were shouting out obscene comments in between taking drags of their cigarettes.

In a grave error of frustration the teacher turned his back towards them, intent on writing the subject matter on the old blackboard with a piece of screeching chalk. Mr Watts had broken the primary, golden rule 'never turn your back on a wild animal' particularly if, as in this case, they hunt in packs. Everything that was not nailed down or in some other way restrained, was launched violently at the frantically scribbling teacher, from spit balls and wads of chewing gum to text books and whole contents of geometry sets, including their actual brass-coloured tin boxes.

"You animals! You swine! I don't deserve this, I'm an educated man!" Mr Watts shouted, the pulsing veins in his temple engorged with blood, standing proud of the surface like a zig-zag thread of flesh. "You'll never learn anything, you're un-teachable scum." he bellowed, trying desperately to make himself heard above their howling, jeering and whistling.

"Piss of wanker and take yer Frog verbs with yer, we don't need them." they called to him, some adding, "We're not goin' t'France, we fuckin' live 'ere."

"Yes you do and hopefully that's where you'll all stay, please God!" he shouted, tears of rage welling up in his eyes.

Less than a quarter of an hour after stepping into the classroom, a crushed, broken, formerly dedicated teacher walked back out pulling the door shut behind him. As he stood shaking in the vile smelling, narrow, claustrophobic corridor, he lit one of his favourite French cigarettes, saying "Merci, mon Dieu, c'est fini."

Natural Born Skinhead 1971 •72

He would never attempt to teach another lesson in that school or any other.

"Good effort lads!" Stamfo called out, simultaneously releasing a massive, protracted fart, "Now fuckin' pay up, I said he'd last no more than fifteen minutes, so let's have yer money. Mitch do the honours will yer and make sure no cunt misses out." Once again the house collected as it always did.

At this opportune moment Sharkey returned from his final visit, one of many, to the dentist, having had a false palette made with four new, regularly shaped teeth attached.

"Alright sir, havin' a quick crafty smoke are yer, I don't blame yer, these kids in 'ere would get on anyone's tits, you carry on sir, I won't tell no one." he said smiling broadly, proud of his new immaculate dentures.

The general pandemonium and testosterone charged atmosphere suddenly calmed as Sharkey entered the reeking room, each rival faction momentarily united in silence by the unexpected arrival of the previously vanquished heavyweight Skinhead.

"Alright Sharkey lad, glad t'see yer back, take a seat over 'ere." Vox called out, gesturing to the youth to sit with his crew, nearest the door, holding out a lit cigarette offering it to him.

Liam and his supporters stared without making comment at the enemy camp for a few seconds then resumed their card playing and pornography reading. A brief period of relative peace followed until Stamfo's gambling craving overcame him once more, leading him to encourage Mitch to provoke some fresh, possibly lucrative entertainment.

"How's yer new fangs Sharkey?" Mitch called to the denture wearer.

"Alright thanks Mitch lad, they're good enough t'take a bite out of anyone." Sharkey replied, unintentionally taking Mitch's bait.

"Fuck! You better watch out there Liam, sounds like this cunt is gonna try and take another piece out of yer." Mitch continued his work, smiling slyly.

"Yeah, well if he does, he'll be losin' those fuckin' teeth as well." Liam responded now also hooked.

Natural Born Skinhead 1971 • 73

Sharkey was on his feet in an instant, quickly crossing the wooden boarded floor, coming to a halt by the teacher's desk and vacant chair. "You won't get the fuckin' chance, yer ginger twat. Come and gerrit boy!" he shouted, crouching forward, stretching out both hands, palms upward.

Throwing his blazer from him, Liam sprang from behind the desk where he was seated next to Jay Mac and raced forward to do battle with his grinning adversary once more. "Those new fangs of yours are gonna be joinin' yer old ones, I've got a space waitin' for them in me other boot, yer fat cunt!" he shouted as he closed with Sharkey.

Even as Liam came within range of his stocky opponent, Sharkey quickly stepped back, his left hand resting on the top rail of the heavy, old, wooden chair. In one swift, continuous movement he pulled it in front of him then using both hands raised it above his head, before slamming it down upon the charging Liam.

"Get down there yer fucker!" Sharkey called out as he repeatedly struck his downed foe with the dark wooden piece of furniture, determined that there would be no repetition of his earlier defeat.

The kneeling Liam was stunned but desperately tried to defend himself from his gloating enemy's blows.

"Sharkey, yer fuckin' cheatin' bastard, no way are yer doin' this." Terry (H) and others of Liam's crew shouted, leaping to their feet and joining the fray.

"They're jumpin' in on Sharkey, everyone in." Vox responded, immediately leading his gang forward.

Within seconds the supposed re-match bout between two eager individuals turned into a wild mêlée with the opposing mobs punching and grappling each other, impelled by a murderous rage. Fortunately for them all, after releasing his pet sadist, Mitch, to pick victims as he pleased from either side, Stamfo chose to remain neutral and sat back laughing at the rear of the heaving room like a bloated Roman Emperor, watching the bloody struggle as if it were offered entirely for his entertainment.

Cringing in the corridor outside, knowing that he should do something but too afraid to intervene, Geoffrey Watts ran from the scene calling for help as he did. While the desperate conflict

Natural Born Skinhead 1971 • 74

swirled around the classroom with both sides' original champions wrestling each other across the filthy floor in the centre of the room, The Boss was already racing in their direction accompanied by two more Brothers, their black cassocks flapping ominously with the speed of their approach.

"Wretched creatures! Damnation awaits yer all!" The Boss roared, charging into the riot with his brethren, canes drawn ready to dispense some righteous, soul redeeming punishment.

Heads, faces, shoulders and arms were violently struck with the Brothers displaying the martial skills of warrior monks. All three were not averse to punching a boy to salvation if necessary, remembering they had not always been men of the cloth. No quarter was given even to those who surrendered and withdrew from the action, all were battered indiscriminately with equal savagery until eventually order was restored; only Stamfo, the seated spectator, remained unscathed.

With the heavily breathing, triumphant trio standing drenched in sweat, staring at their equally exhausted bloodied foe, The Boss delivered his judgement.

"You evil swine, you've cost a good man his job t'day and this school has lost a dedicated teacher. The Almighty knows what you've done and he'll punish yer all when the time comes but yer goin' to pay me now for y'sins. Gerrin t'that yard and line up in silence."

Stamfo was not happy with this proposal, "What about *me*, Brother, I've done nothin'?"

"Of course, Stamford, you haven't done anything have yer?" The Boss asked rhetorically, continuing, "And that makes your sin the worst of all. Will yer look at the size of yer, yer a big lump of a feller aren't yer? These little boys here look to you for leadership and you just sit there like a big sack of potatoes wearin' a stupid grin on yer face, gerrout boy, you're goin' t'get double whatever these fools get."

There was no further discussion, their sins had found them out and the first instalment of their painful chastisement would follow immediately. Standing in total silence in single file, all thirty two boys held out their hands horizontally to either side palms upward at shoulder height, like so many individual representations of the

Cross. With The Boss standing directly in front of the lead boy watching to ensure no one flinched or was accidentally deprived of some saving grace, the other two Brothers began their task, vigorously striking each rigid hand six times with their canes as they slowly proceeded along their respective lines. Not one boy winced or whimpered but all stared blankly forward. Only Stamfo showed any trace of an expression, grinning broadly as he received his extra portion. A far worse punishment would follow with a week of hour-long post school detentions only adding to the term of their sentence in the hated institution.

Jay Mac like the rest of his angry, frustrated, Skinhead classmates knew someone was going to pay dearly for what they viewed as totally unjust treatment.

The sinners would find some errant souls in urgent need of salvation themselves and dispense a suitable penance of their own. Regardless of whoever first set it in motion, the self-perpetuating cycle of violence rolled on.

Saturday 5th September 1970

Shortly before three o'clock on a still, close, Saturday afternoon, gathering together with the rest of the Anfield faithful, the Crown team players, who happened to be Liverpool Football Club supporters, were preparing to mete out some painful retribution to their most hated rivals, the Skinhead crews of Manchester United Football Club.

"Everyone tooled up and ready to get stuck into them fuckin' Mancs?" Tommy (S) asked leading his mixed crew of Seniors and Juniors, the latter of which included Jay Mac and his Cardinals' fellow pupil Terry (H), towards the turnstiles of this hallowed ground. They all answered in the affirmative.

Most of the younger Skinheads were carrying either coshes or knuckle-dusters, although Jay Mac preferred his recently acquired replica Seppuku knife in its shiny black lacquered scabbard. He had not as yet used it in anger but felt it had a certain style, an intimidation value that could prove decisive if it were required to be produced.

"Remember lads we're not dealin' with some no mark blurts here, these are Man United Skins, they're hard bastards and thee'll

Natural Born Skinhead 1971 •76

stand their fuckin' ground," Tommy advised unnecessarily, as they all knew of their enemy's fearsome reputation.

Johno recently 'made man' was ostensibly in charge of the Juniors: Jay Mac, Brain, two diminutive boxing brothers known as 'The Ants', Tank and James 'Treky' McCoy, who had recently obtained a deck-hand's position on the Isle of Man boats and was looking forward to a long, adventurous career at sea.

Treky always had an outspoken opinion about any topic that may come under discussion. "Yer Mancs are hard cunts alright Tommy, yer not wrong there but, they're not as hard as some of the lads yer get on the boats, yer know what I mean?" Treky offered, about to start one of his usual lengthy assessments of regional fighting capabilities but was interrupted sharply by Tommy (S).

"That's great that Treky, useful t'know but we're not on a fuckin' boat in case yer hadn't noticed, so keep that t'yerself and be ready when the time comes, ok?"

Suitably admonished, Treky knew better than to say anything further and followed their leader with his coterie of Seniors including: Dayo (G) his fellow commander, Gaz and the privileged Terry (H), allowed to stand with the rest of the 'old guard' both inside the ground and out.

Once they had all passed through the turnstiles they briskly made their way to their chosen position on the famed Kop terrace, in the centre behind the goal facing the rival supporters across the verdant green turf in the Anfield Road end. It was immediately apparent that unlike the usual forty five to forty eight thousand attendance, the ground was packed to capacity with over fifty thousand eager fans crammed into every possible and, impossible space. An uncomfortable afternoon lay before them where retaining their footing was absolutely vital to avoid being swept over, when the crushing Kop leviathan moved as one undulating mass.

From their position at the top of the terrace steps, just under the rafters, the huge Kings Skinhead team began to make their presence felt, constantly repeating their one word chant, 'Kings, Kings Kings' and unfurling their huge scarlet banners, emblazoned with white letters declaring 'Kings Skins'.

Natural Born Skinhead 1971 • 77

"Yer've got to give it to your boys Jay Mac, thee let yer know they're 'ere." Tommy (S) acknowledged from his place, one step up from and immediately behind the youth, unintentionally reminding him that *he* was not from the Crown Estate and still considered the outsider. Jay Mac did not reply but joined in the rousing L.F.C anthem *You'll Never Walk Alone*, one of the many renditions of this emotive song to be heard that afternoon. Directly across the field in the opposite terraced enclosure, the Manchester United fans responded with a chorus of boos, jeers and their own repetitious one word chant, "United, United, United," similar to that of the Blue half of their city.

After the players were announced on entering onto the pitch and the game had commenced, although the banter and songs continued unabated, there were no real outbreaks of significant violence other than some minor scuffles. Instead both sets of fans whether by design or accident settled into watching a brilliant display of top class football. With United fielding such legends of English soccer as Nobby Stiles, Denis Law, Bobby Charlton and arguably the finest player of his generation, George Best and these masters facing Liverpool stalwarts, Tommy Smith, Emlyn Hughes, Ian Callaghan and Ray Clemence 'the safest hands in the league', the match quickly became a thrilling struggle between two perfectly opposed sides.

Brian Kidd's twenty first minute rocket of a goal put Manchester United in the lead for almost one whole minute, until Alun Evans responded with a thumping strike for the mighty 'Reds' that tore into the back of the net and levelled the game once more. Despite wild exhortations from both sets of supporters and dazzling displays from individual players, the match ended as a one-all draw.

Not usually prepared to accept such an indecisive result and still smarting from the ignominy of finishing fifth in the First Division previous season's race, with their bitter Blue rivals, Everton, securing the title and accompanying bragging rights, today having been privileged to such a quality game, the majority of the Anfield faithful accepted the single point with good grace. When the great Bill Shankly made a post-match appearance on the hallowed turf, walking close to the lower edge of the Kop, wearing his red and white scarf about his neck, the effect was

Natural Born Skinhead 1971 ●78

unintentionally Messianic, the ecstatic crowd surging forward to touch his garb as if all their ills could be cured by this fleeting contact.

Within minutes of exiting the ground, however, a number of the more disgruntled Skinhead teams began to fixate on the unsatisfying draw, blaming the opposing team and by extension their jeering supporters, who felt that coming away to Anfield and securing a point was victory enough. The brief extension of bonhomie soon dissipated and the serious business of hunting the enemy in search of trophies began in earnest.

"'Ey lad, you with the big sidies, are you Tommy Southern from the Crown?" a tall skinhead with not inconsiderable sideburns of his own called to the Crown Team leader, as they left the ground.

"Yeah I am, why, what's it to you?" Tommy (S) called back, casually studying the six foot two male dressed in original kit of Levi's denim jacket, Ben Sherman shirt and Levi's white sixteen-inch parallel jeans with the usual cherry red Airwair, standing in the midst of two dozen similarly attired youths.

"I'm Albie Pitts everyone calls me Pitto, I run the west Kings Crew. You after Mancs the same as us?" Pitto asked.

Jay Mac had also been studying this new arrival and was pleased to finally be able to put a face to a name he had seen scrawled and painted in various locations on his own estate, even as far as the south Kings territory where he lived. He knew of Pitto's reputation as a long-standing original Skin and gauged him to be about nineteen years of age, with his crew comprised mainly of his chronological peers.

Tommy (S) though cautious, was intrigued by this formidable looking character's question, "Yeah, we're after Mancs so what is it yer want from us, yer look like yer've gorra a big enough crew of yer own." he asked.

"This is only part of our crew, a load of our boys 'ave gone off already up to the Lancs Road to do these Manc cunts in their coaches, when thee go through there. What we're after is fuckin' a few of their Skins here now before thee can even get t'the bleedin' coaches. What d'yer say, d'yer fancy jumpin' in with us, 'ave

Natural Born Skinhead 1971 • 79

your boys got the balls for it?" Pitto asked smiling slyly, revealing the odd arrangement of his few remaining teeth.

"You don't need to worry about my crew, these lads are fuckin' rock solid, none of them will shit out." Tommy replied angrily.

"Nice one Tommy lad, I heard you was an hard case. If yer boys can do the business as well, like yer say, we'll 'ave a result 'ere t'day. The Mancs 'ave got their cars and coaches parked all round by the Annie Roadan the other side of StanleyPark on Priory Road, right?" Pitto paused to ensure they were all listening then he outlined his plan. "We can't get near them with all these fuckin' plods hangin' round so what we need is a bit of a distraction like to pull them away, then get a crew of their Skins to chase yous into the park, where we'll be waitin' for them. What d'yer think Tommy, are yer up for it?"

"We'll sort that, don't you worry lad. Our Juniors will get the bizzies off then my crew will go for their Skins, that should bring them after us. You just make sure that your lads are waitin' in that park when we come runnin' alright?" Tommy paused while he received verbal assurances from Pitto and some of his closest companions then he added, "Yer see I've heard of you too Pitto an if you fuck us over, I'll know where t'find yer."

"*As if* Tommy lad, we're all Scousers here aren't we, yer know warra mean?" Pitto laughed then led his two dozen strong crew away in the direction of StanleyPark to prepare the ambush.

The Crown leader immediately began to deploy his troops. "Alright Johno this bits down t'you. Get yer Juniors here alongside some of those dad and lad Mancs, grab a few scarves, hats or whatever, make sure the bizzies come after yer, leave us a gap and we'll do the rest."

"Will do Tommy, no messin'." Johno replied, pleased to have been singled out for what he considered to be a prestigious action. "C'mon lads, let's gerroff!" he shouted to Jay Mac and his fellow Juniors.

Moments later they had selected a likely group of several older males who looked as if they had their grandchildren with them, theoretically a 'soft' target.

For Johno and crew, however, accepting the task of causing a diversion was one thing, actually achieving it proved to be an entirely different matter. A large police presence both of mounted

Natural Born Skinhead 1971 ●80

and foot officers, who were herding the United supporters along the main road towards their waiting cars and coaches, meant there were only limited opportunities to actually make a fleeting assault upon these fans. Both Johno and Jay Mac were acknowledged as two of the fastest runners in the Crown Team and they knew what was expected of them, as they darted quickly into a momentary gap between the shepherding police.

"Got yer!" Johno shouted pulling a red and white bobble hat from the head of a youngster only a couple of years his junior.

"'Ey, yer thievin' Scouse bastard." the boy's heavily built grandfather called out, bringing his massive left fist into contact with Johno's right temple, causing the Crown youth to stumble.

Others now also struck out at the unfortunate farm labourer leading Jay Mac to dash in and attempt to relieve *them* of their hats and scarves. The police patrol failed to respond, remaining close to the hardcore Skinhead faction that they were endeavouring to keep hemmed in, allowing the older fans to deal with the harmless stings of the two Crown gnats. Johno's crew were not the only pests that were harassing the extended column as it trudged on. Further along the line other prowling packs of hyenas tormented the increasingly exasperated United fans. Suddenly there developed a fierce struggle some ten yards to the rear of Johno and Jay Mac's unsuccessful efforts. A mounted officer left the Skinhead contingent he had been corralling, quickly trotting his dark chestnut horse towards the incident; Tommy (S) and his Seniors struck instantly.

"Come on you stinkin' Manc cunts, lets 'ave it!" he roared, leaping into the thick of the momentarily stunned United Skins, punching the nearest convenient face as he did. Dayo (G), Terry (H) and the rest of the old guard followed suit, coshes drawn, knuckle-dusters encasing fists, violently forcing a breech in their enemy's left flank.

"Yer fuckin' dead y'Scouse queers!" one huge M.U.F.C Skin bellowed in return as he strove to reach the Crown players, leading his own wild crew towards them.

Having achieved his primary objective, for the first time in his life Tommy (S) did as requested by the West Kings Team leader,

Natural Born Skinhead 1971 • 81

Pitto and turned to run away, hoping their raging foe would take the bait.

With cries of "C'mon lads, let's have these fuckin' Jessies." and, "Yer Scouse shitbags, we're on yer!" hurling after them, the Crown Seniors raced for the park some two hundred yards ahead, scene of the proposed ambush, intent on making their stand and joining forces with their Kings temporary allies.

"Fuckin' hell don't look back lads!" Gaz shouted, having made that very mistake and seeing the huge mob of thirty plus howling United Skins in very close pursuit.

For the moment the police were reduced to passive spectators as similar outbreaks occurred at numerous intervals along the extended line; reinforcements were urgently needed.

"What the fuck are we supposed t'do now?" Brain asked watching the ferocious Mancunians tearing after the Crown Seniors.

"What d'you think Brain, go home and put on a dress, or go after them cunts and help our boys out?" Jay Mac asked rhetorically.

"Come 'ed lads, lets leg it or it'll all be over before we fuckin' get there!" Johno their captain shouted, determined that he and his contingent would give a good account of themselves.

Racing in through the eastern entrance of the Victorian park, then across the manicured lawns and floral display beds, the Crown Seniors made for the central play area with its backdrop of dense ornamental hedging, where the Kings Skins should be waiting.

"Where the fuck are thee?" Dayo (G) shouted on reaching their destination and finding it totally deserted. "The bastards!" he declared angrily.

They all expressed similar dismay, all except Tommy (S) their leader, if he had any concerns he did not reveal them. With the United Skinhead horde almost upon his crew, he called them to a halt, preparing to face the enemy.

"Fuck this lads, am not runnin' any further, get ready, whatever yer carryin', make it count." he ordered.

The leading runners of the M.U.F.C Skins were delighted on seeing their hopelessly defiant stand, knowing they had their prey totally outnumbered. Coshes and knuckle-dusters in hand, the

Natural Born Skinhead 1971 •82

Crown Seniors stood resolutely awaiting their imminent assault. Tommy (S) had drawn his weapon of choice that he always carried, even though he had never owned a dog. By coincidence similar to the improvised tool that Jay Mac had used recently against the South Docks Skins, a heavy, metal shank, dog lead with a sizeable clasp and thick leather strap handle, had in recent years also become the Crown team leader's favoured implement of war that he used with devastating effect, supplementing his powerful fists, head and boots.

"Come on yer Manc cunts!" he shouted running towards them, meeting their advance with an equally explosive force and smashing their foremost Skin in the face with his metal assisted fist.

"Scouse bastards!" the Mancunians cried out on closing with their hated enemy.

Now all became grunts and shouts, thumps and cracks with wild punches, kicks and strikes of leather coshes filled with lead shot, as the Crown players desperately fought their numerically superior foe, whilst trying to remain standing and not be overwhelmed.

When Jay Mac and Johno, the fastest runners of the younger crew arrived at the scene of the action, at first it was impossible to even glimpse their own Seniors who were completely surrounded and in danger of being swamped by the sheer volume of their assailants. Momentarily Tommy (S) became visible darting from side-to-side, lashing out with his painful weapon of choice then deftly coiling it around his fist cestus style, pounding the nearest enemy within range.

Jay Mac had been aware that their leader used this particular tool but until now he had never seen him in action with it. Even as he watched the master class in progress, he raced forward accompanied by Johno and the rest of their crew to join the fight.

The unexpected arrival of these younger Crown players did little to alter the odds in favour of their Seniors and they were soon absorbed into the raging mêlée. Terry (H), exchanging punches with a huge Mancunian, stumbled close to Jay Mac who was grappling with another United Skin and for a moment they fought back to back.

Natural Born Skinhead 1971 • 83

"Just like the fuckin' Cardinals' Jay Mac," Terry (H) announced with a grim smile.

"Yeah, break time on a wet day." his fellow pupil called back, before they were separated by the action.

Violently thrown to the ground and instantly receiving a vicious boot to the face, Jay Mac panicked and withdrew his slender knife in its black lacquered scabbard. Before he could unsheathe it, the huge Skinhead standing over him kicked it from his hand then pulled out a blade of his own, intent on leaving the fallen youth with a permanent reminder of the day.

"'Ey you... Manc!" Tommy (S) shouted, appearing from nowhere at the left side of the surprised Skinhead, before driving his mailed fist into the jawbone of the knife wielder, fracturing it with a loud crack.

Jay Mac quickly retrieved his weapon and turned to thank their leader but he was already gone, moving back to wherever the fighting was thickest. Despite his sterling efforts and those of his combined crew, the Crown players were being badly mauled and in danger of suffering a major beating.

"Kings Team!" Pitto yelled, finally unleashing his troops from their concealed position, springing the trap at last. With this timely if late arrival of two-dozen fresh reinforcements, the tide of the ferocious battle gradually began to turn in favour of the combined local contingent.

Pitto threw himself into the thick of the fighting exactly as Tommy (S) had done and lashed out in every direction with his own tool, a short length of lead pipe.

Even as the United Skins began to suffer a reprisal battering themselves, all the combatants momentarily froze then disengaged on hearing the dreaded cry of alarm, "The bizzies! It's the fuckin bizzies!"

Accompanied by snarling, barking German Shepherd attack dogs, a wave of uniformed police officers, truncheons at the ready, now came upon the brawlers from the rear intent on inflicting some post-match violence of their own. Everyone, whether Scouser or Mancunian dashed in all directions, friend and foe alike desperate to avoid capture, or suffer some renowned local police brutality. For a few brief moments, in a temporary action-less

Natural Born Skinhead 1971 •84

hiatus, the blood soaked Tommy (S) stood alongside his blood spattered opposite number Pitto and turned angrily towards him.

"You fuckin' Kings bastard, why did yer leave it so long before jumpin' in?" he demanded.

"Ah fuck off yer moanin' Crown cunt, we was lettin' yer 'ave a go but had t'jump in and save yers. Yer should be fuckin' grateful." Pitto retorted angrily.

"I'll fuckin' remember this... and you, yer shit-house," Tommy (S) warned.

"Don't you worry prick, the whole of the Kings Team is gonna know what happened 'ere t'day, you're gonna be fuckin' sorry." Pitto replied, almost spitting his words.

Seeing that a police dog handler was nearly upon them with his canine companion, both leaders ran in opposite directions and escaped from the clutches of the law, while multiple arrests occurred all around.

Neither side, Kings or Crown, would ever forget those events but none of them suspected the enormity of bloody violence that would grow from the evil seeds sown that fateful day.

◇◇◇

Within days the first signs of the bitter reprisals that were to come began to appear after Pitto, who assumed the role of the injured party, had disseminated his prejudicial tale of betrayal throughout the Kings Estate. Even in the southern district where Jay Mac's aunt and uncle's small council flat was located; a new piece of bold graffiti was now superimposed across the existing, almost undecipherable murals that covered every available space on shop fronts and bush shelters. Either in stark black, white or red paint dependent upon the principal colour of the material that they wished to overwrite, the inflammatory slogan 'KINGS GUNNERS, CROWN RUNNERS' was daubed large enough for all to read and for those who knew, to fully comprehend its meaning.

When this message had spread even to the seatbacks of the fleet of green Atlantean public transport buses, which passed through Crown territory en route to the city, *their* publicity agents responded with crude but clear, succinct works of their own: 'Kings Shit-houses Always Run' and 'Kings Queers' being the favourites of these. Some hostility erupted at home games of both Liverpool and Everton with missiles being deliberately launched at Crown supporters from the Kings usual position at the top of the Kop and Gwladys Street terraces respectively but as yet there had been no major incident.

Saturday 31ˢᵗ October 1970

On a bitterly cold Saturday night with a strong north easterly wind blowing, the Junior members of the Eagle crew, Jay Mac included, were gathered outside their regular meeting place, the permanently empty, securely locked and shuttered library. Having failed miserably yet again in their attempt to convince the sceptical bar staff of the eponymous alehouse that they were all eighteen years of age and been refused service, much to the amusement of their team Senior's, Tommy (S) and the old guard, they were consoling themselves with swigging from a number of bottles of cider, that they had at least managed to purchase from the less circumspect proprietor of the off-licence branch of the same hostelry.

"Fuck this lads its bleedin' freezin'." Blue observed unnecessarily, inadvertently reminding them that the warm, relative comfort and convivial atmosphere of the Eagle public house, tantalisingly situated just across the road from their present position, was for the moment denied to them. Ever mindful that his corpulent frame required regular sustenance, he continued, "Let's have a stroll down to Mr Li's and gerra load of nosh, it'll warm us up, yer know worra mean?"

"We all know what you mean Blue *you're* fuckin' hungry... again. Yer've just polished off four bags of crisps yer greedy cunt. Tell us one time when yer not starvin', now that would be scary." Jay Mac grinned as he spoke. Like the rest of the crew he was always amused by Blue's efforts to obtain additional rations, even though they all knew he was considerably overfed at home by his doting mother.

"There's nothin' goin' on up here, so we might as well go down to the Diner and see if there's any birds hangin' round outside." Johno suggested, having recently begun to assume more of a leadership role amongst them.

Natural Born Skinhead 1971 •86

With no more said, all seven youths, including Irish, Glynn, Tank and Brain moved off down the main central road in the direction of Mr Li's Golden Diner, considered the best eatery on the estate and run by the eponymous Mr Li, a formidable Chinese gentleman, whom they were all wise enough to respect.

As they strolled along the Skins zipped up their bomber jackets or fastened their Harrington's, depending on their choice of supplementary garb that they had worn over their usual denim jackets to combat the unseasonably biting cold conditions. Most were also wearing close-fitting, blue or black woolen hats, some even contemplating letting their number one crops grow out to a warmer length in keeping with the season.

Although a fish and chip shop existed in their own mid-estate territory, this was considered substandard and certainly not on a par with Mr Li's establishment, consequently the whole crew almost exclusively tended to eat at the Golden Diner, located at the lower northern edge of the bleak housing development. Unfortunately the negative aspect of its position from the Eagle Skins perspective was that it was in the heart of Heron territory close to that public house, where Yad, his fellow sinister commanders and their followers gathered.

On this cold, blustery night, however only the Heron Juniors were perched along the low perimeter walls of the public house, while their three leaders enjoyed the warmer surroundings inside its crowded, cigarette smoke filled noisy interior. The Eagle players quickly purchased their steaming meals of golden battered fish, thick cut chips, sausage or pie dinners with extra gravy, or one of each in Blue's case and a selection of hot, crispy, chop-suey rolls, the latter as a nod to the healthy option. Apart from a canon of appreciative grunts and belches, there was little other communication between the ravenous youths, while they tore into their heavily salted and vinegar drenched comfort food.

Just as they were completing their meals their luck ran out and the atmosphere changed rapidly.

"Alright lads... and Jay Mac," Yad began on approaching with his two co-leaders Macca (G) and Weaver, "Come down 'ere for some decent scran, ey? I don't blame yers, that chippy of yours by the Eagle is shite but like yers already know, everything's better

Natural Born Skinhead 1971 • 87

down'ere in the Heron crew. If you's all ask me nicely I might think about lettin' yers join, except for you Jay Mac, we don't want any tarts in our crew." Yad smiled slyly as he spoke.

"No, fair enough Yad, I can see that." Jay Mac agreed. "There wouldn't be any room not with the biggest fuckin' tart on the estate already runnin' the crew."

The Eagle players laughed but a seething Yad responded quickly, "Are you callin' Macca a tart, or maybe yer mean Weaver, is that it?"

Jay Mac looked from one to the other of this pair before replying. Macca (G) the sexual sadist, whose only real pleasure was derived from someone else's pain was a tall, rangy character with a unique feature that often caused him ridicule from the Seniors, who could not seriously consider him as a fellow Skinhead, with his long, dark wavy hair that he refused to cut. Alone amongst a cohort of cropped haired youths of generally similar size and physique he stood out, even though he wore the exact same uniform as them.

Weaver in stark contrast appeared in many respects like a twin of Tommy (S), although marginally less stocky but also possessing impressive sideburns and uncannily similar, steel-grey, triangular eyes. He was a vicious fighter whose primary enjoyment came from permanently marking his victims with his weapon of choice, a solid steel toffee hammer, which he used with lightning fast dexterity.

Jay Mac nodded to them both then returned his gaze to the grinning Yad, "Macca and Weaver know I don't mean them, just like you know it, yeah?" he answered firmly. Keeping his eyes fixed on Yad, waiting for the slightest tell-tale movement.

"We got knocked back in the Eagle again, tryin' to get served." Blue suddenly blurted out, drawing the attention of all three new arrivals towards himself and away from Jay Mac.

"Shut it fat arse, we're not interested." Macca (G) snapped angrily, annoyed the moment had passed and that Yad was distracted by Blue's outburst.

"What's that Blue, yous couldn't get served in the Eagle again, is that right?" Yad asked with a broad smile.

"Yeah, that's right Yad, it was fuckin' embarassin' cos Tommy (S) and the boys were all there." Blue continued unabashed.

Natural Born Skinhead 1971 •88

Yad belched loudly "There y'go lads, smell that, there's five pints of brown mix in there, see if yers can get pissed on that." He laughed at his own sparkling wit, "Yer see I've told yers come down 'ere, ask us about joinin' the Heron crew and I'll see what I can do about gettin' yers served in our alehouse. Sid, the landlord knows better than to cross us three."

"Or yer brother Dayo and his mates yer mean?" Jay Mac offered with a smile.

Before anything else was said four young boys aged no more than ten or eleven years, part of the increasing number of feral children who seemed to wander the estate at all hours of the night and day, usually accompanied by a scrawny, Heinz 57 of a dog, ran around from the garages directly towards the combined crews.

"Come with us will yers, big lads 'ave stole all our wood for the bonfire." one of them cried, clearly distressed, with a trail of dried snot and blood running from his nose onto his chin.

"Yeah, thee said the fields are *all* theirs now and when Benny told them it was ours thee twatted 'im." another excited grubby boy advised.

"What the fuck is goin' on? Yous better not be lyin' yer little shits." Yad warned.

"No we're fuckin' not, thee was all big lads and thee came over from the Kings side of the road." the bloodied Benny replied, causing Jay Mac to experience a sinking feeling.

"Come 'ed, if its Kings rats, they're fuckin' dead." Yad bellowed before racing to the corner by the rear of the burned out garages, leading both crews, seething with rage tinged with delight.

When they arrived by the farmer's old field, which lay to the rear of the Heron and shops, extending several hundred yards to the north and on its western edge to the man-made, bisecting boundary of the Lancashire highway, at first they could not see any sign of the alleged intruders. After squeezing through the convenient gap in the rusty old perimeter railings, they quickly though carefully made their way to the roadside, leaping across the stinking river that meandered through the fields at a specific crossing point where its muddy banks were closest to each other.

"There thee are." the keen eyed Johno shouted on observing a gang of youths carrying large pieces of timber on their shoulders,

Natural Born Skinhead 1971 • 89

disappearing into the dense screen of tall grass and weeds that thrived in this section of the field on the Kings side of the road, long abandoned by the farmer after the main thoroughfare had split his considerable acreage, without leaving him an access bridge or crossing.

"'Ey you, yer fuckin' cunts stop where yer are!" Yad roared, totally without any effect. "'Ey y'shitbags, come on let's 'ave it!" he demanded, equally to no avail.

All of the Crown Skins advanced further, dashing out between the fast moving inbound traffic, gathering on the central reservation, starkly lit under the yellow beams of the tall highway lights. Even as they were about to cross between the outgoing traffic to the far side of the busy dual carriageway, they heard, "Kings, Kings, Kings!" being shouted by several dozen voices.

Deciding to halt on the central reservation, they could all hear the familiar chant growing louder and rapidly coming closer to them. Without any further warning at least three dozen Kings Skinheads burst out from the curtain of grass and weeds, raced to their edge of the road and commenced delivering a salvo of bricks and stones directly onto the Crown players, marooned as they were in the middle of the highway.

Pelted and struck by a hail of missiles on the head, shoulders and upper arms, launched by a numerically superior force, they had no alternative other than to fall back. Sprinting once more between the speeding traffic, they regrouped on their side of the carriageway and began searching for ammunition to return fire. By the time they had gathered sufficient suitable material it was too late, the enemy force had slipped back into the darkness of their natural cover and departed carrying their wooden trophies with them.

The mixed Crown crew of Heron and Eagle players trailed disconsolately back through their own field, only to be stopped in their tracks by a further glaring insult.

"What the fuck!" several of them called out as they stared in disbelief at the long, continuous, ten foot high brick wall that spanned the southern edge of the field below the grey, high rise tower blocks.

Natural Born Skinhead 1971 •90

'KINGS SKINS RULE OK!' was painted in broad white letters, each at least six feet tall, along two thirds of the brick boundary's length.

The recriminations were immediate and direct, "This is down t'you Jay Mac, yer fuckin' Kings rat, you probably knew thee where comin' here t'night." Yad roared angrily.

"Piss off Yad, that's fuckin' bollocks, and you know it." Jay Mac responded equally irate.

At this point, Johno felt that his seniority and by extension, leadership, was being called into question and stepped between both raging youths. "Listen Yad I'm gettin' really fucked off with you always goin' on about this lad. He's part of the Eagle crew and I'm the Senior Eagle Skin here, so I'm tellin' yer... back off."

Now Macca (G) and Weaver thought their fellow leader was being challenged, which reflected badly on them, "Watch where yer goin' there Johno, yer not a bad lad don't make me use me hammer on yer." Weaver warned genuinely.

"No disrespect to you Weaver, or you Macca but like I said, I go t'work not school, I was put up to senior by Dayo (G) himself and if anyone's got any fuckin' doubts about Jay Mac, go up to the Eagle and ask Tommy (S), or even closer, go into the Heron and ask Dayo, Yad's brother. They'll both tell yer what happened when we was up against the Mancs." He paused and let them all absorb what he had said, then added, "Thing's looked fuckin' bad in Stanley Park, Jay Mac could've got off, he could've said I'm not even a proper Crown Team Skin but he didn't, he got stuck in just like the rest of us, yeah?"

When the indignant farm labourer had finished his honest assessment of his fellow Eagle player and LFC supporter, nobody made a further comment and they all trudged away in the direction of the Heron public house and dilapidated shops.

Later, after the Eagle crew had returned to their own usual perch outside the presently windswept library, Jay Mac thanked his friend for his intervention and straight talking.

Johno remained impassive, responding flatly "I only told the truth Jay Mac, that's all. What's right is right otherwise I wouldn't have said anythin'."

Natural Born Skinhead 1971 • 91

Irish had not intervened previously, feeling that the steadfast Johno had adequately dealt with the situation but now warned his school friend, "I'd stay away from the Crown for a while Jay Mac, I don't think yer gonna be welcome round 'ere until things settle down. I'll see yer back in the Cardinals' on Monday and tell yer how it's goin', see yer." With that he walked away to his nearby home in the road behind the central shops.

The others also departed leaving the miserable youth to wander back down to his bus stop on the lower edge of the estate. Jay Mac the illegitimate child of a drunken mother, who barely recognised his existence, always wanted to belong, rejection and possible ostracism from his likeminded, sub-culture peers was worse to him than any physical beating that he may have suffered.

As he stood waiting at the deserted bus stop not far from the Heron and its row of shops, the discarded newspaper wrappings of earlier consumed greasy fare, came flying across the road, airborne on a gust of blustery wind and firmly enfolded about his legs.

"Fuckin' great, that's just about right." he observed dejectedly.

Chapter 4

I'm a Neanderthal Man

Spring/Summer 1971

For the next few months Jay Mac followed his friend's well-meant advice, in part. He curtailed the frequency of his visits to the Crown Estate, kept away if possible from the Heron territory, or at least ensured that he did not rise to any of Yad's provocative remarks, whenever he accidentally came into his company. Apart from these avoidance procedures he also slightly altered his route from the lower bus stop to the centre of the estate, where the Eagle crew met.

In doing this fate then intervened and led him into the acquaintance of three entirely different, disparate characters, all of whom would have a significant impact upon the impressionable youth.

One of these, known as Tony (G), an apprentice electrician, scooter enthusiast and capable Skinhead scrapper, was a popular member of the team and rightfully belonged at its centre. Due to family circumstances, he happened to lodge in the house of his parents' friends who themselves had one son, Malcolm 'Mal' Chadwick. Mal was a genuinely weird young man, who had no desire to belong to any group, only wishing to be a loner, an outsider. Stylistically he represented the antithesis to the majority of the estate's Skinhead youths, choosing to dress in the fashion of a late 1960s Hippie, though even here his choice was deliberately intended to set him apart from his peers, not through any wish to associate with this particular cultural movement. He had only one passion, a compulsive obsession with the occult, in particular attempting to contact the dead. Mal had his own reasons for this and he kept them to himself, even his gregarious house guest, Tony (G) had no understanding of what motivated his bizarre quest. The presence of this popular Skinhead, however, gave Mal ingress into circles where he would not normally be welcome, the other Skins being prepared to tolerate him for Tony's sake. When Jay Mac became friends with the one, he also became an acquaintance of the other.

Natural Born Skinhead 1971 • 93

The third of these differing individuals was Michael Pemberton, an overweight, relative newcomer to the estate, whose acne covered flabby face instantly earned him the unkind sobriquet Mickey 'pimple'. Though unlike the charismatic Jay Mac who was generally popular with most of the Crown team players and their leaders, apart from Yad, Mickey, who dressed in his own version of the Skinhead style, was exactly the same in one respect as the Kings' renegade, he also was desperate to belong.

During the fateful year of 1971 with the Skinhead cult showing no signs of abating, other than some significant stylistic changes towards the later months, the paths of all four would be inextricably woven together with painful consequences.

Spring-Summer 1971 - Friday 23rd April

Whatever major or minor events were occurring on the Crown Estate, Jay Mac and his fellow Skinheads of similar age, if they had not already left school as in Johno's case, still had to endure one final term before the great release came. After nearly five years trapped in the dark dungeons of the Cardinals' hellish institution, a faint ray of light at first no more than the size of a pinhole, pierced the dense fog of ignorance and abuse and through that tiny aperture into the hot sulphurous atmosphere came a tantalising, sweet scent of freedom. The Fifth Year boys recognised it instinctively and knew that finally the end was in sight; the Brothers and masters also recognised these signs, reluctantly acknowledging that their brutal reign of terror was almost over, at least for these fortunate pupils. In addition they knew that discipline would be even more difficult to enforce and watched closely during each long day, waiting for the growing restlessness and defiance to take expression in the form of open revolt, cognisant that their own response would have to be Draconian and excessively violent in order to crush any outbreak, before it could spread to the lower years.

The Fifth Form pupils, the majority of whom like Jay Mac, Irish and Terry (H) belonged to aggressive Skinhead teams across the city, were preparing to initiate their own long dreamed of revenge with a series of orchestrated actions of wild anarchy and mayhem known as 'National Riot Days.' When the opportune time arrived the signal would be given and organised chaos would

Natural Born Skinhead 1971 •94

ensue, no surrender and no quarter were to be contemplated, only when a sufficient degree of retribution had been achieved would the hostilities cease. With this exciting prospect uppermost in their minds, the various Skinhead crews wandered about the school during breaks and lunchtime, with greater swagger than usual, flagrantly disregarding any attempt to impose authority, waiting for that one flashpoint incident.

"Come 'ed yer little bastards, where is it?" Mitch asked the two terrified First Year boys, that he had captured near to Mr Arkwright's woodwork rooms.

He was dangerously close to blinding one of them as he pressed the thumb of his right hand deep into the crying boy's eye socket, forcing the soft, watery orb back within.

"Where's that fuckin' cat? Tell me or his eye's gonna get popped instead!" Mitch demanded of the boy's companion.

"Alright Mitch lad, havin' a bit of trouble with these two little bummers are yer?" Liam asked casually as he and his crew came alongside.

"There's a fuckin' stray cat hidin' somewhere in this shit-hole and these little cunts 'ave been feedin' it. Thee know where it is but thee won't say." Mitch snapped angrily in reply, increasing the pressure on his intended eye-gouging victim, while simultaneously firmly squeezing the testicles of his other captive with his left hand.

Both boys were now crying but refused to reveal the whereabouts of this foolish feline that had sought shelter in the dilapidated old building, willing to pay for its lodging by disposing of several mice from the innumerable horde that infested its rotten fabric.

Liam looked at the boys then back at Mitch who was salivating with delight, "Ok Mitch they don't know nothin' about any fuckin' cat, thee would've told yer by now, so let them go, yeah?" Liam ordered calmly.

"Fuck off yer ginger twat. I'm enjoyin' meself, get yer own First Years if yer fancy a bit of fun." Mitch responded with a sneer.

Instantly Liam threw his left arm around Mitch's scrawny neck, catching hold of his right wrist with *his* right hand and pulling

Natural Born Skinhead 1971 • 95

Mitch's hand away from the agonised boy's face, as he lifted the struggling torturer off the ground.

"Go'ed, fuck off kids, Mitch wants to talk to us now." Liam shouted, increasing the pressure of his choking lock on the gasping sadist.

As the tearful boys walked away Jay Mac raised the thumb of his left hand and called to them, "Nice one lads, yer done well."

"Right Mitch, tell us where this fuckin' cat is cos we really wanna know," Liam demanded, grinning to his friends.

"I don't fuckin' know do I?" Mitch gasped, his face now purple, his eyes bulging. "Please Liam, let me go, yer chokin' me." he pleaded.

"Sorry Mitch, me hearing's fucked, I've been practising on the rifle range with the cadets, yer'll have t'speak up." Liam advised.

Mitch was now close to unconsciousness and cried out as best he could, "Please Liam let me go!"

Finally Liam released him, "Go on Mitch, piss off before I really hurt yer."

Once he was at a safe distance Mitch called back "You'll be sorry yer ginger fuck, when I tell Stamfo what yer done."

"Do one yer little bitch." Liam replied then pelted Mitch on the head with a well-thrown, *Refresher* sweet from a pack which they were all sharing.

The crew laughed but they felt uneasy about Liam's actions.

"Yer know he'll tell Stamfo some fuckin' story that will get him after you, don't yer?" Terry (H) observed.

"Well, like I've said Terry, mate, no point worryin' about the fuckin' consequences, sometimes yer've just gorra do what yer've gorra do and fuck it." Liam replied philosophically as the bell rang to end morning break.

A couple of hours later, after a substitute teacher of French had bravely tried to keep them in the classroom if not actually studying, during their lunchtime, Liam, Terry (H), Jay Mac and Irish separated from the rest of their crew, choosing to patronise a fish and chip shop located slightly further afield that they preferred.

It was not just this particular eatery that attracted them to this specific location. Not far from this original 'fast food' shop was

Natural Born Skinhead 1971 •96

another high street vendor of an entirely different nature, *Madame de Paris, Purveyor of fine Corsetry and Exotic Lingerie*, was a somewhat incongruous establishment occupying as it did a corner site between the fish and chip shop on one side and the sombre funeral parlour on the other, suggesting that either or both earthly pleasures could only lead to one end.

Apart from casually observing some of the fascinating garments on offer in its two large window displays and storing mental images for subsequent pleasant fantasising, what principally drew the boys to this purveyor were the young female, usually attractive, sales assistants that the canny Madame tended to employ, a feature which also brought older, discerning male customers to peruse her tantalising wares.

"'Ave yer ever noticed that in the five years we've been lookin' in these friggin' windows, womens' tits'ave got less an less pointy? Thee could've had yer eye out with some of the kit thee've had in 'ere." Jay Mac observed before greedily forcing another handful of vinegar doused soggy chips and Vienna loaf into his already overstuffed mouth.

"It's not their tits that've changed shape, soft lad, it's just the fuckin' gear thee hold them up with." a knowledgeable Liam advised, almost choking on his extra-large portion of fish and chips that he was rapidly devouring.

"What about those birds in America who go round burnin' bras; what the fuck's that all about?" Irish asked curiously in between lighting a post lunch cigarette to aid his digestion.

"Thee don't just burn any fucker's bra, Irish, thee do their own and let their jugs 'ang out." Terry (H), who was clearly another keen student of these matters, advised.

"There y'go... see, what've I told yers? That's another good reason for movin' to the States... yer've got great big knockers with no bras, right in yer face, everywhere yer fuckin' look." Jay Mac, the obsessive Americana fan, who was always extolling his perceived virtues of life in the USA, concluded.

As they all finally finished their meals and lit their cigarettes, except Jay Mac, they stood outside Madame de Paris' establishment, casually studying the intriguing items on display.

Natural Born Skinhead 1971 • 97

Liam suddenly had a disturbing thought, "Wait a minute, what if *every* bird burned her bra? That could be fuckin' scary."

"Yeah, I know what yer mean Liam; imagine those two arl broosters who serve the sloppy shite in the canteen with their bags flappin' away. Fuck! It's enough t'give yer nightmares." Jay Mac conjectured, much to the horror of his friends.

"There'd have t'be an age limit. I mean, look at me Ma, she's a woman, I think, and I wouldn't want *her* doin' it." Irish added even more alarmingly.

"Fuckin' hell Irish no one would want that, not even yer arl feller." Jay Mac advised genuinely.

They all laughed, even Irish, allowing Terry (H) almost the final word on this fascinating subject. "Hang on there Irish, don't be too fuckin' hasty with yer age limit. There's a few tasty arl birds with a good set of lungs on them, that I wouldn't mind seein' wirrout a bra."

"Let's just say we'd only allow it if the bird was decent, otherwise... do us a favour girl... keep the fuckers tied up an out of sight." Liam finally concluded, receiving approving nods of agreement all round.

"'Ey lads, lookout! We've gorra live one in the next window, come 'ed." Terry (H) noted on observing the latest of the Madame's pretty, young female assistants entering into the window on the left of the centrally positioned door.

Given the prevailing fashion for micro-mini skirts and dresses was still at its all revealing height, it was not necessarily the most practical garb for working on a window display, which was already situated a few feet above ground level. As the embarrassed, blushing girl stepped out of her low heeled shoes and bravely attempted to arrange a new selection of nylon stockings, some 'worn' on upturned, detached mannequin legs, adding here and there packets of more functional, if less alluring, tights, she could not avoid revealing her own choice of underwear, which again following the prevailing trend where worn over her American Tan coloured tights.

"Well in girl!" Liam shouted appreciatively, adding unnecessarily, "Look at the arse on that!" His three fellow voyeurs also called out ribald observations, "Yer'd have those knickers down no problem." Terry (H) conjectured as he studied the girls

Natural Born Skinhead 1971 •98

tiny white with pink flowers underwear, tantalisingly positioned at the boys' eye-level, with only the frustrating pane of glass separating them from her well rounded bottom. When she stepped back a pace and brought her pert rear into contact with the window, all four pushed forward as if trying to place their hands on the prize even through the obstructing pane.

Finally the girl finished her arrangement, turned to exit the window display area and raised two fingers in victory salute towards them. At the same moment, while making this gesture, she smiled pleasantly in their general direction, prompting each of them to believe that this was a positive sign meant for him alone. Almost instantly even before they had turned from the window the door of the shop was pulled open from inside with a loud ringing of its bell. Madame de Paris also knows as Cynthia Prendergast, formerly of Central Lancashire, dashed out angrily towards them.

The once stunning brunette, proud possessor of an enviably top-heavy hourglass figure, kept herself well-manicured and attractively attired, knowing exactly which foundation garments to choose to ensure that her goods were always displayed to their best advantage. Standing before them now in her fitted silk blouse, tight pencil skirt and stilettos, she epitomised the attractive older woman fantasy figure to these appreciative, lustful young males.

"Get away from here you dirty little pigs, before I go and complain to the Brothers!" Cynthia warned, instantly recognising their infamous uniform.

"There's no need for that missus, we were only admiring your new girl's assets." Jay Mac pleaded, making a gesture as if tugging his non-existent forelock.

"Were you now? You wouldn't even know what do to with a *real* woman, if y'fell over one." she responded firmly but with just the briefest of smiles.

"Why madam, that's a most generous offer on your part, challenge accepted." Jay Mac replied and then bowed formally.

"*You*! you're only a boy, don't make me laugh." Cynthia chuckled and raised her well-plucked eyebrows, hinting at a playful, girlish nature.

Jay Mac pressed on momentarily experiencing the briefest spark of electricity between them. "On the contrary madam, I'm

Natural Born Skinhead 1971 • 99

sixteen years of age, fully primed and ready for action. How should we go about this? Perhaps you could lie down and I'll fall over you then see where that leads us."

Cynthia blushed, "Go on be off with you, that's enough cheek from you." she advised, this time allowing a pleasant smile to light her attractive face for more than a fleeting instant.

The boys strolled away in the direction of the Cardinals', smoking their final cigarettes before their lunch break ended.

"Now that's one golden-oldie I'd help burn her bra." Terry (H) began.

"Too fuckin' right mate, did yer see the size of the set on her?" Liam agreed, adding, "I tell yer what, she's got the hots for you Jay Mac, I bet she'll be given 'erself a little feel later on, thinkin' about this feller on the job." They all laughed even Jay Mac, who, though still fixating on the stimulating mental images of the young shop assistant, was also briefly visualising some equally erotic thoughts about the shop's voluptuous owner.

Irish was his usual critical self, observing, "Fuck, can yer imagine if those two beauts got loose, yer'd be suffocated in tit."

"Now that's the way yer'd wanna go, with a fuckin' big smile on yer face, thanks Irish, I'll be thinkin' about that all afternoon, when I'm havin' a few tugs in double Physics." Liam advised.

These four young studs had no comprehension or understanding of who they were dealing with, or that they would be totally out of their depth if ever they were fortunate enough, to find themselves in the company of the vastly experienced, more than capable Cynthia.

Twenty seven years previous, at the age of sixteen, Cynthia had helped a handsome, young American G.I. to relieve his pre-Normandy landing's anxiety, effectively calming his nerves in the most natural and basic way possible. He survived his tour of France, returning to England for the final embarkation, Stateside; the naive Cynthia being almost crushed in the throng as she waved him goodbye from the quay at Liverpool docks. Promising to send for her, the smiling, grateful young man blew her a kiss from the top deck of the huge transport ship. The longed for letter never arrived, only the goodwill 'package' he had left her with, nine months later.

Natural Born Skinhead 1971 ●100

Johnny went marching home again back to his adoring wife and young son, who were waiting patiently for him on another dockside three thousand miles across the Atlantic, the car salesman from Detroit with the easy charm picked up the threads of his life, leaving Cynthia to do the same with the fragments of hers. She put the child up for adoption, moved from Central Lancashire to Liverpool and pursued her passion as a seamstress, eventually making enough capital to open her own lingerie shop; she never married. Men were allowed into her life only when she desired to admit them, when her appetite for pleasure was sated, they were soon dismissed.

Just as the Skinhead quartet were approaching the side entrance to the old, crumbling, mid-Victorian school building, which had long since ceased being fit for purpose, they encountered a group of First Year boys loitering nervously near the dark green, wooden door.

Jay Mac noticed that amongst them were the two earlier captives of Mitch 'the Torturer'. "What's happenin' youngsters? Not too keen on goin' back in for the afternoon 'ey?" he asked casually.

"No there's another Fifth Year after us and everyone says he's worse than that Mitch lad. Thee say he does real bad things t'yer." the red eyed, gouging victim advised.

Instantly all four youths knew who the terrified boy was referring to; Dennis 'Denny' Grimshaw, otherwise known by a range of homophobic alias: 'Denny Shirtlifter'; 'Denny Arsebandit,' or more usually 'Denny the Bummer'." An asthmatic, sickly boy, with pale skin, dark ringed heavy bagged eyes, a permanently blocked crusty nose and excessively prominent bad teeth, all topped with a mop of hair as equally stylish as that of Jay Mac's cousin, Margaret. He had initially enjoyed some success as a serious contender to Mitch for the prestigious title of 'official school torturer.' When his particular *modus operandi*, that of pulling down boys trousers and underpants then vigorously pretending to mount them, while squeezing their testicles, had become a little too repetitious, even for his coterie of grinning assistants, revealing too much of his own

Natural Born Skinhead 1971 • 101

suspect private penchant, he was quickly 'outed' from his flimsy closet. Less concerned with his sexual orientation, viewing him more as an exotic curio, Denny's chronological peers no longer aided him in his capture and assaults, leaving him to act either alone, or to rely on the goodwill of younger, less perceptive pupils.

"Lads, just wait 'til yer hear the bell then dive in quick and remember, never go anywhere near those fuckin' bogs." Jay Mac advised.

Terry (H) adding, "Anyway if one of yer gets gripped by Denny, stay together, don't fuck off an leave yer mate, if four of yer pile on and get into him, he'll back off, he's a total shit-house.

The boys seemed reassured and thanked their experienced seniors for their sound advice.

Jay Mac then asked, "Was there a cat, or did Mitch gerrit wrong?"

"Yeah, there's an arl moggie down in the cellar where Arkey keeps his wood. We saw it go in through that broken window outside when we was comin' into school on Monday, we've been feedin' it but it looks like its dyin'." Mitch's other victim replied.

"We'll have a little pipe around there in last break and see what's happenin'. By the way lads, how did Mitch find out about this cat?" Jay Mac asked.

"A prefect stopped us when we was comin' out the canteen with some milk and we told him. He said he wouldn't tell no one but then he brought that Mitch lad after us." the red eyed boy answered.

"Dark, wavy haired fucker, with a bad case of spots was it, by any chance?" Irish asked perceptively.

"Yeah that's right." both boys replied.

"Sound, we'll deal with him, see yer lads." Jay Mac said as he entered the foul smelling lower corridor with his friends, before making their way to the yard for the afternoon line up.

After a single lesson of Commerce and another of Geography had finally ended and during the quarter of an hour break before the dreaded, mind-numbing double period of Physics began, Jay Mac and Irish quickly made their way to the cellar entrance, outside the Woodwork rooms. The door was bolted with heavy iron fittings but unlocked.

Natural Born Skinhead 1971 ●102

Mr Arkwright was considered a reasonably fair teacher by most of the boys, though they also acknowledged his fearsome reputation for excessively painful punishments, administered via specially selected pieces of hardwood that he personally chose. Consequently nobody wished to transgress and incur his wrath. The large, clear notice secured to the cellar door which read 'KEEP OUT, or SEE ME! Mr Arkwright' was usually sufficient to deter any prospective trespassers. Only the bold or desperate would willingly enter into this dark, cold domain of musty labyrinthine passages. Jay Mac and Irish both thought it was worth the risk to save this unwary feline from a much more cruel fate than death, at the hands of Mitch.

Fortunately not long after descending the uneven stone stairs, by use of Irish's matches to supplement the one struggling shaft of natural daylight entering via the single broken narrow window, they soon located the aged Tom cat sprawled out on a length of freshly planed timber with a saucer of milk and a well-meant, uneaten Mars Bar in front of him.

"Fuckin' hell Jay Mac, this arl feller's on his last legs, I don't think he'll see out the day." Irish noted, sadly.

"Well he can't stay 'ere, he'll 'ave t'piss off back to wherever cats go to die. It won't take Mitch long to suss out where he might be, not with that rat of a prefect Daniels helpin' him out." Jay Mac replied pragmatically. "Come 'ed, let's help him back up through that broken window, before it's too late."

Both Skins carefully handled the lightly mewing old tabby cat as they climbed up onto the timber and raised him towards the opening. Even as Irish pushed the misplaced moggie from the Stygian depths into the warm fresh air outside the forbidding, educational institution, they both heard urgent footsteps on the stairs not far behind them. Turning about they saw Mitch standing with his reviled escort the prefect Reggie Daniels, a notorious informant known by them all as 'Daniels the Rat.'

Daniels shone a small torch that he was carrying in their direction and Mitch asked, "What are you two fuckin' queers up to 'ey? Bummin' the arse rings off each other, I'll bet." He did not wait for a reply but pressed on, "'Ave either of yer seen this fuckin' cat that's supposed to be livin' down 'ere?"

Natural Born Skinhead 1971 • 103

"No, no cats down 'ere, too fuckin' damp for anythin' like that." Irish advised, with Jay Mac adding, "Yer more likely to find a fuckin' arse sniffin' rat Mitch."

"What's that Mack, are you tryin' t'take the piss?" Mitch asked angrily with his companion shuffling nervously, keeping close to him. "'Ave you still got yer foreskin boy? Cos I'm doin' a nice line in circumcision at the moment, free of charge." the sadist enquired.

"No thanks Mitch, kind of yer t'offer but I think I'll keep the old Jap's eye with his hood still on, yer know, with the winter comin' on like." Jay Mac replied.

"What about you O'Hare, fancy a little snip off yer Irish prick?" Mitch asked extending his generosity further.

"Ah no, not right now thanks Mitch, I'll leave things as thee are for the moment." Irish replied. "What did yer want with the cat anyway Mitch, did yer wanna take it home, like?"

"Are you fuckin' bent or what? I want its eyes, that's what." Mitch advised genuinely.

"Oh yeah, cat's eyes, tryin' t'see in the dark, 'ey?" Irish suggested.

"What the fuck are you on about bum boy, I wanna pop its eyes, yeah? I fuckin' love poppin' cats' eyes." Mitch replied, again entirely truthfully.

"Right we'll have a look round for yer, keep an eye out so to speak." Jay Mac offered.

Mitch decided there was no point remaining in the dark cellar. "I'm off, you two can get back t'yer bummin' y'pair of fuckin' queers. Remember if yer see that fuckin' cat bring it straight t'me."

"Sure right enough there Mitch, straight to you no one else." Irish replied.

"We'll even throw in a few mice if we find any." Jay Mac added with a grin.

"No fuckin' mice! I hate them horrible little cunts, with the scratchy claws and sneaky faces." Mitch warned as he began to ascend the stairs followed closely by his own pet.

"See yer Daniels, yer fuckin' rat." Jay Mac unwisely shouted after them.

Natural Born Skinhead 1971 ●104

Less than a quarter of an hour into the first of the double period of Physics, Daniels exacted his revenge, Jay Mac and Irish were sent for by Mr Arkwright.

"Stand there y'disgustin' pair of trespassers." the totally bald headed, stocky Woodwork teacher ordered as they entered the room, which was filled with a First Year class learning basic joint methods. Mr Arkwright's shiny, pink scalp gleamed under the stark strip-light as if it had been French polished. He drew himself up to his full six foot height and began his preamble to their imminent punishment, addressing the whole class who were stood to attention in readiness to observe justice being done.

"These two boys, Mack and O'Hare, call themselves Skinheads, think they're tough guys." he began, whilst scanning the room for the slightest movement, "Well I'm the only 'skinhead' in this place that you need to be scared of." He paused then turned to the smiling prefect, "These are the two you saw trespassing in my cellar, is that right, Daniels?"

"Yes sir, I told them not to go in but they said they didn't care about your notice, or you sir." the informant replied.

"Did they now? We'll see about that. Right, do either of you characters have a good reason, why two young men would want to be alone in a dark cellar?" Mr Arkwright asked with a contemptuous sneer.

"Well sir as we're leavin' soon, we thought we'd have one last look around the old school, for all those happy memories, sir." Jay Mac replied straight faced.

Some of the First Year boys laughed, much to the annoyance of their teacher.

"Always got to say something smart, haven't you Mack? Well just for that you're first and you can have a few extra, bend over that bench now!" he ordered angrily.

Jay Mac did as instructed bending across the rough wooden workbench, grasping the other side preparing to receive yet another beating, one of a thousand he had endured, either deservedly or not, throughout his five year term in the Cardinals'. Using a three foot long strip of Peruvian mahogany, his favourite implement of punishment, the excited teacher set about his task with relish, delivering blow after blow with all the strength that he could

Natural Born Skinhead 1971 • 105

muster. After regaining his breath and second wind, he repeated his vicious performance with Irish as his victim. Neither boy made a sound, trying desperately to remain poker faced, despite the terrific stinging pain.

As Irish stood up stiffly from his punishing position, Jay Mac, close by, deliberately barged into the smiling Daniels who had moved too near, whilst enjoying the spectacle.

"Won't be long now rat, you'll be gettin' yours." he said quietly.

The startled prefect sprang back out of harm's way, declaring, "Sir, sir, Mack has just threatened me."

"Have you now Mack, you never learn boy, do you? I'll be doing Monday and Tuesday detentions next week and you'll be joining me, this workshop could do with a good cleaning. Now get out of my sight you disgusting pair." He turned to the audience as Jay Mac and Irish moved towards the door pointing with an accusing finger after them, "There they go boys, they were scum when they came to this fine old school and they've chosen to leave the same way. Look at Daniels here, he is the model pupil, never been in any trouble, always keeps the teachers well informed of any wrong-doing. Look up to him boys, make him your example."

The silent watching First Year's arrived at their own conclusions as to who had triumphed in this physical-psychological contest and chose their own paradigm from those on offer to emulate for the next five years.

Wednesday 28th April 1971

'It's an ill wind that blows no good,' so the saying goes and Jay Mac's two evenings of detention, however unjust, served to be fortuitous in a way that he had not considered. With Mr Arkwright keeping his detainee until after five o'clock each day, ensuring that all tools were correctly stored and every wood shaving or pile of sawdust was thoroughly swept from each bench and the entire workshop floor, Jay Mac's late departure from the school coincided with that of the pretty assistant from the shop of Madame de Paris also.

On seeing her exit from the lingerie store, he quickly darted between the busy traffic across to that side of the road, intent on making some initial contact. Unfortunately for Jay Mac, one of the

Natural Born Skinhead 1971 ●106

vehicles in that same traffic was the bus that she was hurrying to catch at the stop some twenty yards from the shop.

"Hi, hello, me name's Jay Mac..." he called, almost catching up with the anonymous girl, who turned, looked at him blankly then stepped up onto the rear platform of the old open-ended London bus as it arrived at the stop.

"Cor, she's a bit of alright." said the leering conductor, admiring the pretty girl's form while she ascended the spiral staircase. He quickly stepped up behind her, fully enjoying the view of her pert bottom that his vantage point afforded, as her micro skirt left little to the imagination.

Jay Mac turned and walked away to his own bus stop, determined to improve his luck the following day.

Just after five o'clock on a warm Tuesday evening, the eager youth escaped from his final detention in the Woodwork rooms and raced over to his planned assignation. Once again the pretty girl left the shop and made her way to the nearby bus stop, only on this occasion the waiting Jay Mac was already in situ.

"Alright, don't you work in the shop on the corner?" he began.

"Why, what d'you wanna know for?" she replied curtly.

"No, er... it's just I... er thought... me name's Jay Mac by the way and ..." he attempted.

"Right, ok. I remember you now, you're one of those dirty little school boys who was lookin' up my dress when I was in the window. What d'yer want? Come for another look have yer?" she asked angrily.

Things were not going according to plan and Jay Mac's reply only made matters worse, "No, I mean yeah, no, not up yer dress, I just need a bit longer... to talk to yer I mean."

The untimely arrival of her bus and its lecherous conductor ended their brief discussion.

"'Ello darlin', plenty of room on top." the smiling conductor advised, preparing for a repeat performance, one that he happily enacted dozens of times each day.

Jay Mac walked away once more in dejection but was already forming a plan that he hoped would ensure a better outcome tomorrow.

Natural Born Skinhead 1971 • 107

"Im bunkin' this afternoon, I can't be arsed goin' back." Jay Mac announced to his friends as they were strolling along from the fish and chip shop on that sunny Wednesday, towards the end of their lunch break.

"You goin' somewhere?" Irish asked with a casual interest.

"Nah, I'm just gonna gerroff, thee owe me a bit of time with doin' those fuckin' detentions anyway." Jay Mac lied in answer.

"Yer'll end up gettin' some more if yer get caught." Terry (H) warned.

"Yeah I know Terry but like Liam always says, 'fuck it'." Jay Mac answered, and then left them to wander back in the direction of the old school in time for the quarter-past one bell, which signalled the end of lunch.

He had other plans, furtively loitering between the bus stop and Madame de Paris' establishment, knowing that shortly almost all the local shops would shut for the traditional Wednesday early closing.

Jay Mac did not have to wait long as within minutes he heard the pretty assistant calling farewell to her employer and pulling the door to, behind her. Standing expectantly midway twixt stop and store, he quickly realised that something was amiss; the young girl was not walking in his direction but remained just outside her place of work near to the kerb. Accepting that even the best laid plans can go awry; Jay Mac improvised and briskly marched towards his intended date.

"Hi, alright, sorry we didn't gerra chance t'finish our conversation yesterday." he began on arriving next to the startled girl. "Like I said, me name's Jay Mac and I was wonderin' if..."

The short, instructional reply that she mouthed was fairly clear, even though totally drowned by the blast of twin air horns announcing the arrival of her scooter-borne boyfriend.

Pulling in close to the kerb on his magnificent Lambretta SX200 fully accoutred, bearing a long front rack packed with an array of spotlights and mirrors, plus additional chrome-work in the form of a front mud guard rail, sweeping Florida bars and backrest, the Centurion helmet wearing rider was dressed in full denim Skinhead uniform, including a well-polished pair of cherry red Airwair.

"Alright Penny, is this boy botherin' yer?" he asked angrily.

Natural Born Skinhead 1971 ●108

"Not really Dave, I think he's just a bit soft in the head." Penny replied smiling.

"Was there somethin' yer wanted lad?" Dave asked in a condescending manner, as if dealing with somebody who was mentally deficient.

Jay Mac stared vacantly at Penny, then Dave, replying, "Nah, I thought there was but I was wrong."

"Hadn't yer better get back t'school before yer marked late?" Penny enquired sarcastically, fastening the chin-strap of the spare helmet.

Jay Mac did not reply but watched as she mounted the back of the scooter, allowing him another generous view of her minimal underwear, momentarily rekindling his interest. He looked at the superb scooter and the pretty Penny, wishing he was the rider of both, 'I've gorra get one of those Lambrettas, they're fuckin' bird magnets,' he thought as Dave sped away with Penny fully displaying her shapely legs, straddling his machine.

"Hey you there, why are you hanging around outside my shop?" Cynthia asked, standing in the doorway of the emporium. "You're too late if y'wanted to buy something, we're closed for half day."

"I don't think yer sell what I want." Jay Mac replied with a grin.

"That all depends on what *you* want." Cynthia quipped, casting her gaze over the rangy, athletic young male.

Jay Mac stood dressed in his red, white and blue checked short sleeved Jaytex, sixteen inch parallel off-white Levi's, red half inch braces and obligatory cherry red Airwair. He was holding his blue-black blazer in his right hand, having previously removed his colourful striped school tie and stuffed it into the inside pocket.

Cynthia now recognised him, "Wait a minute... you're that cheeky boy from the other day... you look different, are you supposed to be dressed like that for school?"

"Am not in school am I, it's me afternoon off." he lied, failing to mention that he had already been caned by one of the Brothers for coming to school without the regulation white shirt and grey trousers.

Natural Born Skinhead 1971 • 109

"Is that right? Maybe y'can help me with something?" she enquired with a smile.

"Am all yours madam, lead on." he replied.

"C'mon then, y'can make yerself useful in here for a bit." Cynthia offered as they stepped into the cool, dim interior out of the stark sunlight.

"On yer own in 'ere, Mr de Paris not around then?" Jay Mac enquired.

"No, that ship sailed long ago. I prefer me own company, most of the time anyway." Cynthia replied. "Here, I've got some new stock to put up on the top of these shelves, it'll save Penny doin' it in the mornin', she's never much use the next day after she's been out with Dave." Cynthia laughed, then asked, "Now d'you want to stack or hold the ladder?"

"I think holding the ladder could be more interestin', cos I'm not really good with heights I'm better lookin' up than down, if yer know warra mean?" he replied, grinning.

Cynthia led Jay Mac behind the counter and stood on the bottom broad step of a short wooden ladder. "Those boxes there please, if yer don't mind," she said pointing to a stack of slender cardboard boxes on the floor nearby.

"My pleasure madam." he replied, passing her the first box.

Cynthia ascended the next few steps and reached up to the top of the tall, old display unit. Her wide beam, large rounded bottom was exactly at the same height as Jay Mac's appreciative eyeline and as he studied her shapely, curvaceous form, he began to feel very pleased with his choice of this afternoon's lesson. By the time he had passed her three of the boxes, Jay Mac began to visualise himself in a scene from a tacky 'Carry On' film, or an episode of 'Benny Hill' and considered whether to have a peek under the hem of her loose-fitting, just above the knee length, skirt, curious to see where the perfectly straight seams of her dark tan, nylon stockings may lead. Emboldened by his curiosity and raging hormones, he casually placed his right hand on the back of her warm, soft calf, waiting to see what reaction this may elicit.

Cynthia said nothing but carried on with her task, though a fleeting shiver passed through her and revealingly transferred down her elegant legs.

Natural Born Skinhead 1971 •110

"You'd be better off if you used both hands," Cynthia advised, much to Jay Mac's delight and surprise, until she added, "...to pass me those boxes, I mean."

The excited youth quickly withdrew his hand.

A few moments later Cynthia stepped down from the ladder, lightly brushing past Jay Mac with her well-endowed bosom, firmly supported by her expensive corsetry that was almost visible through her revealing fine-silk blouse.

"I just need to get these an then I'll give yer something for y'trouble." she promised tantalisingly.

"No trouble madam..., honestly, it really *is* my pleasure." Jay Mac announced, genuinely, his growing enthusiasm now difficult to conceal.

Cynthia bent down apparently to examine some of the stock in the remaining boxes on the floor, raising her large round bottom, fully outlined by the straining material as it clung to her considerable curves.

'Fuck it.' Jay Mac thought, his brow covered in beads of perspiration, 'Am not missing this chance, whatever happens.'

Stepping immediately behind the bending woman, he thrust his right hand forward and firmly grasped her more than ample posterior.

"Don't start something you can't finish," she called calmly, adding deliberately provocatively, "Are y'sure you're capable?"

In one swift movement Jay Mac placed his left arm around her waist whilst keeping his groping right hand in place and swung Cynthia up and round onto the obliging counter.

"I'll show yer if I'm capable or not, let's have yer knickers off," he answered, pulling her skirt up revealing her flesh coloured lace panties, which barely contained her fully rounded bottom. After unzipping his Levi's, Jay Mac struggled to pull them and his straining Y-fronts down with one hand, as he tugged Cynthia's expensive underwear to her knees with the other.

Once his throbbing erection was released, without further ceremony, he forced himself into her quivering flesh, burying his manhood to its base within her receptive woman's moistness.

Natural Born Skinhead 1971 • 111

Driving himself on, plunging back and forth against the willing Cynthia's curvaceous bottom, he reached around to unleash her huge breasts.

"I'll do it." she advised breathlessly, before unfastening the mother-of-pearl buttons and allowing her considerable orbs to be revealed, barely contained in their similarly coloured bra.

Jay Mac roughly squeezed and mounded her bosom, no longer responding to anything other than primal sensory pleasure.

"You could have at least let me lock the door." Cynthia called then moaned loudly as he exploded inside her with a violent orgasm.

"Not enough time." he gasped referring to her request and his performance.

After a short post-coitus pause, Cynthia straightened her clothing and crossed the room to secure the front door. Turning towards him, she called casually, "First time was it?"

"No, no way, are you jokin'?" Jay Mac answered, embarrassed.

"Second then," she replied, smiling. "Not to worry tiger, we've got all afternoon, if yer fancy gettin' in a bit more practice."

"Too fuckin' right... sorry, I mean... yes please madam." a delighted Jay Mac responded.

"Let's go to my flat upstairs, we'll be more comfortable there and when you're ready, we can go again." the obliging Cynthia offered, catching hold of his warm hand and leading him up the stairway to heaven.

During that passionate afternoon and each of the three subsequent Wednesdays, under the expert tuition of the experienced Cynthia, Jay Mac obtained an exquisite education in giving and receiving pleasure, in her bed, on her couch, floor and kitchen table. Even when his repeated absence from official lessons on these afternoons was noticed and he was challenged, he carried on regardless. He suffered the brutal beatings, endured the long hours of detention as his punishments for truanting with a resigned stoicism. All pain was negligible when balanced against the precious pleasure that briefly bloomed in the spring of his youth.

Only after the fourth of these Wednesday assignations, when Vox, who had been serving a late detention himself, was passing

Natural Born Skinhead 1971 •112

by the shop, seated on the upper deck of his bus and saw Jay Mac leaving the supposedly closed premises by the main entrance, did the situation change dramatically. The following morning, as Jay Mac entered the school yard he was greeted with shouts of "Granny fucker!" and "Wrinkly shagger!" Plus speculative questions either of a general curious nature, "What's it like shaggin' a hundred year old bird?" or the anatomical, "How far down do her tit's hang when she takes her bra off?" or even the gynaecological, "Hasn't her minge dried up years ago?" By lunchtime Jay Mac was receiving notes containing even more extensive questions in a similar vein, or fantastic cartoons of his partner's supposedly sagging physique or he and a grotesquely wrinkled Cynthia engaged in the 'Act'. When Irish, Terry (H) and Liam also joined in the 'fun', the uncomfortable, callow youth decided there would be no further exciting trysts, abandoning his expectant paramour without notice.

Cynthia waited for him, looking toward the closed door eagerly but he did not arrive. After half an hour had passed she retired to her upstairs flat, fully aware of what had occurred. Slipping her tight stiletto shoes from her aching nylon stocking-clad feet, she reclined on her comfortable couch, listening to an old 78rpm of Glenn Miller's *Moonlight Serenade*, on her record player, poured herself a cup of strong tea and unwrapped a bar of Cadbury's Dairy Milk.

"Ahh, that's better than a man anytime," she said out loud on finishing her chocolate, "Satisfaction *always* guaranteed."

Friday 28th May 1971

The morning of Friday 28th May, dawned with a fiery red glow up-lighting the pale blue sky and to be fair to the weather gods, they were not being disingenuous when they chose to provide this traditional shepherd's warning of a gathering storm. Events of that day would prove to be both momentous and painful for a number of the Fifth Form cohort, even if they did not suspect it as they prepared for school that morning.

Although the majority of their chronological peers were Skinheads, there were also other cult affiliations, including: 'Trogs,' 'Walleys,' bike-less aspiring 'Greasers' and 'Civilians'. Taken together, however, they only presented a small contingent

Natural Born Skinhead 1971 • 113

providing a situation analogous to the uncomfortable co-existence of Neanderthals and Homo-sapiens. Though in this case in a reversal of historical precedent, the violent Skinhead Neanderthals would prove triumphant, the meek would not be inheriting this particular patch of Earth.

"What the fuck's goin' on?" Terry (H) asked Jay Mac, who was standing next to him in the crowded, stifling gymnasium that sometimes doubled as an assembly hall, on the rare occasions that they were all gathered together for an address.

"Fuck knows, Terry, must be somethin' big for them to risk bringin' us all in 'ere at one time." Jay Mac replied.

"Yeah, look at those fuckin' Trogs over by the wall, shitting themselves in case anythin' kicks off." Liam noted with a grin.

The Trog, or Walley grouping, both names being interchangeable, were comprised of boys who preferred rock music or folk ballads to Ska, Reggae or Tamla Motown. They grew their hair long, usually to shoulder length, risking ridicule from the notoriously homophobic teaching staff, before they were ordered to have it cut and wore army, or R.A.F. greatcoats over their school uniforms, with suede boots or 'desert wellies' as their choice of footwear. Almost without exception they were the more intelligent pupil, pacifist in nature, spending their break times discussing music and profound philosophical issues, whilst furtively passing herbal 'joints' between them; they avoided trouble as far as that was possible trapped in this junior prison environment.

A hush gradually fell over the mixed assembly as the Boss entered the room, with four of the Brothers and a number of secular staff. Brother Mulcahy stepped up onto a low sports bench to use this as his platform, there was no stage or raiseddais, this would prove sufficient for his purposes, as long as he could see and be seen was all that he required.

"Quiet, you wretched creatures, the Almighty is watching you, every one of you, even as I speak. Do not make Him angry or *I* will bring His righteous punishment down upon yer." He paused, scanning the room looking at each upturned face, checking for the slightest sign of any perceived disrespect. "Your time at this outstanding educational institution is nearly at an end. No doubt being the ungrateful, wretched creatures that you are, you're planning some devilment, some nasty prank during the coming

Natural Born Skinhead 1971 ●114

week after half term... but I tell you, that will not be happening. When you walk out of this building at the end of today, you will only enter again when you have an exam and at no other time." There were a few spontaneous cheers from several brave souls, which momentarily caused the Boss to pause once more. "Oh yes, cheer now, you wicked boys but let me see if you're still cheering when you're without work, homeless, starving, lying in the gutter begging for some spare change. May God forgive you." He stopped for one final time then continued, "You will go about your business and attend all your lessons, just like any other day. If one boy in any class steps out of line, all boys will be punished. Now go from here and make the most of your last few precious hours, do the Lord's work while yer still can."

Stepping down from his impromptu rostrum, the senior Brother had no idea that he had just announced the formal commencement of 'National Riot Day'.

Standing in the centre of the Skinhead throng, Stamfo beamed, he looked about him, saying openly, "When I say... wait for my word."

His fellow Skins smiled in return; the Trogs, Greasers and Civilian population, which included the reviled informant 'Rat' Daniels, rightly shuddered expecting that the worst day of their school lives was about to begin.

Walking away from the gym towards their classrooms, the boys all speculated as to when and where the flashpoint may occur, Jay Mac could not have imagined that he would be the one to light the fuse and provide the vital spark. The first two periods, however, gave no clue as to what was to come and passed without incident or interruption, other than the normal, deliberately loud outbreaks of belching and farting that punctuated every lesson, usually though not always necessarily, emanating from the pupils alone.

As Jay Mac sat daydreaming at the rear of his boiling, smelly classroom, he idly considered his journey from schoolboy to Skinhead. When first he assumed the identity of a Skinhead, the uniform and the cropped hair meant something more than just a style choice. As an obsessive American popular culture fan and superhero comic collector, he instantly adopted an ethos and classic line for his new identity from Marvel's Amazing

Natural Born Skinhead 1971 • 115

Spiderman 'with great power, comes great responsibility,' believing that if something was obviously right it had to be upheld and if it were glaringly wrong, it had to be challenged. On Jay Mac's arrival at the Cardinals' five years previous, from his strict, disciplined primary school, he felt that he instinctively knew right from wrong but the longer he spent in his present perverse education establishment, that distinction was becoming increasingly blurred, when to act and when to ignore no more an obvious choice. During the first morning break, which was rapidly approaching, an incident would occur that would provide instant clarity, leaving him with only one option.

Standing with the rest of his crew in the crowded yard, rapidly eating the contents of two packets of smokey bacon crisps, purchased from an entrepreneurial Third Year, whose father owned a mobile shop and was keen to encourage his junior protégé to take his first steps in the business, Jay Mac was suddenly distracted on being called urgently by a group of rapidly approaching First Year boys, one of whom he recognised from the earlier 'cat' incident.

"Jay Mac, help us please!" they cried, almost running into him. "Help us please, thee've got Joey and their takin' him to that place."

"Calm the fuck down boys", Jay Mac began, "Yer lucky we're standin' here in this part of the yard for lower school or yer'd all be fucked. Now warra yers goin' on about?"

"Some lads... we think thee was Second or Third Years... grabbed Joey... thee said Denny was waitin' for him in 'Andersonville'." they warned alarmingly.

On hearing the name of this dread place and who was lurking in it for the unfortunate boy to be brought to him, Jay Mac and his friends all blanched, even the hardened scrappers, Liam and Terry (H). When they had been First Year pupils themselves a series of collectible bubble gum cards entitled 'Civil War News' was re-issued, immediately becoming a hit with all the boys because of the colourful, gory images of violent action that they depicted. Featured on one particular card was the notorious Confederate prison camp, 'Andersonville,' a name synonymous with horror and torture. The pupils of the Cardinals' institution quickly adopted this as a fitting title for a dark, store cupboard positioned under an old wooden staircase to the rear of the building, where terrified

Natural Born Skinhead 1971 •116

victims were taken for sickening assaults to be carried out upon them. Nobody ever went near this vault of nightmares willingly.

The Skins knew that if Denny was presently occupying his favourite hiding hole, lying in wait like a grotesque, human trap-door spider, the unlucky boy would indeed be about to suffer an excruciatingly painful, depraved attack.

"Come 'ed, we'll have to go and sort this out, that kid's decent, we can't let Denny get his hands on him." Jay Mac suggested naively.

"Hang on there Jay Mac, what's it gorra do with us... and before yer start, remember Denny's connected *all* the way up." Liam warned, for once abandoning his own careless philosophy.

Terry (H) concurred and they both walked away without another word.

"Fuck it! I'm gettin' that kid outa there whatever 'appens," Jay Mac announced, then sprinted across the school yard, heading for the lower corridor where the old wooden staircase was located and below it, Andersonville.

"Hold on yer mad fucker, I'm comin' wit yer!" Irish shouted, throwing down the stump of a cigarette that he had been sharing with Liam and Terry (H), before running after his friend.

Within moments of racing down the narrow, foul smelling corridor, throwing other pupils to one side if in any way they impeded his progress, allowing his rage to grow with every angry step, Jay Mac arrived at the enclosed stairwell at the base of which was a pale blue painted, sloping cupboard whose raking height rose from one to five foot, following the gradient of the wooden stairs. A mixed group of Second and Third Year boys were loitering in the dingy stairwell, passing a cigarette between them, when the furious Skinhead came upon them, closely followed by Irish now equally roused.

"Gerrout of my fuckin' way!" Jay Mac shouted, immediately punching the first two faces that came within range, not waiting for them to comply.

Irish caught hold of this pair, then flung them into the corridor where their two associates quickly joined them, receiving hard kicks to their backsides as they did.

Natural Born Skinhead 1971 • 117

"Denny! You fuckin' sick bastard, open this door before I boot it in!" Jay Mac demanded almost apoplectic with rage on hearing the muffled cries of the young boy within.

The asthmatic Denny wheezed his reply, "Fuck off lad, don't mess with me when I'm havin' me fun."

Utilising all the strength that his keen runner's legs could muster, Jay Mac delivered an awesome boot to the old wooden door, kicking it through, almost taking it off its hinges. For a moment he froze in horror on seeing the vile image that lay before him. The First Year victim, who had previously almost been blinded by Mitch, was bent double, face down with his trousers and underpants around his knees. Denny had pulled *his*own regulation grey trousers to a similar position but as yet had not fully removed his filthy, stained underwear, though it was obvious he was very excited as he clung onto the boy's privates with his right hand.

"Please stop him, please." the tearful boy cried fully, with Denny's restraining left hand now removed from around his mouth.

"Come 'ere you fuckin' piece of filth," Jay Mac roared, grasping Denny by the throat and dragging him from his lair into the open.

The depraved sexual sadist screamed in terror as he was flung to the base of the stairs for Jay Mac to begin his reprisals.

"No, no, please someone help me." he cried out, these being the last intelligible words that he would utter for some time.

Repeatedly punched about the face and throat until his features were almost unrecognisable, Denny lay in a pool of his own blood, still with his trousers around his knees. Moaning incoherently, he tried to mouth a plea for mercy but Jay Mac the avenger was not yet sated, transferring his fury from his fists to his gleaming, cherry red Airwair, putting them to good use.

"Jay Mac, Jay Mac... come on man... snap out of it will yer!" Irish called to him, genuinely worried that his wild friend would commit murder.

Others were now also racing to the scene, Denny's helpers having gone for assistance to his protector, Vox.

"Mack! You cunt! What 'ave yer done t'Denny!" Vox shouted on arriving with Sharkey and two others of their crew and

Natural Born Skinhead 1971 ●118

finding the semi-conscious, bloodied pervert lying on the hard floor.

Without waiting for an answer and totally disregarding Irish's presence, all four set about the heavily-breathing Jay Mac, as he stood over his battered prey, grinning insanely. Irish knew he had to act quickly and dashed out from the stairwell into the corridor. Seconds later he returned carrying the best improvised weapon that he could find, a full sized metal dustbin packed with reeking contents. With great effort he raised the heavy object, often used as a receptacle for unwilling pupils who were forced into it head-first, before slamming it horizontally into Jay Mac's quartet of attackers as they pounded the youth, who was by now reduced to his knees.

"Come on man, let's get the fuck out of 'ere." Irish called, dragging his friend to his feet and out into the narrow corridor.

Dazed, though soon recovered, Jay Mac did not require a second invitation, joining Irish sprinting along the claustrophobic passage towards the schoolyard door with Vox and company in hot pursuit.

Even as they reached the open doorway, one of the Brothers was about to step into the overcrowded, stifling yard, carrying the bell to announce the end of break.

Irish and Jay Mac collided with this rotund, elderly male, separating him from both bell and the iron ring of keys that he carried loosely tucked into the sash, which he wore about the waist of his deepest black cassock.

The untimely collision however fortuitous in delivering up an essential set of keys, unfortunately hampered the escape of the two Crown Skins and they were quickly overtaken by their enemies, all six stumbling into the coarse gravel-covered yard, punching, kicking and grappling wildly as one struggling mass.

His attention drawn to the action, the lugubrious Stamfo, located in his usual position slouching against the rear wall, rose fully to his feet, deciding the moment had arrived and bellowed from the depths of his considerable lungs, "National Riot Day!"

Echoed dozens of times over, resounding off the old brick walls on three sides and grimy glass panes of the staff room's French windows on the rectangle's fourth, madness and mayhem were

Natural Born Skinhead 1971 • 119

unleashed amongst six-hundred plus overheated, raging male animals. Instantly realising his position of serious jeopardy, 'Rat' Daniels the informant, ran for the door and escape. He was too late, a smiling Third Year boy, who had also been a victim of his tell-taleing, slammed the heavy, aged wooden door shut, locking it with the keys that he had judiciously retrieved from the floor, leaving the distraught snitch trapped on one side and the embarrassed Brother, his only hope of salvation, on the other.

Banging desperately on a small dirt-stained window, one of several that ran along the outer wall of the corridor, Daniels screamed for help; the barely visible image of the Brother made the sign of the cross then joined his hands in prayer, as if acknowledging the inevitability of the infernal fate that would soon overtake the hopeless boy. Turning from the window the 'Rat' ran shrieking into the midst of the mass brawl, seeking refuge in the eye of the storm. It was a futile gesture, *all* old and new scores would be settled that day, Ragnarök had dawned. Friend and foe alike must fight, as the new sort to oust the old. First and Second Years laid into each other en masse, while the Third and Fourth Year boys joined forces to assault their hated Fifth Form overlords. In all the prevailing insanity, a score of individual engagements were also taking place with equal ferocity. Jay Mac and Irish, though initially overwhelmed by Vox's crew, were now fighting in a more evenly matched bout, having been joined by Liam and Terry (H).

Watching from the safety of the staffroom, a mixed group including Brothers and secular teachers, continued drinking their tea, eating their biscuits and smoking their cigarettes or pipes. No one was particularly concerned; they had seen it all before, several times.

Brother Mulcahy, 'The Boss' calmly addressed them. "Well, there it is, it's been comin' for some time, the young fellers lettin' off a bit of steam." He paused to sip his dark brown, stewed tea and light another Capstan full strength cigarette. "The hot weather and all those hormones they're t'blame, every couple of years it ends like this. We've seen the Teddy Boys and we've seen the Mods, now it's the turn of these Skinheads, God knows what we'll be seein' next." He paused again to take a long relaxing drag of his cigarette, looking out across the yard filled with the teeming

Natural Born Skinhead 1971 •120

mob, victors and vanquished alike fully blooded, now truly initiated into the rights and ethos of the Cardinals', 'give no mercy and expect none.'

Suddenly the Boss's gaze was drawn to a lone figure running towards the staffroom windows, as if to seek sanctuary. Wearing only his socks, shoes and underpants, bleeding from numerous wounds, Rat Daniels almost made the final few yards to what he perceived as a place of refuge, before he was overtaken by a howling mob. Desperately clinging to a badly chipped once painted, though now barely recognisable, life-size statue of the Sacred Heart of Jesus, he was forcibly dragged away for further revenge at the hands of his captors.

One of the teachers turned toward The Boss and said, "What about Daniels, Brother, shouldn't we try to help him; he's been very useful to us in the past?"

"No, let him stay where he is, he'll have t'learn t'deal with his own kind now. Anyway, he's leavin' today with the rest of them, so he's of no further use to us." The Boss answered before taking another sip of his tea, whilst casually finishing his cigarette.

There was a sudden blinding flash of lightning immediately followed by a dramatic roll of thunder. "Ahh, just in time, here comes the rain, that'll cool them down a bit. The Almighty dispenses his Justice on the innocent and the guilty at one and the same time." he concluded.

While the mass brawl raged on, the heavy rain became torrential, though it appeared to do little to dampen the combatants' enthusiasm. Gradually wounded individuals who had been badly injured and some who had just lost their appetite for the fight did, however, begin to withdraw to the sidelines, leaving the central arena open for the more determined scrappers to settle bitter feuds of their own.

Jay Mac and Vox had become separated from their original crews and were totally oblivious to what was occurring around them as they tore into each other, still seething with blind rage. Mitch, Stamfo's pet torturer, had been unleashed and abandoned by his master, who was content with strolling about delivering devastating punches to friend and foe alike, as he saw fit. Coming upon Jay Mac and Vox just as the Crown Skin had finally achieved

Natural Born Skinhead 1971 • 121

the upper hand, having downed his opponent, Mitch, accompanied by two of Denny's younger 'helpers' keen to learn the trade from the master, leapt upon Jay Mac from behind, clutching him round the throat, with one hand, whilst grabbing hold of his testicles with the other and wrenching them backwards violently. After instructing his two eager assistants to seize his struggling captive's arms, he called to the floored Vox inviting him to take his revenge. Vox happily complied, springing to his feet before commencing a flurry of hard punches to the immobilised Jay Mac's face and stomach.

Suddenly Stamfo wandered onto the scene of this unequal encounter and he stopped momentarily to casually watch the sickening assault. Something began to stir within his stagnant brain as he observed his once close friend Jay Mac taking such a ferocious beating. Lumbering forward he steadily gained pace until like a charging Juggernaut he ploughed into Jay Mac's tormentors then began flinging them in all directions. Saving the terrified Mitch until last, Stamfo seized him around the throat and raised him fully into the air, before repeatedly smashing the screaming torturer into the nearest crumbling brick wall, continuing until the limp mannequin in his huge hands ceased to move. Ragnarök was almost at its end, the twilight of the Skinheads was passing as it must for the new order to rise in its place.

Stepping out through the open French windows, The Boss loudly rang the bell that he was carrying in his firm grip. He stopped by the dishevelled Sacred Heart statue and called to his pupils whilst continually ringing the bell like a sombre-looking town crier.

"Well, well boys, yer've all had a great time playing out here in the rain, instead of goin' to y'lessons, haven't yer?" he asked rhetorically, pausing for a few seconds, watching them gradually begin to settle, whilst the hammering rain bounced off his white cropped head and broad frame. "Alright now, yer've had yer fun and God knows it's probably cleared the air for a few of you fellers, so I'm going t'be even more kind than usual. Stop what yer doin' right now, bring those keys over t'me and then we'll let yer back into yer nice dry classrooms, where y'can sit quietly with

Natural Born Skinhead 1971 ●122

yer teachers until mid-day and then I'll allow school to finish early for yer all. How's that sound boys?"

All eyes turned from The Boss of the school to the King of the Yard, Stamfo.

"Nice one Brother." he boomed back across to the smiling cassock-clad male, then called out to his peers, "You 'eard The Boss, everyone line up now, move yerselves."

A First Year was sent running to Brother Mulcahy carrying the keys and a few minutes later, the entire teaching staff, canes and straps drawn at the ready, stood in front of the waiting lines.

"How many for each boy Brother?" Mr 'Lenny' Wilkinson asked eagerly.

"Ahh, just make it half a dozen strokes each, I'm feelin' generous today." he announced with a grim smile. "I must be gettin' soft in me old age."

All the pupils complied, there was no further resistance, they had had their National Riot Day.

Stamfo climbed down from the lofty pinnacle of the blood-drenched pyramid that day, leaving his hollow crown and worthless title where it lay to be claimed by the next victorious contender. He had been the undisputed 'cock of the school' for several years, now he joined the adult world of work as a 'can lad,' on a building site, the boy who made the tea or performed any other menial task as instructed. He had gone from King of the Hill to Bottom of the Pile in a few short days, the rest of his peers would soon follow suit as apprentices, factory hands or cadets and begin a far more desperate struggle with much greater odds, that of trying to earn a living.

Natural Born Skinhead 1971 • 123

Chapter 5

Within You and Without You

Monday 19th July 1971

On the warm Monday morning following his eventful trip to Southport, Jay Mac managed to secure the provisional offer of employment as a junior office boy in the distinguished old shipping company of Edwin Roach, Symes and Butterworth, at the princely sum of £5.00 per week. It was a poor wage even by contemporary standards for similar positions but despite having attended several dozen such interviews throughout the seven weeks since the 'National Riot Day' premature dismissal from school, in between completing his required exams, this was the only prospective employer to even consider him as a potential employee.

Jay Mac's old soldier uncle had told him, in no uncertain terms, that he must accept any offer of work, irrespective of wage or conditions, adding that he could not continue to live off the generosity of others for the rest of his life and that his food would actually taste better when he began to pay towards it. The youth complied without protest, knowing full well how futile this would be. He failed to mention to his guardian that the offer was subject to receipt of satisfactory references from his former school, the Cardinals' were still controlling his fate even after he had escaped from their brutalising institution.

Having directly approached the school immediately after his interview, Jay Mac was told to return on the Friday of that week when the office would be open and he could obtain a reference from a member of the senior staff. He decided that as Irish may also require a similar testimonial, he would invite him to attend on the same day, feeling that somehow together they may be able to illicit a more positive response and preferring not to face the Brothers, or possibly The Boss, alone.

That same evening he had just alighted from his bus at the municipal depot stop on the lower edge of the Crown Estate, when he was called to by a portly youth who lived in one of the small terraces in the row immediately facing the garage and repair sheds.

Natural Born Skinhead 1971 •124

"Alright Jay Mac, come over mate, I've got somethin' ace t'show yer." Mickey 'pimple' Pemberton shouted.

"Alright Mickey lad, I'll be straight over." Jay Mac replied with a smile, though cursing himself for having accidentally wandered into the path of this unpopular youth.

Mickey 'pimple' Pemberton was of a similar height to the athletically built Eagle Skin but he was noticeably overweight, podgy and unfit with an unfortunate case of raging acne covering his round face. Mickey had only lived on the bleak estate for less than a year and he was desperate to belong, to fit in. Amongst the group of violent, rangy, adolescent Skinheads who were almost obsessive about the very specific uniform that they wore and in particular how it looked, the corpulent Mickey had little, if any, chance, of being accepted.

"What 'ave yer got there Mickey?" Jay Mac asked feigning an interest, "I bet it's some hot bird needin' a good seein' to, am I right?" he enquired, grinning.

"No mate, sorry, I wish it fuckin' was." Mickey replied, also with a grin then stepped into the shared alley that ran between each pair of houses in this long row.

"What d'yer think... it's a beaut isn't it?" Mickey asked, beaming, on returning wheeling out a Vespa GS150 scooter which bore no additional embellishments and had been badly re-sprayed in an amateur manner to a finish of blue and orange.

Jay Mac was momentarily lost for words as he stared at the garish machine and its owner in his bursting, short-sleeved, fitted Ben Sherman shirt, as it struggled to contain his pot-belly.

"Yeah Mickey, it's definitely got a look of its own, mate." he finally answered then asked, "I don't wanna piss all over yer parade Mickey but can I just ask yer why yer've picked a Vespa? They're great machines like... but all the lads round 'ere 'ave got Lambrettas?"

"It was me dad, he gorrit for me cos I've joined 'im on the bread van, now that I've finished school, he bought it off his mate." Mickey advised.

"Fuck me! He actually paid good money for it?" Jay Mac observed with genuine astonishment, "Well, I suppose y'could always do it up and maybe sell it on."

Natural Born Skinhead 1971 • 125

"Oh no, I wouldn't sell it, I'm gonna get a fly screen and all the chrome gear and I'm gonna put 'Mickey P' 'Crown Skins' in gold letters on the side panels." he announced proudly, much to Jay Mac's amusement and horror.

"Whoa there Mickey lad, I'd give that last bit a miss if I was you. Tommy (S), or maybe Dayo (G) down in this part of the Estate, says who's a Crown team player and who isn't, thee might not take that too good, if you just lash on a few letters, without clearin' it with them first." he advised seriously.

"D'yer think so? Maybe yer right Jay Mac, I'll ask them and see what thee say. Are yer goin' up t'the Eagle t'meet the crew now?" he asked eagerly.

"Not yet, I've got t'see Irish about somethin' then we'll be goin' over to the Eagle." Jay Mac replied.

"D'yer wanna come in and have some cakes, we've got a load of left-overs off the van, that 'ave gorra be ate today." Mickey offered temptingly.

"Nah but thanks anyway, I'll have to gerroff." Jay Mac replied.

"Ok, I'll come with yer, yer can'ave a lift on me new scooter." Mickey suggested hopefully.

"No fuckin' way... I mean... I'm goin' a different way... up past Tony (G)'s then round to Irish's but thanks, see yer." the shallow youth advised knowing that he would now have to alter his route to that which took him through the narrow back street, where Tony (G) lodged and across the old field which lay behind this particular cul-de-sac.

Quickly hurrying away Jay Mac left his overweight acquaintance behind, still admiring his reward for beginning his career as an assistant to his father, delivering bread and cakes from a local bakery. 'Talk about puttin' temptation in his way.' Jay Mac thought, 'That boy's got no fuckin' chance'.

A few minutes later on entering the short street where Mal Chadwick's parents' house was located, Tony's temporary accommodation, Jay Mac saw his friend standing by his gleaming Lambretta LI 175 and called to him.

"Alright arsehole, how did yer gerron with my bird?"

"Jay Mac, yer missed out there mate, we got the three of them back to her place, which was one of those fuckin' big detached efforts and then we all got paired off." He paused and made an

Natural Born Skinhead 1971 •126

arm gesture with his right forearm being thrust up at forty-five degrees over his horizontal left forearm. "I tell yer what, that Sharon was a right goer, I had those pink knickers of hers down in no time."

"Thanks for that mate, that's made me feel a lot better." Jay Mac replied, "I'm really glad t'know you was on the job while I was gettin' fuckin' soaked, tryin' t'get back from bleedin' Southport."

"Better luck next time. Maybe y'should think about gettin' yerself a scooter, the birds love gettin' their legs around somethin' hot and throbbin'." Tony advised, grinning.

"So I've noticed." Jay Mac replied, adding "I'm startin' work on Monday so I might be able to save a few bob for a scooter of me own."

"Where y'startin', over the road in the factory, or on the site?" Tony asked casually, causing Jay Mac some discomfort.

"Er... it's more like a sort of shippin' type of job, if yer know warra mean."

"On the boats 'ey? Nice one Jay Mac, the birds love a sailor." Tony replied with a wink then noted, "At least yer haven't ended up in a shop or worse... in an office... like some fuckin' fruit."

Jay Mac said nothing further about the matter and changed the subject on hearing the dull, rhythmic bass beat of Mal's favourite record *Come to the Sabbath* by Black Widow, loudly playing upstairs in the front bedroom of the nearby house.

"Shite, does he ever change that bleedin' record?" Jay Mac asked, looking in the direction of the open window.

Before Tony could answer, as if summoned by Jay Mac's query, Mal leaned out and called to them, "Alright Tony, got one of the unbelievers with yer, 'ave yer? Jay Mac isn't it? Come in my friend and let's see if I can convert yer. My master always likes new converts, he only punishes the guilty and those who refuse to believe." he sniggered exposing his yellow, decayed teeth, wrinkling his long, prominent nose as he did.

"No yer alright thanks Mal. I'm a Catholic, so I already know all about guilt and punishment." Jay Mac replied, raising the thumb of his right hand and smiling.

Natural Born Skinhead 1971 • 127

"Some other time then, Jay Mac, I'll pray for yer soul." Mal offered before disappearing back into his incense filled room.

"Fuck, must be a laugh livin' here with that cracked cunt." Jay Mac observed.

"He's alright; I just keep out of his way. D'yer fancy a lift up t'the Eagle, cos I'm goin' t'meet the crew at the Hounds an I can drop yer off on the way?" Tony asked.

"Too right mate, I could do with a lift." Jay Mac replied smiling.

Within moments the two youths were mounted on the speeding Lambretta, heading away from the narrow street, leaving Mal to continue his incantations and chants undisturbed.

After Jay Mac had been conveyed to Irish's residence on his favourite form of transport, Tony (G) departed for his rendezvous with the Crown's scooter crew in the car park of the Hound's public house. When the door was answered by Mrs O'Hare, she told Jay Mac that her middle son, Patrick was at his friend Oliver's house, which was located in the street immediately behind the one where the disappointed youth was currently standing. Resolute in pursuing his objective, Jay Mac strolled off in the direction of the abode of his ideological nemesis, Oliver Furlong.

Oliver, or 'Ollie Beak' as he was usually referred to, based on a popular puppet representation of a fluffy know-it-all owl, wearing a school cap, featured in a long-running children's television programme, was also most recently named 'Tiny Tim' because of his uncanny resemblance to a bizarre American ukulele player who had a hit record entitled *Tiptoe through the Tulips*. Jay Mac felt both nick-names were equally apt and used them interchangeably as he felt appropriate.

The Eagle crew member detested Ollie, not because he was bright, capable and smug, or that he had attended a prestigious grammar school and on recently completing his A-levels had received provisional offers from Liverpool, Manchester and BirminghamUniversities to read philosophy, sociology and politics. It was because, to Jay Mac, Ollie represented the quintessential, arrogant, opinionated, ultra-liberal, champagne socialist while deluding himself that he was a working class hero who would gladly sacrifice all at the barricades when the

Natural Born Skinhead 1971 •128

revolution came, as long as his own personal safety was never compromised, of course.

Jay Mac felt that Ollie was one of the finest examples of the totally detached from reality, bullshit spouting, middle class hippie and their infrequent heated discussions stayed just within the boundaries of verbal argument without becoming physical confrontations, principally because the avowed pacifist, Ollie, abhorred violence in any form. In stark contrast Irish, sat cross-legged at the great pontificator's feet eagerly consuming any edifying morsels that fell into his lap. He believed Ollie was a philosophical oracle, whose intellectual sounding pronouncements perfectly encapsulated the *real politick* of life for the downtrodden proletariat, under the oppressive regime of 'The Man' who controlled 'The System.'

On reaching Ollie's address and ringing the doorbell, Jay Mac was admitted, reluctantly, by Mrs Furlong who stared down her own considerably large, hooked nose in contempt at the youth's distinctly working class Skinhead attire and his cuts and bruises.

"Oliver is in the parlour talking to his friend Patrick. I'd rather you didn't stay too long, he has got a lot of planning to do with all of his university offers." the tall, greying female of a-sexual build said in her sniffy manner, her huge magnifying lensed spectacles perched precariously on the curved ridge of her prominent proboscis.

"Right you are madam. I'll get straight in there, give Ollie a bit of advice and back out again." Jay Mac said, grinning, pretending to doff an invisible cap. "Thee can be dangerous places, these universities, I remember when I was a young Fresher, some of those older buggers were always trying to de-bag us but not to worry, I'm sure Ollie can hold his own with the best of them."

When he entered the well-decorated front room with its comfortable furniture and colourful prints of works by Picasso and Pollock, Barry McGuire's *Eve of Destruction* was playing on the turntable of the teak veneered stereogram, Jay Mac continued in a similar vein, "Good evening Ollie old chap, how are you? I hear you've got a bit of a dilemma about which uni could best contain your ego."

Natural Born Skinhead 1971 • 129

"Oh look out, its Jay Mac the Skinhead rogue, he always tries to say something funny because he can never say anything clever." Ollie responded with a sly smile.

"Yeah sorry about that Ollie, you'll have t'teach me t'talk total bullshit, I know you're fluent in it." Jay Mac immediately replied, before sitting down uninvited in one of the dark red leather armchairs.

Irish decided to intervene, "Hey, leave it will yer Jay Mac. We was just talkin' here and you have t'kick off."

Ollie smiled, "Yes, I've been hearing all about your latest disgraceful escapade in Southport, I've told Patrick not to have anything further to do with you, or these Crown Team thugs."

"Have yer now?" Jay Mac responded, "Still givin' free advice where it's not wanted, in between savin' the planet, I see."

"Someone's got to try, not everyone is a capitalist war-monger like you and your American heroes."

Jay Mac knew exactly where the conversation was being taken but could not refuse this particular challenge. "Ollie, yer outa yer depth, you know nothin' about the war in Vietnam, or the lads who fight in it, your views come from Hippie protest songs and poems, not from any real understandin'."

"Is that right Jay Mac, what about the My Li massacres, or what happened at KentState, is that real enough for you?" Ollie retorted.

Jay Mac, the obsessive Americana fan and keen student of all events related to the protracted war in South East Asia was well aware of these tragic incidents but neither dented his support for the ground troops or 'grunts' who daily endured the gruelling conditions, privations and horrors. "Like I just said Ollie, you know fuck all, only the lads who are there now, or the vets who've been there have the right t'speak, not any long-haired protestor, sleazy politician or windbag prick like you." Jay Mac advised calmly but firmly.

For a moment Ollie looked as if his pacifist ideology and manner may just be in danger of slipping, as an expression of murderous rage passed over his awkward features. He threw back his long, stringy, unkempt hair away from his reddened face and asked, "What is it you actually want Jay Mac, say it and get out. Nobody wants your type in their company."

Natural Born Skinhead 1971 •130

"Well Ollie my friend, that's where yer wrong once again. I have this very morning been offered a top position in a major shipping company, in the city. All that I require is a reference and I thought that Patrick here may wish to accompany me to our beloved old school on Friday to collect our testimonials." Jay Mac replied with a smug grin.

"Alright Jay Mac, I'll go with yer on Friday mornin' to the Cardinals' give us a knock about eleven o'clock, ok? Like Oliver says, I think yer better go now mate, cos trouble always seems t'follow you around." Irish replied coldly.

"Fair enough Irish, I'll see yer on Friday." Jay Mac began, "Could you show me the door please Ollie, then you can tell your mother it's safe to put the silverware back out, thanks for the chat, I hope that's cleared things up for you."

A short time later, after a brisk walk back down to the lower edge of the estate, he called in to see Mickey Pimple, determined to help him resolve his cake problem.

Friday23ʳᵈ July 1971

"There y'are fellers, two glowin' references for yer, so everyone will know *all* they need to about the pair of yer." Brother Mulcahy said with a broad grin, passing them each a brown envelope containing the requisite document. "Startin' work on Monday, 'ey, young Mack, that'll be the makin' of yer. Always remember wherever yer go in the world, you're Cardinals' boys."

"I don't think we'll ever forget that Brother." Jay Mac replied smiling.

"Well, off y'go now and don't come back, unless yer've made yer fortune and want t'share a bit of it with yer old school." the Boss suggested, ushering them both under the carved motto and down the steps out of the dim entrance hall, which still managed to reek of rotten eggs and wet fish, even in the absence of its six-hundred plus male pupils.

Outside in the stark sunlight of this hot, late July day, Jay Mac breathed a deep sigh of relief and glanced back over his shoulder at the dark, forbidding edifice which somehow looked yet more disturbing and incongruous than usual in this pleasant weather, as

Natural Born Skinhead 1971 • 131

if it should permanently be wreathed by black storm clouds pouring a torrent of icy tears of rain onto its crumbling shell of a sepulchre.

"Fuck me that place still gives me the creeps and that's after I've escaped." He half expected that if he should glance again the house of cruelty, pain and torment would have vanished back to its own dimension, like that in an episode of his favourite American Sci-Fi series, *The Outer Limits*.

Soon it would be the only reminder of a long gone age as the whole area, comprised of small Victorian workers' terraces and large artisan's houses, would be demolished as part of the continuing slum clearance programme in this original core of the city.

"The arl bastard!" Irish exclaimed on reading his own reference, despite it being addressed *'To whom it may concern.'* "Look what he's put!" he shouted indignantly then began to read aloud. *"Patrick, Seamus O'Hare has attended this school for five years. He is a boy of fair ability and was a popular pupil. Signed, Brother Brendan Mulcahy."* Fuckin' hell what am I supposed to do with that?"

"I know what yer mean, I'd be pissed off too if I'd been named Seamus." Jay Mac advised, smiling, whilst tearing open his own 'confidential' envelope. His smile soon faded as, except for the name John Michael Mack he read exactly the same reference for himself. "Shite, this is not good!" he declared.

"I never knew you was called Michael," Irish noted.

"Confirmation mate, I thought I better pick one of those top saints, yer know the Archangel feller, who battered Old Nick and lashed him out. Seemed like a good choice at the time, yer never know when yer might need a bit of help from the other side." Jay Mac advised, while they both casually strolled along the worn pavement of the cobbled street, re-reading their matching testimonials.

Suddenly Jay Mac bumped into a long-haired, unkempt, bearded young man in his late teens, who was wearing a dirty tie-dyed pink and blue granddad vest, filthy wide flared, dark green satin loons, crusty open-toed sandals and carrying a tattered maroon leatherette shopping bag.

Natural Born Skinhead 1971 •132

"Watch where yer goin' yer fuckin' Hippie scruff." Jay Mac snapped angrily, although the collision was entirely his fault.

"Sorry man, peace and love, yeah?" the older youth replied walking on.

"What did you say then? Are you takin' the piss, yer smelly cunt?" the Eagle Skin called to him.

"No man, like I said... sorry, chill... ok?" he unwisely replied.

Now Jay Mac strode after him, "Hey, stop where yer are you. Don't you fuckin' tell me t'chill." he began, as the hairy male complied and stood still on the far corner of the street of condemned shuttered houses. "Where yer goin' tramp and what's in the fuckin' bag?" Jay Mac demanded.

"Nothin' man, I'm just goin' home with food for the family." the Hippie replied nervously, looking into the angry, unreasoning face of the young Skinhead.

"The Family, the fuckin' Family, who are yer, Charlie fuckin' Manson, is that it?" Jay Mac roared.

"No man, he's one bad dude, bad karma." he answered, clearly afraid, then pleaded, "I just wanna go home man t'my family, please."

The raging youth looked at him coldly before stating, "Home, round 'ere? Nobody lives round 'ere, these are all derelict houses lad."

"I do man, honest, just down the road with my family." he advised foolishly.

"Jay Mac, stop actin' the cunt and let him go." Irish said firmly, momentarily snapping his friend out of his temporary fit of anger.

"How d'yer afford t'live round 'ere hey? I bet yer don't even go t'work like everyone else has to do yer? I fuckin' hate spongin' Hippies." Jay Mac began again, though less raging than previously. "And yer probably wanna bring down 'The System' that feeds yer, don't yer? Go 'ed, piss off."

The nervous young man was grateful that all he had suffered was a verbal tirade and nothing worse. He shuffled away into the long street that was adjacent to the corner where the two Crown players were still standing.

Natural Born Skinhead 1971 • 133

"Fuckin' hell Jay Mac, Oliver was right about you, yer a fuckin' trouble magnet wherever y'go." Irish observed, adding "Why did yer start on that poor bastard, he's done nothin' t'you?"

"Because he was in the right place at the wrong time, that's why." he answered continuing, "and do me a favour Irish, tell Tiny fuckin' Tim t'keep his massive beak out of it, or he won't be goin' to no university. There'll be one less know-it-all, do-nothing parasite, Hippie to suck the blood out of the rest of us."

Irish did not respond but began to walk away towards the bus stop on the main road. His angry friend lingered for a few moments watching as the long-haired young man reached his destination then gave a distinctive knock on one of the boarded, lower bay windows. The battered, heavy, old wooden front door was opened for him to be admitted and a malevolent plan began to form in the grinning Eagle Skin's mind.

A short time later having caught up with Irish, they both passed by Madame de Paris' shop on the opposite side of the busy road, en route to their bus stop heading for the city centre. Cynthia, femme fatale and obliging mentor to fortunate, lustful young men of her choosing, happened to step outside for a few moments to check a new window display.

"Aren't yer gonna say hello t'yer bird?" Irish asked, much amused.

"Nah, we was just two ships that passed in the night, shagged our arses off then moved on." Jay Mac replied dispassionately.

As if the light, warm breeze had carried his words directly to her ears, Cynthia turned and smiled knowingly.

Within twenty minutes of catching their bus and following an uneventful journey, they arrived at the business quarter of the city close to the waterfront and its collection of iconic buildings.

Both youths entered the musty old chambers of the shipping firm, where Jay Mac was due to commence employment the following week and climbed the flight of stairs to the first floor reception. Once there Jay Mac tapped on the frosted glass, sliding window of the vestibule.

Instead of the moveable pane being slid to one side as they expected, the door to the room's gloomy interior was quickly

Natural Born Skinhead 1971 •134

pulled open and a large, elderly male dressed in a black uniform with red piping down the seams of the trousers and carrying a white topped, peaked cap in his left hand, stepped out briskly to meet them.

Jay Mac offered him the brown envelope saying "Alright mate, here's me reference. Could yer see it gets to the right person, thanks?"

"Mate? I'm not yer mate." the powerfully built individual stated, snatching hold of the proffered envelope. "I'm Mr Atkins to you boy." he advised sternly then continued, "So y'got the job then? I wouldn't have took yer on, I'd have told yer to sling yer hook."

"Why's that then Mr Atkins?" Jay Mac asked.

"The look of yer, the way y'dressed an yer cuts an bruises, yer can't fool me, seen too many of your sort in the army." he replied.

"Oh yeah, an... er... what sort's that then?" Jay Mac pressed on.

"Trouble makers, y'can always tell. Yer not a scrapper, oh no... yer haven't got the look of a scrapper. You're more the sort that starts trouble then runs away when it gets a bit rough." the elderly expert observed, before taking a few satisfying puffs of the old briar pipe that he was holding in his right hand.

At six foot two and seventeen stone, the seventy-one year old former Royal Artillery B.S.M. was still an imposing figure. With his thick, grey, heavily Brylcreamed hair cut in a regulation short-back-and-sides style and his bristling moustache, he looked every inch the terror of the parade ground.

"Right, well, thanks for that Battery Sergeant Major Atkins, I'll bear that in mind, next time it all kicks off." Jay Mac replied, turning to walk away.

"'Ey, hold on, how did you know I was a B.S.M?" the old soldier asked curiously.

Jay Mac turned back to face him again and replied, "The badges on y'sleeve an yer cap *'Everywhere Wither Right and Glory Lead'*, I recognised it, me uncle was a Royal Horse Artillery Gunner. He joined as a regular when he was eighteen, served in India in the last days of the Raj before the war, then was part of the

Natural Born Skinhead 1971 • 135

B.E.F. in France and later fought the rear guard action, until he was captured at Dunkirk."

The intrigued veteran listened carefully to all that the youth said then drew on his pipe again, before responding, "I see, well that's different; maybe I was a bit quick, after all yer've got a decent haircut and those boots look as if thee've had some effort put into them." He paused again then concluded, "Alright young Mack, we'll see you at o'eight thirty hours, Monday and see how yer shape up. Just remember one thing, I'm the fuckin' boss!"

Jay Mac sprang to attention and executed a perfect, crisp salute answering, "Yes sir, B.S.M. Atkins, sir." then walked away with the grinning Irish who observed, "Fuckin' hell Jay Mac from one Boss to another, there's no escape."

As they strolled out to the first floor landing, they collided with an excited, tousle- haired, frail looking boy, who was dressed in a heavy, blue-grey, R.A.F great coat, despite the warm weather, over his flowery pattern shirt and matching 'kipper' tie, with dark blue flared trousers and sand-coloured 'desert wellies', suede boots.

"Not again, I don't believe it," Jay Mac stated, adding a repeat of his earlier warning, "Watch where yer goin' Hippie."

The terrified boy sprang back in alarm on seeing the two Skinheads in full uniform. He covered his face with his arms and called out, "Please, please don't hit me, I've got no more money, or luncheon vouchers. I've already told Josh I'll give him some when I get paid next week."

Irish caught hold of the boy's arms and lowered them to his sides saying "Calm down lad, we don't know what the fuck yer talkin' about and we don't want yer money or anythin' else."

The nervous youth began to relax slightly and looked first at Irish then Jay Mac, "I thought Josh had sent yer for more 'protection' money, sorry." he said.

"Mate, we're Crown Skins and we've never heard of any fuckin' Josh tit, whoever he's supposed t'be." Jay Mac said reassuringly.

"Josh runs the South Klan Skins. I went to school with him and we all used to have t'pay protection to his boys. When I left last year I thought I'd got away, once I got me job here but he started workin' in town a few weeks later." the boy advised.

Natural Born Skinhead 1971 •136

"You work 'ere do yer, with that arl feller, is that right?" Jay Mac asked.

"Yeah, me names Timothy Murphy, are you the lad who's startin' on Monday?" the nervous boy asked.

"Yeah I am, me name's John Mack but everyone calls me Jay Mac. I'll see yer on Monday, Timothy." the Eagle crew member replied, adding "and don't worry too much about that Josh wanker, he's not the only Skinhead round 'ere no more."

"Ok Jay Mac, thanks. By the way am not a Hippie, I'm a Trog and a T-Rex fan, yer know, Marc Bolan?" Timothy replied.

"Trog, Walley, Hippie, same difference, yer all fuckin' scruffs, see yer." Jay Mac shouted back with a grin.

That evening after demolishing his meal of fried eggs, bacon and chips, supplemented with five rounds of salty, margarine-smothered bread and washed down by the aid of two cups of dark brown tea, Jay Mac happened to mention to his uncle that his immediate superior would be a former B.S.M. from his old regiment.

"Is that right?" his guardian began, "Then you had better watch yerself boy. Those fellers didn't get t'be called Bastard Sergeant Major for nothin'." he observed before returning to his pipe and newspaper.

Jay Mac thanked the veteran for his advice, finished polishing his gleaming cherry-red Airwair then threw on his Levi's denim jacket before departing, for the Crown Estate. When he left the low rise block of tenements, he quickly scanned the surrounding area before sprinting over to the vandalised, precast concrete slab bus shelter. The anxious youth was becoming more careful while the evenings remained light, not wishing to be identified by any of the local Anvil public house crew as an enemy player. As soon as his bus arrived he leapt on board, stayed on the lower deck and kept his head down.

Half an hour later, having met Irish, Blue and Glynn at their usual library perch, Jay Mac outlined his plan for a diversion to their normal routine of wandering the estate, looking for something to do.

Natural Born Skinhead 1971 • 137

"Listen I was thinkin', instead of hangin' round 'ere tonight, why don't we have a change of scene." Jay Mac began, "We know that cunt in the Eagle won't serve us and no one fancies tryin' the Heron, not with Yad and the other two arseholes bein' down there."

"Go on... this sounds interestin', let's see where yer goin' with this." Irish said before taking a long drag on his cigarette.

"Now before y'start, Irish, I'm just sayin' here's an idea for a few grins, that's all." Jay Mac paused, waiting for his cynical friend to interrupt again but instead Irish merely waved his hand dismissively. "Ok, so today me and this miserable git went down to our old school to collect our shitty references. Well I was thinkin' we could go back there tonight and leave some references of our own. Put a few windows in and do a bit of paintin' or sprayin'. What d'yers think?" Jay Mac asked with a smile.

"I don't mind, it'll make a change from walkin' around this shit-hole." Glynn offered.

"Ok, I'm up for it, if there's a decent chippy round there." Blue agreed.

"Oh yeah mate, there's a top chippy alright, not as good as Mr Li's but not far off, it's a Greek one, so y'know it's gonna be decent." Jay Mac advised, continuing to promote his suggestion.

"This wouldn't have anythin' to do with a certain scruffy Hippie prick that we bumped into while we was there, would it?" Irish asked perceptively.

"Look Irish, I'm just suggestin' somethin', if we happen to come across a squat packed full of sweaty Hippies and their dirty birds at the same time, well we'd... er... just have t'see what happened next." Jay Mac replied smiling slyly.

"Hold on, are you sayin' there might be some spaced out pussy in a house by this school of yours?" Blue asked eagerly, adding, "Cos if that's the case, I'm well in, them Hippie birds will do anythin' when they're off their fuckin' heads."

Jay Mac momentarily felt some disquiet over where his suggested 'adventure' may lead but this quickly passed. "So, all we need is some paint and a few brushes, any offers?" he asked.

"Me arl feller's got a couple of half empty tins in the bin cupboard, I'll grab them and a brush." Blue offered generously on behalf of his father, without his knowledge.

Natural Born Skinhead 1971 •138

"I've got an arl brush and a rucksack in the yard, we might as well use that too." Glynn added.

"Brilliant, come 'ed its Blue's first, then down to Glynn's." a delighted Jay Mac beamed. Only the dour Irish remained silent.

After collecting two half-filled tins of gloss paint, one red and one white and two almost worn out brushes from Blue's home, they obtained the promised rucksack, which itself was covered in mould and paint spatters and an additional brush from Glynn's neat terraced residence. As they walked towards the bus stop closest to Glynn's home, they were called to from the ground floor entrance of the flats opposite.

"'Ey, where are you girls off to with yer paintin' gear, doin' yer boyfriends' places up are yer?" Yad shouted, emerging from the entrance, zipping up his jeans.

Before anyone could prevent him the garrulous Blue blurted out, "No, we'er goin' to their old school to wreck it and knob some Hippie birds while we're there."

Immediately Yad was joined by his two fellow commanders Macca (G) and Weaver, the Heron trio then strolled across to the Eagle quartet.

"What about Skank?" Weaver asked Yad casually, referring to a local girl who was just beginning her 'career' in providing relief, at a cost, to those in urgent need.

"Fuckin' leave her there with Peza and the boys, she's only doin' ten pence tosses tonight with her bein' on the rag, and I've had mine, so I don't give a fuck." Yad replied coldly.

All three arrived at the bus stop where the four youths were waiting.

"So go 'ed then, let's hear the fuckin' lot." Yad demanded.

"Blue's havin' yer on Yad." Jay Mac began, "We're just goin' down to our school to do a bit of damage, give them some payback for all those happy years, that's all."

"Yeah and don't forget the Hippie birds in the squat." Blue interrupted excitedly, leading Jay Mac to add, "And there's supposed to be some Hippies livin' nearby in the arl houses."

"This sounds fuckin' promisin', what d'yer think lads, should we join them?" Yad asked his peers.

Natural Born Skinhead 1971 • 139

"Too fuckin' right." Weaver said, producing his famed toffee hammer and spitting on it for luck."

"Defo, an if there's some Hippie snatch in need of a bit of pain, all the better." Macca (G) agreed, adding, "Let's call back to ours for a minute, I've got a stash of nicked spray cans in loads of colours, so we can do a proper job and let them all know the Crown Team have done them."

Motion proposed and carried, there was no further discussion and all seven youths, six of whom were full Skinheads and one who presented an incongruous long-haired boot boy, set off for the sexual sadist's extensively modified terraced house at the lower edge of the estate.

Once they had fully loaded Glynn's rucksack, which they all agreed they would take turns in carrying, they waited for the first green Atlantean bus bound for the city centre to leave from the nearby terminus.

"Alright lads, goin' somewhere are yers?" Mickey Pimple shouted pulling up alongside them on his gaudy Vespa and now sporting an old style, peak-less, steel coloured helmet, with an unfortunate central vertical thin black stripe running from the front of the crown to the rear.

"No, we're just standin' here, waitin' for a fat tit with a dick on his head, to come and ask us a fuckin' stupid question." Yad replied angrily.

Mickey ignored the Heron co-leader's sarcastic reply and addressed his next question directly to Jay Mac.

"Alright mate, how areyer, haven't seen yer passin' by lately." he began, much to the shallow youth's embarrassment. "I've got plenty more of them cakes that yer like, so anytime yer fancy slippin' in, we can get stuck into them."

"Oh yes please Jay Mac, slip it in, then the two of yer can get stuck right in there." Yad observed smiling slyly.

Now all of them, other than the mortified Jay Mac began to laugh.

"What the fuck are you talkin' about, yer fat twat? Piss off will yer!" Jay Mac snapped angrily causing the surprised Mickey to sit back in his seat and look curiously at the youth, whom he thought was a friend.

"See yer lads." he said as he rode away on his unique scooter.

Natural Born Skinhead 1971 •140

"Pity that, I fancied a few of them cakes." Blue noted, while the driver of their bus boarded his waiting vehicle and started the engine.

When the seven youths leapt onto the platform one after the other and threw down their customary ten pence payments, the mid-forties, overweight, balding male made no objection and closed the doors with a hiss of the hydraulics, before pulling away from the terminus stop.

It was only a half hour journey to the area where the Cardinals was located but Jay Mac felt it was never ending as he sat listening to Yad's jibes, beginning to regret that he had ever suggested the venture.

"Fuck me, I thought the Crown Comp was a dump but this looks like a fuckin' haunted house." Macca (G) observed when they arrived in the deserted cobbled street not far from the busy main road, as the late evening sun began to slip behind the tall, dark, silent houses.

"So this is where yer learned to bum, hey Jay Mac?" Yad continued his usual line of insult.

"There's only one expert in bummin' round 'ere Yad an I'm talkin' to *him* now." Jay Mac responded dryly.

"Come 'edlet's get started before it goes dark." Glynn suggested, interrupting them both.

"What's the rush Glynn, scared of the fuckin' dark are yer?" Macca (G) asked with a sneer.

"No, course not but it might help if we can see what we're fuckin' doin', yeah?" he replied sharply.

Without any further comment, the group set about their work competing to achieve the biggest, most noticeable piece for the benefit of the dead-eyed buildings opposite and the ghosts of their long-gone original tenants.

As if commissioned by a wealthy patron they continued diligently, until finally they stepped back to admire their combined efforts. 'CROWN SKINS RULE OK' read the main proclamation, which covered the area between the once smooth-cast base plinths up to the rotting windowsills of the ground floor, in huge letters of dripping white paint. Accompanying this were individual

Natural Born Skinhead 1971 • 141

inscriptions either completed with brush or a flourish of spray can, declaring simply 'CROWN TEAM' or 'FUCK YOU' finished either in red or black, depending on the whim of the artist.

Yad began to include the 'names' of those Heron crew present, beginning with his own, followed by that of Macca (G) and Weaver, finishing with the name of the eponymous alehouse. When Blue began to follow suit, both Irish and Jay Mac told him to omit their sobriquets, knowing that they were already carved into numerous desks in different classrooms around the old school and this would provide too much of a clue as to the identity of the culprits.

"What's the problem, ladies? Too fuckin' scared to 'ave yer names seen are yer?" Yad asked on hearing their instructions to Blue.

For once it was Irish who responded to his challenge rather than Jay Mac, "No there's no problem Yad, just like you wouldn't be bothered if we put every fuckin' window in the Crown Comp in then wrote your name outside."

"Fuck the pair of yer, I don't want the names of two losers anywhere near mine anyway." Yad concluded.

"What d'yer think of this?" Macca (G) called to them all, drawing their attention to his piece de resistance, a huge circumcised, erect penis with massively inflated testicles, wildly ejaculating a torrent of semen like some primitive totemic pagan fountain. "It's fuckin' good aint it?" the self-congratulatory artist suggested. "I modelled it on meself of course."

They all laughed at the idea, even Weaver the psychopath who was rarely amused. "Right, enough pissin' about with paintin' let's get down to business." he ordered, the smile quickly vanishing from his grim visage.

Abandoning their materials for the moment, they ran across to the nearest derelict building, which had been part demolished and collected sufficient ammunition for the next phase of their school improvement scheme. Window by window was smashed either by a single shot or a combination of well-aimed missiles, until only the very top panes under the eaves remained.

It was acknowledged among them all that Jay Mac was not only a peerless runner but also, usually, a deadly accurate shot with a variety of projectiles. Both he and his arch enemy Yad now strove

Natural Born Skinhead 1971 ●142

to reach the highest, small circular window immediately positioned under the apex. The Heron co-leader threw first and struck the old wooden frame but the lead strip that bound the segments of coloured glass held. Jay Mac stepped further away, paused studying the target like a darts player at the oche, focusing on the bullseye. With one perfectly aimed shot his small piece of brick rubble smashed through the dead centre of the ancient window, instantly reducing it to dozens of coloured fragments.

"Well in Jay Mac!" Irish said with others, including Weaver, also congratulating the Eagle player.

"Lucky shot that's all. I weakened the frame with mine, that's why it went in with just a weak tap." Yad concluded angrily, adding, "Anyway fuck all this playin' with stones that's only f'kids, where's these Hippie cunts that need a kickin' and their dirty bitches?"

Jay Mac now totally regretted that he had even suggested this mission but he did not yet know the extent of remorse the events of that night, would induce within his troubled mind.

"Listen Yad no one said anythin' about any Hippie birds, except Blue." he began nervously. "I can't even remember where the hairy scruff went to, to be honest."

"You better be fuckin' jokin' lad. D'you think we came all this way t'this bummers' school, to do a bit of paintin' and stone throwin'?" Yad roared furiously then continued, "Hang on, 'ave you just got us down 'ere out the way, so your Kings shitbags can do a little raid on the Crown? Have you fuckin' set us up?"

"Piss off Yad, yer know that's total bollocks!" Jay Mac shouted in reply then driven by his anger, offered "Come 'ed, I'll take yer to the fuckin' Hippie house and I'll get us all in."

"Lead on boy, lead on!" Yad replied grinning.

Darkness had fully fallen and was greeted by a pair of random streetlamps flickering reluctantly into life, as the seven youths came upon the decaying Victorian villa. A faint glow of light was escaping from within, between the gaps in the shuttered windows, around the badly fitting front door and through spaces left by missing tiles on the aged slate roof.

Natural Born Skinhead 1971 • 143

Unfortunately for Jay Mac, despite his faithful reproduction of the distinctive knock, three short taps, three long and three short again, none of the occupants responded to his internationally recognisable S.O.S. Undeterred, the resourceful youth raced around the side of the large end terrace and into the reeking entry at the rear. Initially he thought he was to be thwarted again on seeing that the usual burglar deterrent practice, of cementing broken glass shards along the top of the yard wall, had been put into place here. When he tried the rotten wooden door however, he felt it would give with minimum force and by means of one swift kick, he burst it open detaching its rusty latch and bolt. Quickly scanning the small yard filled with a mound of mixed detritus, comprised of food stuffs and junk, including a battered old tin bath, Jay Mac spotted exactly what he was looking for, a half open lower, sash cord window, in the rough-shod outbuilding annexed to the main house. He whistled a signal to his waiting companions and they ran round to join him.

"Alright, I'll slip in through the window, open that back door and let yous in, right?" he offered.

"Go 'ed then, what's fuckin' keepin' yer?" Yad asked angrily.

Jay Mac ignored him, carefully stepped across the minefield mound of rubbish then climbed up onto the broad sandstone sill and squeezed through the narrow gap into the dark interior of the amateur extension.

Once inside the gloomy pantry he was immediately aware of a sweet sickly smell of burning incense, floating on the cool air that filled the confined area. Passing through a connecting doorway into the main kitchen, he also became aware of low rhythmic chanting, the sound entering from the dark narrow lobby that lay just beyond this present room. Quickly he unlocked the rear door with the large key that was conveniently protruding from that fitting, unbolting it at the same time.

"We're in." he announced with mixed feelings.

"Sound, let's find these Hippie scruffs and have some fun." Macca (G) said, smiling slyly.

Moving along the lobby they quietly opened the door to the first room that they came to. Apart from the dim light from a small selection of candles of different sizes, the room was almost completely empty, without ornaments or furniture other than a

Natural Born Skinhead 1971 •144

number of filthy sleeping bags, laying scattered about. Even as they approached the main front room further along the lobby, they knew there were occupants present, as the originally indistinct chanting now became clearer and insistent, suggesting several people were inside.

Grasping hold of the ivory doorknob with his left hand, having slipped his favourite solid brass knuckle-duster onto his right, Yad flung the door open and leapt into the candle-lit room, his crew of Eagle and Heron players following immediately behind.

On the old, weathered wooden floor, each seated in the lotus position forming a loose circle, were five long-haired males wearing beards of varying lengths. They were bare-chested but with their pale flesh covered in a selection of tattoos including letters, numbers and serpents, each bore the image of a stylised eye ball in the centre of their upper sternum just below the clavicle. The chanting stopped; the figure positioned furthest from the door and facing them looked vacantly in their direction, saying, "Welcome brothers, we've been waiting for you, we 'saw' you coming."

Yad sprang forward crossing the circle before smashing a vicious straight right, metal encased fist into the speaker's face, cracking his front teeth. "Did yer see that one comin' as well, yer fuckin' tit?"

Not to be outdone, Weaver drew his weapon of choice and struck the head of the nearest seated male, shouting, "I'm Weaver I done this to yer, I'm Weaver."

Seemingly roused from their meditative torpor the three remaining males rose to their feet intent on escape. The one closest to Jay Mac tried to push past him, hoping to reach the door but was seized by the hair, butted in the face then flung back down to the bare boards. Irish and Macca (G) equally effectively dealt with the other two fleeing hippies, punching and kicking them until they offered no further resistance. As yet without any opponents, Blue and Glynn were for the moment consigned to being spectators only and Yad called to them, "Watch that fuckin' door yous two, we don't want any of them gettin' out to warn the pussy." He turned his attention back to the male who had originally welcomed

Natural Born Skinhead 1971 • 145

them, now lying on his back with a bleeding mouth. Yad quickly straddled him and began his questioning.

"Right shit-head, I don't know if yer with me or not but I just wanna know one thing from yer then y'can go back to whatever the fuck yer was doin', when we came in". Yad paused, catching hold of the long hair on either side of the head of the non-responsive Hippie.

"Before I smash yer bleedin' head into this floor tell me where your birds are, where's the fuckin' pussy, 'ey?" he demanded.

With an impassive, resigned expression on his thin face, he replied, "The 'sisters' are not for you man, you're unclean, your karma is out of alignment."

"What the fuck is this cheeky cunt sayin'?" Yad shouted indignantly, "He fuckin' stinks of shit like he's never had a wash in 'is life and he say's I'm unclean!" With that Yad commenced knocking some sense into his clearly deluded victim, repeatedly banging the young man's head onto the floorboards.

While the raging Heron co-leader conducted his interrogation Jay Mac casually studied the room's interior, his eyes having adjusted to the low light of the numerous candles and the one paraffin lamp, which was standing on the otherwise empty hearth. All around the walls were large posters containing colourful images of Hindu deities including; Shiva, Kali and Vishnu, juxtaposed with these where copies of enlightened Buddhist teachings.

Above the tall ebony mantelpiece was a huge stylised depiction of an all-seeing eye painted directly onto the wall, though sadly for the Hippies, in this instance, it had woefully failed in its apotropaic function of warding off evil. Standing immediately in front of this was a small bronze statuette again of the multi-armed, cosmic dancer, Shiva. Burning josticks of varying fragrances were set all about, giving off a strong intoxicating grey vapour.

As Jay Mac finished his brief inspection and while Yad continued his useless pounding of his victim's head, the Eagle player's eyes settled on a cream coloured Bush radio in the left hand alcove nearest the hearth. It was switched on but tuned to an off-station frequency so that only the white noise of static could be heard. Jay Mac was pleased to have finally traced the source of

Natural Born Skinhead 1971 •146

this irritating sound, which he had been aware of since they entered the room.

He was not the only one to have been surveying the room and Weaver's gaze also fell upon the battery-powered transistor radio at the same moment. Whereas Jay Mac took it to be some form of harmless aid to meditation used by the group, the crazed psychopath felt it was somehow a direct affront to him, taking exception to its presence. In an instant he had seized it, flung it against the wall then ensured it was completely destroyed by several rapid strokes of his hammer.

"No man, what have y'done?" the Hippies', including Yad's bloodied captive began to shriek as if in pain. "The voice has gone, they've killed his voice, kill them! Magog help us! Magog help us!"

Within seconds the five long-haired bearded males transformed from passive acceptance to wild resistance, leaping upon the stunned Skinheads while Yad's prone victim seized him around the throat and began choking the life out of the Heron player.

"Magog help us, Magog!" they kept calling at the top of their voices, whilst punching, clawing, kicking and spitting in a frenzy, trying to pull the youths close to them as if to bite into their flesh.

Blue and Glynn abandoned their door duty and attempted to assist their companions as best they could, all of whom were trying to avoid being bitten as much as defeat their own opponents, who each now seemed to possess the strength of ten men. Suddenly the door burst open once more and the biggest, hairiest Hippie any of them had ever seen crashed into the room carrying a huge, disturbingly still glistening, flesh coloured hard plastic vibrator as his primary weapon, Magog had come to the rescue of his disciples.

Having previously felt surplus to requirements, Blue and Glynn transferred their attention to this new arrival, tackling him around the waist and shoulders. Only momentarily hampered by their combined attack Magog struck them both with his smelly, sex toy weapon; much to their disgust then flung them from him as if they were infants. In no more than two lengthy strides the giant leapt onto the back of Yad and began thumping him about the head, using his 'tool' like an erotic mace.

Natural Born Skinhead 1971 • 147

Jay Mac was the first to ultimately dispatch his adversary by repeatedly head-butting him then slamming his hairy skull into the nearest wall.

"Blue, Glynn, grip that fucker's arms, get hold of one each!" he shouted, allowing his semi-conscious foe to slump to the floor before running across to Yad's aid.

Positioning himself directly in front of the struggling Heron co-leader, Jay Mac first stamped on the face of *his* original opponent, hoping to remove him from the fight then snatching hold of Magog's wild hair he shouted to Yad, "Keep yer head right down!" With that warning he delivered a powerful knee strike fully into the face of the 'giant' repeating this devastating move over and over, while Blue and Glynn clung to Magog's flailing arms, doing their best to restrain him.

Weaver hammered his own crazed opponent across the forehead, bridge of the nose and mouth in rapid succession until he ceased to resist and eagerly joined Jay Mac in his rescue of Yad.

"Giz a go Jay Mac, mind over!" he shouted then began an exhibition of frenzied hammering about Magog's bloodied face and skull.

Battered as he was the raging late-twenties, hairy male struggled ferociously, trying to extricate himself from the grip of his attackers. Finally with Yad's interrogation victim having been repeatedly stamped under Jay Mac's boots, he gave way to unconsciousness, released the Heron co-leader's throat as his hands fell away, joining the rest of his motionless body on the bare boards.

"Get this fucker off me!" Yad roared, staggering to his feet and raring to add to the combined assault.

All five Crown skins punched, kicked and hammered the brawny older man, while attempting to grapple him to the floor. With supreme effort they eventually managed to down him, instantly switching to a vicious, ten-legged, Airwair-clad kicking machine.

"Boot this cunt till he's dead!" Yad ordered, unnecessarily as they were all making a determined attempt to do just that.

Irish and Macca (G) had also beaten their opponents into submission and they wandered over to casually watch the 'sport'.

Natural Born Skinhead 1971 •148

"Lads, I think he's fuckin' croaked." Irish observed. "He's even let go of his false dick." he added in support.

Exhausted by their efforts all five kickers stepped back to admire their work, "That was one tough fuckin' Hippie." Glynn concluded.

Jay Mac was not convinced that the black leather, sleeveless jacket wearing giant *was* a Hippie. "I don't think he is one of them, look at his kit, the back of his jacket and his filthy fuckin' Levi's and those motorbike boots, this cunt's a friggin' Greaser."

"Yeah, is that right Sherlock, well he's one dead fuckin' Greaser now." Yad retorted.

Jay Mac was in fact correct in his deductions. Although Magog bore no motto, emblem, top or bottom rocker revealing a motorcycle club affiliation, or no specific badge, if they had had the opportunity to study the front of his black leather waistcoat, they would have seen two small, though distinctive, patches: one saying 'Vice President' the other declaring proudly '1%'.

Derek 'Magog' Richards a twenty-six year old drifter from the North East, had been a significant member of a Chapter of Greasers with aspirations to be recognised as affiliated Hell's Angels. Unfortunately for Derek and his crew they pushed their ambition and luck too far once they began wearing the famous skull and war-bonnet image on the back of their jackets, as if they were the genuine article. It was not long before this sacrilege attracted the attention of a real hardcore Chapter, who soon exacted an appropriately violent revenge on these upstarts, removing their colours forcefully.

Once disbanded, the various members went their separate ways with Derek's route eventually bringing him to a Hippie squat in a deserted back street, in the old Victorian centre of Liverpool. He quickly established himself as their leader, mentor and protector, charging only a nominal fee of free board and lodging, plus his choice of females, or males, as the sexual fancy took him.

"Tie this cunt up with his belt and then we'll 'ave a sniff around for the pussy." Yad ordered with the observant Macca (G) adding "Yeah, and from the smell of that fishy fuckin' dick, it's been in 'action' pretty recent and we don't want this crazy bastard interruptin' us again, when we find that muff."

Natural Born Skinhead 1971 • 149

After securing the enemy giant and checking the condition of the wounded Hippies, who had reverted back to docile pacifists, the Skins set off on the hunt for the much anticipated treasure trove.

This was a large family residence, occupying three floors and an attic and the youths were now more cautious as they searched each darkened room, not knowing what they may find. Finally by process of elimination, they approached the master bedroom situated at the rear of the second landing. Yad again assumed the leadership of his Heron peers and the Eagle crew, grasping the handle then flinging the heavy door wide open. "Yes! Fuckin' Jackpot!" he shouted with delight as he stepped into the room lit by an assortment of candles, similar to that of the ground floor 'prayer' chamber.

"The dirty fuckers!" Macca (G) exclaimed, equally pleased, adding "Now that's what I call a party."

All seven youths stood transfixed just inside the doorway, gazing voyeuristically at the writhing tableau set out before them, in a mix of fascination and incredulity. Two pale skinned emaciated males with long scraggy hair and matching beards, their flesh also covered in the same selection of tattoos, were being entertained and, to a lesser extent, entertaining two females with equally undernourished physiques.

Slouching with his back resting against a wall, one of the totally naked males was having his penis enthusiastically sucked by a squatting female who in turn was receiving a thorough gynaecological 'inspection' from the lapping tongue of the skeletal hippie lying supine below her, his head firmly pushed up between her willing thighs appearing as if she was giving birth to a full grown male. The 'fun' continued with a second obliging 'lady' positioned on her hands and knees, bottom raised invitingly in the air, whilst she too engaged in a vigorous fellatio performance on the supine cunilingus practitioner. Only she was without a reciprocal partner and it did not take long for the boys' fevered imagination to conclude whose vacant orifice, Magog may have been previously filling with his mechanical aid.

Their suspicions were entirely correct and the only missing piece of the entire 'adults only' jigsaw was the one containing the image of Magog ramming the device into the kneeling girl, while

Natural Born Skinhead 1971 ●150

simultaneously being feverishly masturbated by his favourite disciple of the group, the presently slouching male. Together all five had formed a perpetual motion circle of base sex, exchanging bodily fluids as they were produced.

The seven onlookers were split into three distinct camps: those who wished to join in; those who were unsure and those who wanted to keep their own genitals safely where they were.

An overpowering smell of sweat, which was freely running all over the participants' pale, glistening bodies, combined with that of their unwashed for several months flesh, particularly their unwiped rears and added together with the pungent mix of jostick vapours to produce an aroma at once primaly exciting and yet perversely repugnant.

"Right let's gerrin there." said Yad, unzipping his jeans.

Weaver needed no invitation and immediately threw the standing Hippie to one side, pulling the squatting girl onto her back for a more conventional missionary encounter. Yad booted the supine male in the ribs then seized the crouching fellatio exponent, preparing to mount her from behind.

"Nice one Yad, turn the bitch round t'face me, she can put her mouth t'good use round a real man's cock." Macca (G) shouted, releasing his straining erection from his Y-fronts and unzipped jeans.

Blue and Glynn loitered pensively just inside the room, both almost wishing they had taken the initiative but conversely partly relieved that they had missed the 'opportunity.'

Their Eagle crew companions, Jay Mac and Irish watched the show for a few moments as the two stupefied, dead-eyed girls swapped from hippie to Skinhead partners without any objection, or discernable reaction. Neither youth particularly wanted to become active participants and were about to leave the scene, intent on exploring the remaining rooms while their Heron associates were being entertained.

"Gettin' off are yers?" Yad called, while thrusting hard into his non-responsive kneeling partner. "I don't blame yers, yer know yer can't compete with us 'big' lads. Go'ed, fuck off, unless yer fancy sloppy seconds."

Natural Born Skinhead 1971 • 151

"Yad, in case yers hadn't noticed, that's what yous are gettin' now, or thirds or fourths." Jay Mac shouted in reply, adding, "I'll go and get yer that false knob so yer can shove it up yer arse and make yerself feel really at home."

"Piss off and take yer two bum boys with yer, they're puttin' me off me stroke!" Yad shouted angrily, driving himself on into the virtually comatose female.

"Yous comin' with us or watchin' these three gettin' their bell-ends wrecked? Hang around and 'ave a go, if yer feel like joinin' them down the V.D. clinic." Jay Mac said to Blue and Glynn, who were still watching the ugly performance in grotesque fascination.

"Yeah, come 'ed, I defo wouldn't fancy goin' into either of those two skanks, not after them three fuckers, or those Hippie skeletons 'ave been there." Glynn replied honestly.

Slowly and even more cautiously, like a quartet of soldiers on a house-clearing mission, the four Eagle Skins moved from room to room checking for occupants, hoping not to find another Magog, or an even more ambitious sexual entanglement. Just as they had completed their tour of the upper landing they heard a distinct thump on the ceiling immediately above their heads coming from the attic. With the narrow staircase that led to this top storey room just outside the door of their present one, Jay Mac assumed the lead position with Irish, Blue and Glynn following immediately behind in that order.

"Stealth it lads, we don't know what the fuck's up 'ere." he said in a whisper to them grasping hold of the worn wooden doorknob and turning it slowly.

They quickly and quietly filed inside the long based isosceles triangle shaped chamber with its steeply raking roof sides. Only a single paraffin lamp whose light was dwindling illuminated this draughty room. Jay Mac was first to see the sight that for him personally was the worst he could imagine.

There in the far corner under the eaves was a rickety wooden cot containing a crying infant, a toddler of about eighteen months, standing holding the bars with a snot encrusted nose, wearing a filthy t-shirt and in urgent need of feeding and changing. What proved too much for the horrified youth was the harness which was strapped around the child's chest, with its reins tied in secure knots

Natural Born Skinhead 1971 •152

to the bars opposite those that the child was grasping, ensuring that its movements were restricted.

If an exact mirror image of himself at that age was too painful to bear, when Irish drew his attention to the body of the mother slumped against the opposite wall, with a trail of thick porridge-like vomit pouring from her mouth and down her equally filthy front, Jay Mac finally snapped.

"Fuckin' hell! Not again, no, no!" he yelled, his mind cruelly tormenting him with images of his own drunken mother, passed out in the bedroom after another heavy drinking session, while a party raged on downstairs leaving the similarly restrained child at the mercy of any of those same party animals.

"She's still breathin'." Irish advised, leaning close to the reeking woman. "John, snap out of it, you're the fastest, go and get an ambulance... John... can yer hear me?"

Jay Mac looked at his long-standing friend but did not see him, he spoke as if in a trance, "Get an ambulance... I can run."

"Fuck, what's the matter with him?" Blue asked.

"Yer don't wanna know." Irish replied.

Glynn, himself the abandoned child of an errant father, whose own mother entertained a number of over-friendly 'uncles' shuddered and remained silent.

In an instant, without another word, Jay Mac was gone. Leaping down the flights of old wooden stairs, sprinting past the room where the Heron leaders were still enjoying the hospitality of the obliging residents. When he came to the first floor staircase, his path was blocked half way up by the raging Magog, now released from his bonds by his faithful disciples.

"You! I'm gonna fuckin' start with you, yer bastard!" he bellowed, his face scarlet, drenched in his own blood.

At any other time he would have had little difficulty in achieving his objective but at this moment Jay Mac's own rage was unparalleled, rendering him unstoppable. Grasping the bannister rail with his right hand and flattening his left against the wall opposite, he sprang up and forward delivering a powerful thrust kick with both feet, sending the roaring giant crashing, heels over head, down the hard stairs.

Natural Born Skinhead 1971 • 153

Lying at the bottom with a dislocated neck, he was incapable of further movement; Jay Mac cared not whether he was alive or dead and leapt over his twisted body then raced along the narrow lobby to the front door.

The one functioning red telephone box in the vicinity was located just beyond the bus stop, where he had waited for Madame de Paris' pretty assistant and Jay Mac sprinted towards it like he was competing in yet another vital race.

Irish, Blue and Glynn followed their companion's lead, making their way as quickly as possible to the ground floor exit, stopping only to warn the Heron crew and briefly admire Jay Mac's felling of Magog, the ex-Greaser giant.

When the ambulance arrived all six youths were already boarding their bus back to the Crown estate; the crazed Eagle player was nowhere to be seen.

"I'll fuckin' do that grass when I see him, ruinin' our fun." Yad warned angrily.

"Nah, yer won't Yad, not after I tell your Dayo what happened tonight and how Jay Mac saved yer twice from that dick-carryin' monster, cos if he hadn't have stopped him on those stairs that cunt would've been rammin' that plastic cock up all yer arses right now." Irish warned with a deadly seriousness.

Yad paused and considered what had been said, "Yeah, well maybe I'll let him off this time. Just do me a fuckin' favour, the lorra yers, don't ever mention this to our kid, or anyone else."

Their bus sped on through the warm night; Jay Mac wandered about drenched in his sweat, unseeing, using his own middle eye for guidance as he tried to find his way back from the nightmare infested dark caverns of his mind.

Natural Born Skinhead 1971 •154

Chapter 6

O Fortuna

Saturday 24th July 1971

"What's the matter with you John?" the old soldier and proud postman asked his nephew while lighting his pipe, after finishing his meal of mixed offal. "It's not like you to be off yer food an that's best tripe on yer plate."

Jay Mac looked at the dish of quivering white tripe, swimming in vinegar and covered in onions with a side helping of fried liver and kidney and somehow he found it less appetising than usual. Normally whatever was placed before him, other than the dreaded boiled-to-a-mush cabbage, was greedily wolfed down as if it were the first meal the youth had been fed in years and he was always grateful to receive it. With the events of the previous evening still playing over in his disturbed mind, as they had been continually during the three miles he had walked as part of the seven that separated his school from the Kings Estate, before finally deciding to catch his bus for the remainder of the journey, he did not feel particularly hungry or talkative.

"Yeah it's funny how somethin' can just do that to yer." he answered cryptically. His uncle puffed on his pipe until he was satisfied that the glowing strands of St Bruno tobacco were fully lit, then said, "Y'couldn't just leave yer food like that in my day, my arl feller would've strapped the hide off me."

"Yeah, sounds great." Jay Mac replied disinterestedly.

"Does it, well maybe a bloody good hidin' is what you need?" his guardian observed becoming angry, adding, "Or in the army, the other lads would've thought y'was queer if yer'd played with yer food like that."

"Thee thought you was queer just for breathin' the wrong way, from what yer've told me." Jay Mac responded unwisely.

"'Ey, don't you be knockin' the lads. Thee were a great bunch of real men, not like the fuckin' fruits yer get everywhere nowadays." his uncle snapped, momentarily removing his pipe from his mouth.

Natural Born Skinhead 1971 ● 155

The Eagle player had the sense to say no more and rose to leave the table prompting his guardian to warn, "Anyway, it'll be waitin' for yer when y'come back, good food's not gettin' wasted, yer can 'ave it cold tonight."

'Fuckin' great.' Jay Mac thought, 'Cold tripe an onions, that's somethin' to look forward to.' but answered with a request instead, "Any chance y'could iron me cream parallels, I need yer razor-sharp creases down the front?" Whenever military precision ironing was required, he always asked the veteran for this favour and in most instances he was happy to oblige, always maintaining 'a smart appearance maketh the man.'

"Aye go 'ed, I'll just 'ave a look at me paper then do them before the *Black and Whites* comes on the telly." he responded now more amenable, looking forward to watching his favourite television programme, *The Black and White Minstrel Show*, which knocked even Val Parnell's *Sunday Night at the London Palladium* and *Songs of Praise* into a tied second place, in the old soldier's order of viewing preference.

A few moments later while he sat relaxing in one of the well-worn armchairs reading his paper, in the small living room, he called to Jay Mac, "Your boys in 'ere again, causin' more trouble."

Jay Mac froze in the midst of polishing his cherry-red Airwair to their parade ground finish, wondering how their assault on the house of the Hippies had become a news item already. "What are yer talkin' about, we've done nothin', we was on the estate all night listenin' t'records..." he offered by way of an alibi, before being interrupted.

"What the fuck are you goin' on about?" the older man asked quizzically, "I'm talkin' about 'Skinheads', your boys, yer know, 'Bovver Boys'. Says 'ere they've been doin' more of this beatin' up of Pakistanis, thee call it 'Paki Bashing' according to the paper."

A relieved Jay Mac answered, "That's just somethin' the rag newspapers come up with for arl ones like you t'get excited about, the way the *News of the World* does on Sunday with its roundup of the weekly rapes. I've never heard of any Skins round 'ere doin' that. Anyway just 'ave a look where we live, I don't think I've ever seen anyone on this whole friggin' giant estate whose *not*

Natural Born Skinhead 1971 ●156

white. They've got more sense than to come to a shit-hole like this."

"Ey, if it's not good enough for you, lord fuckin' snooty, yer can piss off!" the veteran shouted angrily then persisted, "I thought your boys just went round havin' little play fights with each other, thinkin' you were hard cases." He paused to draw on his pipe and continued; "Now I don't mind if yer'ave a go at them long haired Hippie Jessies, I can understand that, some of them need a good kickin' but I'll not 'ave yer bein' part of any racial prejudice bollocks."

"Fuckin' hell d'yer really think I'd be part of any shite like that?" Jay Mac asked becoming angry himself.

His uncle considered the position for a few moments then replied, "No, I know yer wouldn't, or I'd take me fuckin' belt to yer."

"Listen, bein' a proper Skinhead's got nothin' t'do with that shite, that's just for sad loser cunts who've got no understandin' of what it is to be a Skin. We're into the gear, the sharp style, the music, most of which is Black anyway and the action. We wanna be seen, to be recognised, t'be somebody, not just fuckin' nobodies." Jay Mac answered honestly.

"Well, Mr Somebody, let's see how yer feel after yer've done a week's work. Yer startin' on Monday so yer better make the most of yer weekend lad, cos yer'll be fuckin' glad of it once the bosses own yer." the paradoxical Queen and Country – Socialist advised before turning back to his newspaper.

Within a quarter of an hour, after his uncle had ironed his immaculate twenty-inch cream parallels to their pristine best, Jay Mac was getting dressed in the tiny kitchen listening to the small transistor radio, currently tuned to the Radio One frequency, playing The Tams *Hey Girl Don't Bother Me*. As the youth put on his well-scrubbed Levi's denim jacket with bleached white collar and pocket flaps, over his light blue short-sleeved Ben Sherman shirt and before he gave his gleaming Airwair a final wipe with the soft polish-stained cloth that he always carried, Jay Mac's uncle appeared in the doorway now smoking one of his full-strength Capstan Navy Cut cigarettes.

Natural Born Skinhead 1971 • 157

"Is that what's botherin' yer?" he asked, feeling that the title of the popular record may have provided a vital clue. "Birds, is that it? Well there's no solvin' that one lad, y'know what thee say about women, 'you can't live with them and you can't live without them'." After dispensing that pearl of sagacity and on hearing the theme tune to his favouite variety show, the old soldier returned to his armchair ready to sing along with a selection of classic ballads. His wife was already seated on the couch reading one of her Agatha Christie murder mysteries with her hearing aid switched off, so that she need not listen to either.

"I wish it was that bleedin' simple." Jay Mac said without being heard as he strolled through from the kitchen and out into the even tinier hall, ready to depart.

During his relatively short journey to the Crown Estate he managed to supress the disturbing images of the previous night, by replacing them with what he considered to be righteous anger at the suggestion of any racial prejudice slur being associated with his choice of youth culture movement. Virtually everyone he knew was of white, working class origin and he could not recall them ever expressing any such view, for him personally any concept of one race being superior to another was anathema.

Jay Mac, the obsessive Americana fan could never reconcile the incongruity of segregation occurring in the nation that was founded on the principles of egalitarianism, feeling that somehow this great wrong must be righted. From his regular reading of all articles connected with the United States, particularly the Vietnam War and the Civil Rights campaign, he could not help but be exposed to the profound teachings of a man that he came to regard as the humanitarian giant of the twentieth century, Dr. Martin Luther King. The impressionable young male believed that if you actually listened to the unembellished elequoence of his speeches, you heard the truth, the simple, irrefutable and self-evident truth, that *all* men are created equal. In the way that everyone who was alive at the time of the assassination of President John F. Kennedy was supposed to know exactly where they where when they received that terrible news, which in that instance included the then eight year old Jay Mac, so too was the case for him when he heard of the dreadful tragedy of the assassination of Dr. King.

Natural Born Skinhead 1971 •158

Roused from his thoughts on reaching his stop the youth alighted from the bus at the lower edge of the estate and walked across to the long row of terraces, to begin his trek up to the Eagle public house. Even before he had gone ten yards he was uncomfortably confronted by the presence of the rotund Mickey Pimple, standing in his path with his colourful Vespa parked by the kerb.

"Alright Mickey how are yer?" Jay Mac called to him.

"Sorry are you talkin' t'me, I didnt think you knew who I was." Mickey replied coldly.

"Come on Mickey lad, I was only jokin' mate, I had things on me mind, ok?" Jay Mac offered by way of a partial appology.

"Yeah, nice one." Mickey answered still unsmiling, adding "I'd ask yer in for a few cakes but I know yer not really that keen on them, you were just tryin' to humour the sad fat boy weren't yer?" He paused for a moment then pressed on before Jay Mac could reply. "On y'way up to the Eagle now I'll bet. All smartened up 'ey, big night for yers all isn't it? Everyone except me, 'Mickey Pimple', that's what yers call me, am I right?"

"Listen yer wrong, I call yer Mickey that's all. I've got no fuckin' control over what the others say or do, yeah?" Jay Mac answered feeling his anger rise, not wishing to be falsely accused of another slur.

Mickey considered what the Eagle player said then replied, "Ok, that's fair enough and to show yer I've got no hard feelings, I'll even give yer a lift up the Eagle on me scooter, how's that?"

Jay Mac felt he was trapped and accepted the inevitability of his fate, "Sound Mickey, soon as yer ready mate."

With that he climbed on board the still unadorned, garish blue and orange Vespa, while Mickey kick-started the vehicle into life, after placing his ill-fitting steel helmet on the top of his round head.

"'Ey Mickey just in case yer thinkin' of offerin' me a spare lid like yours, don't bother, I wouldn't want it to ruin me hair." Jay Mac called smiling, having no real hair to speak of, his latest number one crop being cut at his local barbers mid week.

Within a few minutes they arrived at the library perch of the Eagle crew, opposite the eponymous alehouse to a mixed

Natural Born Skinhead 1971 • 159

reception. Most of Jay Mac's chronological peers, who were about to become Seniors, were gathered around the building and gave both scooter riders the benefit of their considered opinions.

"Now that's one ugly fuckin' scooter." Tank shouted.

"Yeah, it matches the riders." Bobby Anton, the elder of the 'Ant' brothers noted.

"Fuckin' hell Jay Mac, yer arrivin' in style tonight." Irish observed.

"Whose yer fat fairy Godmother?" Blue asked unkindly, pleased that there was now someone slightly more overweight than him.

Mickey's delight of finally having a pillion passenger soon turned to dismay, while the shallow Jay Mac cringed with embarassment. As the insults grew crueller and cruder the Eagle player dismounted without speaking to his driver. "Ok, joke over, leave it will yers?" he asked in vein.

"Go 'ed fat boy, piss off with yer shit scooter, it's given me a fuckin' headache just lookin' at it." Johno, the only existing Senior among them advised, bringing the frivolity almost to an end.

Mickey wheeled his vibrant blue and orange machine about after adjusting the strap on his awkwardly positioned helmet, "See yer then lads." he called, disregarding all they had said, prompting Glynn to ensure that he *had* got their message, "'Ey, and squeeze that fuckin' big zit on the top of yer head will yer!" he shouted as a parting riposte.

Jay Mac joined the crew who were all dressed in their best kit, some wearing similar cream parallels to his own, others choosing petrol blue or the popular blue-green two-tone version. Most had well-scrubbed denim jackets with bleached white collars and, or pocket flaps though Irish, Blue and Tank all wore their Harrington jackets in shades of dark blue or maroon. Everyone had their Airwair polished as if waiting for an inspection except Irish, whose dull black pair looked entirely out of place, though he was unconcerned by any incongruity.

"Alright lads everyone 'ere? Who're we waitin' for?" Jay Mac asked looking about.

"We was waitin' for you." Irish advised.

Natural Born Skinhead 1971 •160

"How're yer feelin' Jay Mac, after last night like?" Blue asked without thinking.

"Me..? I'm sound Blue, ready for the big night, fuck whatever happened yesterday." he replied disingenuously, adding, "We all off to the Eagle then?"

All nine youths strolled over to the nearby public house, through the opening in the long low walls that surrounded the permanently empty carpark and stepped up into the entrance porch. Once they crossed the threshhold that night they would no longer be seen as mere Juniors but instead would be formally admitted to the upper ranks and acknowledged by all as Crown Team Seniors. Tommy (S) their leader would instruct them to mark the back of their denim jackets with the distinctive black outlined crown, containing the word 'Skins' at its hollow centre.

Only Jay Mac the non resident of this estate would remain an outsider, considered by all a worthy Senior auxilliary but not quite a fully fledged team member. He was acutely aware of his position but made no protest accepting that the rules devised by the 'founding fathers' could not be broken, however legitimate his right to full membership may be.

When they entered through the swing-door with its single frosted glass panel, the crew found the lounge was already packed and the usual crowd of Saturday night regulars were enjoying their noisy revellry. This stuffy, nicotine smoke-filled room was meant to be the marginally more plush of the two drinking chambers offered by the establishment, in that it had a fitted carpet, though now well worn, heavily stained and covered in inumberable cigarette burns, as oppossed to the tired, bareboards of the adjoining bar. The latter being the preserve of the hardcore, dedicated drinkers, who included Irish's father and the male parents of many of the crew, the youths tended not to bother with this rough, basic bar, leaving it to be 'enjoyed' by its own particular clientele.

Core to the considerably livelier ambience of the lounge was its well-stocked juke box, with its eclectic selection of contemporary hits and older popular tunes. As the nine former Juniors entered to join their existing Seniors and the old guard, Jim Reeves' *Welcome to My World* was currently playing, raising a smile from them all.

Natural Born Skinhead 1971 • 161

"Alright lads, grab some stools an join us over 'ere." Tommy (S) called warmly to them from his central position in the semi-circular, red leatherette backed, seating arrangement at the rear of the rectangular room. He was, as usual when in attendance, flanked on both sides by his company of loyal retainers with the privileged Terry (H) to his immediate left and Gaz to his right.

The new arrivals did as instructed pulling low stools and chairs about the already heavily laden small round tables, to form an opposing inward facing curve matching that of the rigid arrangement.

"We'll get yers a drink in, then yer on yer own." Tommy offered generously, "Pints all round, ok? I'll just get Col the barman." he advised then raised his right hand and gestured for the surly mid-thirties barman to come to him, even though waiter service was not available and the bar was near capacity.

Leaving the safety of his battered wooden counter he approached the crew carrying his sodden bar towel. "Yeah, what is it Tommy, we're really busy tonight?" he asked without changing his dour expression.

The Skinhead leader looked up into the barman's sweating face "You fuckin' alright Col? Not got a problem or somethin'?" he asked.

"Nah, I'm fine but like I said we're dead busy." Col answered acerbically.

"Must be your charm that brings the punters in, Col." Tommy observed then placed his own pint of amber bitter down on the small table. "Anyway Col, better to be dead busy than just fuckin' dead, yeah?"

Colin the overworked barman, understood the younger man's remark and said no more, for the moment. Instead he took the order of each youth and walked back to the counter to pour their drinks. When he returned, carefully balancing a tray containing nine pints, Tommy paid him, included a tip and some additional free advice, "These lads are gonna be yer regulars from now on Col, make sure yer give them good service, ok?"

A few moments later when the whole crew had a drink in their hand, Tommy raised his pint to the nine youths and said "Cheers lads, welcome to the team. Yer Crown Seniors now, never forget it."

Natural Born Skinhead 1971 •162

Everybody responded happily to his salutation including Jay Mac, even though he knew he was being received as an associate rather than a full member.

Tommy continued his brief informal speech, "Not one of yer would be 'ere tonight if yer hadn't shown yerseleves as bein' up for it. Yer've proved yer've got what it takes, don't ever fuckin' let the side down, we're a team, The Crown Team."

Again everyone cheered his rousing comments and then began to drift into their own conversations, shouting to be heard amongst the general clamour and the juke box now playing The Ethiopians *Train to Skaville*

After several minutes spent talking to the favoured Terry (H), the leader leaned forward to where Jay Mac was sitting almost directly in front of him with Irish, Blue and Glynn at one of the small circular tables. "Listen Jay Mac you know the score." he began, continuing "You're a good lad, I've seen yer in action and yer've got heart." He paused to take a drink of his pint, "but yer don't live on this estate, you're from the Kings so yer can't be a proper Crown Skin. Don't get me wrong, we still want yer on board, no doubt about it." After pausing for another drink he moved on, "Anyway, I hear there's a fat boy from the lower estate called Mickey Pimple who's keen to join the team and he's matey with you, am I right?"

"Yeah, sort of Tommy, I've only spoken to him a few times. He's a bit of a fat twat and he looks more like an unmade s bed than a Skin but he's not a bad lad." Jay Mac replied, wondering where the conversation was heading.

"Jay Mac, I don't give a shite what he looks like, or if he's as thick as a brick. Take yer mate Irish, he's a friggin' scruff but he'll get stuck in, or Brain, he doesn't know which way's up but he wont run when it all kicks off." He paused allowing Jay Mac to absorb his meaning then continued, "If he wants t'be part of this team an he can prove he's got the balls, then that's good enough for me, after all *he* does live on the Estate. Keep an eye on him Jay Mac and when the time comes give him a shot, I'll go with what you say, ok?"

"Will do Tommy, I won't let yer down, if he shows 'imself good enough for the team you'll be the first to know." the

Natural Born Skinhead 1971 • 163

disheartened youth answered honestly, ending their brief conversation. 'So that's all it takes,' he thought, 'if Mickey Pimple shows any sign of balls, he's fuckin' in cos he lives'ere but I can't be considered no matter what I do... fuck me, nothin' ever changes, yer either belong or yer don't.'

While the leader returned to his conversation with Terry (H) and the old guard, Jay Mac laughed and joked with his peers, making the most of finally being at least admitted to their hallowed bastion, The Eagle public house. Well worn, both in furnishings and decor, stuffy and overcrowded, ugly and tacky it may be but it was their alehouse, the hub of their circumscribed world and they would defend it if the need arose against all-comers.

In a curiously paradoxical way, although they were all rampant, heterosexual, young men, many of them having at least casual girlfriends, they tended to socialise almost exclusively with their own male peers. There were females present in the lounge bar but they were either the wives or girlfriends of past players now fully or semi-retired, no unaccompanied, unattached young women where anywhere to be seen and they in turn tended to socialise with their own sex usually in their homes. The only girls who frequented the vicinity of the alehouses were those who loitered near the entrance looking to barter sexual favours for small change, bottles of ale, or, a few cigarettes. Apart from the weekly discotheque organised by the council for fifteen to eighteen year olds, where both groups finally came together in a social setting, they remained two separate, discrete genders.

"I'll get them in." Glynn shouted as his turn arrived to buy the ale, after several golden hued pints of Double Diamond had already been quaffed by the crew.

"Fuck, he must be gettin' pissed, offerin' to get the round in without bein' reminded." Irish observed with a grin.

"I'll go with him to the bar." Jay Mac offered, adding, "We dont want any fuckin' spillage, y'know warra mean?"

Both youths weaved their way through the tightly packed throng seated at the numerous tables and the standing punters, eventually arriving at the small crowded bar.

There were three barmen serving that night, one of whom was the landlord. He tolerated the presence of the crew members, viewing them as a necessary evil and felt that they at least offered

Natural Born Skinhead 1971 •164

some degree of protection from other unsavoury factions, if not themselves. Acknowledging Tommy (S) as their overlord, he rarely challenged his actions or rulings, if the young commander said that these new Seniors were old enough to be served then that was all the confirmation he required. Unfortunately his most recent addition to the bar staff, the thirty five year old surly Colin, was less amenable and resented the very presence of these cheeky upstarts. It was he who happened to be in attendance at the lounge bar when the youthful, blond Skinhead Glynn accompanied by the angry Jay Mac were attempting to be served.

"What d'yer want lad?" Colin asked angrily.

"Four pints of Diamond when y'ready mate." Glynn answered, smiling.

"No lad, I mean what d'yer want in 'ere? This is an alehouse not a fuckin' sweet shop." Col responded with a sneer.

Other drinkers nearby laughed, momentarily, until they caught a glimpse of the murderous rage contorting the face of the dark haired Skinhead, clenching his fists as he leaned on the wooden counter.

"Lad, I don't know what yer fuckin' problem is but me mate 'ere has just asked yer nicely for four pints of Diamond, not fuckin' sweets, so do us all a favour and serve us now, alright?" Jay Mac demanded, staring directly into the face of the barman.

"Or what boy? What are *you* gonna do, gerrout yer pram and hit me with yer rattle? he asked with a grin.

Jay Mac looked along the bar with its small collection of recently returned empty pint glasses, considering with which to strike the older male and wipe the smile from him. Even as his left hand closed around the base of one of these, Tommy (S)'s strong right hand clamped his forearm. "Leave it Jay Mac, I just wanna quick word with Col." the leader said, positioning himself immediately in front of the six foot two, heavily built, mid-thrities, Colin, whose facial expression had totally altered.

"Alright Tommy, did y'want servin' mate?" he asked nervously, while fumbling beneath the beer stained counter for the foot-long, wooden club that was secured there.

In a blur of movement the team leader's right hand shot from Jay Mac's forearm to the barman's flabby throat, grasping his

Natural Born Skinhead 1971 • 165

trachea in an iron grip. Squeezing tightly, drawing him forward and down to his own five foot nine height, so that Colin could glimpse his steel-grey, glass splinters of eyes and become transfixed in fear as if staring at a wild animal, Tommy almost allowed a brief smile to form on his virtually non-existent thin lips.

"Listen to me shit-head and listen good, cos I won't ever tell yer again. These lads are Crown Seniors, that means you fuckin' serve them everytime thee come t'this bar and yer gonna be happy to do it. You say one more fuckin' word that I don't like an I will drag you over 'ere and smash your face in so bad even yer own Ma won't know yer." He paused, squeezing the purple-faced barman's windpipe until he could barely breathe. "Ok, when I let y'go, yer gonna say 'sorry lads, four pints was it?' Right?"

Colin was released and after clearing his pained throat, did exactly as instructed, serving Glynn and Jay Mac without any other comment or delay. Tommy (S) strolled back to his central position in the semi-circular seating arrangement, from where he surveyed the entire room listening to his friends nearby while simultaneously watching out for his troops, even at a distance, ready to intervene if any perceived challenge arose.

As the night passed and the alcohol consumption increased above and beyond intoxication levels, the ribald humour and loud, exaggerated tales of sex and violence rose in accord occasionally accompanied by spontaneous communal singing. When *Natural Sinner* by Fairweather, sprang onto the turntable of the busy juke box, a cheer erupted from the whole crew. Everyone joined in the chorus adding their own words to this favourite song of the Skins:

> *"I'm a natural Skinhead, born a Skinhead's son*
> *Evil's been my motto, fuck up everyone"*

As Colin the barman watched and listened to them all, he knew this would be his last night working in this alehouse, or any other on the bleak estate.

"'Ere he is, the lad 'imself!" Tommy (S) shouted, acknowledging the arrival of his fellow team commander, Devo (S), who had just entered the heaving cauldron of the lounge and was standing close to the door by the blaring juke box, now playing Dave and Ansell Collins *Double Barrel*. In stark contrast

Natural Born Skinhead 1971 •166

to the generally warm welcome from his peer, the sinister Unicorn Crew overlord uttered a brief response, staring about him with a dark scowl on his battered countenance.

"Come over Devo an 'ave a pint, yer miserable cunt." Tommy offered.

Devo made his way to where the assembled Skins were gathered and stood amongst them facing the Eagle leader. "'Ey wolfman, am not fuckin' miserable." he advised apparently unconcerned about the other part of the appellation. "I don't wanna pint, I hate this shitty boozer, give me the Unicorn anytime."

Jay Mac and Irish were nearest to him and glanced up over their shoulders in his direction, curious to see the infamous knifeman, whose fearsome reputation was known across the estate, at such close quarters. Though of fairly average rangy build with a dark number one crop similar to most of the team, his badly damaged facial features, particularly his prominent brow ridge and crushed right orbital socket, gave him a chilling, deranged appearance. Both youths wisely looked away before he noticed their fascinated gaze.

"Come 'ed let's get this young feller into town and give 'im a night t'remember." Devo said with a faint trace of a smile, gesturing for Terry (H), the leaders' favourite, to finish his pint and join him and Tommy (S) for an adventure that he would never forget.

"Yeah, c'mon Terry mate, drop yer ale and let's gerroff into town, on the pussy hunt. Fuck anyone who gets in our way tonight." Tommy observed smiling.

"Let's hope some soft cunt does. A few bevvies, a hard shag and dishin' out a fuckin' good beatin', that's what I call a top night." Devo advised, entirely genuinely.

The crew laughed but they also knew the dangerous psychopath was being completely honest. Tommy (S) and Terry (H) rose to their feet and joined Devo before making their way to the door.

"See yer lads!" Terry shouted back to the assembly.

"God help any poor sod who gets on the wrong side of them three." Jay Mac noted.

Natural Born Skinhead 1971 • 167

"I think even the Almighty would turn a blind eye if he saw those fellers up to no good." Irish observed then returned to his pint.

Tommy (S) had done his duty and admitted his new Eagle Seniors into the fold, Devo having done the same at the Unicorn prior to joining him and Terry (H). Down on the lower edge of the estate, Dayo (G) had also welcomed his initiates to the team, including Weaver, Macca (G) and his own brother, Yad, fulfilling his obligation as one of the three principal leaders of the Crown Skinheads. He had no idea that before the long, eventful night passed, he would be forced to assume sole command, with his fellow leaders and their brightest future prospect, removed in one bloody incident.

Shortly before midnight after visiting numerous hostelries, downing dangerous amounts of alcohol and accosting almost every female that they encountered, whether unaccompanied or not, the Crown trio arrived at the bottom of Mathew Street, their intention being to round off their night with a visit to the world famous Cavern Club. Fate now engineered a chance collision that would alter the fortunes of many other than just those individuals caught in the immediate impact. A seven-strong group of Kings Skins led jointly by Pitto of the West Kings and the middle brother of three who ran the huge North Kings, Steven 'Steg' Griffiths whose elder sibling had founded that crew as Mods in the mid 1960s and was now serving a lengthy prison sentence for his part in a failed warehouse robbery with extreme violence, had just emerged from a nearby public house as the Crown Skins passed by.

"Fuckin' hell, I don't believe me luck." Pitto announced on recognising Tommy (S), his hated rival. "There's that Tommy Southern cunt from the Crown with two other shitbags." he advised Steg his fellow commander for the evening.

Steg observed the three youths, guaging their size, physiques and possible fighting potential. "I've seen Southern before and I think I've seen that other fucker at the match meself but I don't recognise the one with the smashed in face, he looks like he could be a bit handy."

Making their drunken progress at a suitably retrogressive pace taking one step forward to every two backward, the three Crown

Natural Born Skinhead 1971 •168

Skins did not immediately suggest that they were formidable fighters, two of whom were ranked at the very pinnacle of their peers' listing.

Tommy (S) was wearing a black Harrington jacket over his short sleeved, white, Ben Sherman shirt and Prince of Wales check twenty inch paralells, with his gleaming cherry red Airwair. Both Terry (H) and Devo were similarly attired in jackets and trousers with the former preferring a maroon coloured Harrington and twenty inch cream parallels and Devo a navy blue version of the ubiquitous item and two-tone blue-green eighteen inch parallels. Again there was nothing in their dress that gave an obvious indication as to who they actually were. Unfortunately for the Kings Skins this encouraged them to make a grave error of judgement and they quickly caught up with the trio, encircling them for the intended 'kill'.

"Southern! You wankin' shit-house, let's have it!" Pitto shouted breaking the circle and leaping onto the unsuspecting Tommy (S) from behind.

Steg simultaneously made to grab hold of Terry (H), with two of the remaining five reaching for Devo. Armed with short, heavy, flexible leather coshes encasing lead shot as their pricipal weapons, they pounded their ensnared foe mercilessly, hoping to reduce them to their knees quickly and inflict a total battering with minimal risk to themselves.

Any normal group of youths taking such a ferocious beating may have quickly succumbed but these were not average individuals. Terry (H) had received a brutal tutelage at the hands of his own hard-working stevedore and part-time unlicensed boxing champion father, from an early age and could absorb tremendous punishment. The amazingly resilient Tommy (S) seemed impervious to pain, giving no outward sign of agony or displaying any change in demeanour, calmly allowing his Kings attackers to dissipate their fury and exhaust themselves. In stark contrast to his stoic co-leader, Devo actually appeared to be enjoying receiving the beating, almost as much as he would if delivering it.

"Fuckin' get them to the floor!" Steg roared, slamming his cosh against the back and shoulders of Terry (H).

Natural Born Skinhead 1971 • 169

"Go down you fuckin' Crown queers!" Pitto demanded incensed at his own failure to achieve this objective.

Hard punches and powerful kicks complemented wild strikes with heavy coshes as the seven attackers raged about their trio of 'victims.' A small crowd had gathered, drawn from the passing drinkers, who casually lit cigarettes, or swigged from dark brown ale bottles watching the street theatre, some idly speculating on what they thought would be the inevitable outcome.

Inebriated, beleaguered and outnumbered as they were, all three Crown Skins were about to deliver a devastating response of their own. Without his usual weapon of choice, his short, heavy steel shank dog lead with leather handle, Tommy (S) was still in possession of his secondary tool for close-range work, a solid brass knuckle-duster. Terry (H) carried a similar item; both had reached inside their jackets and managed to slip these implements into place on their respective fists, ready to bring them into play. The sinister Devo, however, did not bother with such half measures, instantly changing the balance of power and the dynamics of the struggle when he drew his cherished, family heirloom, combat knife.

A tight circle of seven attackers rapidly opened to one of a much greater radius with a strange staccato dance of crouching, lunging figures, rotating about looking for an opening. Devo struck first slashing two of his opponents across their chests and upper arms, their coshes proving ineffectual against the razor edge of his otherwise dull, stained blade. Tommy (S) closed with Steg who had replaced Pitto as the opponent facing him. Punching with tremendous force even while being coshed, the Crown Skin repeatedly hit him about the face and head, drawing fresh blood with each blow. Reducing the distance between him and his multiple assailants, Terry (H) leapt into them, delivering powerful punches of his own with equally damaging effect.

Now swollen in number the crowd had also become excited and animated, shouting encouragement almost universally in favour of the three valiant Crown scrappers, watching the tide of battle turn. Falling to the ground on top of his immediate foe, Terry (H) continued pounding him with his metal-assisted fist in the temples and forehead, with Tommy (S) repeating an identical performance against the heavily bleeding Steg, though concentrating his blows

Natural Born Skinhead 1971 •170

more to his enemy's face, particularly around his eyes. Devo would not be outdone changing his tactic from wild slashing to thrusting and stabbing. Unable to avoid one of his adversary's violent lunges Pitto became the most grievously injured casualty of the night, as Devo's blade burst between his lower left ribs, narrowly missing his vital organs but puncturing one of his lungs. Staggering about clutching his scarlet gushing side, Pitto gasped for his life's breath, while those Kings Skins who were still standing drew away from the fight.

The psychotic Devo laughed insanely shouting "Come on, who's next, you fuckin' Kings shit-houses?"

Tommy (S) rose up from the unconscious Steg who lay with his mush of a face totally rearranged and one burst eye of no further visual use. He grasped hold of Devo's knife hand firmly by the wrist warning, "Leave it Devo, we've gorra gerroff."

Then snatching the still punching Terry (H) by the collar of his jacket, he pulled him also to his feet, "Leg it lads, the fuckin' bizzies will be 'ere in no time, come 'ed let's do one."

Racing desperately through the city centre, unsurprisingly unable to convince any of the taxi drivers that they hailed to accept them as fares, the blood-stained trio ran for the Pier Head bus and ferry terminus, not realising that the last vehicles to all destinations, including the Crown had already departed.

On arriving at their hoped for getaway site and finding every parking bay for the fleet of green Atlanteans empty, they decided to remain within the shelter complex while they fully assessed their predicament and until they felt it safe to depart. Devo though, did not wish to leave anything to chance and sprinted across to the elevated, manicured gardens of St Nicholas' church, which rose majestically on its sloping site nearby across the main arterial road.

"I'll be right back, I've gorra do somethin'." Devo advised.

When he returned a few minutes later, Tommy (S) observed, "I didn't know you was a fuckin' religious type Devo."

"I'm not Tommy but I can't risk 'him' bein' taken, y'know worra mean?" he answered cryptically, having secreted his precious knife, determined to save his soul.

Unlike the amateurish, badly timed attempts of the estate police to enforce some rudimentary law and order, the city constabulary

Natural Born Skinhead 1971 • 171

were already out in force, this being a usual lively Saturday night. Arriving at the scene of the serious incident, the police officers were immediately made aware of the identities of the fleeing Crown Skins by their willing Kings informants, breaking with the usual accepted practice of non-cooperation with this particular agency.

It was only a short matter of time before the outlaw trio were traced to their terminus hideout and then surrounded, trapped within the confines of the glass cloister shelters. Soon the wailing black Mariah's arrived filled to capacity with huge, heavy-set riot officers eager to 'quell' these three 'armed and extremely dangerous' youths.

"Throw down y'weapons, put yer hands in the air and come out into the open!" the massive police sergeant boomed without requiring any artificial amplification.

The Skins' pragmatic leader, Tommy (S) accepted the inevitability of their fate and advised both of his companions to comply, dropping his own knuckle-duster with a dull clang to the ground. While Terry (H) repeated the gesture, Devo flatly refused even though in reality he was unarmed and when they stepped into the warm night, reduced to three starkly lit caricatures by the tall, overhead, pale orange street lights, he acted as if he was still in possession of his blade.

Almost immediately the waiting anticipatory throng of blue-black gorillas pounced, truncheons drawn and began battering the surrendering trio with relish, inflicting far more damage than their seven original Kings assailants.

"Fuck this yer pig bastards!" Devo roared above the thuds of the multiple dark wooden baton strikes, reaching into his jacket as though to draw his beloved knife once more. "Come on, come on!" he shouted attempting to make a wild arcing slash before his wrist was fractured by a powerful downstroke of one of the officer's truncheons, forcing him to release the stump of a Betting Office pen 'weapon' that he was holding. The beating that rained down upon them following this vain gesture continued long after they had lost any capacity to resist.

Natural Born Skinhead 1971 ●172

Sunday 25th July 1971

By the time Jay Mac arrived at the crew's usual library perch on that humid, grey, overcast Sunday evening, looking forward to a repeat session in the Eagle before commencing his employment the following morning, wildly exaggerated rumours had been circulating about the bleak estate throughout the day, none of which he was aware of.

"Fuckin' hell Jay Mac, are yer mad comin' here tonight?" Johno asked with a look of genuine surprise on his face.

"Nah, am alright thanks Johno, am only gonna 'ave a few pints then gerroff, so no need t'worry mate." Jay Mac replied equally surprised by his friend's seeming concern.

"He's not talkin' about yer havin' a few bevvies before startin' work tomorrer, soft arse." Irish advised sharply then realising that his friend had no knowledge of recent developments, added, "He means with what happened last night to our boys in town."

"What the fuck are yer goin' on about Irish?" Jay Mac asked intrigued.

Brain decided to provide the necessary information, giving his version of the embellished tale that he had been told. "It was your boys... er... I mean Kings Skins... a fuckin' load of them jumped Tommy (S), Devo and Terry (H) by the Cavern. Tooled up with all kinds thee were, them fuckin' big knives, hatchets, I heard thee even had a shooter. Fuckin' blood everywhere, a couple of their crew 'ave already died, I think." the storyteller concluded his fantastic myth and lit a cigarette as if to steady his nerves.

"Fuckin' hell is he on somethin' or what?" the astonished Jay Mac blurted out. "What did 'appen to our boys?"

"Gripped by the bizzies, been charged with murder, got them locked up in the cells now... poor bastards." Irish offered his own misinformed missive.

Before any further discussion could occur, Peza, one of the crusty-nosed, scruffy new apprentice Juniors from the Heron, directly under Yad's command, arrived at the scene.

"Yers 'ave gorra come down thee Heron now, Dayo wants a word with yers." the raggedy, green-nostrilled herald announced.

Natural Born Skinhead 1971 • 173

All nine Eagle crew who were present made their way down to their estate rivals' public house, following Peza who worked constantly to remove much of the restrictive dried mucus from his permanently blocked nose.

"Remind me not to shake hands with that fucker." Jay Mac observed with a grin.

"Jay Mac now's not the time for fuckin' jokes, I'd keep it zipped if I was you, when we get there." Irish warned wisely.

When they reached their destination, the bottom row of shops and the adjoining Heron public house, after a brisk march down the main central road, Jay Mac decided to follow his friend's well-meant advice and be more guarded with his comments. A large crowd had gathered both in the car park of the alehouse and under the overhanging balconies of the low-rise tenement block, constructed above and along the length of the collection of shops. None of them looked pleased to see the Eagle crew, their hostile gaze focusing particularly on the outsider, Jay Mac.

"I've got t'give yer some credit there lad." Macca (G) began, pausing momentarily from his insistent groping of a young, bedraggled looking girl who was sitting on his knee as he sat upon the low perimeter walls outside the Heron. "Comin' down to the Crown the night after a crew of your shitbags 'ave jumped our boys, that's one thing but comin' here to our alehouse, well, yer've either got some balls or yer fucked in the head." he observed then returned to squeezing the girl's small breasts over her thin blouse with his right hand, while exploring between her legs, under the hem of her ridiculously short skirt with the other, as she remained ambivalent to his actions, feigning only a weak token protest. "I've told yer Gary I'm still 'on' so there's no use goin' there, it's not gonna happen t'night." Molly 'Skank' Brown advised prosaically.

"That's never stopped yer before Molly." Weaver noted with a sly smile, adding, "Or me, I'll get me fuckin' nuts whatever state the muff's in."

Macca (G) laughed, "Nice one Weaver mate, that's tellin' the bitch." he stated, though nevertheless, withdrawing his left hand a few inches back along her grimy, laddered tights-clad thighs.

Jay Mac and the rest of the Eagle crew made no response; instead Johno instructed a group of Peza's friends to vacate their

Natural Born Skinhead 1971 •174

position on the wall perch. "Gerrup Juniors, we don't fuckin' stand while yous sit down. What's happenin' anyway, why does Dayo want us 'ere?" Johno pressed on speaking for them all.

"He's in the alehouse usin' Sid's phone, tryin' to find out what the fuck is goin' on with our boys. When he comes out he's gonna tell us what he wants us to do with those Kings shitbags." Macca (G) advised.

Suddenly without warning Jay Mac was siezed from behind in a powerful headlock thrown by the furious Yad. "I've gorrim, the Kings rat, everybody he's 'ere, I've gorrim!" he shouted so that all those assembled could hear.

Jay Mac cursed his carelessness for making such a basic error of allowing himself to be taken by surprise in this manner. The Cardinals had taught him from his first days 'never leave your back exposed' and 'always keep your eyes open for potential trouble'. By not following these golden rules and failing to scan the area for his enemy's presence, he had been complicit in his own capture.

Yad, who had been enjoying a more vigorous groping session of his own with one of Molly's associates at the rear of the alehouse, had been even more excited when he saw his hated rival sitting on the low wall, with his back towards him.

"Come on Kings rat, tell us all why yer set our boys up, yer fuckin' grass." Yad demanded increasing the pressure of his lock on the purple faced Jay Mac. "Won't fuckin' talk 'ey, I'll choke the life outa yer then, that'll teach yer t'be a Kings rat, lettin' the lads walk into a fuckin' trap."

"Leave it Yad." Johno ordered rising to his feet, warning "Am not jokin', let him go, he's one of our crew."

"Fuck off farm boy, yer've got no right t'be givin' orders down 'ere, this is Heron territory." Yad responded equally vehemently.

In an instant Johno leapt over the wall through the gap in the line of youths where he had been sitting and threw his own powerful headlock around Yad's neck. Nobody else moved, they all watched the unfolding drama in anticipation.

"I will snap your neck Yad, don't push me lad, am lovin' it." Johno warned in deadly earnest, increasing the pressure of his hold exponentially.

Natural Born Skinhead 1971 • 175

Yad felt the icy grip of fear sieze his heart, he knew he was no match for the super strong farm labourer and slowly released his lock on the gasping Jay Mac.

"Come on Johno, fuckin' let 'im go, he's done what yer asked." Weaver demanded, reaching into his denim jacket for his prized toffee hammer.

Johno was in the clutches of another equally powerful emotion, rage and as it burned through him, he lost all sense of reason, giving no thought to Weaver's warning, only indulging his angry pleasure.

"Please Johno... please." Yad gasped, reminding Jay Mac and Irish of the sickening torturer Mitch, when he was in a similar position at the hands of Liam.

"Leave it Johno, let him go now." Dayo (G) ordered, having approached from the porch of the Heron. He placed his own strong hand on the Eagle player's left wrist, grasping it firmly.

"He fuckin' started it Dayo, he just wouldn't leave it." Johno advised.

"Am sure he did lad and now I'm finishin' it, let him go right now or take me on." the team leader said, delivering his ultimatum.

For a few pregnant seconds it appeared as if Johno would accept the challenge in order to eliminate Yad then, common sense finally prevailed and he released the choking Heron player.

"You bastard Johno, I'm gonna..." Yad began, spluttering but was interrupted by his brother.

"You'll do nothin' soft lad except shut yer fuckin' mouth and think about how you're gonna explain to the arl feller why yer couldn't break a headlock... yer tit." Though clearly livid, Yad said no more rubbing his chafed red throat while contemplating how he would face his father that night.

"Am glad you showed yer face tonight Jay Mac, if yer hadn't I'd of thought that was a bit suspect. I'll wanna word with you later, right?" Dayo advised before crossing back to the step of the entrance porch, intending to use this platform as a makeshift rostrum for his address. "Alright, all of yer quiet." he bellowed turning to face them, backlit by the small stormlamp fitted above the door.

The crowd quickly fell silent and waited for their team leader's words.

Natural Born Skinhead 1971 •176

"Yer've probably heard loads of mad stories about what 'appened in town last night to Tommy (S), Terry (H) and Devo." he began then paused to drink from a bottle of Guinness that Gaz passed to him. "That's better, right, I've just spoken to Devo's arl feller on the phone in 'ere and he's told me the score. Our three lads are bein' kept locked up in the Lanes nick and from what I've 'eard, the bizzies 'ave give them a proper kickin'." He paused to allow for their spontaneous cries of outrage.

"Fuckin' bizzies" and "Bizzie cunts." being the main theme.

"Ok, yer right but the good news is that's about all that's 'appened to them. Devo's dad said thee've got some bad cuts and bruises but nothin' major; yer Kings shitbags weren't so lucky. Seven of them jumped the lads accordin' to Devo's dad and three of them are in hospital in a bad way. One of them's been blinded, ones had his skull cracked and another one had his lung done in."

There were more cheers from the assembly whose spirits were suitably lifted.

"So what it comes down to is a right result for the Crown Team, three fuckin' nil."

The crowd were ecstatic and although he had no previous experience, or deliberate intention of rousing them to such a level, Dayo had been thrust into the spotlight of sole leadership and made an excellent start to his new role. He was, however, about to face another more serious challenge almost immediately.

At this entirely inopportune moment the local police made an appearance in the less than intimidating form of a small, patrolling, blue and white Panda car bearing two occupants, an overweight driver and a young, willowy, nervous constable. The entire assembly turned towards the vehicle as it parked alongside the kerb immediately opposite the low walls of the public house.

"Evenin' lads." the tall, thin constable called, stepping out of the car, totally ignoring the presence of Molly Skank and her associates. Though receiving no response he carried on regardless, "I wanted to 'ave a few words with some of yer, ask if yer knew anythin' about an incident in the city centre last night, involvin' some local lads."

Natural Born Skinhead 1971 • 177

The stone-faced crowd looked blankly at the lone officer, his colleague remaining within the relative safety of the vehicle's cramped interior.

"What about you mate, standin' on the porch there,'ave you got a few moments to spare?" the constable enquired naively.

Dayo swigged from his bottle of Guinness, belched loudly and answered calmly, "Fuck off pig, stick yer snout somewhere else."

Before anymore was said several bottles were thrown from the packed throng positioned towards the rear of the car park, "Do one bizzy, piss off!" someone shouted, leading to a repeat chorus of similar forceful requests, accompanied by a hail of glass projectiles and loose stone. Like a raging forest fire, once ignited, the flames of revolt spread throughout the crowd in a matter of seconds.

Bravely if unwisely, the young officer tried to remonstrate with them, even as the bottle 'shells' burst around him on the ground and the roof of the patrol car, until a well-aimed stone dislodged his peaked cap.

"Step on it Peter, sharpish." he called, quickly getting back into the beseiged vehicle; a fresh torrent of mixed amunition crashing onto its top and bonnet like a storm of angry hail.

"Yer don't have t'tell me twice Dennis, let's fuck off while we can." Peter the sweating driver replied, putting his foot on the accelerator, intent on making a speedy getaway.

He was too late; the howling mob leapt over the low walls, ran out from under the balconies of the tenements and surrounded their Panda car, pounding, hammering and kicking it from every side.

"Don't worry about knockin' any of these fuckers down, Peter, just belt them." Dennis advised, no longer concerned about anything other than escape.

Outside of the police officers' metal shell, Weaver was working frantically with his toffee hammer like a dedicated panel beater, while Brain, apprenticed in this trade, settled for a fragment of brick as he attemtped to reshape the vehicle's right front wing.

"Out the fuckin' way!" Johno roared racing forward, holding an empty beer keg he had 'borrowed' after forcing the previously locked door to the rear yard of the public house. Lifting it above head height to his full arms length, he launched it into the front windscreen of the battered patrol car, shattering the reinforced glass into thousands of sparkling splinters.

Natural Born Skinhead 1971 •178

"Fuck this! Hold on Dennis." Peter announced, his face streaming with blood having being peppered with the tiny, razor sharp fragments.

Forcing the gear stick into reverse, pushing the accelerator pedal to the floor, he released the handbreak and rocketed away from the scene, dislodging the clinging marauders striking some in the process. Unfortunately for the desperate driver, his vision was impaired both by the scarlet rivulets running from numerous forehead cuts into his eyes and the completely crazed glass of the rear window. Within less than twenty yards he drove over some scattered rubble, mounted the kerb and backed violently into one of the eyeless, pre-cast concrete lampposts, much to the wild delight of the cheering mob.

"Come on! The fuckin' bizzies are down, let's do them!" Weaver bellowed sprinting in their direction, hammer raised to deliver the first blow.

"Peter, leave the radio it's fucked, it's no use, we've gorra run for it." Dennis warned having already exited the crumpled vehicle.

The heavyweight, badly bleeding driver joined him, reluctantly abandoning his wreck of a patrol car to the fury of the wild Skinhead horde. With his colleague Dennis, the young, raw recruit helping him, the portly policeman ran and stumbled as best he could manage out into the speeding streams of traffic on the main highway, in a vain hope of a passing motorist stopping to assist them.

"Get the fuck back 'ere now!" Dayo roared from the steps of the Heron entrance porch, determined to regain control of the team and the chaotic situation.

Satisfied that they had chased their reviled enemy from their area, the pursuers ran back to their leader at least obeying this command. Yad however, felt the moment had arrived where he would challenge his brother's authority, feeling that a large number of youths present were either Heron crew or their Juniors, who owed their loyalty to him.

"Grab the fuckin' Kings rat, bring him to me!" he screamed, "*I* say what's happenin' to him.., he set our boys up."

Jay Mac looked into the sea of unreasoning, hostile faces where only a handful that were friendly remained. Even in his desperate

Natural Born Skinhead 1971 • 179

position, he could not help but be reminded of classic black and white cinematic images of a crazed mob of archetypal central European villagers, brandishing their flaming torches, intent on killing the definitive Frankenstein's monster as portrayed by the often imitated but never equalled Boris Karloff. He raised his fists defiantly in a futile gesture without any real hope of defending himself.

Across on his rostrum, Dayo smashed his ale bottle against the hardwood frame of the entrance porch, leapt from the low steps and quickly strode across to the desperate youth, arriving immediately alongside him. Yad beamed with delight believing that at last his brother was about to deal out some summary justice, to this unwanted interloper.

"Stay the fuck back!" Dayo shouted, "If any cunt tries to lay a hand on Jay Mac they're gonna 'ave t'go through me first." he warned, adding for the sake of clarity, "That means *anyone*."

The altruistic heroism of his act and the intimidating image of this hirsute Skinhead ape standing resolute, clutching his primitive weapon, somehow entered their combined psyches at a primal level and they ceased almost at once, becoming perfectly still exactly where they were.

For a few moments all that could be heard was the sound of their heavy breathing in the warm, clamy night.

Dayo called to the members of his old guard, placing them in charge, while he attended to a pressing issue, "Keep these fuckin' mad pricks in order until I get back." he ordered then turned to Jay Mac, "Right you, inside with me now, we're gonna find out what y'do know about this fuck up."

Again a smile returned to Yad's face as he stated, "About time, now the Kings rat's fucked, our Dayo will beat the truth out of 'im."

Once inside Dayo ordered two pint glasses and four bottles of Guinness from Sid the obliging landlord then sat with Jay Mac, at a small circular table in the relatively empty bar, where only a few elderly male curmudgeons were engaged in a game of dominos. *Resurrection Shuffle* by Ashton, Gardner and Dyke was playing on the juke box as the team leader began his interview.

"Jay Mac, Tommy (S) tells me yer a sound lad, he's gorra lorra time for yer, Terry (H) says the fuckin' same. I've seen yer in

Natural Born Skinhead 1971 •180

action 'ere and at the match an I know yer've got heart." He paused to drink some of the dark stout that he had poured into his glass "but I've got to ask yer face t'face what yer know, if anything, about what 'appened last night in town?"

Jay Mac drank from his pint of Guinness before replying, "First of all thanks for steppin' in, I won't forget what yer did." he paused and took another deep draught. "I'm sorry yer feel yer've gorra ask me that question Dayo. I've been comin' here to the Crown for five years, I've been in school with Terry (H) and Irish all that time and never once 'ave I let them down either there or 'ere. Since you, Tommy and the others formed the team, I've tried everyway to be part of it an am gonna keep on doin' that. Nothin' would make me betray the team."

Both Skins finished their pints in silence with only the sound of McGuinness Flint's *When I'm Dead and Gone*, playing on the juke box.

"Ok Jay Mac lad, that's all I wanted t'hear, well in mate." Dayo responded, indicating for the Eagle player to join him at the entrance.

"Right, shut the fuck up the lorra yer." Dayo began as he addressed them for the final time on this night of madness. "I've spoken to Jay Mac an what he's told me is all sound. So like I've said before, both Tommy (S) and Terry (H) say this is a good lad and we're lucky to 'ave him 'ere and not with the Kings Team." He paused and looked about waiting for any dissent but there was none. Only Yad ground his teeth and clenched his fists in raging frustration. "Anyone whose gorra problem with Jay Mac has gorra problem with me, is that clear enough?" Dayo shouted without response. "I said is that fuckin' clear?" he bellowed, this time to affirmative shouts and some cheers. "Alright, that's good. As for the Kings Team, well they've got the ball now, let's see what they wanna do with it, ok? So do us all a fuckin' favour an piss off 'ome the lorra yer, those cryin' pigs will 'ave ran back to their sty an a fuckin' crew of them will be on their way 'ere anytime now. Gerroff, stay in and keep yer fuckin' mouths shut if yer do get asked anythin'."

With that piece of wise advice received and understood the mob began to slowly disperse. Yad was still standing close by as

Natural Born Skinhead 1971 • 181

if struck motionless by his burning anger; Dayo crossed over to him and said in a low voice, "Twice tonight you've caused me a fuckin' problem. You ever challenge me again an yer out of this team permanent an I'll forget yer my brother."

Lowering his head Yad turned and walked away, his silent coterie falling in behind him. "I'll kill that fucker, when the chance comes." he said not indicating whether he meant Jay Mac the outsider or his own flesh and blood, Dayo.

"Alright John, havin' an early night before yer start yer job tomorrer." Jay Mac's uncle observed, surprised at the youth's premature return to the small council flat. "Not like you to do somethin' sensible." he added puffing on his pipe enjoying the final smoke of the evening whilst sitting in the kitchen and tuning the transistor radio to the BBC news, waiting for the ten o'clock bulletin.

"Yeah, dead funny that, yer should be on the stage." Jay Mac replied disinterestedly, searching for any available items of food in the cupboard or larder. "Is thee any chance of there bein' somethin' decent to eat round 'ere?" he asked unwisely, placing his foot fully into the snare that was always ready and waiting.

"Something decent, is that what yer after? Well that depends on what yer call fuckin' decent, doesn't it? To a fussy little bleeder like you, nothin' is good enough but any normal lad would be fuckin' grateful for the bloody good food that gets put on that table." the old soldier advised, becoming angry as he always did at any perceived slur regarding the fare on offer that his meagre wage paid for. "Anyway, there's a pig's trotter I've not started on in there, so 'ave that if yer fancy it, your Lordship!" he suggested with a smug grin.

"Fuckin' hell did yer's get every part of that bleedin' pig from the robbin' butchers? I bet yer've got his fuckin' dick in yer sarnie box for yer carry-out, haven't yer?" Jay Mac replied, laughing at the idea of the porky penis sandwiched between two slices of bread, waiting in the veterans own lunchbox.

His uncle changed the subject having listened to the news broadcast. "'Ey, yer bloody smart arse Yanks aren't doin' too good over in Vietnam are thee, where's John Wayne when thee need 'im?" he observed laughing at his own sparkling wit.

Natural Born Skinhead 1971 •182

"Yeah, well we'd all 'ave been fucked wirrout them by now and carryin' little red books on the 'Thoughts of Chairman Mao." Jay Mac responded candidly, adding, "and worrabout World War Two, what would we have done *then* without Uncle Sam?"

"Shut up boy, you know fuck all about anythin', yer still wet behind the ears, and keep that trap shut about the War, or yer'll get the back of me hand." his uncle snapped.

The youth said no more, not because he was any longer particularly afraid at the threat of a physical beating but more out of respect for the veteran, who had endured nearly five years of harsh captivity and experienced some horrors that he had never fully recovered from.

"Am off t'bed, make sure yer do a good day's work for a good day's pay tomorrer." his uncle advised, giving Jay Mac once more the benefit of his own principalled work ethos.

After preparing a bowl of cornflakes for himself the youth retuned the transistor to the Radio Luxemburg frequency and listened to a selection of recent chart hits. As he sat and ate his 'breakfast' supper with Norman Greenbaum's *Spirit in the Sky*, playing in the background, he smiled at the extent of venomous dislike his guardian could instantly produce at any reference to America or Americans, particularly its troops. 'Overpaid, oversexed, and over here' was his usual assessment, even though the latter element of his cliched criticism had not applied for many years. Jay Mac and his elderly uncle could not have been more diametrically opposed in their opinion of the leading super power nation, one an obsessive Americana fan, the other fervently anti-'Yank' on every issue.

"Lot of noise from your fellers' tonight." his aunt called from the living room, rousing him from his mental ramblings."

"What d'yer mean, *your fellers*, what are yer talkin' about?" he called back as he strolled into the small room to join her.

"Skinheads like you, Bovver Boys, all round 'ere, all bloody night. I could hardly concentrate on me Agatha Christie, shouting, swearing, making a terrible racket thee were." she advised without raising her gaze from a well-thumbed murder mystery she was re-reading for the dozenth time.

Natural Born Skinhead 1971 • 183

Jay Mac was intrigued; normally his aunt and uncle did their best to ignore the local youths and their boisterous behaviour. This developement suggested to him that this must have been of some significance for her to pass comment.

"Did yer 'appen t'look out the window and see where thee went?" he enquired curiously.

"I did, actually with all the bloody noise thee were makin'. Dozens of them there was, all with those cropped heads. Round to the Anvil most likely, looked as if thee were goin' to a meetin' or somethin'." she replied before opening a new ten-pack of Embassy filter tipped cigarettes, determined to finish her novel before the night ended assisted by a steady nicotine supply as required.

Jay Mac took the backdoor keys from their hook in the kitchen and quickly made his way to the communal yards at the rear of the tenement block, from where the gable side of the similarly empty carpark of the Anvil public house could be viewed.

Crouching low, close to the rusty iron railings that ran along the outside edge of each designated yard space, he could see from his elevated position at least three dozen denim-clad Skinheads, gesturing and shouting excitely. Though the full content of their discussion could not be heard, the odd snippet or word that he did receive made it clear what the topic was. This was a war council, one of many that were occurring across the vast estate that night, with its normally rival crews preparing to join forces to annihilate their common enemy, the Crown Team.

When Dayo (G) had said the ball was with the Kings Skins he was correct but the kneeling Eagle player knew that as he observed the angry youths not far distant below, that same ball was about to come rocketing back to the Crown Estate with devastating effect.

Later that night, despite his best intentions, when he lay on his couch-bed, after his aunt had finally retired to join her thunderously snoring husband in their room, Jay Mac was unable to sleep. His restless mind was in turmoil as he continually played over some of the disturbing events and images of the past forty eight hours, the rapidly approaching world of work was the least of his worries.

Natural Born Skinhead 1971 ●184

Chapter 7

Get Down and Get With It

August – September 1971

"All rise." the court usher instructed those present in an official capacity and as interested members of the public, on the day of sentencing of the three Crown team players. As the issue of their guilt had previously been established beyond doubt, this hearing was merely a formality to allow their respective punishments to be allocated; it was a much less crowded affair, with only a handful of spectators seated in the gallery.

The elderly, gaunt judge who appeared so pale and grey that if he should sneeze a cloud of dust particles would detach itself from him and he would crumble like an ancient parchment, wasted no time after taking his seat in imposing the appropriate penance, with reference to judicial precedent, allowing only scant mitigation.

"Terrence Harper, in view of your age I have erred on the side of leniency and sentence you to three months in a young offenders' institution. Thomas Southern, I believe you did, as in Harper's case, act in self defence, nevertheless, the extent of physical injury that *you* inflicted far exceeded that which would have been sufficient to subdue your attackers. You are hereby sentenced to twelve months imprisonment. I come now to Sean Devlin, who in my view should be regarded as a danger to the public. Your ludicrous attempts to convince the court that you were only in possession of this betting office pen and no other weapon, almost amount to contempt. However, in the absence of the actual knife, which witnesses have all testified to your use of in this deplorable incident, I have, after consideration, decided to impose a custodial sentence of three years imprisonment, with the suggestion that you should be subject to regular psychological assessment."

There were no outcries either from the representatives of the victims' families or those of the Crown youths. Neither was there any false bravado or defiant gesture as all three were taken down to begin their sentences immediately. Justice had been seen to be done and all those involved appeared to accept the outcome.

Natural Born Skinhead 1971 • 185

Alone among the parents of the the three Crown Skins, Mr Devlin smiled as if contented, which indeed he was. His son's sentence had been of some genuine concern and it was not this that made him smile but rather due to his immeasurable pride in the fact that Sean had refused to reveal the whereabouts of their prized family heirloom, combat knife, even under sustained, persistent interrogation. Only he, the boy's idolised father, had been told of its location during their brief conversation shortly after Sean's arrest.

Immediately on leaving the Lanes Police Station that very night, Michael Devlin had hurried to church for the first time in many years. Once he arrived in the city parish and entered the grounds of Our Lady and St Nicholas Church, close to the Pier Head bus and ferry terminus, he quickly detatched the broken piece of old cast iron downpipe, nearest to the rear door and retrieved his precious blade from inside. He was a happy man, Sean had done his duty, now he could fend for himself during his three year prison sentence, it would be the making of him, it would transform him, his misguided parent actually believed, in some ways he was completely correct.

Wednesday 25th August 1971

Shortly before one o'clock on a warm August afternoon, with a pleasant light breeze blowing up from the restless, dark brown, River Mersey, Jay Mac the Skinhead office boy accompanied by Timothy his Trog fellow junior, was almost back at their joint place of employment, Edwin Roach, Symes and Butterworth shipping office.

"I'm just nippin' in'ere Tim to get another pasty, I'm friggin' starvin'." the Eagle player advised, about to enter a conveniently located Cubbon's bakery shop.

"Gosh, don't you ever stop eating?" the nervous, tousle-haired boy asked.

"You should see me mate Blue, he's a fuckin' eatin' machine." he replied, adding "Go 'ed, you gerron, I'll catch yer up, I wouldn't want yer to be late an get a bollockin' off arl arse Stan."

Timothy hurried along, his heavy R.A.F blue-grey great coat flapping about his frail body. He did not wish to return to work

Natural Born Skinhead 1971 ●186

late, he was afraid of their septuganarian, ex-B.S.M boss, just as he was afraid of everything else in life.

A few minutes later, greedily eating his excessively hot, ridged Cornish pasty, while casually strolling along Castle Street, Jay Mac stopped suddenly on seeing a disturbing incident taking place not far ahead.

Timothy was being dragged about and slapped across the face by two tall rangy Skinheads. Though he had not previously encountered these youths, the Crown Skin took them to be either the cowardly bully Josh with one of his minions, or two of his crew.

"Please leave me alone, please; this is all I've got." Timothy pleaded as he offered his last remaining luncheon vouchers to the grinning pair.

'Walk the fuck away.' Jay Mac heard himself say in his mind, even as his raging body betrayed him running at full speed toward the ugly scene.

"Alright girls, I've told yer not t'play rough." he shouted, almost crashing into the trio.

"What the fuck ...?" the tall, albino Skinhead began, before being interrupted by Jay Mac who stuffed the remains of his scalding pasty into his surprised face.

"'Ere y'are tit, and remember to chew yer food." he advised, forcibly feeding the bully, while shoving his partner violently to one side with his right forearm.

Timothy was released from their combined clutches by virtue of the shock effect of Jay Mac's swift, unexpected attack.

"Fuck off Tim... now." he ordered, receiving a blow to the stomach and being siezed himself.

"You cheeky fucker, do you know who I am?" the albino Skin began once more.

"Save it lad, I'm not fuckin' interested, I've heard it all before." Jay Mac answered trying to appear nonchalant.

"'Ey Josh I think he's fuckin' tapped in the 'ead." the assistant bully suggested, inadvertently confirming the identity of the principal player.

"I don't care if he's totally fuckin' nuts Mugga, nobody does this t'me." Josh warned, wiping the meat, vegetable and pastry

Natural Born Skinhead 1971 • 187

residue from his angry face then asking curiously, "What the fuck are you grinnin' at boy?"

"Any minute now you're either gonna be gettin' off or gettin' gripped." Jay Mac advised as if he had suddenly acquired the gift of prophecy.

Mugga looked over his shoulder in the direction that the youth was staring then immediately warned his leader, "Josh we better get off mate, fuckin' quick style."

Both Skinheads now saw the excessively tall menacing figure of a well-built middle aged male, dressed in a pink frock coat with long tails, black trousers with a broad red stripe running down them, gleaming patent leather shoes and wearing a black silk top hat precariously balanced on his head. Looking like a surreal cartoon character known as an 'Apple Bonker' as featured in the fantastical animated film of the Beatle's quest to rescue Sgt. Pepper's Band from the Blue Meanies, entitled *'The Yellow Submarine'*, this angry giant was in fact one of the distinctively dressed doormen of the nearby local branch of the Bank of England.

"Hey you two nasty buggers, what the fuck d'you think y'doing? I've been watchin' your antics for the last ten minutes, y'pair of bullies." He paused ensuring he had a firm grip on the Harrington collars of both Josh and Mugga. "Pickin' on that little skinny feller and now this lad, you make me sick, y'better piss off before I call a Bobby and have y'pulled in." With that warning he shook them both violently then released them.

Walking away the two disgruntled bullies looked back angrily at the smiling Jay Mac. Once they had reached a safe distance Josh called "This isn't over lad, we'll see you again!"

"No thanks boys, am not queer but thanks for offerin'." Jay Mac shouted in return defiantly but knowing that Josh was correct, this was not over and had only just begun. It would require a bloody, painful show of force to ultimately resolve this burgeoning feud. He thanked the huge doorman for his intervention, who replied with a grin, "That's alright lad, I saw what yer done, trying to help that little feller, I fucking hate bullies meself."

Jay Mac walked on, speculating as to what sort of bullies this solid individual may have encountered, 'Fuck me, I'd hate to have seen the size of those cunts.'

Natural Born Skinhead 1971 •188

"Yer late boy, fuckin' late!" Stan shouted in Jay Mac's face as he strolled into the small reception office, "If you were in the army now, yer'd be on a fuckin' charge." he advised.

"Well thank fuck am not in the army then... anyway how late am I? Oh yeah, three minutes, sorry sir, I'll stay another five tonight to make it up, how's that?" the youth offered.

"How's that? Yer cheeky pup, yer lucky I don't tell the wages clerk to stop yer half a day's pay." Stan replied angrily, fastening the jacket of his uniform before placing his peaked cap on his grey head. "I've got to go out and the partners are havin' a workin' lunch which means the caterin' delivery will be'ere anytime now. You'll have to sign for it and take it up to the boardroom; Tim's already settin' the places." He paused as he stepped out of the drab, claustrophobic room, warning, "Don't fuck this up boy, or you'll be gone by the end of the week."

Jay Mac did not reply but merely smiled to himself. Having been employed for almost a month under the direct supervision of the old soldier, he knew exactly what Stan's euphemism 'I've got to go out' meant. With his own alcoholic mother having used a similar expression herself every evening, as the temptation of the drink called to her and she grew increasingly irritable, Stan's ruse quickly became transparent after Jay Mac's first few days in his office junior position.

Only moments after his boss's departure for the Eight Bells public house located a short distance from the shipping company's premises, Jay Mac opened the sliding, frosted glass window on hearing a firm knocking on the vestibule door.

"Yeah, what can I do yer for?" he asked disinterestedly, before stopping almost mid sentence on recognising the catering firm's delivery boy.

"Alright Jay Mac my man, so this is where yer workin' is it?" Floyd asked with a grin, "Tony (G) happened to tell me you were on the boats or somethin', hows that then? Have y'gorra boat in there?"

"Well... er... its more a dryland sort of shippin' job... if yer know worra mean." Jay Mac offered, red faced with embarassment.

Natural Born Skinhead 1971 • 189

"Yeah, I know what yer mean mate; yer an office boy in this shit-hole and the nearest you get to any boats is walkin' down to the Pier Head t'look at the ferries." Floyd replied with a sneer.

"'Ey Floyd, before yer get too carried away takin' the piss, just tell me what sort of apprentice chef gets sent out deliverin' fuckin' seafood sarnies *to* a shit-hole like this?" Jay Mac immediately responded, looking the uber-cool Crown player up and down, studying his white jacket and baggy trousers with their small blue and white checked pattern; not quite his usual sharp Skinhead attire.

"Yeah well... fair point man. I *am* an apprentice chef but I 'ave to do deliveries as well sometimes. Anyway this is a bit of luck you workin' in 'ere Jay Mac." Floyd replied cryptically.

"Why's that man? Cos I can tell yer it's no fuckin' use to me." the Eagle player stated.

"Jay Mac, there must be some birds workin' here, typin' pool, secretaries, even the fuckin' cleaners. Birds means fellers and that means cash for me an you." Floyd continued, explaining "I do a nice line in aftershaves, watches and other items as I come by them, if yer follow me."

Jay Mac began to understand what his entrepreneurial team mate meant and smiled as he replied in turn "Nice one man, I think we can do a bit of business between us."

"Listen I'll sort out the details with yer back on the Crown, I'll meet yer in the Eagle Friday night, ok... partner?" Floyd said smiling offering his hand for them to seal the deal with a formal gesture.

Jay Mac shook hands with his new associate cementing yet another mercantile arrangement in this place of business.

"Now yer better sign for this lot before thee go off." Floyd said passing Jay Mac an invoice and pen, pointing to a stack of slim, rectangular, cardboard boxes.

"Will do, what's in them anyway?" Jay Mac asked with a casual interest.

"Seafood platters man, all fresh ingredients; y'king prawns, mussels, battered squid, octopus, all on a salad bed." Floyd paused, looking at his salivating team mate and advising, "an before yer go helpin' yerself, y'should know me and the lads spat on every one of them before we packed them up."

Natural Born Skinhead 1971 •190

"Thanks for that Floyd, I'll take them straight up to the partners, thee sound just right for those snooty fuckers." Jay Mac replied smiling.

"Don't forget man, let's keep our business to ourselves... yeah?" Floyd said with a grin, adding, "Tell yer partners 'bon appetit' from me. See yer."

"Oh I will do Floyd, an if there's any leftovers am sure me boss Stan would like t'give them a try, see yer." the grinning youth called as he carried the eagerly anticipated luncheon along the narrow corridor, to the waiting shipping magnates.

Almost nine hours later Jay Mac was desperately trying to clinch a deal of an entirely different nature together with Irish, Blue and Glynn and most of the combined Eagle and Heron crews. They were standing among the tightly packed ranks of young predatory males at the weekly, council-run, Wednesday night Disco. With the magic hour of ten o'clock almost approaching, the houselights would soon be turned up fully, revealing too many temporarily love-struck couples that their passionate partners throughout the evening were not quite the Prince Charmings or Cinderellas they had hoped for.

Only two dances now remained, one regular paced and the final slower tempo number of the night, securing a member of the opposite sex for the latter often depended on the performance of the prospective individual during the former. This was real social Darwinism, natural selection at its rawest, with shuffling males lined up to face the rows of gyrating females, ready to be chosen or end the evening in the ignominy of rejection. There had been a new exotic ingredient introduced to add a certain spice to this Wednesday's proceedings, three fresh, nubile, attractive girls had arrived, apparently on the invitiation of one of their fellow schoolfriends. While the boys were generally pleased with this development, it was almost universally despised by the regular girl attendees, altering the balance of power and odds in favour of being selected significantly.

"Am goin' in lads." Jay Mac announced bravely, as if about to attempt a suicide mission, which in some ways he was.

Natural Born Skinhead 1971 • 191

"Go for it Jay Mac." Blue encouraged uncharacteristically sportingly, considering he had attempted the same feat earlier and been totally ignored, one of the worst ways to crash in defeat.

"I'm with yer Jay Mac, come 'ed," Glynn announced, having now had sufficient illicit whiskey poured into his watery orange juice, to induce the necessary level of Dutch courage.

"And me, am havin' the blonde with the short hair, so keep yer fuckin' paws off." Macca (G) instructed grinning slyly, though somewhat more amiable than usual in the surprising absence of his two co-leaders Yad and Weaver.

"Alright me name's Jay Mac, what's happenin'." the youth shouted above the blaring sound of the D.J's penultimate selection Bob and Earl's *The Harlem Shuffle,* as he placed himself in front of a pretty brunette, whose shoulder length hair was cut and back-combed in an earlier Mod style, rather than some of the more aggressive feather cuts that several girls had begun to choose.

"What's happenin', I'm dancin' that's what, soft lad." she replied sarcastically though with a pleasant smile and crucially without telling him to move on, or changing places in the extended line herself, the ultimate rejection.

"I'd ask yer what a nice girl like you is doin' in a place like this but I don't think yer'd give me the answer am after." Jay Mac tried speculatively.

"What answer's that then?" she called back.

"Lookin' for the love of yer life, or maybe just the love of yer night, if I'm lucky?" he replied smiling, believing that he had nothing to lose at this juncture.

She did not reply at first and continued her rythmic movements, allowing him to enjoy her undulating curves.

"Yer a cheeky git, aren't yer?" she asked rhetorically though still smiling, adding "and how far d'yer think yer'd get if I said I'd just found him?"

"Now that's my kinda question, maybe we could both find out the answer, when this disco's finished, what d'yer think?" Jay Mac enquired hopefully, leaning in close to her, allowing her intoxicating perfume to envelop him.

She responded by moving closer too, placing a soft kiss on his lips. "If there's a slowie after this, stay where yer are." the obliging girl instructed much to Jay Mac's delight.

Natural Born Skinhead 1971 •192

"To be honest I'd probably find it difficult to move off anyway," he advised genuinely, adding, "Do yer 'ave a name by the way, or do yer just answer to 'gorgeous'?"

"Yeah, usually I do, it depends on who's askin'." she replied smiling then added, "Me name's Samantha, what did y'say yours was again?"

"Jay Mac." he replied.

Before anything else was said the record finished and all the girls relaxed from 'shaking their tail-feathers' while the council employed, forty-something, D.J made his final selection for the night. As Marvin Gaye's cool, smooth voice began to sing his haunting, simple elegy to *Abraham, Martin and John,* those fortunate enough to have secured partners for this last dance eagerly embraced them, making the most of the three minutes of the 45rpm vinyl play time.

Passionate kissing and wandering hands were the order of the day for both male and female temporary paramours, in this briefest of encounters, extended by some to post disco assignations.

"Goodnight and safe journey home." the D.J called, his turntable now silent and the harsh lighting at full wattage, awaking many a beautiful dreamer to an ugly reality. Once downstairs and outside the civic function hall, which was located above the extended row of battered shops in the middle of the estate, Jay Mac, Glynn and Macca (G) had managed to persuade their respective partners, the three new arrivals, to linger for a while before catching their bus back to the Meadow Green area where they lived. Quickly resuming their enthusiastic exploratory clinches, the couples joined several other amorous pairings in the semi-darkness of the overhanging balconies, leaning against the graffiti covered, metal-shuttered windows and doors of the few brave retail outlets that struggled to survive on the bleak housing development.

Macca (G) was particularly insistent as he raised the hem of his partner's micro-mini dress and began massaging her pert bottom greedily, with both hands.

"'Ey girl! What the fuck d'yer think yer doin' with my feller?" a familiar shrill voice enquired urgently. Suddenly all the restless, gropings in their immediate vicinity ceased as several couples

Natural Born Skinhead 1971 • 193

stopped what they were doing, unsure whom the question was being addressed to and in anticipation of another form of excitement.

Molly 'Skank' Brown had arrived at the scene, none too soon she felt, as she stood glaring furiously at the Heron co-leader and his dishevelled female partner in crime.

"Am fuckin' talkin' to you... yer blonde slut... if that *is* the colour of yer hair!" Molly screamed, the cheeks of her grimy, heavily made-up face glowing even more red than her excessive blusher. Her four fellow 'traders' formed a loose semi-circle behind their 'business manager' prepared to assist in this venture also, if necessary.

"Who *is* this ugly bitch, Gary, d'you know 'er?" the equally furious short-haired girl asked.

"Nah, I don't know 'er Brenda, she's just some fuckin' skank who can't get a feller." he replied cruelly.

Brenda stepped toward Molly and warned, "Go 'ome girl, stick yer 'ead in a bucket of water and cool off." she began then added, "It might wash some of that shite off yer face, yer look like a fuckin' clown."

Molly struck first with a powerful straight right to Brenda's open mouth, splitting her lower lip on contact but Brenda did not back away, instead she unleashed a flurry of accurate punches of her own, both to Molly's face and body; the duel for the affections of Macca (G) had begun.

"Bitch fight!" a number of enthusiastic boys shouted, drawing a crowd of keen, mostly male, spectators from the immediate area and the eponymous public house across the road.

Both girls were soon bloodied, though they maintained their ferocious boxing contest unabated. Cries of "C'mon Molly fuck that bitch!" generally dominated those in favour of the newcomer, with many neutrals just happy to enjoy the spectacle. Soon it changed from punching to grappling, Molly finding herself at a distinct disadvantage, her opponent having no real hair for her to grasp hold of. As clumps of her own scraggy, unkempt mane were being torn out, while she was simultaneously receiving vicious kicks from Brenda's heavy ox-blood Brogues, the local girl fell to her knees, laddering her dark brown tights even worse than they

Natural Born Skinhead 1971 ●194

usually were. Brenda kept a firm grip on Molly's hair, relentlessly kneeing her to the face and abdomen.

"Molly's fuckin' had it." several pundits agreed.

"Yeah, I thought she was a better fuckin' scrapper than that." others concluded disappointedly.

Like a proverbial phoenix rising from the ashes of an inevitable defeat, Molly made good by unleashing a ferocious punch directly to Brenda's most private part, instantly dropping her to a similar kneeling position. Now the wrestling could begin in earnest and the two desperate females rolled over and over, revealing all to the appreciative spectators.

"Bloody hell, am glad I didn't miss this one." one of the old curmudgeons from the Eagle bar observed, shuffling his bottom set of false teeth about excitedly.

"Fuckin' hell, I tell yer what, her indoors doesn't wear knickers like that, thee look like two pieces of stickin' plaster, hardly big enough to cover their essentials." his smiling corousing companion advised.

"Thank fuck for that say's you." the dentally challenged original speaker noted, unable to transfer his gaze from the stimulating spectacle.

When Molly tore the front of Brenda's dress, revealing her barely contained breasts in their white bra beneath, in contrast to the grubby black item she was wearing, which had been exposed early in the struggle with her flimsy blouse soon ripped open, the non-paying crowd cheered wildly, feeling they had well had their money's worth. As the fight degenerated into an unedifying stalemate of scratching, biting and one-sided hair pulling, there were calls to separate the two exhausted combatants. Some of the older spectators were already drifting away towards the alehouse remarking, "If that's all that's comin' off, am goin' back t'me pint."

Irish and Johno eventually did the necessary, though manhandling both females enthusiastically whilst disengaging them from each other.

Brenda was first to speak, "'Ey love, if yer want 'im that bad yer can 'ave 'im, his fuckin' breath stinks anyway." she advised

Natural Born Skinhead 1971 • 195

before wiping her bloodied face with the back of her grazed and cut hand.

"He already is *my* feller yer fuckin' bitch, and I don't care if his breath does stink, so go 'ed, fuck off." Molly replied, making no attempt to cover her exposed chest, or remove the blood from her own spattered face.

After somewhat selfconsciously checking his breath against the palm of his hand, Macca (G) spoke directly to Molly, "What's fuckin' wrong with you, yer stupid little scrubber, am not your feller and your not my bird, yer anyone's whose got a bit of spare change, or a few ciggies, or a couple of bottles of ale, piss off will yer."

If life had not already torn every last vestige of self respect from the unfortunate girl or had not crippled her emotions, she may have burst into tears. Instead she stood staring blankly at her unrequited love and died a little more inside. Turning to walk away she was instantly elated as Macca (G) called to her again.

"Molly before yer go," he began.

"Yes Gary, did yer want somethin'?" she asked hopefully.

"Yeah I do, you owe us three lads three good shags, so we're havin' them now." he advised.

"What, all of yer jumpin' me, Gary? Well, if that's what yer want...." she offered obligingly.

"Not you 'skank' we've *all* been there. Let's 'ave three of yer girls, now, for free and we'll call it quits." he demanded.

The crestfallen Molly said no more, other than to instruct three of her four associates to join Macca (G), Jay Mac and Glynn.

"In the fuckin' alley yous girls and get ready for a good seein' to, cos I'm in a right bad mood." the sadistic Heron co-leader ordered.

Jay Mac looked at the sorry trio, all similarly dressed to Molly in ridiculously short skirts, thin blouses, laddered tights and down-at-heel shoes, then across at the attractive, smartly dressed, well-scrubbed Samantha as she strolled away towards the bus stop nearby. Not being even partially inebriated unlike the stupidly grinning Glynn, he did not feel that this substitution was of like value, or a suitably enticing alternative. Following his two team mates and the girls into the reeking alley, the usual central location for vigorous, impromptu sexual encounters, not always necessarily

Natural Born Skinhead 1971 •196

consensual, he decided to make the best of the situation and get some much needed relief.

On walking only a few feet along this foul-smelling dark entry, stepping as best they could over the mixed detritus, including human and animal droppings, that litterd its floor, the all pervasive, overpowering stench that filled the warm night air was almost sufficient for them to reconsider, almost but not quite.

The anticipation, though less heightened than it may otherwise have been with their original prospective partners, of an al-fresco sexual liaison with these willing, capable females, still proved enough motivation to lead them on.

Reaching the first rear doorway of the shops, Macca (G) caught hold of his chosen girl by the waist and threw her violently; face forward, into the slim recess. Pushing her micro-mini skirt up he grasped the top of her panties and tights, ready to drag them down prior to his aggressive, immediate penetration of her.

Walking on with Glynn and the two other females, Jay Mac heard the Heron sadists 'victim' shout "Why d'you always have t'be so fuckin' rough Macca?" To which he replied, "Shut y'mouth bitch and push yer arse back 'ere."

Glynn was the next to stop, though in his case it was out of natural necessity, as he quickly unzipped his petrol-blue twenty-inch parallels and urinated a torrent of whiskey and ale smelling fluid onto the existing dank material at their feet. He collapsed back against the door behind him for support, saying, "Ahh, that's better, listen love I don't think I can get the fucker hard enough t'go up yer, I feel a bit rough."

"That's alright lad, don't you worry, I'll give it a few sucks and see how yer go, ok?" his kindly partner offered, taking his dripping, flacid penis in her right hand and giving it a good shake before slipping it into her ruby red lipstick-covered mouth.

When Jay Mac and his consort arrived at their doorway recess – 'chamber of love', he decided to at least make some rudimentary attempt at foreplay, before proceeding to the main event.

Putting his arms around the girl and placing his hands on her skinny bottom, he lifted her towards him, about to kiss her on the mouth. The sight of the ring of crusty scabs surrounding her lips

Natural Born Skinhead 1971 • 197

made him draw back instantly, causing the girl to ask, "What's the matter, is somethin' wrong?"

"No it's nothin' honest... er... its just me, I've got things on me mind." he answered only partly lying, still thinking of what might have been with the attractive Samantha.

"If it's me mouth yer don't need t'worry, the doctor said it's clearin' up nicely, now that I've had the injections." she advised then asked curiously, "What is your real name anyway Jay Mac?"

Slightly surprised and also a little relieved he answered, "Well I suppose it had to come out in the end... Nigel Fortesque Smythe the Third, don't yer know..., love-child of a famous aristocrat.., got 'imself killed in a duel over a lady's honour."

"So yer not gonna tell me then." she responded before changing tack slightly, "Some of the girls say you live rough in a bin cupboard on the Kings Estate, is that right?"

Jay Mac laughed at the idea but answered, "Its worse than that a bin cupboard would be luxury, it's a cave filled with other wild animals. Now... about those knickers of yours are thee comin' down, or do I have to tear them off with me claws, or sharp teeth?"

"Ooh, yes please, yer kinky devil." she replied invitingly with a giggle, though obligingly pulling down her underwear herself.

Jay Mac unzipped his cream, twenty inch parallels and freed his growing erection from his Y-fronts. Unfortunately as he pulled her undernourished frame towards him, placing his right hand between her moist, parted thighs onto her downy thatch, a powerful smell of rotting fish emanating from that region filled his nostrils, making him almost retch. The pungent aroma of dirty underwear, stained with urine and other regular discharges, was eye-wateringly strong and instantly penis deflating, in one toxic combination.

"What's happened, 'as the little feller gone t'sleep?" she asked, blissfully unaware of any possible cause.

"Yeah, it must be all the ale I've drank." he lied.

"Well I could just suck yer off if yer like?" his obliging partner offered in a similar kind-hearted gesture to Glynn's companion.

Looking at her crusty mouth and with the fishy fragrance rising from her nether regions, Jay Mac decided to opt for the basic package.

"I tell yer what, I think I'll settle for a good old fashioned hand-job, I know you girls are tops at that."

Natural Born Skinhead 1971 •198

"Alright if that's what yer'd like, hang on a second." she said, before spitting into the palms of her hands to remove some of the ingrained grime, "Can't be too careful, I wouldn't want yer t'catch somethin'." the smiling girl warned then placed her left hand under his testicles, as if giving him a medical examination, grasped his member in her right and began tugging firmly with her experienced hand, until she achieved the throbbing hardness she required to start in earnest.

Moans and groans filled the stinking alley as other couples who had also ventured into this impromptu love den, added their ecstatic cries to the cacophony reverberating off its brick built walls. Crescendos were being reached and climaxes peaked all around while undulating pairs gave way to their primal needs, ignoring all but this primary concern.

Whilst being fucked, sucked and wanked the three not-so-wise monkeys all thought they heard an urgent request being shouted by an excited male voice, as if placing a time limit on the services of their obliging partners.

"Come quick everyone, come quick for fuck's sake!" rang out repeatedly, growing louder with each chorus. When the cause of the alarm was added they all knew it was time to finish their pleasure and get ready for business.

"It's the Kings Team, they're here, fuckin' loads of them, the Kings Team!" Mickey Pimple acting like an overweight, modern-day Paul Revere, riding on a mechanical steed, gave the dire news that a company of contemporary Kings men had crossed the border into their territory, necessitating an instant response from these Skinhead minute men.

Sensing his urgent need to depart, Jay Mac's skilled masturbation exponent brought their exciting encounter to a speedy, satisfying conclusion. With his explosive ejaculation only narrowly missing her already stained clothing, their 'affair' was over and the grateful youth put away his spent member.

"Thanks for that... er... what's yer name by the way? I forgot to ask before." he enquired disinterestedly.

"Me name's Donna, not that it really matters does it, we're hardly gonna be sendin' each other Christmas cards are we?" she replied, wiping her sticky hands on her short skirt.

Natural Born Skinhead 1971 • 199

"No I suppose not, anyway like I said thanks Donna, I'll see yer around." Jay Mac replied then rapidly exited the reeking alley. "What's happenin' Mickey, what's goin' on?" he called to the scooter rider who had pulled his garish vehicle into the kerb, outside the library.

"It's the Kings Team; they're all comin' across the fields, loads of them. Yad sent me up 'ere to get everyone." Mickey advised.

"Yad sent yer? Now I know this is a fuckin' windup, why would he send you?" Jay Mac asked sceptically.

Glynn and Macca (G) left their respective partners and emerged from the alley also both much relieved and then joined the Eagle player, with the Heron co-leader advising, "Yad sent Mickey because he's one of our boys now, well almost. Anyway yous didn't want him in the Eagle, so that's your loss."

Jay Mac looked at Mickey's Vespa noticing the deep blue fly screen that had been added, with small gold adhesive letters proudly proclaiming 'MICKEY-P' across its centre.

"Yeah, Yad said he's gonna make me a full Crown Team player, if I do good." the corpulent youth advised excitedly.

"Good luck with that one Mickey." Jay Mac responded.

A dozen more Skins had arrived either from the Eagle public house or other stimulating diversions. In the absence of any old guard or senior leaders, Johno assumed command. "Grab every bottle yer can and let's get runnin'." he ordered.

Everyone complied without question, loading the pockets of their denim jackets with glass ale or milk bottle ammunition, before falling into place for a team sprint to the lower edge of the estate and the Heron public house.

Even as they reached their destination after racing down the long, bisecting, Central Road, they realised that Mickey's information was out of date, the Kings Team were not on their way but had already arrived. Turning the corner of the end terrace to their left and diagonally facing the Heron public house across the road from them, they could see at least two-dozen Kings Skins swarming around the alehouse like angry, denim-clad wasps attacking a rival's nest.

Above the general clamour of angry shouts, the thumping of wood being struck by bricks and boots, and glass being shattered,

Natural Born Skinhead 1971 •200

Macca (G) called to Mickey "I thought you said there was fuckin' loads of them?"

"There was, honest Macca, thee must've split up." Mickey replied nervously.

For once the deviant commander used his intelligence for something other than his own sadistic pleasure. "Right Mickey, get the fuck off on yer scooter and scout around along the front. There's only the bus sheds thee could be after, so check there then get back to us." he ordered acting like the leader he was supposed to be, adding, "Johno, this is Heron territory I'm takin' over, right?" Johno acquiesced, even though the bulk of the relief party were Eagle crew.

"Ok, I don't think they're tryin' to break into the Heron, it looks to me like they're keepin'our boys trapped in there while their other crew does whatever thee really came for." He briefly paused to quickly let them assimilate what he had said. "Right form a line 'ere and then let them 'ave some."

Everyone fell into place forming a loose, extended, hollow arc then released a withering salvo of glass projectiles which smashed into the angry Kings Skins from above and to the rear, striking heads, shoulders and upper backs.

"Come on; let's have them, Crown Team!" Macca (G) roared, leading the mixed cohort, racing across into the pub car park, intent on inflicting some painful reprisals on these invaders.

Almost at the same moment with the dazed Kings Skins falling away from the main entrance porch, the wooden door they had been battering was wrenched open, with Dayo (G) the raging gorilla at the head of his old guard, followed by Yad, Weaver and the remainder of the Heron crew.

Revenge may be a dish best served cold but in the angry white heat of this two-prong attack, it was cooked to perfection, proving too much of a meal for the appetite of the badly mauled Kings Team as they desperately tried to retreat.

"Fuckin' hurt them, leave yer mark!" Dayo called, the familiar order unnecessary in this instance as everyone who could reach one of their rivals, punched, kicked or head-butted them mercilessly in an orgy of frenzied violence.

Natural Born Skinhead 1971 • 201

Running, stumbling and falling to the ground, the two-dozen Skinheads of the Kings secondary target crew desperately scrambled for the old, uncultivated fields and the busy dual carriageway beyond.

Though all the Crown Team players were enjoying dishing out their brutal reprisals, Weaver was ecstatic as he ran from victim to victim breaking noses and splitting lips with his solid steel toffee hammer, shouting his eponymous war cry, "I'm Weaver, I did this to yer, I'm Weaver!"

Eventually their own appetites for revenge sated the rescuers and the rescued stood smiling as they caught their breath, admiring their night's work. Dayo (G) called them all to order. "Right, pack it in now, they're fucked, I think thee've learned a good, hard lesson tonight." He laughed as he spoke, until Macca (G) warned of the possibility of another attack occurring elsewhere on the Estate. Just at that moment, Mickey Pimple came racing back on his Vespa calling, "Yer right Macca, there's another crew of them in the bus sheds. I don't know what the fuck they're doin' in there."

Dayo quickly scanned his troops before making an executive descision to split his own forces, "Johno, Jay Mac, you lads are the fastest, take yer Eagle crew over to them sheds and flush those Kings fuckers out. Everyone else with me, we're gonna chase those other cunts out of our territory, then we're gonna wait for their mates to come our way. With the Eagle crew chasing them and us waitin', this could be a fuckin' good result for the Crown."

Without another word both crews raced off after their respective prey, bouyed by Dayo's words and the prospect of snatching a stunning victory out of the Kings thwarted surprise attack.

Both Eagle sprinters arrived almost together at the broad opening of the municipal bus depot, where the city's northern fleet of Atlantean vehicles were garaged, repaired and maintained. There was also a large canteen on the site with most of the off-duty drivers and conductors enjoying their break in its warm, convivial surroundings, leaving only a minimal, skeleton security staff on duty patroling the grounds.

"Get down lads." a crouching Johno instructed as their comrades joined him and Jay Mac.

Natural Born Skinhead 1971 •202

"There thee are, over to the far left." Jay Mac pointed out quietly, adding, "They're strippin' all the bus poles out, the cheeky fuckers."

Mickey Pimple was parked across the road, close to his own home, watching for a signal. Waving him over to them, Jay Mac gave the scooter rider a basic instruction.

"Ok Mickey, we're gonna sneak in there and surprise those cunts, there looks to be about eighteen of them so we're not far off in numbers. You wait 'ere by the openin', an if they come runnin' out twat into them with yer bike, knock the fuckers down, ok?"

"Okay Jay Mac, you can rely on me, they won't get past me." Mickey promised, delighted to be included in the action.

Keeping low, moving stealthily the fourteen Eagle players crept towards their enemy, who were intent on stealing the four foot long, gleaming, aluminium poles from within each vehicle, these being considered as prized weaponry for close combat. Careful as they were in their approach, the youths had been spotted by two Kings Skins who were engaged in a separate task, spraying slogans and their logo on an unattended vehicle that was shortly due to commence its route, passing through the Crown Estate to the city centre.

"Crown shits! Look out lads, there's Crown shits comin' on yer!" they warned urgently.

With no need for any further stealth, the Eagle crew raced into their rivals although they were at a distinct disadvantage, being mostly unarmed and not in possession of any similar weapons themselves.

"Come 'ed Crown shits, lets 'ave it!" an angry Kings Skin shouted, lashing out with his gleaming bus pole.

Johno, the nearest to him parried the blow with his sturdy forearms and charged directly into his opponent. Now it was a case of fists and boots against vicious strikes of extended, aluminium batons as a desperate, close-quarter struggle began. In this type of encounter the Crown's two diminutive, amateur boxer brothers, Liam and Bobby Anton, 'The Ants', came to the fore throwing expert punches with devastating effect. All around individual bouts were taking place, with both sides giving as good as they received.

Natural Born Skinhead 1971 • 203

After several minutes of inconclusive action with only the sounds of bodies and faces being thumped and cracked, there began to emerge a distinct feeling that the Crown Skins were gaining the upper hand as several Kings players retired from the game, too badly injured to continue.

"Maza, Chrissy, get those fuckin' poles and run for it!" a fair haired Skin with a hard angular face instructed.

"Will do Danny." the pair replied, scooping up an armful each of the prized weapons, a number of which had been dropped during the desperate contest. Instantly on hearing the urgent order, Jay Mac turned to the direction from where it came. He briefly thought that he recognised the speaker but put this out of his mind as he threw his own opponent to the ground, temporarily disengaging from the immediate fight and shouting, "Now Mickey, for fuck's sake, drop them runners!"

The overweight, aspiring team member was parked near the entrance, sitting astride his scooter. As yet he had not been involved in the action but his moment had now arrived. Mickey kick-started the engine, revved the throttle, preparing to mow down the two Kings runners as they neared his position.

Jay Mac was struck a violent blow to the face by the raging Danny, the apparent leader of this present Kings crew. Both then grappled each other, crashing into the rear engine bay of one of the silent, green Atlantean buses as they did. Slipping on a thin slick of oil just below their feet, Crown and Kings Skin fell to the floor still punching and being punched, each determined to gain the dominant position. As Danny momentarily achieved this he tried to throttle Jay Mac, who, from his disadvantageous underdog position still strained his head and neck to obtain a topsy-turvey view of Mickey's action; the Kings runners now almost parallel with him. Suddenly without any warning or shout, Mickey Pimple wheeled his scooter about letting the enemy run past him, making no attempt to impede them then drove rapidly away from the scene.

"You fat shit-house!" Jay Mac called enraged, even while having his head banged onto the hard floor, Danny deciding to crack his opponent's skull instead of choking him.

Natural Born Skinhead 1971 •204

"Wait a minute, I fuckin' know you, yer cunt, you're from the Kings..." Danny blurted out, pausing in surprise at his recognition of Jay Mac.

"Yeah, do yer, well know this as well...!" Irish shouted, booting the stunned Kings leader hard in his left cheek bone, disengaging him from his floored opponent. "Gerrup Jay Mac only you and Johno can catch those two fuckers, off y'go." Irish advised as he assisted his friend to his feet.

Johno was of a similar mind and, having battered his opponent into submission, he nodded to Jay Mac for the race to begin.

A bizzare chain of chasing groups now organically developed. Maza and Chrissy the two original Kings runners were a clear twenty yards ahead of the rapidly gaining Jay Mac and Johno but behind them, having decided flight was the best policy, came Danny leading his wounded troops, intent on escape. Running at their heels confident that further along this stretch of the main highway, their own Crown team mates, under Dayo (G), should be lying in ambush, came Irish and the rest of the Eagle crew.

Watching this strung out race intently from their concealed vantage point, crouching in the long grass and weeds of the uncultivated field, close to the gable wall of the bus sheds, were the eager Heron Skins.

"Let's dive out and grab the two Kings cunts with the bus poles, they're nearly 'ere." Yad suggested on observing how rapidly Jay Mac in particular was gaining on the pair, with Johno a close second and wishing to deprive them both of any glory.

"Nah, we won't fuckin' do that Yad." Dayo advised his brother, "We're gonna let our boys do their job, if thee can. Just wait and watch all of yers."

Jay Mac felt the familiar burning in his stomach and lungs and as always he ignored it; legs running of their own accord whilst his disengaged mind focused on a spot just ahead of the Kings runners; that place called victory. To achieve it he must increase his pace still further, disregard all pain, the physical sign of weakness leaving the body and overtake them both, not just catch up to them.

He did not know what mental images inspired or motivated his running team mate Johno, he was only peripherally aware of his

Natural Born Skinhead 1971 • 205

presence close to his right side a few paces behind, when he launched himself forward to tackle the Kings lead runner around the waist and bring him down. Within a heartbeat Johno repeated the move, dragging his prey also crashing to the hard ground. Now all was elation for the Crown Skins both in front and those pursuing.

"Crown Team!" Dayo roared, bursting forth out of the dark green natural screen. It was too late for Danny to stop his own party from colliding with these fresh Heron troops and he knew they must battle through the throng if they were to have any hope of escape that painful night. This time however, it was a more one-sided contest, unlike at the bus sheds battle. Danny's crew took a hard beating as the rested, refreshed Heron Skins set about them enthusiastically, even as their own Eagle comrades closed from the rear to add to the onslaught. In a matter of minutes the battered Kings Team players were overcome and calling out in surrender.

Dayo (G) was magnanimous in triumph, quickly bringing the Crown Team's mixed contingent to a halt.

"Who's yer fuckin' leader 'ere?" he demanded with his own force surrounding the exhausted, bleeding enemy.

"I am, me... Danny (H) from the Anvil Crew, South Kings." the fair haired Skin offered defiantly, blood running down his face from a number of wounds.

"Well listen, Danny (H), from the Anvil Crew, yers have had a kickin' tonight from the Heron and Eagle crews of the Crown Team, right?" He paused and stood menacingly glaring into the pale youth's face, like a hirsute prehistoric caveman curiously studying a clean-shaven member of a rival tribe. Catching hold of Danny's lower jaw in his strong, hairy hand, Dayo drew him forward to ensure that he could clearly see the murderous intent in his own dark, cold eyes.

"You ever come down on this estate again lookin' for trouble, I'll be waitin' and I will fuckin' personally snap your scrawny neck. Now get y'boys together, get movin' an keep goin' till yer back in yer own South Kings shit-hole, cos this is the Crown Team's ground."

He released Danny with a shove then stepped back while the shaken Anvil Crew leader gathered his troops before walking

Natural Born Skinhead 1971 •206

away, in complete silence. Only once did he glance back over his shoulder and it was not Dayo (G) that he stared at.

"I think that's the fuckin' end of the Kings shitbags." Yad announced beaming, "Thee won't be comin' back 'ere after what our Dayo's just said, thee'll be stayin' home shittin' themselves, too fuckin' scared to even come out the door."

Everyone laughed and was in good spirits as they began to drift away from the scene, some carrying the captured aluminium weaponry, as if lifting the javelins and spears of a defeated enemy in an ancient Greek Hoplite encounter.

Alone of them all, Jay Mac knew Yad was entirely wrong. This ignominious defeat would only further serve to unite the numerous, warring teams of the vast Kings Estate and bring violent reprisals from a horde far greater than the raiding party they had seen this night.

Dayo suddenly called to the two Eagle runners, "Jay Mac, Johno, yer done well lads, really well, good effort."

They acknowledged his praise and thanked him before going their separate ways, Jay Mac leaving with Irish, Blue and Glynn, making their way along the lower edge of the estate back towards the bus sheds and Mickey Pimple's house opposite. The angry Eagle runner was determined to confront the corpulent scooter-rider and find out exactly why he had fled the scene.

A smiling Yad watched them walk off and shouted, "'Ey, if yer goin' to Mickey Pimples tell 'im we don't fuckin' want him anymore, yer can 'ave him back in the Eagle crew where the fat shit-house belongs."

"What do yous want, bloody knockin' on my door at this time of night?" the heavyweight, late-forties male asked angrily, on opening the faded coroporation green front door of his small mid-terraced house.

"Alright Mister Pemberton, sorry t'bother yer this late, we was just wonderin' if we could have a quick word with your Mickey." Jay Mac replied politely, with Irish, Blue and Glynn standing just behind him.

"No yers fuckin' can't, he's in bed, gorra be up early to 'elp me on the delivery round. Anyway, he's not feelin' too good, so he

Natural Born Skinhead 1971 • 207

wouldn't wanna see yers, even if he *was* still up." Mr Pemberton advised, preparing to close the door on his son's callers.

"What's the matter with 'im, it wouldn't be his guts would it?" Jay Mac enquired sarcastically, leading Mickey's father to pull the door quickly open once more.

"What's that lad, are you tryin' t'be fuckin' funny?" he asked angrily then continued, "I don't know if one of yous has upset him but I do know something's botherin' him and I won't have it, so keep away from my son, or yer'll be answerin' to me. We didn't move 'ere for our Michael to be hangin' around with the likes of you lot, now clear off or I'll have the law onto yer." With that warning he slammed the door shut, leading to some more flakes of the tired green paintwork to shake loose and fall to the ground.

"I don't think we'll be gettin' any free cakes tonight lads." Jay Mac observed as they turned to walk away.

"What was thee like Jay Mac, these cakes that he gave yer?" Blue enquired eagerly.

"Fuckin' hell Blue, thee was like cakes, what else can yer say? Yer eat the fuckers and forget them, yer don't start gettin' excited and askin' them out on a date." Jay Mac replied with a grin then turned to Irish, "Any chance of me kippin' in yours, if I miss the last bus?"

"I'll ask me Ma, it should be alright, me arl feller's on nights, come'ed let's cut through by the back street to the field." Irish replied, lighting one of his final cigarettes of the night from the glowing stump of his previous smoke.

All four youths turned into the narrow street that led to the small field at its rear, a short-cut that Jay Mac often used on his route from his usual bus stop. They had walked only a few yards when they heard the familiar throaty sound of a scooter's two-stroke engine, entering the steet behind them.

"Alright lads." Tony (G) called to them on passing, before bumping his immaculate Lambretta LI175 up onto the pavement and bringing it to an eventual halt outside the end terrace, where he lodged.

"Hello Skinheads, how are you tonight?" Tony's pillion passenger, the bizzare Mal greeted them, as he dismounted the vehicle, allowing Tony to wheel it into the shared alley between the two final houses of this row.

Natural Born Skinhead 1971 •208

Though they all knew who Mal was only Jay Mac had ever spoken to him and this for the briefest of conversations. The Skinhead quartet looked curiously at the strange character while he fumbled in the deep pockets of his heavy, grey-blue R.A.F. great coat for his keys.

Dressed in his incongruous winter coat on this warm night, exceedingly wide, purple loon flared trousers, mud covered, pointed toe, Chelsea boots and carrying his old army surplus bag across his shoulder, he represented the stylistic antithesis of the Skins' clean-cut, sharp, aggressive appearance. Flicking his unkempt centre-parted, long mousey fair hair away from his weasely acne-scarred face, he opened the front door and called to them as they were chatting with their own Skinhead peer, Tony (G).

"Come in gentlemen, all are welcome in my master's house." Mal offered.

"Some other time, thanks Mal," Jay Mac replied on behalf of them all.

"What's the matter Jay Mac, scared are you? I don't bite, unless you want me to." Mal hissed in reply, sneering at the Eagle player, and then added as inducement, "There's lots to eat and drink inside, we could all relax and have a nice chat. What d'yer say?"

"Sounds alright t'me." Blue replied enthusiastically, easily ensnared.

"Why not, I'm fuckin' starvin' meself," Irish added with Glynn also in agreement.

"Fuck it, if that's what yers all want, let's do it." Jay Mac bowed to the consensus and acquiesced.

Once inside Mal showed them into the well-decorated living room, with its comfortable furniture and welcoming glow of several table lamps and wall lights.

"Sit down and relax, there's some bottles of beer and cold chicken in the fridge, I'll bring it in for yers." Mal offered generously.

Shortly all six youths were sitting in the ambient surroundings, five of them ravenously devouring a selection of oven-grilled chicken breasts and thighs, while quaffing the accompanying cold

Natural Born Skinhead 1971 • 209

beers, in this instance both pale ales and Guinness, provided by their gracious host for this impromptu supper, Mal.

Having placed Led Zepplin's albums, I and II, on the turntable stack of the teak veneered stereogramme, though keeping the volume turned low as a nod to his hard-working parents already asleep upstairs, Mal began to roll a cigarette for himself using a paper from an orange Rizla packet and some of his own 'special' tobacco.

"Anyone else fancy one? Its good stuff this." he again offered, leading Irish, the only other genuine smoker to accept.

"I don't mind if I do, it'll make a change from me own brand." he advised.

"Oh yeah, what brand's that?" Mal asked niavely.

"It's called 'knock-off', yer don't see it advertised on the telly that much but its got its own great, smooth taste." Irish announced with a grin.

Mal laughed exposing his badly stained, yellowed teeth, wrinkling his long, prominent nose. "Nice one, I'll 'ave to try that brand meself sometime."

"Been out anywhere decent tonight, Mal?" Jay Mac asked, genuinely curious.

"Tony very kindly picked me up from the cemetery. I told him I'd be waitin' there sittin' on the wall, when I'd finished." Mal answered before taking a long drag of his herbal cigarette, then added, "There'd been a funeral earlier today, so I wanted to 'pay me respects', so-to-speak."

"Sorry to hear that, was it someone yer knew?" Blue asked politely.

"No, I never knew her previously but I do now." Mal replied cryptically.

Blue had not fully understood Mal's words and pressed on, "Young bird was she, local girl from round 'ere?"

"She wasn't local, I don't bother with 'local' but she was young and a virgin." Mal answered smiling slyly.

"Fuck, thee put a lot of information on them gravestones don't thee?" Jay Mac observed sarcastically with a grin.

"There was no gravestone; she'd only just been buried." Mal snapped, becoming momentarily less friendly.

Natural Born Skinhead 1971 ●210

"Then how did yer know all that about her?" Glynn asked, intrigued.

"She told me herself." Mal answered with a wicked grin.

"Lots of virgins up there are there?" Blue asked licking his greasy fingers, having finished his food.

"There's virgins aplenty if y'know where to look." Mal replied without further explanation.

Irish laughed, beginning to feel the effects of his relaxing smoke, "'Ey they're fuckin' good ciggies these Mal, I'll have t'get some of that baccy and start rollin' me own." he stated then began laughing again.

"You lads were busy yerselves tonight weren't yer, over in the bus station?" Mal suddenly asked.

"Yeah we were, how did you know that, one of those virgins didn't tell yer did she?" Jay Mac asked sceptically.

"Not quite, I hear lots of other things when I'm 'talking', it's a gift." Mal replied, wearing an expression that implied genuine belief in what he said.

"So you told 'im did yer Tony?" Jay Mac asked his friend.

"No mate, it's the first I've heard of any trouble over at the bus depot. I've been up at The Hounds all night, hangin' round with the scooter crew." Tony replied honestly.

Mal grinned with satisfaction and Irish laughed heartily either at what had been said, or some private joke of his own.

For the next hour or so, they all sat listening to LPs (albums) whilst discussing the meaning of life and other imponderables. When finally the four Eagle Skins departed and were walking across the small field on their way to the middle of the estate where three of them resided, with a thin sickle moon hanging in the dark night sky, they gave their considered opinions of their host.

"Yer know what, he's not a bad lad really." Glynn concluded.

"Yeah, he's alright and pretty decent with the food and drink." Blue concurred.

Irish simply nodded and continued laughing randomly to himself. Only Jay Mac felt uneasy, as if someone had just stepped over his grave. Mal's cheap seduction would cost them all dear, some more so than others.

Natural Born Skinhead 1971 • 211

The unusually long, hot summer slipped past the end of that season and extended into the next, giving a false sense of security regarding the continuing pleasant, comfortable weather. Almost as if a switch had been flicked, once beyond the middle of September a particularly cold though glorious autumn arrived with all its attendant features; shorter days beginning with frosty mornings and punctuated by random sharp showers and lengthening nights of dropping temperatures. At the same time a new item of apparel, that had been glimpsed in the peripheral wings of the Skinheads' distinctive style scene, now moved to centre stage, quickly becoming essential de rigueur fashion, the Crombie overcoat.

This dark blue or black, smart, businessman's formal wear ousted the sheepskin coat that many original Skins wore during the colder weather, acquired dominance almost instantly and transformed the principally utilitarian workwear look of the youths, morphing them into the next stage of the cycle that would eventually spawn the Boot Boy. When worn with blue-green two-tone parallels, or cream, or Prince of Wales variants and a pair of highly polished ox-blood loafers or brogues, the members of this violent, aggressive sub-culture acquired the appearance of young financiers, junior solicitors, trainee accountants, city gents in the making. Paired with twenty-inch parallel blue Wrangler or Levi's jeans or white bakers trousers and the ubiquitous, gleaming, cherry-red Airwair, the wearers assumed a bizzare mezamorphic look, juxtaposing white collar professional elegance with traditional blue collar industrial pragmatism.

Across Liverpool, in keeping with all the other major English cities, if you wished to retain your Skinhead credibility, acting the part was not sufficient, you must also project the latest image, possession of a Crombie was a vital pre-requisite if you wanted to be taken seriously and belong to the 'in-crowd'.

As both Kings and Crown Team players began to embrace this stylistic trend, with early appearances of either team's Skins clad in these formal, dark overcoats, coincidentally beginning on the arrival of the first real cold snap of the autumn, Jay Mac and his companions were desperate to acquire their own Crombies as soon as possible. Eventually by mid-October, after several weeks of saving and with his funds partially augmented by 'commission'

Natural Born Skinhead 1971 •212

from his sales of Floyd's aftershave range, Jay Mac was able to purchase a dark blue, reasonably priced version from a city centre department store, Owen Owen. He could now join his friends in the Eagle crew and legitimately be considered a 'Smoothie', a 'Suedehead', or a 'Crombie Boy', although they all remained very much Skinheads at their core.

Irish, who normally eschewed ephemeral whims of the fashionistas, surprised them all by arriving one evening at their eponymous alehouse base, wearing a well-cut, expensive black Crombie, bought from the more up-market emporium of Jackson the Tailor, his mother having obtained it for him in an effort to smarten his appearance and possibly improve his employment potential. It was not long, however, before he had managed to add sufficient food particles and cigarette ash to the coat's front to bring the garment in line with his usual dishevelled appearance.

While these major stylistic developments were occurring, the Kings Team steadily increased the frequency of their random incursions onto their Crown rivals' territory, sometimes arriving as a large company of combined public house crews or on occasion as small raiding parties, probing for weaknessess and gathering information. During one of these Kings 'intelligence' missions, an unfortunate, semi-retired, old guard member, previously a Crown Mod, Phil 'Smigger' Smith happened to disturb some Kings Crew commandos while they were spraying slogans on the walls of the low-rise tenement block where he lived at the lower edge of the estate. Unwisely approaching them, believing that he could single-handedly deal with these young Skins if necessary, he was overcome and dragged away to their side of the busy highway to be tortured in the old, uncultivated field of tall grass and weeds. This unused acreage had recently been the subject of a compulsory purchase order by the local council, allowing construction of a huge, six-lane flyover, which would permanently join the two warring estates, to begin and at the same time inadvertently providing the opposing Skinhead teams with a magnificent arsenal of varied weaponry, from mixed shale ballast to heavy pieces of concrete rubble and a selection of differeng guage metal bars, used in the building process.

Natural Born Skinhead 1971 • 213

Although Smigger suffered appalling damage to his face after being repeatedly beaten with a piece of half-brick, a rescue party of Seniors led by Dayo (G), crossed into the enemy's territory and saved Smigger from any worse punishment. Even though they were successful it had taken Dayo's ferocious individual duel with the Kings raiders' leader Yoz, where the Crown Skin fought his rival to a standstill using his favourite weapon, a metal studded, thick leather belt with heavy buckle, pitted against Yoz's wooden baton replete with rusty nails, to secure the captive's release. As with many a minor skirmish, not all the Crown Team were even aware of its happening, although the totally battered facial features of the freed Smigger bore testament to the cruelty of his captors and earned him an equally unkind new epithet, now simply 'Mash'.

All of these attacks, whether small raids or large assaults, led to an increasing bitterness between the Kings and Crown factions, with the feud growing into a genuine deep hatred of the enemy. Jay Mac passed between both estates regularly; he fully realised that his precarious duality of living on one massive industrial factory and domestic housing development, while fighting for their much smaller, microcosm rival, was becoming exponentially more dangerous with each new incident.

Sitting at the rear of the Heron public house, though for the moment still under his brother's command, Yad brooded on these developments and Jay Mac's apparent blasé attitude, becoming convinced that his team mate was a turncoat, an informer, a double agent who had successfully duped them all, except him. Somehow he would bring about the bloody downfall of this traitor, Yad told himself and then everyone would know he had been right all along.

Natural Born Skinhead 1971 •214

Chapter 8

Wand'rin' Star

November-December 1971

Monday 1ˢᵗ November 1971

"That looks ace that does thanks." Jay Mac announced returning to the cramped living room, after admiring his uncle's sewing handywork in the larger mirror of the bedroom dressing table.

"Are you sure y'should be wearin' this badge, lad? Cos I wouldn't be happy with someone havin' my old regiment's crest on his breast pocket, if he wasn't entitled to." his uncle advised, before taking a satisfying draw of his glowing briar pipe.

"Nah, no one's bothered, we've all got them on our Crombies, thee look cool." the niave youth replied, partially telling the truth in that most of the Crown Skins, had begun adding distinctive British Army regimental insignia to the breast pocket of their Crombies, complementing the neatly folded triangles of red or white silk that they already wore tucked into this pocket and secured with a faux semi-precious stone stud, usually either a diamond, ruby or garnet. Jay Mac knew that he was lying when he stated that there were no objections to this distinctly local trend, having already been questioned by the elderly shop assistant in the gents' outfitters where he had purchased his splendid 'White Horse of Hanover', passant above the motto of the Kings Liverpool Regiment ; '*nec aspera terrent*'. The young Skin felt that the literal translation 'nor do difficulties deter' was particularly apt for his circumstances and was proud to wear it, even if not officially entitled.

"Are you in the army sonny, cos you don't look old enough? I wouldn't want to sell this to you and then you get into trouble for wearing it." the curious shop-keeper had enquired.

"Oh yes, been in the army for a couple of years now, I just look young for me age." Jay Mac had replied, quickly completing the transaction with the appropriate amount of cash.

Natural Born Skinhead 1971 • 215

"You off somewhere decent John, with yer smart kit on?" his aunt asked feigning some minimal interest in his evening activities.

"Yer never know with us lads, could turn out to be a good night for some lucky birds." he replied smiling, though knowing he had no real plans other than to meet the crew in the Eagle and well aware that a cold Monday night was not usually conducive to a stimulating encounter with any obliging members of the opposite sex.

"Well don't get into any mischief with this being Halloween." his aunt warned incorrectly, before returning to her 'latest' lurid murder mystery, opening a new ten packet of Embassy filter tipped cigarettes.

"That was yesterday, its the first of November today, so yer don't need to worry about any Halloween nonsense, the 'queer feller' had his chance last night, see yer." Jay Mac replied then stepped into the tiny hall to check his appearance once more in the bedroom mirror, now tilted to an angle where he could inspect his gleaming boots.

"'Ey, you just be careful, Old Nick's always hangin' around to cause trouble, even if today is All Saints day." his aunt called to the departing youth in warning.

It was a bitterly cold night, feeling more like late December than the beginning of November. Even as Jay Mac travelled on his short journey to the Crown Estate a wild squall of icy rain and hail battered the roof and sides of the bus. Trying to peer out into the darkness beyond, through the dirt stained, grimy window at the rear of the lower deck of the vehicle, Jay Mac concluded, 'Fuck smart gear, for this freezin' wet, country, y'need a bleedin' trawlerman's kit and wellies up t'yer balls.'

Once he had alighted at his stop he decided to briskly march up to the narrow back street where Tony (G) lodged and use the shortcut across the small field to its rear. Passing close to his friend's end terraced residence and briefly glancing up at its upstairs windows, he was surprised to see Mal sitting motionless, staring down at him. The window of his room opened and he called "Hello Jay Mac, I've been waiting for you to go by, I knew you would."

Natural Born Skinhead 1971 •216

"Shit, they're not showin' where I go every night on the telly again are thee?" Jay Mac replied, intending his comment to be their final words.

"No they're not, like I said, I *knew* you'd pass by. Anyway, listen it's gonna be fuckin' bad outside tonight so why don't you and yer three friends come round again? There's loads of food and drink in, if yers fancy it." Mal offered generously then on appearing to sense Jay Mac's reluctance, added, "'Course if you four tough Skinheads are too scared of one lone ex-Hippie, well, yers better leave it."

"Hey Mal, believe me nobody's scared of you. We'll probably see yer later you just make sure yer've got plenty of scran, because when Blue starts eatin' he *is* fuckin' scary." the Eagle Skin advised before quickly moving on.

A few hours later, having exhausted their combined funds in the eponymous alehouse, with no other reasonable alternative venue on offer and only the prospect of wandering about the bleak estate in the worsening weather before them, Jay Mac decided to reveal Mal's invitation.

"So 'ang on Jay Mac, are you sayin' he's got a stash of food on offer and a few beers?" Blue asked excitedly.

"Yeah, sounds like it." he replied.

"Is there a chance of any birds bein' there?" Glynn speculated.

"Glynn, I think that's stretchin' it mate. I don't know whether this cunt's AC or DC, yer just can't tell." Jay Mac advised.

"Still it's off the streets and we'll be gettin' fed, so why not?" Irish decided, leading them all to stroll away from the Eagle and down towards Mal's house, near the lower edge of the estate and the bus depot.

Glynn considered the possibility that there may be another 'attraction' available. "Hey, he looks like a right kinky bastard, I bet he's got a fuckin' load of hard core porno mags for us to 'ave a blimp at."

Jay Mac smiled at his friend's naivety, "Mate, if Mal's got a fuckin' porno stash, I don't think any one of us is gonna be wantin' to look at it."

Natural Born Skinhead 1971 • 217

Following their brief journey to Mal's house with the rain and hail constantly lashing them, Jay Mac rang the bell on the well-painted front door.

"Alright Mal, we thought we'd take up yer offer, if it's still goin'." he enquired politely.

"Of course it is; I *knew* you would accept." Mal replied, opening the door fully for them to enter.

Once inside they hung their wet Crombies on a rectangular wooden coat rack, attached to the wall adjacent to the living room then passed into that comfortable salon.

"Been keepin' busy have yer Mal?" Irish asked, lighting one of his cigarettes and offering the pack to Mal, who declined.

"No thanks Irish, I prefer me own rollies." He paused to prepare one of his special smokes then continued, "Yeah, I'm always busy, my work's never done."

"What is it yer actually do Mal, what is yer job... like?" Blue asked, genuinely curious.

"Helping lost souls find their way, preparing for 'the arrival'." Mal offered in reply without further expansion.

"No wonder yer fuckin' busy then, cos there's loads of lost arseholes staggerin' out of the Eagle every night, who can't find their way home." Jay Mac advised grinning.

Mal made no comment but instead went into the kitchen to collect their food which was already prepared and waiting for them. Once again he proved a generous host and the hungry Skins greedily devoured a selection of cold meats, slices of pie and numerous bottled beers. All the while Mal played an eclectic mix of tracks from different albums that he particularly liked, including: *Happiness is a Warm Gun* and *Helter Skelter* from the Beatles *White Album,* Led Zeppelin's *I'm Gonna Leave You* and *Dazed and Confused;* Atomic Rooster's *Death Walks Behind You* and *The Devil's Answer.*

Everyone was in good spirits and relaxed even though the chosen songs were not exactly uplifting, sing-a-long numbers.

"Anyone fancy tryin' a board game that I've got upstairs?" Mal asked with apparent innocence.

"What sort of game's that then?" Irish, who was a capable chess player, asked.

Natural Born Skinhead 1971 ●218

"Oh it's only somethin' simple, harmless really. It's what yer might call a communication game. I'll show yers if yer like, it's in my room upstairs and I've got more records up there that are a bit different." Mal answered, smiling slyly.

All four youths were intrigued and agreed to try their hand at this apparently innocuous game.

When they entered Mal's bedroom, which was the largest in the house, his doting mother and father having long since relinquished it to their excessively spoilt child, the Skins each experienced a momentary feeling of disquiet, there was a noticeably similar atmosphere to that of the Hippie house they had 'visited' during the summer. Mal's bed was a simple mattress lying on the bare-boarded floor; the walls bore only torn fragments of the expensive embossed paper he had ripped off and the exposed plaster was covered in strange symbols, obscenities and figures as was the door to the room. No light bulb hung from the ceiling pendant holder, the dark chamber being lit only by a low watt, purple shaded lamp supplemented by a number of flickering candles. Mal gestured for them to squat on some of the larger cushions, that where loosely set about a low wooden table with short stumpy legs.

"Sit and relax, listen with your minds." he began, then placed his favourite record Black Widow's *Come to the Sabbath* on the turntable of a standard mono record player that he had had Tony (G), his electrician houseguest wire additional speakers to.

"Fuckin' hell Mal, whose yer decorator, Dracula? Y'room looks like it's a set from a Hammer Horror film." Jay Mac observed genuinely.

"Good, I'm glad y'like it. Now let us begin the game." Mal smiled broadly, fully revealing his rotten, yellowed teeth.

Opening a simple, modern, melamine-veneered, fibreboard wardrobe that had originally been plain white in colour but was now also entirely covered in similar markings as the walls and door of the room, Mal produced a heavy, wooden, circular board which he had difficulty in lifting into place on top of the low table. All four youths looked at its unusual markings, consisting of the letters of the alphabet written in both upper and lower case, in a black Gothic font, around its edge as if radiating from the large,

Natural Born Skinhead 1971 • 219

stylised eye positioned at its centre, the latter reminding them all once more of their encounter with Magog and the Hippies.

"What sort of game *is* this, Mal?" Irish asked as he studied the smooth surface of faded sepia on which the letters and image where printed, having the appearance of an ancient parchment or early cartographer's attempt to map the celestial rotation of the heavens, almost sensing the aura of great age that exuded from it.

"It's a game of fortune really, seeing what might come to pass through the help of others, just harmless fun." Mal answered placing an up-turned dark green, glass tumbler that appeared of equal age to the board, on top of the 'all seeing eye'.

Jay Mac was becoming more uneasy by each moment, particularly when his vision adjusted to the gloom and he spied an image that he found disturbing, high in the darker recesses of the wall above Mal's bedfixed just below the artexed ceiling that of a foot long, inverted wooden crucifix with an alabaster figure of Jesus Christ.

"I won't be takin' part in this shit Mal." he announced, adding, "None of yous should bother with it either, yer fuckin' with somethin' yer don't understand and you shouldn't mess with."

"Of course Jay Mac, that's what I knew you'd say." Mal acknowledged with a sly smile, continuing, "That's why I've only set four places, you're not invited, you're not wanted. Could you do just one thing for us?" Mal asked rhetorically. "Write down whatever is revealed on that notepad by my bed, with this pen.

At first Jay Mac was reluctant to be involved even as a scribe but after receiving peer pressure from his friends he acquiesced and sat away from the table, on the floor, with the pad on his knees and pen in his hand.

Mal's favourite record had now ended and the room fell silent. He placed his right index finger lightly on top of the tumbler's base instructing them to follow suit. "When the 'visitor' arrives, let yourselves be guided, make no sound offer no resistance." he advised in a soft low monotone voice as if he had already drifted into another realm, devoid from his surroundings.

For several minutes there was no sound, no movement other than the flickering light of the candle flames, set in their varied sconces around the room. Suddenly Mal appeared to be in the grip of a seizure, a bodily spasm, with his eyes rolled up in their sockets

Natural Born Skinhead 1971 •220

to reveal only their blood-shot whites. Though it appeared that he could not see where the now animated tumbler was being directed, he still called out each letter in turn as it was 'selected'; Jay Mac the scribe recording them all the while. This seemingly unaided motion continued for some time, changing pace either from a slow ponderous choice to quick, direct revelation, all four youths maintaining contact with the oracle tumbler by their single digits.

Jay Mac had recorded almost a paragraph of scribble before a cryptic communique of sorts could be extrapolated from the letters, if combined in a particular sequence. As a possible meaning began to reveal itself, it was clear that a prophetic warning of dire events was the intended message; Jay Mac noticed two distinct developments beginning to occur. His friends' expressions had all changed from fairly lighthearted enthusiasm to that of stark fear; Irish in particular looked as if he was caught in the grip of a terrible nightmare. Added to this unsettling sight, the temperature in the room had perceptibly lowered and even though they were all shallow breathing, each emitted a small vapour cloud as he did.

"I want t'stop now." Irish asked though not quite sounding like himself.

"No one stops until I say." Mal snapped in a low gutteral voice.

"Please, I don't wanna go on." Irish pleaded, again appearing in a somnambulistic state.

"You will not stop!" Mal roared with his newly acquired primeval tongue.

"Fuck this crap!" Jay Mac shouted as he sprang from his seated position and booted the heavy board from the low table, causing the antique, green glass tumbler to crash to the floor and shatter into thousands of glittering fragments as if thrown from a great height.

"No, no, you've ruined it!" Mal screamed, writhing in agony before leaping onto Jay Mac, siezing him by the throat.

Both youths fell awkwardly, knocking over the purple shaded lamp which rolled about erratically, toppling some of the candles, one of which set light to the flimsy net curtains.

"Master, help me, give me the strength to punish this unbeliever!" Mal cried out digging his thumbs into Jay Mac's

Natural Born Skinhead 1971 • 221

trachea, choking the life out of him, even while receiving thumping punches to his face and body from the struggling Eagle Skin.

As Glynn tried to extinguish the fire which quickly consumed the highly flammable curtains, both Irish and Blue punched, kicked and then grappled the raging, maniac Mal trying to free their companion from his death grip. Eventually after a ferocious struggle they managed to subdue their maddened host, allowing Jay Mac to regain his feet and breathe once more.

"You've ruined it! You've ruined it! Get out of *our* house, never come back!" Even as Mal spoke the previously closed window burst open admitting the freezing night air, flinging a squall of hail and sleet into the unholy chamber.

The four Crown Skins hurriedly exited the room with Jay Mac at their rear, turning to warn Mal in a hoarse voice, "Be careful what yer doin' Mal, yer don't know what yer fuckin' with"

Mal did not reply but stood totally immobile, glaring at the departing Skinhead, continuing to focus on where he had stood; even after he had descended the staircase retrieved his Crombie and passed out into the rain swept street. A smile now appeared on Mal's thin lips and he began to laugh uncontrollably, only pausing randomly to utter a stream of obscenities and gibberish.

Sometime later, when his doting parents returned from their overtime twilight shift in the local washing machine factory, they found him in exactly the same position.

"There, there, it's alright now, mummy's here." Mrs Chadwick said, placing her arms around him, while her husband filled the kettle, hoping that a good strong cup of tea may be of help. Neither home comforts made any difference to Mal's condition, leaving his bleary-eyed parents to sit through the long night choosing the only option left to them, prayer.

Jay Mac, Irish, Blue and Glynn all thought they had seen the last of Mal after that disturbing night and they were partially correct. Other than random sightings of the macabre youth wandering the estate, going about his business, neither of the two latter Eagle Skins had any further contact with him. Their crew mates were not to be so fortunate; the troubled Mal still had at least one more prominent role to play in their lives.

Natural Born Skinhead 1971 •222

Sunday 14th November 1971

On a bleak, wet, Sunday evening shortly after Jay Mac and Irish had finished a substantial meal of roast chicken, roast potatoes, several ladles of peas and carrots, plus half a loaf of thick sliced bread, heavily margarined and most of the contents of the family size, glazed brown teapot, courtesy of Mrs O'Hare, both youths were ready to find some interesting diversion to while away the long, dark hours that stretched out before them.

"D'yer fancy the Eagle for a few pints?" Irish enquired, casually lighting a post-meal cigarette as he and Jay Mac stood in front of their usual library perch, watching the driving rain falling in a silver grey curtain from the overhanging tenement balconies.

"Nah, it's only seven o'clock, there'll be no one over there yet, except the arl fellers cryin' in their ale." Jay Mac answered, turning up the collar of his Crombie and glad that he was wearing his Levi's denim jacket underneath as the sharp cold weather of recent weeks had continued unabated, the temperature dropping all the while. "How about a stroll down to Mickey Pimple's and see if we can scrounge some cakes for afters, if his miserable cunt dad's not there? The fat bastard owes us a bit of scran after pissin' off that night at the bus sheds." Jay Mac suggested, in the absence of any other more attractive alternative and with none of their usual crew present on this foul night.

"Right enough, I don't think any of the boys are gonna show up for a bit anyway, so we might as well try some scroungin' off fat arse Mickey Pimple, sure *he* won't miss a few cakes." Irish concurred, turning up the collar of his Crombie too before they set off on their foraging mission.

As they made their way down to the lower edge of the estate the rain began to lessen in intensity and the accompanying wind dropped also, both being replaced by a much colder air.

"It's fuckin' freezin' man, if it carries on like this we're gonna have a hard frost and probably a load of snow." Irish observed just as they arrived at Mickey Pimple's residence.

"Thanks 'Mr fuckin' depressin' weather man.' I bet yer read all that in the *Echo* didn't yer?" Jay Mac responded grinning, ringing the newly fitted bell on Mickey's front door.

Natural Born Skinhead 1971 • 223

"Yeah, what d'yers want lads?" the corpulent youth asked, opening the door only part way, looking to see if they were alone or with others.

"Well, what it is Mickey, we don't know why yer fucked off that night at the bus sheds but we're prepared to put it down to nerves, like a stage fright sort of thing and we'll let it go at that." Jay Mac offered diplomatically, being no stranger to fear himself and understanding there was only a thin line between what someone did in response to that fear, which had them considered either a hero or a coward.

"Thanks, that's decent of yers but I've heard Yad said if he sees me out anywhere he's really gonna hurt me." Mickey replied nervously.

"Fuck 'im, he's always talkin' out of his arse." Jay Mac advised, adding, "Anyway, just keep out of his way when yer out an about on yer scooter, then, when another chance comes, make sure yer show yerself t'be up for it, don't fuckin' shit out."

"Yeah Mickey, like Jay Mac says if there's another kick off with the Kings or any other crew, get stuck in, even if yer take a bit of a kickin', don't just fuckin' run." Irish concurred also advising, "If you shit out again yer finished round 'ere."

Mickey listened intently to what both Eagle Skins were saying then answered, "Ok lads, thanks, am with yer. Next time somethin' starts I'll dive right in there; I won't let the team down again, honest." He paused, looking from Jay Mac to Irish, waiting for a sign of acknowledgement.

Both youths eventually nodded with Jay Mac offering, "Don't worry Mickey, we're a tight crew, we've always got each others backs, if one of us goes down we'll all step in and help him."

Mickey seemed much relieved and responded, smiling, "'ang on lads, I'll be right back." A few moments later he returned with a large paper bag filled with a selection of out of date cakes, including both varieties of doughnuts, ring and filled, a number of custard slices and some Danish pastries.

'Result!' Jay Mac thought as he looked across at Irish, who gratefully accepted the bag with an expression that suggested he was thinking exactly the same.

"There y'go lads thanks f'calling round..., see yers." Mickey said before closing the door on his two satisfied visitors.

Natural Born Skinhead 1971 •224

Walking away from the grateful youth's house greedily devouring his mixed assortment token of appreciation, they met their fellow crew mate Johno.

"Alright lads, been to see the fat shit-house have yers?" the immensely strong farm labourer called to them, as they approached arguing over the last dry custard slice.

"Alright Johno, 'ere yer are, 'elp yerself, there's a couple of stale doughnuts left in there." Irish offered generously having magnanimously decided to split the sought after slice between himself and Jay Mac, displaying the wisdom of Solomon, except in this instance both parties agreed to the division of the disputed item.

Johno quickly disposed of the two hardened doughnuts then advised, "I'm off up to the Eagle before it starts pissin' down again, are yous goin' there yerselves?"

Even before either of his crew mates could answer, as if in response to the youth's tempting of fate, the angry weather gods opened the heavens once more and released another torrential downpour.

"Fuck this, let's nip through the side street and over the field." Jay Mac suggested.

Almost immediately on turning into this short street they found Tony (G) kneeling in the road, reaching into an open four door, mark II, dark blue Ford Cortina diligently working within. "Jump in the back lads, I'll give yers a lift. I'll 'ave this beaut started in a minute." Tony said in a low voice.

All three Skins gratefully got into the rear of the vehicle, while their electrician team mate sparked the ignition wires sufficiently to bring the engine to roaring life.

"Hello boys, how are you tonight?" Mal asked sitting up from his slouched position in the front passenger seat.

There was no time for any response or objection, to the disturbed ex-Hippie's presence, with Tony quickly jumping into the driving seat and racing the vehicle away from the deserted street.

"Right lads everyone up for a bit of joy ridin' around the city? The tank's three quarters full so we've got no worries there." Tony asked driving through the dark rainy night in the stolen Cortina, the

Natural Born Skinhead 1971 • 225

legitimate property of a thrifty neighbour who had saved for months to purchase the coveted car.

"We don't mind Tony, its better than walkin' these friggin' streets anytime, as long as this fuckin' fruit cake doesn't start his weirdo shit." Jay Mac replied on behalf of all three Eagle players.

"Be nice Jay Mac, I know you haven't got much time left so I won't bother you again, it's too late to save you now." Mal replied grinning slyly.

Jay Mac did not respond, prompting Irish to ask, "What the fuck's he talkin' about, was there somethin' on that piece of paper you were writin' on that we all need t'know about?"

"Nah, it was only a load of fuckin' nonsense, forget about it." Jay Mac answered, refusing to be drawn further.

For the next couple of hours they drove around the city with no specific destination in mind, enjoying the comfortable warmth of the vehicle and the tinge of exhilaration of knowing they were breaking the law. At one point this excitement became a little too close for comfort when they attracted the attention of the occupants of a police panda car, which instantly began a fruitless, though at times hair-raising pursuit of them. It was an uneven contest the much larger cylinder capacity engine of the Cortina easily outpaced its smaller rival.

When they were completely satisfied they had evaded their police pursuers, their arrogant confidence even led them to stop at an off-licence store to purchase some much needed liquid refreshment, for the remainder of their trip. As they passed two large bottles of Woodpecker cider and several bottles of Double Diamond ale around, each of them drinking freely from them, including Tony the driver, everyone became relaxed and in good humour including, it seemed, the usually morose Mal. Eventually after a number of close calls and near misses, speeding through junctions and traffic lights without stopping or taking observation, they returned full circle to the bleak rainswept Crown Estate.

All were mildly intoxicated, Mal appearing more so than the rest, though this did not deter him from insisting that he be allowed to drive. Tony finally, reluctantly agreed conceding to his landlord's son's demands and pulling the vehicle over to the kerb on the main central road, only a few hundred yards from the Eagle to enable him take over the wheel.

Natural Born Skinhead 1971 ●226

"Fuck this bollocks! I'm out, come 'ed lads, leave nut job t'drive 'imself into a brick wall or somethin'." Jay Mac stated as he exited the vehicle, followed by Irish and Johno, who were all in agreement.

"Come on Tony, man, don't stay in there with this cracked cunt at the wheel." Irish warned, Johno also calling similar advice.

Tony looked at his team mates then at the pleading loner, Mal and said, "It's alright lads, its best if I stay with 'im, his mum and dad would never forgive me if I let somethin' happen to 'im.

Mal wound down the window closest to him and shouted, "Go on piss of yer chickens, I don't need anyone, my master looks after me." With that he roared away from them, the wheels squealing and smoke pouring from the exhaust.

It was just as Jay Mac, Irish and Johno were downing the dregs of their second dark amber pints, with their crew mates in the Eagle, listening to *Hey Joe* by Jimi Hendrix on the juke box that the unmistakable sound of a terrific crash shattered the convivial atmosphere and brought them all rushing to the door. Some of the usual female, underage, entrance porch dwellers called out alarmingly "We seen it all, thee went up on the kerb an into the lamppost, they're all fuckin' dead!"

Jay Mac, closely followed by Johno, his Eagle sprinting partner, were the first to reach the scene, with a breathless Irish not much later in joining them.

The dark blue Cortina, only recently purchased by its hard-working proud owner, after months of double shifts and Sunday overtime, was destroyed, a write-off. It had mounted the kerb as reported and struck one of the dead-eyed, precast concrete lampposts, crumpling the entire front of the vehicle, forcing its engine back into the cabin and violently launching Mal, the intoxicated, insane driver head-first through the shattered windscreen. Lying partially on the distorted metal bonnet, his broken legs still trapped by the steering wheel, Mal's left arm and collar bone were shattered and his skull was fractured, dying his long, mousey, fair hair scarlet matting it to his mutilated face. What was a large, prominent nose, had been sliced through at its tip, leaving two exposed nasal cavities that, even despite

Natural Born Skinhead 1971 • 227

subsequent attempts at cosmetic surgery would lead to the youth acquiring the epithet of Mal 'The Pig'.

Jay Mac glanced at the badly injured Mal but he was more concerned with aiding his team mate, Tony (G), though as he ran around to the passenger side of the smoking vehicle, he realised there were other casualties in need of immediate help also.

"Get a fuckin' ambulance someone... now!" he called on finding a ludicrously dressed girl lying with her back on the pavement but both broken legs still trapped within the front of the cabin, similar to Mal and with her almost unrecognisable scarlet face peppered with dozens of glass splinters. "Johno mate, see if yer can ease this girl out while I take a look in the back." Jay Mac asked, not certain whether it was right to move the injured female but more concerned with the black smoke now pouring from the engine bay. Both Irish and he opened the rear doors on either side and found another girl similarly dressed though a much frailer individual, her face having been bashed in by violent contact with the back of Mal's head and having sustained multiple fractures and internal injuries. Jay Mac looked across at her momentarily even as he pulled his semi-conscious, equally injured friend, Tony (G) from the wreck. A sudden sad recognition occurred to him and he knew that the obliging Donna, Molly 'Skank's' associate would have even more difficulty selling her wares, in the brutally cruel market place of her chosen profession.

After lying Tony carefully on the pavement, Jay Mac knelt down beside him and tried to offer some reassurance, "Alright Tony, yer doin' great man, a few cuts that'll leave some cool scars that's all mate, yer know the birds fuckin' love them." he advised smiling.

"Don't... tell me ma... or me da.., please." Tony gasped then fully lapsed into unconsciousness.

The ambulances arrived and the considerable crowd that had gathered watched in silence as the four casualties were lifted into the vehicle, before being sped away to the local hospital's emergency unit.

Returned to their eponymous alehouse base, the Eagle crew sat drinking their pints and considering the evening's events.

Natural Born Skinhead 1971 •228

"Why the fuck did Tony let that cracked cunt drive?" Tank asked, with Glynn adding, "And why was there birds in the car? I didn't know Mal the weirdo ever fancied girls."

"Well not those that are still breathin' anyway." Jay Mac noted, only part in jest, reaching into his Crombie inside breast pocket, checking for the crumpled note paper that he had taken that fateful night, the spectral warning of dire fates awaiting some of those present; so far Mal's had come to pass earlier than predicted. With Jimmy Cliff's *Many Rivers to Cross* playing on the juke box, Jay Mac wondered who would be next.

◇◇◇

Irish the amateur weather forcaster had been correct in his predictions. During the remainder of November and the first two weeks of December conditions worsened significantly, bringing hard, sustained frosts followed by heavy falls of snow, prompting some pundits to speculate on the exciting possibility of a white Christmas. Work on the rapidly progressing, estate-connecting, multi lane flyover, slowed and became sporadic until it was finally decided to call a halt to all construction on the two parallel facing sites, allowing for an early, extended, seasonal holiday for the workers. Both Kings and Crown Team Skins appreciated the gesture, which allowed them largesse to wander about the twin developments whenever they wished, selecting brick, concrete and iron weaponry as the situation demanded. During the raids that followed the acquisition of these convenient arsenals, there were increasing casualties and more serious injuries than usual on either side. Whereas the huge Kings Team could easily absorb its losses, having an army of eager substitutes waiting to join the ranks of combatants, the Crown Team, dwarfed by comparison, felt the significance of each and every wounded player who was forced to withdraw. Any new blood recruits where welcomed, even the untested Juniors being accepted to fill gaps in the frontline defences and the return of a seasoned veteran was a cause of genuine celebration.

Saturday 18th December 1971

With a bone-chilling wind sweeping around the bleak housing estate, howling through the chasms formed between the grey

Natural Born Skinhead 1971 • 229

concrete, highrise tower blocks and flinging blinding snow flurries randomly about, hampering the movement of vehicles and pedestrians alike, the warmest atmosphere was to be found in the packed lounges and bars of the area's five public houses. The lounge of the Eagle was particularly lively and convivial on this inclement evening as the eponymous crew gathered to celebrate the return to the fold of Terry (H), released from custody only the day before.

Shouts of "Good t'see yer Terry!" and "Glad t'have yer back mate!" abounded, with the young Skins genuinely pleased to have one of their Senior players and a renowned scrapper back in their midst. Sat at the very centre of the semi-circular seating arrangement, a position that the still incarcerated Tommy (S) would normally have occupied, Terry was flanked on his right by Irish and his left by Jay Mac, his former schoolfriends, with the rest of the crew radiating out in a broad arc from either side. A thick, grey fog of stale cigarette smoke hung unmoving just above their heads, hazing the light from the ceiling fitting and wall sconces, while the clink of beer glasses and ale bottles vied with the loud shouted conversations and the blaring juke box currently playing Simaryp's *Skinhead Moonstomp*.

"How did yer find it in the nick, Terry, was it hard goin' like?" Brain called out one of his usual obvious questions.

"Well it wasn't exactly a fuckin' Butlin's Holiday Camp, Brain." Terry answered, before taking a lengthy draft of his pint of brown bitter.

"That depends on the Butlin's doesn't it Terry?" Jay Mac asked grinning.

Speaking in a more quiet tone to his two fellow ex-'Brother's' victims, Terry observed, "It was alright in there providin' yer made sure that thee *all* knew not t'fuck with yer. Yer had to stand up and do the business when it was needed, those poor cunts who didn't, well... their time was hard... real fuckin' hard." He paused and drained his pint then threw back his whiskey chaser in one gulp. "Yeah, it reminded me of the Cardinals only yer couldn't gerroff at the end of the day, y'know warra mean?" he asked rhetorically, knowing Irish and Jay Mac fully appreciated his analogy.

Natural Born Skinhead 1971 •230

"Was thee a cock of the nick, Terry?" Blue asked genuinely interested, replacing Brain as the random questioner.

"Yeah, thee was Blue, everyone called 'im Baltic." Terry replied, his facial expression changing from smiling to dour.

"I bet you fuckin' sorted 'im out didn't yer Terry?" Brain observed unwisely, causing their returned commrade to put down the fresh pint half filled with bitter that he was topping up with brown ale, onto the small table in front of him.

"No Brain, I fuckin' didn't sort 'im out, he was called Baltic cos he was that fuckin' cold, right? He didn't give a shit. The lad came from the Gorbals in Glasgow from what I 'eard, he was one big, horrible, hairy Jock, built like a brick shit-house covered in scars and tattoos. I couldn't understand a fuckin' word he was sayin' but I knew enough to keep the fuck out of his way and pay up me ciggie ration whenever he wanted it."

Terry ended his brief edifying tale then finished pouring his pint, before taking another long drink.

"Was he a Skinhead from a Jock team?" Jay Mac asked curiously.

"Jay Mac, I don't know what the fuck he was, he could've been a friggin' caveman for all I could tell. If he was from a team, then thank fuck JockLand's a long way off, cos I wouldn't wanna be goin' up against a crew of 'Baltics'." Terry laughed at the very idea then gulped down his pint in a series of rapid swallows.

The rest of the crew shared the sentiment, laughing also, equally grateful that the far North remained just that.

For the next couple of hours the youths relaxed and enjoyed themselves telling the usual exaggerated stories of unlikely sexual encounters and other vigorous physical actions they were supposed to have been part of. All the time the pints of beer and spirit chasers kept apace with the tempo of their good humour, while the cigarette smoking majority of the crew did their best to ensure the thick, grey, nicotine cloud was never in danger of dissipating. Shortly before ten o'clock with barely an hour's drinking time remaining, Terry (H) announced that he would have to depart for another celebratory venue.

"Right lads, I'll have to be gettin' off, I was supposed to be meetin' Dayo and the old boys down at the Heron about half an

Natural Born Skinhead 1971 • 231

hour ago." he advised, finishing his final whiskey shot in one swallow, before throwing on his Crombie preparing to leave.

"I bet you'll be goin' to Mr Li's for a fuckin' big fish supper when yers 'ave finished in the Heron, 'ey, Terry?" Blue asked speculatively, thinking of his own dietary requirements, whatever the occasion.

"Yeah Blue, yer dead right lad. Of the two things that I've really missed in the nick, one of them is a friggin' massive fish and chip supper with extra helpings of everythin' from the Golden Diner." Terry advised genuinely.

"What's the other thing then Terry?" Brain enquired, equally genuinely.

The recently returned Crown Senior stared at the naive crew member and replied, "Sittin' here talkin' to you of course Brain, what d'*you* fuckin' think?"

They all laughed including the slower witted youth, even though he was not entirely certain whether Terry was being disengenuous or not.

Jay Mac could see from Blue's expression that he was still contemplating the prospect of enjoying the aforementioned massive fish and chip supper with all the trimmings and asked him the ultimate rhetorical question, "D'yer fancy goin' down t'Mr Lee's yerself Blue, for a bit of scran?"

Blue's Crombie was hastily thrown on while he rapidly gulped his remaining half pint of ale, rising to his feet as he did.

"I take it thats a 'yes' then Blue," Jay Mac said with a grin, adding, "Anyone else fancy a stroll down to Mr Li's with Terry being on his way to the Heron?"

Almost the entire crew were in agreement; clearly feeling the need for some deep fried sustenance themselves and all decamped from their Eagle public house base, ready to brave the elements during a brisk march to the lower estate. With Junior Walker's *Roadrunner* playing on the juke box they filed out of the entrance porch into the freezing night air, to be immediately engulfed by a swirling snow storm.

Their Crombie collars turned up and their hands dug into the pockets of the ubiquitous dark overcoats, they moved at a rapid pace on their brief journey down the main central road, through the blinding, bitterly cold conditions. Soon arriving at the row of

Natural Born Skinhead 1971 •232

battered shops situated on the lower portion of the grim estate close to the Heron public house, even given the appalling weather they were surprised to find the entire area, from shopping concourse to hostelry car park and its low surrounding perimeter 'perch' walls, totally deserted. As they approached the entrance to Mr Li's Golden Diner brightly lit, in stark contrast to every other securely bolted and shuttered establishment, Yad's two junior apprentices, Tommo and Nat came racing from the far side of the eponymous alehouse.

"Fuckin' hell, that's a bit of luck." Nat announced, running the shiny sleeved forearm of his grubby Crombie across his permanently bubbling nose. "Yad just told us t'get up to the Eagle and call yers out. The fuckin' Kings team are on their way, comin' across from the fields."

Terry (H) looked at the crew who were all awaiting his instructions, with him being the most senior player present. "Fuck this one, make yer own minds up lads, cos I'm havin' nothin' to do with it. I only got out yesterday and me arl feller would put me in hospital if I got pulled again." He paused and waited for any objection or criticism but received only nods of agreement from them all. "Alright then, like I said, I'm keepin' out of it am goin' into the Heron t'meet the old boys, 'ave a few more beers, then end up in Mr Li's and stuff me face with fish and chips. You decide lads, it's your call." Terry finished what he had to say then walked across to the Heron without a backward glance.

"Is that it? Do yers really want us to run back to Yad and tell 'im the Eagle crew have shit out?" Tommo the heavyweight junior asked with a sneer of contempt.

"Watch yer fuckin' mouth yer fat shit." Johno warned angrily before assuming leadership of the crew once more. "Alright lads, we all know the fuckin' score, we can't just piss off and leave these Heron cunts t'take all the glory, we'd never hear the fuckin' end of it if we did. So we'll get stuck in *if* there is gonna be a kick-off, ok? Anyone who wants to shit out, better go now while thee still can." Johno announced, seemingly magnanimous, though expecting no dissent.

"Can't we get a bit of scran first Johno, then jump in? I'm fuckin' starvin'." Blue asked hopefully.

Natural Born Skinhead 1971 • 233

"Sorry Blue, yer'll have to 'ang on lad, let's just have a pipe and see what the fuck is goin' on first." Johno advised then led the crew of Skins along to the garages below the high rise tower blocks and towards the old field, with Nat and Tommo, Yad's messengers at the fore.

"Shit, that was quick; I thought you boys would still be hidin' in the Eagle when yer heard about this lot." Yad announced from his elevated vantage point, standing on top of the end garage with his right hand raised shielding his eyes and his co-leader Macca (G) sitting on the roof's edge.

"'Ey knob'ed, I've just told this fat tit to watch his mouth and now am tellin' you." Johno shouted in reply then continued, "What d'yer want us for Yad, it better be good, cos we're missin' out on a fuckin' good scran t'be here."

"'Ave a look yerself Johno, yer can all see them now they're on the move." Yad replied pointing with his left hand in the direction of the flyover construction site, across on the Kings side of the busy highway.

The howling wind had dropped, allowing the heavy snow to fall steadily almost vertically to the frozen ground. Moving through this 'winter wonderland' scene were a large group of Crombie-clad Kings Skins appearing like a column of dark chessmen advancing from their own territory into the enemy's sector of the board, their motion seeming almost staccato against the strobe lighting effect of the dense flickering snowflakes. To their rear, next to the construction site earthworks, could be seen a blazing bonfire raised from a selection of building materials and regularly refuelled by similar items. Even through the partial sound-deadening of the soft white material that was rapidly gathering in drifts and deepening layers on the ground, the screams of females could be heard emanating from this place.

"Yeah, that's right, thee've got birds with them, the jammy bastards." Macca (G) announced by way of explanation for the benefit of the new arrivals. "I dunno what sort of birds they must be, the dirty bitches, gettin' jumped by all them Kings fuckers." he added with more than a hint of envy, before returning to the matter in hand. "Anyway, looks like only half of them are comin' over, so if we can grip them and twat them while their mates are on the job, we'll get a right result."

Natural Born Skinhead 1971 •234

Both Macca (G) and Yad jumped down from the garage roof, joining Weaver with the rest of their troops, then the sexual sadist outlined his plan for the combined crews to hear and appreciate, "If we can get those cunts into the garage alley with us waitin', we can drop them all and give them a fuckin' good kickin' before thee can call for their mates."

Yad then added, "We just need some fuckin' bait to bring them round 'ere an I think we *all* know the fat tit who'd do it." he smiled slyly, looking across at Jay Mac, "You're mates with that fuckin' Mickey Pimple shitbag aren't yer Kings Boy?" he asked, pressing on without waiting for an answer. "Run over to his place and get 'im to do the business on his shitty scooter. Tell the prick if he rides up t'this crew, buzzes them and leads them to us, we'll do the rest an I'll make 'im a full Crown Team member... alright?"

Jay Mac felt sick at the very thought of beguiling the innocent, home-comfort-loving Mickey Pimple into becoming involved in this potentially dangerous action but he was almost equally uncomfortable with how his refusal may be interpreted.

"Alright, I'll do it, I'll try an convince 'im to come out on his bike on this shit night and risk takin' a beatin' but if he's not up for it, that's his choice, ok?" he answered firmly.

"Yeah, sure, just fuck off over there and get yer fat boyfriend out of bed, unless yer don't want yer Kings rat mates t'take a beatin'?" Yad replied smiling.

"Fuck you arsebag!" Jay Mac responded before sprinting away along the lower edge of the estate towards the bus depot and Mickey Pimple's house opposite.

"Alright Mickey lad, listen... er... Yad's asked me to give yer another chance t'show yerself an if yer do good he'll make yer a proper team member but yer'll have t'come now, straight away." Jay Mac said with a smile, relaying the Heron co-leader's words accurately.

"Alright Jay Mac, I don't fancy it but if you're tellin' me I can trust 'im then I'll do it, just say what it is yer want me to do."

The Eagle player quickly explained the plan to the overweight youth who listened intently, believing his chance to redeem himself had finally arrived. Within moments Mickey had wheeled

Natural Born Skinhead 1971 • 235

out his much improved Vespa 150GS, resplendent in all the chrome extras it could hold.

"Fuck me, that's lookin' the part now Mickey." Jay Mac observed genuinely, adding, "Just do exactly what I've said, buzz the fuckers then lead them into the garages but keep yer friggin' distance, don't get too close, right?"

Both youths then raced off in their separate directions, one up the main highway, towards the enemy throng, the other across to the garage enclosure trap.

Laid out in the form of a rectangular cul-de-sac with four garages along either side and three across the base, immediately situated below three high-rise tower blocks facing the old uncultivated fields and busy arterial road beyond, these long abandoned structures had been burned out, vandalised and had become the sole preserve of the gangs. The Heron crew tended to use them for numerous purposes, primarily as a place to store 'weaponry' but also convenient if foul smelling dens for sexual encounters as an alternative to the more exposed alley behind the shops, or rear of the alehouse.

Jay Mac sprinted into the open doorway of the second garage to his right on entering the cul-de-sac. It was already occupied by Yad, Macca (G), Weaver, Johno and Irish and a number of Heron Juniors. The remainder of the mixed cohort of Eagle and Heron crews were ready and waiting in three of the other structures, one adjacent to their leaders and two opposite it.

"Got your feller to do it then, did yer?" Yad asked grinning.

"Do us a favour Yad, keep yer fuckin' mouth shut, it smells bad enough in 'ere without your arse breath makin' it worse." Jay Mac snapped, causing them all to smile, except Yad.

Suddenly they heard the blaring sound of the twin air horns that Mickey had recently fitted to his scooter, signalling he was on his way with the Kings Team Skins in pursuit. He had done exactly as requested, riding directly towards the enemy on the outbound carriageway then mounting the central reservation, on which they were marching en route to the lower Crown estate, only narrowly missing this advancing crew. They took the bait sprinting after the scooter-borne Mickey, wearing his own badly fitting Crombie which struggled to contain his corupulent physique and his equally

Natural Born Skinhead 1971 •236

ill-sized peakless Centurion helmet, as he desperately raced back towards the garage ambush.

"'Ere he comes, the fat tit." Yad announced peering through the narrow central gap, where the two battered old doors failed to meet. "They're not far behind him, get ready, nobody fuckin' move until I say." he ordered.

In the brief moments before their enemy came fully into view, all fell silent. Jay Mac listened to his usual tormenting internal voice, questioning once again whether his fear would overcome him, or, he would rise to the challenge and face the foe, giving a good account of himself.

Mickey was almost at the open-mouth of the yawning cul-de-sac, the array of lights on his scooter cutting hazy beams of yellow and white through the rapidly falling snow, with the overweight youth only visible as a dark silhouette behind. Four leading Kings Skins runners were closing on him from the rear armed with their glinting, aluminium bus pole lances, dressed in their black Crombies flapping as they ran like four medieval foot soldiers in sombre livery chasing a lone beleaguered knight on his colourful charger. Just before he reached the safety of the long, low, pre-cast concrete redoubt, where his own rough villein companions were waiting to inflict terrible injury on the Kings men, a well aimed half brick thrown by one of his pursuers struck him fully in the back of his helmet enclosed head. The coruplent rider lost control of his vehicle, skidded on the treacherous surface then crashed violently to the ground, becoming separated from his badly damaged machine.

Howling with delight the four Kings Skins increased their efforts, sprinting to the fallen Crown youth determined to give him no quarter. Repeatedly kicking and striking him with their metal poles, they relentlessly battered their victim as he rolled about in agony on the snow covered surface. In terrible pain as he was and receiving a ferocious beating Mickey did not cry out, he did not call to his supposed friends and risk revealing their position, instead only the dull thuds of the Kings Skins boots and weapons could be heard by them all, as they watched through the gaps in the rotten wooden doors of their garage hiding places.

Natural Born Skinhead 1971 • 237

"Come 'ed Yad, let's go, we've gorra help 'im, he's done his bit." Jay Mac urged.

"Shut it you, Kings Boy, the fat knob hasn't done what I said, they're still outside the fuckin' trap." Yad replied angrily.

Jay Mac looked to Macca (G) then Weaver, Yad's co-leaders in a vain hope that they would give the command but they both remained impassive, while the sickening sounds of Mickey's torment continued, coming from just a few yards further ahead.

With his own heart pounding in his chest as if it would burst and no objective directing him other than to stop the beating of the fallen Mickey, Jay Mac darted out from between the doors of his shelter and sprinted towards the enemy quartet, who were imminently about to be joined by a dozen of their fellow Skins.

"CROWN TEAM!" he roared, before leaping into the momentarily stunned Kings pack, crashing to the ground with them like a collapsed rugby scrum in a sprawling heap.

"Come on, Crown Team!" Johno exhorted followed by Irish, Weaver, Macca (G) and finally the reluctant Yad as they ran to join their companion.

The element of surprise was lost, the ambush failed; now everything relied on speed and ferocity with the whole mixed crew of Eagle and Heron Skins tearing into their rivals. Iron bars, pieces of wooden plank of varying length, empty milk and ale bottles, knuckle dusters and led shot coshes were employed by the Crown Team contingent against an equally eclectic array of improvised and regulation weapons used with painful efficacy by their Kings opponents. Blood and snot stained the pure white, virgin snow with an occasional tooth being flung into the ugly mix, as a maelstrom of unbridled hate raged about the frenzied combatants. Except for their contemporary clothing and boots these determined, cropped haired youths could have been transposed to a winter's battleground in the late fifteenth century War of the Roses campaigns, their savagery was total and equally unabated.

Occasionaly rising above the din and agonised shouts, could be heard the eponymous warcry of the Heron crew's psychopath co-leader, "I'm Weaver, I done this to yer, I'm Weaver!" he called, repeatedly striking any unrecognised face that appeared in front of him with his prized, solid steel toffee hammer, until his clenched right hand was covered in sticky, scarlet fluid. All the while, as the

Natural Born Skinhead 1971 •238

madness raged about the injured Mickey, who had crawled to where his beloved scooter lay wrecked against the gable wall of the foremost garage, he sat motionless with his hands holding his bare head, the dented Centurion helmet upturned on the floor and rapidly filling with snow. Watching the violent tableau unfold, he sat immobilised in shocked silence, unable to participate or flee the scene.

"Kings Team, Kings Team!" a number of bloodied Skins from that sprawling estate cried out desperately, feeling that the battle was being lost. Equally urgent calls answered from the near distance as their companions, who having sufficiently used and abused their female consorts, came racing to their striken team mates' aid. Relatively fresh reinforcements arriving at this juncture threatened to overwhelm the Crown Skins who fell back into the concrete jaws of their own trap. Corralled in this narrow cul-de-sac their jubilant enemy came at them with renewed vigour, striking with their aluminium poles and hurling pieces of brick and rubble into their more tightly packed ranks.

"Fuck we're takin' a beatin' here, Jay Mac." Johno gasped, raising his bleeding hands to ward off another vicious slash to his head, only to be hit by a half brick across the left temple immediately opening a dark red gash. Before he could reply a large chunk of cement and ballast smashed Jay Mac on his right shoulder, with enough force to cause him to stumble and fall to his knees, receiving half a dozen hard kicks to the face and abdomen as he did.

"We've done them! We've done the Crown shits!" one excited Kings player announced, with another exhorting them all to complete their task, "Fuckin' finish them! Bleed them all, don't let anyone get away!"

Even the crazed psychopath Weaver was almost overcome when a sharp blow to his right wrist with a metal pole, made him drop his hammer into the thickening snow at his feet. Diving to his knees, frantically scrambling about in the cold, white, powdery material, seemingly oblivious to the ferocious blows that rained down upon him from all sides, every Kings Skin who could reach the infamous Heron co-leader instantly surrounded him, determined to kick him to death. Yad had seen enough; he always

Natural Born Skinhead 1971 • 239

followed the old adage of *'He who fights and runs away may live to fight another day.'* Self preservation at any cost was the philosophy he subscribed to. Seeing a temporary gap open in the tight press of the Kings attackers as they swarmed around the kneeling Weaver, he forced his way through and ran from the carnage, momentarily glancing down at the motionless Mickey still lying near his wrecked Vespa GS.

Clearing the garages and running through the driving snow towards the Heron, constantly checking over his shoulder that he was not being pursued by the enemy, Yad abruptly collided with a large group of males heading towards the scene he had just fled.

"What the fuck's goin' on... and where are you off to Yad?" his elder brother, the Crown Team leader, Dayo (G), asked angrily, grasping his sibling by the shoulders of his grubby, stained Crombie.

"There's too many of them... it's the Kings Team... I was comin' to find yous for 'elp." Yad stammered in reply.

"Are you fuckin' tellin' me you, a crew leader, has ran off t'get 'elp?" Dayo demanded, shaking his brother violently. "Why didn't yer send a Junior or one of the runners, Jay Mac or Johno? Don't fuckin' say you've shit out boy?"

"I tried t'get them two to come an tell yer but thee both shit an wouldn't do it... honest." Yad offered in reply, though keeping his head lowered.

"Fuck this bollocks, let's get stuck in lads, the crew's in trouble, there'll be enough time for questions after." Dayo announced then led his old guard comrades and Terry (H) to the rescue of their beleaguered team mates. "Crown Team!" he bellowed, smashing into the rear of the Kings contingent, striking the nearest enemy head with one of the brown ale bottles he was carrying, deferring then to his primary weapon, his heavy studded, thick leather belt.

The sight and sound of their seniors battering their previously jubilant foe inspired and revitalised the wounded, trapped Crown Skins, leading them to surge forward ready to exact a bloody revenge on their tormentors. Without any senior players of their own capable of matching these older seasoned scrappers of the Crown, a debilitating icy fear colder than the freezing night, gripped the hearts of the Kings Skins filling them with one

Natural Born Skinhead 1971 •240

desperate desire only, escape. Forced to run the gauntlet of their merciless rivals enjoying their vicious reprisals, they struggled out onto the main arterial road and retreated back along the snow-covered path of the central reservation, finally crossing to their own territory at the flyover construction site, not even pausing to warm themselves at the glowing embers of their previously roaring bonfire. It may have been another win for the Crown Team but it was a Pyrrihic victory; all the members of the mixed crew ambush contingent were injured, some badly, with flesh wounds that would require several stitches and bone fractures that only time could heal.

On their vast, sprawling estate the recovering Kings Team Skins would pass on the intelligence they had gathered about the topography of their enemies terrain, all of which would ultimately inform the planners of a concerted mass invasion, where a final, bloody, unequivocal result would be determined.

For the angry Dayo (G) standing amongst the casualties of the night's engagement, with the snow falling even more densely, he wanted answers to a number of urgent questions and he began with the Heron crew's triumvirate of leaders, Yad, Macca (G) and Weaver.

"The crew looks fucked, thee've just had a lucky escape nothin' else. I wanna understand what fuckin' happened and how yer's got yerselves trapped in those garages. The main thing I wanna know is who the fuck led the team, who started it, so get talkin'." he ordered angrily.

Yad looked at his two fellow commanders and gestured to them to let him answer for them all. Macca (G) and Weaver smiled as he began his explanation, believing that his reply would absolve them of any guilt.

A short time later having listened to his younger brother's explanation, Dayo dismissed most of the assembly other than several of the Eagle crew.

"Come 'ere Jay Mac, I wanna fuckin' word with you." he began ominously. "Am I right in what I've heard, you're the one responsible for what 'appened 'ere tonight, you decided to lead this team into action, even though Yad told yer not to?"

Natural Born Skinhead 1971 • 241

Jay Mac looked about at the scowling Seniors and his smiling accusers, knowing there was no point in denying what he had done.

"Yeah Dayo, I can't say nothin' different, I ran out an called the team after me. Yad told me t'leave it but I didn't, it's my fault, no one elses." he offered honestly.

"Some fat cunt was on the deck after he fell off his scooter an he was takin' a bit of a kickin' from a few Kings shits, is that right?" Dayo asked, studying Jay Mac's expression and demeanour. The youth again replied in the affirmative.

Struggling away in the distance, pushing his useless wreck of a scooter, the limping Mickey was only just visible to Jay Mac, until the whiteout fully enveloped him.

"So you, a Skin who's not even from this estate ran in to save this fat fuck, even though thee were twattin' him with bus poles and yer could see the rest of them almost on yer? An my brother who warned yer not to do it, was standin' right next to yer watchin' all this, yeah?" Dayo asked his final incriminating question.

Jay Mac nodded in agreement of his guilt and waited for the sentence of the 'judge'.

Reaching out with his large, hairy paw of a hand, the dark cropped hirsute, Crown Team leader siezed hold of the right shoulder of Jay Mac's Crombie firmly then pointed directly into the youth's face with the forefinger of his right hand. "*You* are one crazy fucker, yer've got balls an I don't give a toss about the rules, I'm one of the original Skinheads who started this team... Jay Mac... you are a full member of the Crown Skins... an I'm fuckin' glad to'ave yer on board. Now piss off an get that denim jacket marked up, cos next time I see yer, I'll expect t'find a crown on yer back, lettin' every cunt know who *you* are an what team yer belong to."

Standing in stunned silence with a deposit of snow quickly building on his head and shoulders, Jay Mac smiled while his friends congratulated him and as he watched Yad being led away by his brother; Dayo's heavy arm draped across his dismayed younger sibling's shoulders.

Less than half an hour later Molly 'Skank', the obliging, disfigured Donna and three of their associates made their way back

Natural Born Skinhead 1971 •242

across the frozen fields, passed those same garages and along the front of the Heron public house before entering Mr Li's Golden Diner. Battered and bruised, they had spent a long, painful, arduous night consorting with the enemy. Armed with their meagre wages, from those customers who had actually paid for services received, they could now buy their own steaming hot fish suppers without having to beg from, or barter with any of the boys or older males.

While they stood in the limited shelter afforded by the overhanging tenement balconies, eating their food and smoking some of their tobacco earnings, they stared blankly out into the steadily falling snow and the darkness beyond.

Macca (G) approached angrily from the direction of the Heron. "Where the fuck 'ave you been, bitch, I've been lookin' for you. I fancy a hard one now, round the back of the shops, so move yer fuckin' arse." he ordered with a sneer.

Molly took a long satisfying drag on the cigarette she was holding between the two sticky, nicotine discoloured fore-fingers of her grimy right hand, victory salute style, before raising them defiantly, fixing the sexual sadist in the sights of their badly chipped, bright red nail varnished tips. She pursed the lips of her ruby red smeared mouth and blew a thin stream of grey smoke then replied, "Piss off Gary, am not yer bird, *remember*. Yer too late, this shop's closed... happy fuckin' Christmas to *all* our customers."

The Heron co-leader looked at the dishevelled girl as she continued to stare expressionless into the distance. He was wise enough not to pursue the usually obliging, convenient, temporary object of his desire any further.

Sunday 19th December 1971

The morning that followed the bleak, frozen night was a glorious winter's day, with a far distant sun shining brightly in a clear, pale blue sky and everywhere covered by a deep blanket of crisp, sparkling white snow. By the time Jay Mac had risen and consumed his everything fried, including the bread, breakfast, courtesy of Mrs O'Hare, having stayed overnight at the home of his friend, Irish, there being no public transport due to the appalling weather, the weak rays of the golden winter orb had

Natural Born Skinhead 1971 • 243

managed to at least reduce the previously pristine material lying on the main roads to a dirty, grey-brown slush. Now in a position to be able to return to his own isolated estate, Jay Mac thanked his host and his kindly mother then set off for the lower edge of the Crown and the bus depot. En route he was determined to call at Mickey Pimple's residence, ask about his injuries, the state of his scooter and tell him about *his* good news.

"Alright Mickey, how are y'mate?" Jay Mac asked, stamping up and down, crunching the compacted snow beneath his feet.

Mickey stood with the front door partly open, he was dressed in a casual jumper and wearing his striped pyjama bottoms. He was also leaning on a wooden crutch. "How am I, that's a fuckin' good question." he began then gazed down at his left plastercast encased ankle. "Spiral fracture of the lateral malleolus." he announced, continuing, "Sounds good doesn't it? What it means is me left ankle's fucked and that means I can't help me arl feller on the delivery van, he's been out since five this mornin' an he'll 'ave t'work extra, to make up for me not bein' there. So what's your news then, yer lookin' pleased with yerself?"

Jay Mac was not sure whether to bother telling the corpulent youth what had occurred after he has limped away but felt it might inspire Mickey to follow his example, if he couched his information in the right manner.

"After yer'd gorroff last night, Dayo had a few words with me an er... cuttin' to the chase... he's made me a full member of the Crown Team. I'm in even though I don't live 'ere, d'yer get what am sayin'?" he asked then paused to await Mickey's response.

"Well that's fuckin' great, am made up for yer Jay Mac." he replied sarcastically.

"No, Mickey... yer haven't gorrit mate, what am sayin' is... now I'm in, I'll put a good word in for you with Dayo and yer never know, next thing is he'll be askin' you t'be part of the team, a proper Crown Skin... how does that sound?" Jay Mac persisted, smiling as if offering the possibility of the chance of a lifetime.

Mickey drew himself up to his full height as best he could manage on his artificial support. "Jay Mac, it's you who doesn't gerrit, so I'll make it crystal clear." He paused to ensure that the Eagle player was fully listening, "I watched everythin' that 'appened last night everything yous all did, an I can tell yer, I don't

Natural Born Skinhead 1971 •244

want any part of this mad shite, yer like fuckin' animals the lot of yer. I was wrong... am not like you, I don't want no shitty crown on the back of me coat, or anywhere else and as soon as I can am gettin' away from this fuckin' dump."

Jay Mac looked away from the fuming heavyweight and glanced at the wreck of his Vespa 150GS wedged in the side alley, with its shattered fly screen and dented chrome work.

"Won't be needin' yer bike then I suppose, what are yer gonna do with that?" he asked speculatively, considering whether to make an offer for it himself.

"It's goin' back t'me arl feller's mate, he's already sorted that. Like I said I want nothin' more to do with yer Scooter Boys, yer Skinheads and most of all yer fuckin' precious Crown Team." Mickey replied angrily.

Jay Mac had heard enough, "Alright wind yer fuckin' neck in, you need to piss off while yer still can, you *defo* don't belong round 'ere, yer not a Skin or a Scooter Boy, yer a big, fat nothin'." He turned and walked away even as Mickey slammed the door shut with such force as to dislodge a fall of snow from the steeply raking roof of the small terraced house, which narrowly missed the departing Crown Skin.

Later that day whilst eating his evening meal in the kitchen with his aunt and uncle, only partially listening to Bing Crosby's classic *White Christmas* playing on the small transistor radio in the background, Jay Mac considered why some people would do anything to belong and why for others the cost was just too great. He wondered who really was the coward in this instance, Mickey or himself, one youth was too afraid to stay, the other too afraid to leave.

Friday 31st December 1971

It was New Year's Eve, Christmas had been and gone and despite the urging of speculative gamblers and wishful dreaming of romantics, it had not been white but instead proved to be the usual drab, grey affair with leaden skies regularly unleashing angry bursts of frozen hail throughout the day, as the nearest gesture of picturesque seasonal conditions.

Natural Born Skinhead 1971 • 245

Jay Mac was sitting in one of the old well-worn armchairs in the cramped living room, a broadsheet newspaper across his lap, applying a thin finishing layer of Kiwi ox blood polish over the initial colouring, waxy, Tucson cherry red to his gleaming Airwair.

"Not too bad mate, a bit of fast buffin' and that should do the job." he advised his yawning friend, the old mongrel hound, presently stretched out on the faux fair rug in front of the two-bar electric fire, casually watching the youth in case some interesting form of food may be being prepared by him.

During the time since the bloody garage encounter with their Kings rivals there had been a number of minor skirmishes, though these were almost exclusively distance clashes, involving missiles being thrown from either side of the busy highway. Jay Mac had ensured he had been in the forefront of these actions, using his other talent for accurate throwing, enjoying his new status as a full Crown Team member. Mickey Pimple was soon dismissed from his thoughts and never referred to again by either crew, eventually moving from the bleak estate with his family.

Listening to the small transistor radio while getting dressed ready for an evening's drinking and celebrating with his friends in the Eagle, Jay Mac admired his handywork, the neatly drawn outlined black crown on the back of his Levi's denim jacket across the shoulders, with the word 'Skins' in its hollow centre. It had been a pivotal year for the youth, having finished school, started work and ultimately becoming formally accepted by his peers. Just then Lee Marvin's Westen hit *Wand'rin' Star* began to play, causing the smiling Jay Mac to observe "No more wanderin' for me, am part of the team now, I've arrived."

With the promise of the New Year 1972 lying before him and the possibilities for further adventures that this may offer, for the first time in his life he belonged, he was legitimate. Jay Mac, the natural born Skinhead and Crown Team player was somebody.

THE END

MUSIC

Chapter 1 – *In the Summertime* (Mungo Jerry)
Dion -*Runaround Sue*
Rodgers &Hammerstein -*There is Nothing Like a Dame (South Pacific)*
Chuck Berry-*No Particular Place to Go*
Eddie Cochran -*Summertime Blues*

Chapter 2 – *Everybody's Talkin'* (Nilsson)
The Lemon Pipers -*Green Tambourine*
Traffic -*Hole in My Shoe*
The Four Tops -*Still Waters (Love)*
Desmond Dekker and The Aces -*Israelites*

Chapter 3 – *Natural Sinner* (Fairweather)
Rodgers &Hammerstein -*You'll Never Walk Alone (Carousel)*

Chapter 4 – *I'm a Neanderthal Man* (Hotlegs)
Glenn Miller -*Moonlight Serenade*

Chapter 5 – *Within You and Without You* (George Harrison The Beatles)
Black Widow -*Come to the Sabbath*
Tiny Tim -*Tiptoe through the Tulips*
Barry McGuire -*Eve of Destruction*

Chapter 6 – *O Fortuna* (Carl Orff: Carmina Burana)
The Tams -*Hey Girl Don't Bother Me*
Jim Reeves -*Welcome to My World*
Ethiopians - *Train to Skaville*
Fairweather -*Natural Sinner*
Dave and Ansell Collins -*Double Barrel*
Ashton, Gardner and Dyke -*Resurrection Shuffle*
McGuinness Flint -*When I'm Dead and Gone*
Norman Greenbaum -*Spirit in the Sky*

Chapter 7 – *Get Down and Get With It* (Slade)
Bob and Earl -*Harlem Shuffle*
Marvin Gaye -*Abraham Martin and John*

Chapter 8 – *Wand'rin' Star* (Lee Marvin)
Jimi Hendrix -*Hey Joe*
Jimmy Cliff -*Many Rivers to Cross*
The Beatles -*Happiness is a Warm Gun* and *Helter Skelter (White Album)*
Led Zeppelin -*Babe I'm Gonna Leave You* and *Dazed and Confused*
Atomic Rooster -*Death Walks Behind You* and *The Devil's Answer*
Black Widow -*Come to the Sabbath*
Simaryp -*Skinhead Moonstomp*
Junior Walker & The All Stars -*Roadrunner*
Bing Crosby -*White Christmas*
Lee Marvin -*Wand'rin' Star*

GLOSSARY

In response to the requests of some readers I have included a brief glossary of localised 'Scouse' idioms in use at that time. This is neither exhaustive nor exclusive with some of the specific expressions being more widespread, whereas others were entirely parochial.

Airwair – The name given to Dr. Marten boots in this particular area of Liverpool

Arl – Old (me arl feller = my dad, my father, me arl girl = my mother)

Arl arse – Auld arse, old arse, = older person, usually cantankerous

Baker's – Baker's trousers, white trousers, favoured style of some Skinheads and Boot Boys at the time

Betting Office – A licensed bookmaker introduced in the UK in the early 1960's for off-track betting

Birds – girls or women

Bizzies – Police (Polis – Irish pronunciation for Police)

Blimping – Looking, usually taking a sneaky look

Bobby – Policeman (from Robert (Bobby) Peel founder of British police force

Brass necked – Brazened it out, bold, barefaced, daring, overconfident, impudent

Broosted – In the money, have plenty of money to spend

Chocker – Chocker-block = packed, full to capacity

Clocked – Seen, eg. 'Have you clocked this?'

Come 'ed – Come ahead, come on

Corpy – Corporation = Liverpool Corporation the municipal council providers of corporation houses, their duty being the upkeep and repair of corporation houses for tenants. The guttering and woodwork painted in 'corporation' green.

D.A Style – Refers to men's hair style of the 1950s. D.A = Duck's Arse, due to the way the hair was styled

Defo – Definitely

Feltie – Felt tip pen, usually a permanent marker

Flat – High-rise blocks of flats = apartments

Geoff Hurst – rhyming slang, going for a burst meaning going to the toilet to urinate. (Geoff Hurst famous England football player)

Jammy – Lucky

Jib or Jibbed – To choose not to do something

Kecks – Trousers

Keds – Basketball boots (specifically Converse Chuck Taylor's All Stars)

Lash or lashed – To throw away

Lobby – Small hallway

Loons – Flared trousers often with an additional triangular vent of a different colour, on the outside of the trouser leg, just below the knee

Mild – A medium dark porter

Moggie – Cat

Nowt – Nothing (a Lancashire or Yorkshire word)

'Oller – Patch of ground, where houses had been razed. (Hollow)

On the job – euphemism for having sex

'Ossie – or Hossie, short for Hospital

Pipe or **piping** – To pipe, to take a look. **Piping** – looking

Povo – Refers to a person with no money, poor, poverty stricken

Prince of Wales check parallels – Pair of parallel trousers with a small checked pattern

Ragged off – To rip/pull off violently

Ragged around – To be violently pushed and shoved

R.E.M.E – Royal Electrical and Mechanical Engineers

Scouse or **Scouser** – A person born and bred in Liverpool. Many Liverpool people speak with a Scouse accent (said to be a combination of Lancashire, Welsh and Irish influence). Scouse referring to a type of Irish stew (a staple diet of some Liverpool people. Also may refer to Lobscouse – a Norwegian/Swedish dish, similar to Irish stew.)

Scran – Food

Sta prest trousers – (a stylized rendering of "stay pressed") a brand of wrinkle-resistant trousers produced by Levi Strauss & Co., beginning in 1964. Marketed as wearable straight out of the dryerwith no need for ironing (Note: most people in Britain would not own a dryer – or a washing machine at this time and would use a Launderette

– known locally as the 'bag wash'),. The trousers were very popular among British Mods of the mid 1960s and Skinheads of the late 1960s/early 1970s (as well as among traditionalist Skinheads and Mod revivalists). Lee and Wrangler, produced similar styles of trousers during that same period

Smokey Bacon Crisps – Crisps had previously been unflavoured except for the addition of a small blue bag of salt provided in the packet until the introduction of cheese and onion/smokey bacon and other subsequent flavours

Sound – loyal, trustworthy

Sterrie – Sterilised milk

Tarmac – Tarmaced, Tarmacadamed thick black tar road covering

Tart – female (or derogatory term for male who is not courageous)

Tennies – Tenements, tenement blocks, tenement flats

Thee – Often used in place of they when talking with a Scouse/Liverpool or sometimes northern accent

Tramp – Hobo, Down-and-Out

Turkish – Going for a Turkish is rhyming slang, Turkish Delight = Shite (a Turkish Delight is a popular and tasty chocolate bar)

Twenty-Two inch parallels – parallel trousers with 22inch wide hems

Yer – You/your/you're (though you/your/you're, are sometimes used for emphasis) **Yers** or **Yous** – referring to two or more people, ie. "yous two," "the lot of yers"

Printed in Great Britain
by Amazon.co.uk, Ltd.,
Marston Gate.